THE MISSING HEIR MURDERS

A JOHN GRANVILLE & EMILY TURNER HISTORICAL MYSTERY

SHARON ROWSE

THREE CEDARS PRESS

THE MISSING HEIR MURDERS

A John Granville & Emily Turner Historical Mystery

By Sharon Rowse

Published by Three Cedars Press
www.threecedarspress.com

ISBN-13: 9780987923653

ALSO BY SHARON ROWSE

The John Granville & Emily Turner Historical Mystery Series: (in order)

The Silk Train Murder

The Lost Mine Murders

The Missing Heir Murders

The Terminal City Murders

The Cannery Row Murders

The Hidden City Murders

The Barbara O'Grady Series: (in order)

Death of a Secret

Death of a Threat

Death of a Promise

Death of a Shadow

Death of a Lie

Death of a Dream

Want to know out more? Or be the first to find out when Sharon's next book is coming out?

Check out her website: www.sharonrowse.com

With thanks to my friends and family for their support

FRIDAY, APRIL 13, 1900

John Lansdowne Granville stared at the letter in his hands while the rain battered at his office window. A chill draft, smelling of manure and burning coal, crept in from the street below. "Beware the Ides," he muttered under his breath.

The quote felt apt, even if today was the Ides of April rather than March. And he was no laurel-wreathed Caesar. He grimaced at the thought.

"What's that? Something wrong, Granville?" Scott said, looking up from the ledger he'd been wrestling with. His business partner had a half-grin on his face, but his eyes were watchful.

Granville crumpled the heavy white paper in one fist and tossed it across the mahogany partner's desk the two of them shared. He watched as it landed on an unsteady stack of reports they'd both been ignoring. "Not a thing."

"'Cause I got to tell you, the way you look now, you'd scare off a Mama bear looking for her cubs."

Granville gave a crack of laughter. Truth was, he'd rather face a grizzly than deal with this letter. "We've been offered a job."

Scott eyed the crumpled page, written in a spiked, forceful hand.

A challenging job would be welcome, but Granville's expression and the postmark signaled trouble. "In England?"

"No, here. In Vancouver," Granville said. "We need to find the Earl of Thanet's heir."

"How'd he lose him?"

"Quite deliberately, I assure you. Apparently Rupert Weston is a remittance man."

"I thought they only paid off the younger sons to disappear over here, not the heirs," Scott said.

Behind Granville the windowpanes rattled as the storm increased. "And until a most unfortunate boating accident a few months ago, you'd have been right. It seems Weston's two older brothers drowned in unexpectedly rough seas off the Isle of Wight. Hence the search for the new heir apparent."

"Huh," Scott said. "Wonder what young Weston did that got him sent to the colonies."

"Whatever it was, all will be forgiven now."

"He's unlikely to have reformed any, not from what I've seen of the remittance boys."

Scott was right, but the casual dismissal in his voice grated. Granville had refused to admit it at the time, but he hadn't been far from a remittance man himself, not so long ago.

It had been his father's money that took him to the Klondike, though he'd refused to accept another penny once he'd got there. Which proved to be a mistake, since he and Scott had never managed to strike it rich. Despite eighteen months of hard work in extremely trying conditions.

"True enough," Granville said with a wry grin.

"But now he's the heir none of that matters?"

Granville nodded, amused despite his own misgivings by the incredulous note in Scott's voice.

"I'll never understand you English." Scott tossed the crumpled letter back. "Where's this Earl send the money?"

"Post office here in town—care of General Delivery."

"I'm guessing their letters have been returned?" Scott said.

"You'd be right about that."

"So Weston might still be in Vancouver."

"Might be," Granville agreed. "If he is here, he's laying low."

"Gives us a place to start, though. Sounds easy enough," Scott said. "So what's the catch?"

Granville eyed Scott with affection, grinned. "The catch, as you so succinctly put it, is that Thanet isn't hiring us."

"Then who is?"

"Thanet's brother-in-law, the boy's uncle," Granville said. "And the request comes by way of my brother William."

"The Baron? That William?" Scott said.

"That's him."

"But the job's legit? No reason we can't take it, is there?"

Granville shook his head. "*Et tu, Brute?*" he said mournfully.

"Huh?" Scott said, face blank.

That earned him a half laugh, as it was undoubtedly meant to. "William has never done anything straightforward in his life, and most particularly not when it involves me."

"You don't trust him even on something as straightforward as this?" Scott asked. "Or is there some particular reason Thanet isn't the one hiring us to find his missing son?"

"I gather he's too mired in grief to take any action. But based on hard experience, I don't trust William on anything."

"So what's your dear brother up to, then?"

"Currying favor with the Earl of Thanet, I suspect. Or trying to, through the man's brother-in-law. Probably as close as William could get to the Earl."

Scott gave a bark of laughter. "Probably. So we find this Weston, it's easy money and Brother William's in your debt. Sounds like a no fail plan to me."

"Which means we're missing something. I wonder what happens to the estate if we don't find Weston, or if he's already dead."

Scott gave him a sharp look. "Why should we care?"

"Because William will have looked at every angle of this before involving himself. And the most obvious path is seldom the one he follows. He'll not concern himself if we're injured or killed in pursuit of whatever goal he has in mind—in fact it might sweeten it for him."

"Nice brother. But he's thousands of miles away. How dangerous could it be?"

Granville shrugged. "How dangerous was it up on the creeks when a fellow didn't know enough to provision for winter?"

Scott grunted. "Killed by what we don't know? At least it won't be boring."

"Getting tired of guarding nervous bankers are you? Fine, we'll take the job," Granville said, and flicked a disdainful finger toward the crumpled ball he'd made of the letter. It was probably time he stopped avoiding William and his schemes, anyway.

"That was quick." Scott eyed his partner. "And I've seen that look before, usually right before you get both of us into trouble. What're you planning?"

He was planning to outmaneuver whatever his unscrupulous older brother might have in mind for him. "There's nothing to stop us taking on this case and finding young Weston," Granville said. "Once we have all the facts, we can decide how we want to handle it."

"You planning on bamboozling Brother William, then?"

There was a reason he and Scott had remained friends after their return from the Klondike. "Exactly," Granville said, striding towards the door. "What do you say?"

The grating of wood chair on hardwood floor told him his partner was behind him.

"I'll probably regret this," Scott said. "But when do we start?"

BY THE TIME they'd made their way to the imposing granite-faced Main Post Office on Pender Street, the wind had lessened. Shaking the rain from his hat, Granville was amused to find himself standing in front of a long marble counter that could have been in any post office in London, being glared at by a dapper young man—nattily attired in black and white—who seemed to have hopes of being this century's Beau Brummell.

Granville wondered if anyone had told him how unlikely that was in Vancouver, of all places. As far as the English were concerned, the clerk's focus should be on making money, like all good Colonials.

"No Weston here."

Granville had met friendlier icicles. "But he does collect his mail here?"

"Can't give out that information."

"Fair enough. Can you tell me if you have uncollected mail for him?"

Granville watched the man's eyes dart to a section of wooden pigeonholes. Some were empty, some had a few letters, but one or two were stuffed with mail. Which one was Weston's?

"Sorry, that's classified," came the predictable answer.

"We just need to know when he's expected next," Scott put in.

"And how would I know that?"

"Can you perhaps tell us if he collects his mail regularly?" Granville smiled, put an extra hint of Oxford in his tone. "He's a friend—we lost touch with him in Skagway."

"Sorry."

"Come on, Granville," Scott said. "We're wasting our time here." Gripping his partner's elbow, he half dragged him outside.

"I wasn't done there."

"You were about to try bribing that clerk." Scott settled his hat more firmly in place, turned up his collar against the wind-driven rain and began walking north.

Granville buttoned his coat as he paced beside his partner. "I was indeed. And?"

"And I know the clerk's brother," Scott said. "Very officious family—and all of them hate Brits. No offense."

"Seems to be a common sentiment in this part of the world," Granville said. It was unsettling, and the fact that he found it so just annoyed him more.

Confining as he'd found being a member of the English gentry, he'd always taken the respect that came with it for granted. Now he couldn't.

Scott chuckled, then sobered. "Yeah, well if you'd tried to bribe him, he'd have you arrested for tamperin' with the mails or some fool thing."

"That could have been embarrassing. Especially since the local constabulary are none too fond of us."

"Getting some of them arrested will cause that," Scott said with a straight face.

Granville recalled his first weeks in town with a grin. "True enough. But it saved you hanging for murder. I suppose it was worth it. So where are we headed in this downpour?"

"Newspaper office. I thought we'd advertise for Weston."

"Hmm. News to his advantage or something of that sort? That makes sense."

"Yeah, I thought so. The *Province* is around the corner. It has the biggest readership."

"By all means." Granville swiped absently at the rain dripping into his eyes, pulled his hat brim lower. "We'll want replies to a post office box rather than our office."

Scott thought about it for a second. "Keep this anonymous? Makes sense."

"No point giving away our hand quite yet. What time does the afternoon mail get delivered?"

"Around four, but the earliest we can expect replies is tomorrow morning," Scott said. "The ad won't run until tonight."

"And meanwhile, we'll send a letter to Weston. That will get delivered this afternoon, am I right?"

"Yeah, so?"

"So we can see which box it gets delivered to."

"You're not thinking of robbing the post office?"

Granville hadn't been, but as a last resort, it had possibilities. "Why not?" he said with an inward grin as he watched Scott sputter.

"They'd recognize us."

"Calm down. I'm not thinking of robbing the post office. I just want to know how much mail is sitting in Weston's box, uncollected. If the box is full, Weston most likely left town in a hurry. And hasn't been back."

"Huh. That could work," Scott said.

"I thought so." Granville winked at his partner. "You post the ad. I'll write our letter to Weston. And tonight we'll visit a few poker spots, do a little listening. Weston was always a bit of a gambler."

Actually, Weston had been hopelessly enthralled by it, if even half the rumors were true.

"If we're not in jail by then," Scott said with a scowl that Granville didn't believe for a moment. "And I thought you gave up gambling—wait a minute. You know him? Weston? And you're just telling me now?"

Granville shrugged. "I know of him. The young idiot was part of a wild set at college. Got sent down from Oxford twice."

"Didn't you tell me you were sent down three times? Or was it four?" Scott said, poker-faced.

Granville ignored him.

With both Scott and their apprentice out of the office, it was quiet except for the steady pattering of rain and the scratching of Granville's fountain pen as he dashed off a quick note to young Weston.

It was unlikely Weston would ever see it, but in case other eyes were checking the lad's mail, Granville kept the letter short. It simply asked Weston to contact them at his earliest convenience, for information to his advantage. Sealing it, he added the two-cent stamp, then clattered down the stairs and out to the post box on the corner.

That task complete, he sat down to the harder work of composing a letter to his eldest sister Louisa, now Lady Waybourne. He needed to know more about the Earl of Thanet, as well as the society gossip about the family and especially about the drowning of the previous heirs. Only one name had come to mind.

Louisa still thought very fondly of him, and her social connections were faultless. She would know all the latest *on dits* and family scandals. She was also his favorite sister, and could be counted on not to mention a word to Brother William.

It was well past noon by the time he'd finished the letter. With a little luck, Louisa's reply would come in time to do some good. In the meantime, he'd find out everything he could about Weston. Someone must know where he'd disappeared to.

2

G ranville eyed the battered pine walls of the bar at the Terminus Hotel with distaste. Even in the uneven light of the oil lamps, the place hadn't improved since his first visit here. Was it only three months ago? He now had a business, a fiancée, albeit a temporary one—at least until he could convince her otherwise—financial stability and the beginning of roots here.

The Terminus bar was still dirty and crowded, ripe with the smell of sweat, smoke and nerves—but it resonated with the excitement of high stakes, of money won and lost. Something in him leapt at the familiar tension and Granville's hands itched to hold a deck of cards. He had to remind himself forcefully that it wasn't why he was here.

His letter to Weston had been delivered into a very full box at the post office that afternoon. Clearly the fellow hadn't collected his mail in quite some time. Either he'd left town, or he'd gone into hiding. Granville had hopes that someone here could tell him which.

His memory of Rupert Weston was vague: a tall, thin youth with dark hair flopping over one eye and a not very convincing sneer. He hadn't liked him, but then he hadn't really known him. That was four years ago and Weston had undoubtedly changed. He certainly had.

Remembering his own attitudes four years before had Granville's lips quirking. He'd been sure he knew so much. Then his friend Edward had killed himself, and all of the glamor had gone out of that life.

The memory still hurt.

He found himself taking in the scene around him with revulsion—the smell of compulsion strong in the air, the brittle sense of desperation. He could see it in their faces. The money won and lost was irrelevant to the mesmerizing turn of a card, until the game was done and you realized what you'd wagered.

"I see a fellow I know. Think I'll see if he knows anything about our friend."

Scott's voice at his elbow jolted Granville out of his thoughts. "Right."

"I'll look for you in an hour or so?"

"Good enough."

Scott gave him an odd look, then clapped him on the back and headed across the crowded room.

Granville focused on the faces around him, looking for anyone he recognized. With a start of surprise, he found someone. What was Benton doing here? Quick steps had him standing beside the man whispers called the most powerful gangster in town. They never needed to add that he was also the most feared.

"Benton."

"Granville? Thought you'd given up gambling."

"Only on occasion. At the moment I'm looking for a countryman of mine. Fellow by the name of Weston."

Asking Benton for information carried the risk of being obligated to him, but Granville had done the man a favor or two in the past. He'd chance it.

Shrewd brown eyes assessed him. "Weston, is it? And why would you be looking for him?"

"I have news from home that I think he'll want to hear."

Benton smiled, and the man standing on his other side stepped back. Granville could understand why—it was like looking into the heart of a glacier.

"If he's come into a fortune, that information could be useful to me," Benton said.

"Owes you money, does he?" Granville said.

"Let's just say he's not the most successful gamester." The ice was gone, Benton's normal dry humor back in place.

Granville considered the peeling walls and the feeling of desperation in the crowd that seethed within them. "I didn't realize you had an interest here."

"I have many interests."

That information didn't exactly surprise him, but Granville mentally filed the tidbit away. It could prove useful. "Did Weston play here often?"

"Too often for his health," Benton said. "And he wasn't much better at poker than he was weighing odds on the ponies."

So Weston owed the house more than he could come up with. Was that why he'd disappeared? "Then it could be in your interest to help me find him," Granville said.

"True enough," Benton said. "Yes, I know of Weston. A reckless man, with not much sense of self-preservation."

"He's young."

Benton shot him a look. "And English. He lost far more than is good for him, here and elsewhere. His debts came due, and he vanished."

"When was this?"

"Seven, perhaps eight weeks ago."

Interesting. Granville wondered if it was possible to hide in Vancouver without Benton knowing. "And you don't know where he went?"

"I'd no hand in his vanishing, if that's what you're asking."

It was, but it didn't seem a good idea to admit it. "Has he cronies, friends he might have turned to for help?" Granville asked.

"None my men have found."

It figured. Likely Benton's men would have been thorough in

their quest for a delinquent gamester. Had they found him, Thanet would have lost another heir.

It wasn't a good sign for the search he and Scott were undertaking. "Thanks."

"Don't thank me," Benton said. "Just tell me when you find him."

It wasn't a request.

Granville nodded, acknowledgement rather than agreement. He was thankful he'd never had to accept Benton's repeated offers of employment. Though he rather liked the man, he'd be a demanding and potentially lethal employer.

To say nothing of the fact that he walked on the wrong side of the law. Of course, so did a few of Vancouver's current crop of police officers—despite the open scandals that swirled around them. But he'd rather not have to choose between Benton and the police.

One thing was clear. Wherever Weston was, he and Scott needed to find the fellow before Benton's men did.

And before the fellow's trail got any colder.

THE GAS LANTERNS on the far end of the pier threw a dim light that barely cut through the fog that had crept in after the storm had passed. Under the mournful bleat of the foghorn on the point, Granville could hear the water lapping against the pilings and the boats moored there. The reek of tar and creosote drowned the murky smell of decaying seaweed.

He was glad of Scott's bulk at his back and the weight of the hunting knife at his hip—the docks at one a.m. were no friendlier than they'd been when they'd tripped over Jackson's body some four months previous.

It was too dark to read his pocket-watch, but it must be past midnight. If Scott's informant was really going to meet them here, they should be hearing his footfalls any moment.

The fog distorted sound as well as his sense of distance.

Granville wrapped the wool muffler a little tighter around his throat and wished he hadn't forgotten his gloves. "You're sure he'll show?"

"Wish I was," Scott said.

"I gather your informant is not exactly an upstanding citizen."

"Least I found someone who'll talk. All you got was more trouble. Now we need to find Weston before Benton's men get to him."

"I always did like a challenge," Granville said, jamming his hands deeper into the pockets of his overcoat and squinting into the thickening whiteness surrounding them.

Was that movement?

He walked slowly back the way they'd come and Scott fell into step with him. "Your idea of challenge can get damned uncomfortable," his partner said.

Granville put a hand on Scott's arm, lowered his voice. "D'you hear something?"

Scott froze, head cocked, eyes scanning the pier. "Nothing," he said after a long moment, and resumed walking. "You?"

Around them the fog grew denser and the sound of the waves diminished. Even the moan of the foghorn sounded distant. Clammy whiteness swallowed them until Granville could barely make out Scott's face. It wasn't enough to muffle the sound of the shot, though.

Granville cursed and ducked as he felt something sizzle by his arm.

There was no cover anywhere, nothing but the thick fog. The shooter had to be targeting their voices. He pushed at Scott's shoulder but the big man was already dropping to the dock.

Granville did the same.

He drew his knife, held it ready. But there was nothing to see but fog and more fog. Knowing the shooter couldn't see him either didn't help.

There was a sudden flurry of shots. Bullets danced around where he and Scott had been standing.

Then a long pause.

Lying flat out on the cold dock, alert to any sound, Granville felt like he had a target painted on his back.

A second flurry of shots erupted from the same spot as the first, but came nowhere near them.

Then there was nothing but silence and the movement of the fog. Was the gunman trying to force them to betray their positions? Well, they could out-wait him.

Unless the shooter got lucky.

Granville could just make out that Scott, lying beside him, had his revolver drawn. He too was still, listening and waiting. The minutes ticked by, broken only by the foghorn's wail.

Finally Scott raised his head a little, looked around. "You hear anything?"

"Not anymore." Granville pulled out his pocket flask, took a swig, then proffered it to his partner.

"Thanks," Scott said, accepting the flask and downing a hearty mouthful. "You upset anyone lately?"

Granville stood up slowly and brushed the damp off his clothes, bracing himself for any sound, any movement that meant the gunman was still near. "Not that I can think of. I'm guessing someone really doesn't want us talking to your informant."

Scott stood up, and they began walking back along the pier. "Yeah. Young Weston must have got himself in real trouble. How badly dipped was he?"

Granville still had his knife out, and Scott's gun was cocked. "Bad enough. Seems that it's a good thing Benton's men haven't found Weston yet. Though I don't think they'd be motivated to kill us too."

The fog was thinning enough he could make out Scott's grin. "Likely not. It does mean we won't find our new client in Vancouver, though."

"You don't think he could hide from Benton's men here?"

"Nope. Place is too small," Scott said. "And Benton has too many connections in too many places."

That's what Granville had been afraid of. "So it's time to widen our search. And technically, he isn't our client."

"So who is? Your brother? The lad's uncle? His grief-stricken father?"

"Whoever pays our bills," Granville said with a grin. "Which is certainly not my brother. But you're right, it's finding the lad that matters, digging him out of whatever he's got into. The rest is just bill payments."

"Yeah." Whatever else Scott might have said was lost in a curse as his boot caught on the edge of what had seemed a patch of shadow.

Granville grabbed his partner's elbow, grunting as he took most of the big man's weight before Scott caught his balance.

"I don't believe it."

"Believe what...?" Granville began, then he too caught the rank odor of blood and feces, faint on the cold air. "Not again. Who is it?"

Scott bent over the body that sprawled on the damp boards. "Not enough light to tell. You carrying lucifers?"

But Granville was already bending forward, opening the small silver case and striking a light. Hunching close, both men considered the pasty features of the dead man.

"This your informant?" It wasn't a huge stretch to guess who the dead man might be.

"Yup. This is Horace Norton. Or it used to be him, anyhow."

"Poor man."

"Yeah. I reckon we'd best not report this one," Scott said as he gently closed the staring eyes.

Granville dipped his head in respect, then turned away. "Probably not, much as I hate to say it. We got lucky on that case. This time they'd probably arrest both of us."

"And Miss Emily would have to rescue you as well as me," Scott said as he followed him down the pier.

He smiled a little at the thought of his fiancée. "She'd likely succeed, at that, but I'd rather not put it to the test. Shall we go, while we still can?"

"Yeah. And before the gunman, whoever he is, decides to come back," Scott added.

THE CLOCK WAS STRIKING two as Scott drained his ale, glanced at the inch remaining in Granville's mug and signaled for another round. They sat at one of the long, battered wooden tables that lined the narrow interior of the back alley tavern. Tobacco smoke swirled blue around them, nearly as thick as the fog outside. Their damp coats steamed gently in the warmth of the fire at their backs, and the smell of wet wool vied with the sharp richness of tobacco and the acrid odor of spilled beer on muddy sawdust.

"So who d'you think killed Norton?" Scott said.

"And even more interesting, why were they shooting at us?" Granville said.

"Think someone heard him arrange to meet us?"

"That would be my guess. It seems all very chance-driven, though, don't you think? Coincidences worry me."

"Yeah. Probably worry Chief Stewart even more."

Granville ignored the jest. He'd think about what the newly re-appointed Chief of Police—who was still under investigation for illegal payoffs—would make of their latest quest only when and if he had to.

"Maybe we should think about paying someone off. Could make our job easier," Scott added in an undertone.

It was an old argument. "I don't do business that way."

"Yeah, yeah. Times like this, it'd be handy, though."

He grinned at Scott's wry tone, and finished off his ale as a fresh mug was delivered. "Hmmm. But it would make our lives far too simple. So, back to our friend Norton. I have to wonder if he was being followed. And what information he had that was worth killing all three of us for?"

"Had to be about Weston. No other reason to shoot at us too."

"Bad aim?"

Scott snorted and ignored him. "Norton seemed happy enough to talk to me, as long as I paid him. And I kept it quiet."

"So he knew whatever he planned to tell you was dangerous." Granville pictured the dark shape lying sprawled on the damp boards. "Pity he didn't take better precautions."

"Might tell us something about his killer, though. You don't think Weston himself could have done it?"

Granville raised his mug and half-drained it. The ale wasn't too bad, a fair balance of malt and bitter, and he'd nearly grown accustomed to the local preference for serving it cold.

It didn't bring any clarity to the problem at hand, though. "If he's trying to hide, shooting at us seems an ineffective way to do so," Granville said. "No, I think you were right earlier. Weston's either a long way from here or dead. And after tonight, I'm less hopeful that we'll find him alive."

"Too bad." Scott drained his own mug. "So how do we find him and still keep ourselves alive?"

"We find someone else who knows Weston, and hope they don't get murdered too."

"Just like that?"

"We might want to watch our own backs while we do so." Granville lifted his mug in a mock toast. "I believe you're the one who didn't want to be bored?"

3

SATURDAY, APRIL 14, 1900

I t was late morning and barely raining when Granville strolled towards the office he and Scott shared. Their share of gold from the mine they'd found in January had removed their immediate need to work, but neither of them was cut out for the idle life.

This hunt for Weston might well turn into the major case they needed to build a name for themselves, provided they managed not to get killed in the process. They'd come disturbingly close to dying on their last big case.

Patches of fog drifted past, though it was thinner than the previous night, hardly impairing visibility at all. Granville was alert, but had no sense of threat.

The usual bustle of carriages and passersby thronged Hastings Street, and newsboys on the busiest corners hawked the outcome of the latest battle against the Boers in the Transvaal. Granville spared a moment to be thankful that his nephews were too young to following the family tradition of military careers, though he half wished that he'd had that option.

His second brother Cameron had been the son their late father chose to purchase a commission for, and Cam had distinguished himself as an officer in India before perishing in full glory during the battle for the Khyber Pass. He himself had been destined for the clergy until he'd rebelled, a decision that ultimately had seen him vainly seeking gold in the Klondike.

He grinned at the thought of his father's probable reaction to his current life. The old man would have been proud of his venture into trade, possibly even told him so. Right after he'd laughed long and loud. His sense of humor had been one of the fifth Baron's best qualities—a quality which the sixth Baron definitely lacked. Among others.

So why had William sent business Granville's way?

And where was young Weston?

Pushing open the heavy mahogany doors of the building housing their offices, Granville climbed three flights of stairs, absently noting the slick of damp on the grey-veined granite and the burnt-out lamp on the second floor landing that needed replacing. Was it today Trent was due to return?

Their young apprentice, Trent Davis, had spent the last several weeks with relatives in the Interior, and Granville had missed his presence more than he'd expected. The lad's humor and youthful optimism were somehow invigorating when they faced yet another dead end on a case. The boy's ability to shoot straight and stay cool under fire were assets also, though Granville had yet to reconcile his own reluctance to put the boy in that kind of danger with Trent's desire to be a real detective.

"'Bout time you decided to show up," Scott said from the inner office as Granville strode into the outer office. He ignored the jibe, nothing that Trent's desk—which faced the door and the two chairs in the small waiting area—still sat empty. "Any word from Trent?"

"Nope. You haven't heard from him either?"

"Not so far. He'll be here," Granville said, hanging his damp hat and overcoat on the mahogany coat tree and strolling into the inner office.

Scott gave him a dubious look but didn't comment.

Granville sat down across from his partner, gave the untidy stack of papers on Scott's half of the desk a considering look. "Any response to our advertisement?"

"Nothing so far. In fact we don't seem to be washing up gold in any of our enquiries so far. Now what?"

"From what Benton said, Weston won't be able to resist betting on the horses," Granville said. "If he's in town, that is."

Scott's eyes lit up. "Racing?"

"I assume there's a track around this town. Somewhere."

"Well, it may not be London or Chicago, but Vancouver does run to a racetrack. Pretty decent one, too, except for the stumps in the infield."

Granville debated asking the obvious question, but the barely concealed glee on Scott's face changed his mind. "When do they run?"

"Nothing running 'til next Saturday."

"So we know what we're doing next Saturday. In the meantime, where might the aficionados be found?"

"Aficionados, is it?"

Granville raised an eyebrow.

Scott grinned. "Well, I don't know about aficionados, but most of the racetrack gamblers hang out at your old haunt, the Carlton."

"At the Carlton? Where Frances performs? I'd have expected to find them at one of the high stakes clubs."

"Maybe they like the music."

"Or the dancers. Though I didn't see any gambling at the Carlton."

"There's gambling everywhere."

"True enough. We'll head there later tonight, then."

"Good."

"I've been thinking about your informant, though," Granville said, picturing Norton's white face, drained of blood by the bullet that nicked his carotid artery. "We're assuming the poor man was killed because of something Weston is mixed up in. What if it was the other way 'round?"

"You mean if Weston got too close to something Norton was involved in?" Scott tipped back in his chair, stared at the pressed-tin ceiling. "From what I hear, Norton was a scoundrel—one who dealt in reputations—man probably had enemies. Might not be because of us asking questions about Weston, at that."

"He still didn't deserve to die."

"No, but I'm not sure he deserved to live, either. In any case, he's a dead end for us now."

Granville shook his head at Scott's sly grin. "I'm ignoring that. Until we get a better lead on Weston, we might as well find out whatever we can about your late informant. For starters, whom did he work for?"

"Benton, off and on."

"You're not serious?"

Scott's widening grin was not the answer Granville had hoped for.

BENTON'S OFFICE had grown opulent since Granville had seen it last. The plain walls were now covered with English landscapes and medieval tapestries. Most were poorly done copies, though he'd probably paid well for them. The desk had grown, too, and stretched between them like a still wooden pond.

Granville acknowledged Benton's nod of greeting with one of his own, and got straight to the point. "You'll have heard by now that Norton was killed last night. Who did he run with?"

He could feel Scott's tension beside him, the big man growing more rigid with every word.

The gangster's face was expressionless as he faced them, but harsh lines deepened around his mouth. He pulled on his cigar, and a stream of expensive smoke veiled his eyes. "And I should tell you this because?"

"Norton had information about Weston, or at least he said he did. And whatever he knew nearly got us killed along with him. We need any leads you have."

Benton looked them up and down. "I do hope you're as accomplished as you seem to think you are," he said in a deceptively civilized tone.

Granville grinned. "Of course we are. Right, Scott?"

His partner looked deeply uncomfortable with the direction the conversation was taking.

Benton laughed suddenly. "Are you sure you won't work for me? I like your style."

Granville shook his head. "Much as I appreciate the offer, I doubt it would end well. I don't follow orders particularly well, as both my brother the Baron and Scott here will be more than happy to tell you."

Benton chuckled. "You're lucky I like you," he said.

"And that you owe us for saving your Frances's sister and her child," Granville said.

Scott's face paled at his words, but Benton simply shook his head. "Maybe you'll have better luck than my men did. You're faster on Weston's trail, for certain. Try asking for a couple of sorry gamblers named Willis and Jepson. They knew both Weston and Norton. I'll be interested to hear if you get any more out of them than we did."

Granville hoped the man wasn't expecting a report in exchange for the names. He wouldn't be getting one, but it was a conversation he would rather avoid. "How will I know them?"

"Just get the word out you're looking for them. And make sure you carry that knife of yours," Benton said with a tight smile.

Apparently the man's patience had run out. Granville thanked him and they left. Quickly.

On the plank sidewalk outside, he glanced at Scott, grinning to see his partner rolling his eyes.

"Sometimes I wonder how you're still alive," Scott said.

"You saved me from freezing to death, remember?"

"And you've been trying to get yourself killed ever since. What kind of thanks is that?"

"At least I didn't ask Benton to name Weston's bookie," Granville said, turning his collar against the rain and increasing his pace.

Scott groaned. "But you were going to."

"I decided we could start with Willis and Jepson. Work up to the bookie."

Scott mumbled something under his breath.

"What was that?"

"Nothin'. I'll head for the docks, see what I can unearth on those two low-lifes."

"I'll come with you."

"Better not. They'll talk to me before they'll talk to you."

Scott had a point. "Then I'll see what else I can learn about young Weston. Meet you at the office later?"

"Yeah. Probably late afternoon."

That gave him time to get back to the office and check the afternoon post. "I'll see you then."

BY THE TIME he made it back from Benton's office, Granville was drenched. Trying not to drip on the envelopes, he collected the office mail from the mailbox in the lobby, then nearly dropped it while trying to get the outer door unlocked. Dumping the slightly damp envelopes on the reception desk in their outer office, he shook out his dripping coat before hanging it on the coat tree, then flipped through the mail.

None of the envelopes looked like responses to their advertisement, but he carried them into the inner office to open anyway.

By the time he'd sorted through all the mail—skimming the urgent ones—it was nearly one, and he was getting nowhere. Glaring at the stack of opened mail that had nothing at all to do with the case, he'd just decided it was time to eat when the heavy oak outer door to their office banged open.

Hand on his knife, he waited, muscles braced.

And Trent sauntered in, sprawling in one of the upright wooden chairs. It was a less graceful move than the boy had probably intended, and Granville had to bite back a grin. Trent made no mention of his delayed return, but at least he looked to be in one piece.

Tilting the chair back against the wall, Trent watched him through half-closed eyes.

Recognizing one of his own favorite poses, Granville's smile broke out.

The chair came down with a thump. "What's so funny?"

"Not a thing."

Trent gave him a suspicious look, but didn't pursue it. "Had you heard Horace Norton is dead?" he said.

How had the boy heard so quickly? "You knew him?"

"My pa did. So who shot him?"

"How did you know he was shot?"

"Norton was way too wary to let someone close enough to stab him," Trent said.

Interesting. "Where did Norton hang out, do you know?"

"Not really. Pa talked about seeing him mostly when he'd been at one or another of the dives along the water," Trent said. "I was never allowed to go with him."

It amazed Granville that there was no bitterness in the lad's tone, knowing how hard Trent's father's addiction to drink and cards had made his son's life. "He mention any other names when he talked about Norton?"

Trent shrugged, and tipped the chair back against the wall again. "He sometimes mentioned a man named Willis."

So Benton had been straight with them, at least that far. That was good to know. Granville's thoughts returned to Weston, and the little he knew of the fellow. "Were Norton or Willis fond of the races?" he asked.

"The horse races?" Trent grinned. "I know Pa and Norton were. Probably Willis is, too. Too bad they're not running till next week."

"I gather you're fond of the sport?" Granville said in a dry tone. Surely the boy hadn't already been lured by sleek thoroughbreds and seemingly easy money? He hoped not. It was a hard spell to break.

"It's alright," Trent said, in what he probably imagined was an off-hand tone. "We got any new cases?"

Hiding his amusement at the boy's new professionalism, Granville explained their latest undertaking.

"So we're looking for a remittance man? He's probably dead drunk somewhere," Trent said. "He'll show up."

Not according to Benton, he wouldn't. "He's been missing too long. Which is why you need to go down to the Post Office this afternoon, and watch for anyone responding to our ad or showing an interest in Weston's box," Granville said.

He paused, grinned at Trent. "We find our missing heir, maybe we can afford to pay your salary."

"I don't need it, remember?"

"You need it," Granville said evenly. "Just like I do. We can't appear to have income we can't explain."

And since they still had to keep the existence of the mine a secret, they couldn't spend too much of the gold at any one time. Their detective business provided a very handy, and legitimate, source of income. Apparently the boy was having a problem with the notion.

Trent shrugged. "We've got the money. We should just spend it."

"And the minute we do that, the rumors that we found the lost mine start up again," Granville said. "We nearly got killed the last time that happened, remember? Until that mine is registered, we have to be careful."

And they couldn't register the mine because the rightful owner had fled town ahead of a murder charge, and none of them were prepared to steal from a woman, even a murderous one.

"Yeah, I remember," Trent said, tipping his chair even further back. "I don't get why we don't just go somewhere else, where no-one knows where our money comes from."

"Uh huh. And do what?"

"Nothing at all," Trent said with a wide grin. "Ain't—isn't that the point of having money?"

A few years ago Granville had felt the same way. And had it frozen out of him in the Klondike. "Not exactly. Having money with nothing to do is—pointless. Boring."

"Boring? If you have money, you can drink all you want, and gamble, maybe have a girl." Color slid over the lad's cheeks as he spoke, "And even dance with her, and go to the pictures. What's boring about that?"

So Trent had met a girl. That explained a great deal. "And what would you do when you weren't drinking, or gambling, or with your girl?"

Trent looked at him blankly. Clearly the question made no sense in his world. "Sleep?"

Well, it wasn't so different than the life he himself had tried to live, after they'd kicked him out of Oxford for the last time. And the emptier it had felt, the harder he drank, and the more he gambled. It had taken Edward's senseless death to send him looking for more. Only he'd thought it was more gold he was seeking.

Turns out it was more life.

"You can do all that working for us," Granville said. "You just have to do a few other things in the meantime."

Trent brought his chair back to the floor with a crash. "Like waste my time hanging around the Post Office in case we get mail."

Granville was about to ask him if he had something better to do, then thought better of it. "I thought you wanted to be a detective?"

"I do. I just didn't think it would be boring."

"No? Well, it is. Sometimes. What did you expect?"

"Adventure." Trent gave him a sheepish grin. "Like when we were running from that avalanche, and getting shot at."

Granville shook his head. "That kind of adventure is best only when it's long over, and we're not half-frozen and bleeding. Perhaps it's different at sixteen, though that concussion of yours couldn't have been much fun."

"I'm seventeen. And—everything did kinda keep getting fuzzy. But it felt so good to be still alive I didn't care."

Right. "Besides, it wasn't just Norton getting shot at last night— Scott and I were targets too. Now that you're back, you'll probably be added to that list."

"Oh? Good."

Shaking his head—and hiding his grin—Granville picked up one of the letters he'd just opened, began to read. Trent gave him a suspicious look.

Before their apprentice could say anything, the outer door flung open and Scott came in, dripping and cursing. Through the open door, Granville watched his partner hang his hat and overcoat on the coat tree, then shake himself vigorously, spattering droplets of rain everywhere.

"No luck finding Jepson or Willis?" Granville said as Scott joined them in the inner office.

"Nope. All I get is shifty looks and people clamming up. And a strong feeling I should have brought my second gun."

"Well, at least that tells us there's something there to look for." Granville looked back to find Trent glaring at him.

"You already knew about Willis and Norton? Why didn't you tell me?"

"I was about to," Granville said.

Trent looked like he wanted to argue, but before he could get the words out the outer door banged open and two men blew into the inner office, noses red with cold and rain dripping from their brims of their helmets.

Granville's eyes took in the navy uniforms and rounded helmets, then went from one face to the other. He wasn't pleased to see either of them, and they looked far too happy to be here. "Constables. To what do we owe the pleasure of your company?"

"Cut the funny stuff, Granville. Rumor is you're looking for a guy called Weston. Rupert Weston?"

Granville nodded. Scott and Trent had moved to stand, silent and watchful, at his side.

"Do you know where he is?"

"I have no idea."

Constable Brickle seemed to be their spokesman. He eyed Granville suspiciously, as if he couldn't recognize the ring of truth in his words. "I don't know why you want him, and I don't care. We want him more. If you find any information on him, anything at all, you're to report it to us immediately. Understand?"

"What's Weston done?" Scott said, cutting off Granville's response.

His partner knew him too well, Granville thought ruefully. He hadn't been brought up to tolerate rudeness in those not of his class. And though he no longer thought in terms of class distinctions, he still had a problem with lack of manners. Especially when coupled with stupidity.

Brickle clearly wasn't going to answer, but the other officer spoke up. Granville didn't recognize him. He must be one of the three added to the force after the judicial enquiry into police corruption had resulted in some abrupt departures. "He's a person of interest in a recent murder."

Brickle gave his partner a look Granville couldn't read. Had the younger man said more than he should?"

"Really?" Granville said. "Your information is better than ours, then. We haven't been able to find anyone who's seen him in town in the last couple of months."

The second constable smiled slightly. Brickle scowled at both of them. "He's still a person of interest."

Right.

"Who's dead?" Trent said.

Good for him. Although it was reasonable that they would by now have heard of Norton's murder, there was no point in raising questions about how and when they might have found out about it. Brickle would be more than happy to arrest them if he knew they'd found the body.

"Man named Norton," Brickle said.

"How?" Scott asked.

"Shot," the younger constable said.

"Where?" Trent wanted to know.

"That's classified," Brickle growled, shooting a look at his too-vocal partner. "You don't need to know anything more than that. And we need to hear if you find out anything about Weston. Immediately. Got it?"

"We have," Granville said evenly. What they did with it might be another story.

4

The evening meal was finished and while the servants cleared the dining room, the family sat in the parlor. The room smelled pleasantly of the cedar logs burning in the fireplace. Papa was reading the paper, while her mother and two older sisters were embroidering.

Emily stared at the snarled threads in her lap and fought back a groan. It was supposed to be a "G" for Granville, worked in white on the white linen sheet. Her trousseau.

She glanced at the emerald sparking fire on her left hand and sighed.

If their engagement was still a ruse, then the time she was spending was a waste. If the engagement was now real, and her heart leaped a little at the thought, then she was destroying a perfectly good sheet with her lack of skill.

It had been easier when she'd known their engagement was a fiction. Then her only concern had been to help Granville solve his various cases and get his fledging business off the ground. Now...

The ring of the telephone had her dropping her needle. "I'll answer it."

Ignoring her mother's disapproving look, she raced for the telephone table in the hallway. "Turner residence, Emily speaking."

"Good evening, Emily. Would you care to join me for lunch on Monday?"

"I'd adore it, Granville!" she said, then through the parlor doorway, saw her mother frowning over her lack of formality. "I mean Mr. Granville. Where are you thinking of going?"

He laughed. "I gather your parents are within earshot?"

"Yes. But please, go on."

"I'd thought of going to Stroh's, if that suits you? I know you have a typewriting class and will need to get back on time."

"Stroh's is perfect."

"Before you accept, I should warn you that this is primarily a working lunch."

Emily lowered her voice. "So this is connected to a case? Even better. Can you tell me more?"

"We're looking for a missing man. Have you or your sisters ever met a Rupert Weston? Now Lord Weston."

"Who died?" Emily said, earning herself another glare from her mother and a chuckle from her fiancé.

"You don't miss much, do you?" he said, and proceeded to fill her in on the case of the missing heir.

"But I would love to help," Emily said, remembering to lower her voice again. "I've never met him, but perhaps my sisters know of him. They pay more attention to the social whirl."

"Be careful who you talk to, and what you ask. The man's on the run from something, and asking questions about him could be dangerous. Plus the police are interested in him."

"I'll be discreet, I promise," she said, earning herself a sideways glance and a little smile from Mama. "Perhaps I'll talk to Clara instead. She knows everyone."

"Why don't you ask her to join us?"

She'd planned to anyway. She wondered if he knew that tongues would wag if they lunched alone, despite the fact that they'd been engaged for months now. If a wedding date had been set it would be different, but until they made that final commitment, society—in the guise of her mother's friends—was keeping a watchful eye on her.

She hated it, but she was learning to choose her battles. And Clara really would be helpful. "That's a good idea," was all she said.

"Then I'll see you both Monday at noon, if that is convenient?"

"That's perfect," Emily said, then caught her mother's eye and realized she probably wasn't supposed to sound so enthusiastic, either. Too late now.

And she was enthusiastic. She loved spending time with Granville. And she loved being involved in solving his cases.

It was full dark and the lanterns along the CPR docks were lit by the time Granville and Scott reached the Beaver Tavern. The place drew some of the worst riffraff from that part of town—wharf rats, seamen avoiding the law, thieves too stupid or too violent to operate from a better locale.

It was oppressively dim and smoky, reeking of cheap whiskey and unwashed bodies, reminding Granville of most of the bars in the Klondike. Probably why he liked the place so much.

Scott didn't share his enthusiasm, however. He'd undoubtedly known places like this in Chicago, with less pleasant memories attached. The big man glowered at the crowded room. "We'll probably not even find them here."

Granville refrained from pointing out that coming here had been his suggestion. "Where are the games?"

"Back of the bar."

It figured. He ordered another round, passing an extra bill to the barkeep when it was delivered. "Poker?" he said.

An assessing glance, then the extra money was pocketed and a nod given in the direction of a door at the far end of the bar, which gave them entry.

Granville and Scott stepped into pandemonium. This room was smaller, more crowded and thick with smoke. There was a narrow table serving as a bar and three round tables, each ringed with eager spectators, crowded close. The frantic buzz told Granville the stakes were high, or at least higher than most of those here could easily afford.

"You have any idea what these two look like?" he said.

"Trent says Willis is about medium height, maybe a little less, thin, dark. Short hair, brown eyes. Knife scar on one cheek."

They scanned the room, squinting through the smoke. Scott snorted. "Description fits about a quarter of the men in here."

"Then I guess we'd better take Benton's advice," Granville said. "You have your knife?"

"Knife nothin'. I've got my pistol."

"The cops catch you with that gun, you know they'll be happy to throw you in jail," Granville reminded him.

"Yeah, well I'm not stupid enough to ignore both yesterday's ambush and a warning from Benton," Scott said. "You carrying?"

"Knife."

Scott grunted again, his eyes busy. Before Granville could ask him what he was up to, his partner was leaning forward to say something to an ill-favored fellow with knife scars on both cheeks.

"Ah, hell," Granville muttered, draining his whiskey.

Putting the word out that they were looking for Willis and Jepson was an unsettling experience. Instead of the questions Granville had expected, they were met with silence, the occasional raised eyebrow, and a feeling of too many eyes watching them. By the time they were halfway around the room, he was wishing he'd brought his revolver, illegal or no.

It wasn't long before Willis came looking for them, sidling up to Scott as if he was trying to avoid notice.

"I hear you're looking for me?"

"We are," Scott said. "We wanted to talk to you about your pal Norton. And his pal Weston."

"I don't know no..."

"Benton gave us your name, said you might be able to help us," Granville said before the man could finish his denial.

"Benton?" Willis stood silent for a moment, gnawing on his lower lip. "Well, maybe we should talk. But not here."

"Jepson too?" Scott said.

Willis darted a glance around him. "He's not here."

"Oh?"

"Look, buy me a beer and maybe we can talk," Willis said. Without waiting for a response, he led the way back into the main room.

They took their beers to a small table in one corner. "Well?" Scott said, his eyes on Willis.

Willis raised his mug and drained half of it, his Adam's apple rising and falling with every swallow. Granville watched the smaller man, noting the flush on his cheek and his reluctance to meet their eyes. Getting him to talk would not be easy.

Scott was up for the challenge. "You still saying you don't know Norton?"

Willis thunked his mug down and scowled. "No, I'm not saying that. Can't very well, can I? Not with Benton saying something else. And I'm not fool enough to cross that one."

"Probably wise." Scott grinned at him, and drained half his own beer. "Ahhhh. Now, why don't you tell us what you know about the man."

"Norton's dead," Willis said. "And wasn't much use when he was alive."

"Oh?" Scott said noncommittally.

"Man was a poor gambler and a worse associate." Willis scowled. "He'd sell anyone out for the price of a beer."

Scott grinned. "So I've heard. And yet you hung around with him?"

"We gambled at the same places, that's all."

"Any idea what information Norton had to sell us?" Scott said.

Willis' lips tightened and he shook his head.

"What about young Weston?" Scott said. "You know him?"

Willis shrugged, grabbed for his beer. "Not know him, exactly, but he's a gambler, like me, so I see him a lot. Or used to see him, I guess."

"You haven't seen him in a while?"

"Nah. He was on a losing streak, had to quit for a while. He'll be back."

"He's done that before?" Scott asked.

"Now and again. Sometimes the luck runs against you."

Granville narrowed his eyes as he watched this byplay. That didn't sound like the Weston he'd heard about. He wondered what Willis was working so hard to hide.

And from whom? Keeping his mouth shut, he slowly drank his beer, trying to be invisible. This one was Scott's.

"When did you last see Weston?" Scott was asking.

"Dunno. Must be a few weeks now," Willis said.

"Best we can figure, he's been missing since the ninth of February, or thereabouts. You seen him since?"

Willis frowned as though trying to remember, but Granville thought he looked wary now. Before he'd just looked nervous.

"February ninth?" Willis said. "That's a while ago. But I think maybe it was that week I won the pot at the Balmoral. Early February, anyway. I was pretty busy celebrating for a while there, and my memory's a little fuzzy."

He tried out a smile on them.

It failed, and Willis began talking faster. "He was there that night, Weston I mean. I remember 'cause he was ribbing me about finally beating him. Don't recollect seeing him after that. How come you're looking for him, anyway?"

"We've some information to his advantage. Believe me, he'd want to hear this."

"Yeah? Well, wish I could help you more. Sorry," Willis said, looking anything but.

"What about Jepson?" Scott said. "We'd like to talk to him too, see what he might know."

"Jepson?" Willis' voice rose a little higher. "He left town."

"Oh?"

"Yeah. Left right after Norton was killed."

"Interesting." Scott grinned broadly and Willis looked worried. "So when's he planning on coming back?"

"I doubt he'll be back. He went back home—family business."

"And where is home?" Scott said.

"Illinois," Willis said.

"Whereabouts? I'm from Chicago myself."

Willis grabbed his pint and took a few deep swallows. Setting it down, he wiped his lips on his sleeve and stared at Scott. "You'd have to ask him. Some small town or other. Can't remember the name of it because I don't much care."

He was lying, and not very well. Why? Granville wondered.

Scott shrugged. "It was a long shot anyway. Thanks for your help."

"Don't mention it," Willis said, and swigged back the rest of his beer.

"Want another?" Scott asked him.

"Sure, but I'd better get back to my game."

"One last question then," Scott said. "Any idea why Weston left?"

"Nope."

"Anyone have it in for him?"

Willis swiped at his forehead with a filthy handkerchief. "Why would they?"

"Well, that's kinda what we'd like to know. Because from what we know so far, he's either running from something or he's dead."

"Dead?" Willis said, his voice rising.

"You think he's alive?" Scott asked.

"Of course he's—why wouldn't he be alive?"

"But you haven't seen him?"

Willis' eyes darted around the room, settling on another table on the far side of the room before moving back to Scott. "No. I already told you."

Granville decided it was time to step in. "You haven't told us a thing," he said. "Yet Benton seemed to think you'd be of some assistance. Should I tell him that you weren't able to help us?"

Willis went pale. "Yes. No. I mean..." He wiped his forehead again. "Look, I knew Weston a little. I liked him. But I don't know where he's gone or why. I'd help you if I could."

It felt like a lie. But which part? "But you do know something. What?" Granville said.

Willis started. "I—I—I only know that Weston seemed kinda nervy, the last couple weeks."

"Nervy?" Granville asked.

"Umm. Not himself, jumpy, like."

"You know why?" Scott said.

"No. Maybe the luck ran against him," Willis said. "But I think he ran. I think something got too much for him, and he ran."

"Where'd he go?" Scott asked.

"Not back to England," Willis said. "He hated it there."

It was the first thing Willis had sounded certain of.

"If not England, then where?" Granville asked.

"He'd be looking to gamble," Willis said. "Somewhere he could make some money. Maybe he went back to Frisco."

"San Francisco? Why there?" Granville asked.

"When Weston came out from England, he landed there, spent some time before he came north," Willis said.

"Why'd he leave?" Scott asked.

Willis shrugged. "Who knows? Prob'ly lost too much, the town got too hot. But it's been a few years. Maybe he went back."

It made sense. But Willis still looked far too nervous, and he kept checking who else was in the room. They weren't likely to get any more out of him now, but who was Willis afraid would see him talking to them? And why?

"Know anyone else we could talk to?" Scott said.

Willis shrugged. "Weston used to pal around sometimes with a couple of guys. "Mac" McAndrews and Toby Kerr. Mac's a redhead and Kerr is short and bony. They're gamblers, too, but that's all I know," Willis said. "Or maybe try Weston's bookie."

"Who'd he use?" Scott asked.

"You never heard it from me, but a guy named Graham," Willis said. "Todd Graham. And now I gotta get back to my game or I won't be paying my rent this month."

As he and Scott exited onto Water Street, Granville drew in a deep breath of the salty air, savoring the chilly freshness of it. The gaslights along the street were worse than useless. Even after the dim lighting inside, it took a moment to adjust to the dark of a moonless night, and his eyes felt gritty from the smoke in the bar.

"Well, that was a waste of time," Scott said, walking towards uptown. "I'd love to know who's making all of 'em so nervous."

Granville matched his friend's long stride, their breath rising in frosty clouds above them. "At least we know Weston arrived via San Francisco. It might be useful to know why he came here. Maybe your sister knew him in Frisco?"

"Frances? I doubt it, but I'll ask her."

"And we have another couple of names," Granville added. "McAndrews and Kerr. Wonder how they fit in?"

"Not to mention a lead on the bookie," Scott said. "But at this rate, young Weston will be dead before we can even confirm he's left town."

"He may be dead already. Even if Willis doesn't think so."

"Yeah. Interesting that Jepson took the first freight out," Scott said.

"Not surprising. Their buddy Norton's dead."

"And us asking about Weston worried Willis more than any questions we asked about Norton. You notice that?"

"I noticed he couldn't wait to get away from us," Granville said. "He seems to think Weston left town long before Norton was killed, though."

"Cops don't think so. But no one's seen hide nor hair of Weston in weeks. I can't figure why the police are so interested in Weston for Norton's murder."

"I'm surprised you didn't ask Willis that."

Scott grinned. "He was nervy enough already. Whatever Weston's got himself into, Willis wants no part of it."

"I noticed that," Granville said. Whatever Weston had got himself into was likely not good news. For any of them. "Think it's too late to track McAndrews and his buddy down tonight?"

"Night's young yet."

It was the reply Granville had expected. "The Carlton, wasn't it? You go on ahead. I'll meet you there."

His partner gave a quick nod, and increased his pace. They'd played this game before. Granville watched Scott go, then turned the corner onto Columbia, his thoughts on Weston.

And two men fell on him from a dark alley, hard fists driving into his face and his stomach.

No guns this time, so they weren't trying to kill him, the disciplined part of Granville's mind noted. He left his knife in its hidden sheath. Spun and went low.

He caught the one on his left with a driving upward blow to the nose. Blood sprayed everywhere.

A hard right to the chin and the second man was laid out flat.

The first man—still bleeding heavily—got in a shot to Granville's kidneys that nearly dropped him. They knew what they were doing.

But so did he.

A quick uppercut to the chin, a hard left to the stomach, and the first man was down. The other was getting groggily to his feet, fists clenched. Granville set his stance, ready to knock him down again.

But the first man hadn't stayed down, either.

Granville caught a hard blow from behind that half-stunned him. "Leave this one alone, if y'know what's good for you," the first man said.

Shaking it off, Granville spun and returned the blow, noting the Cockney accent. The fellow moved pretty fast too, he thought, dodging another blow.

Granville got in a hard hit of his own. "And which one is that?"

"You know. Stop looking for the toff."

The toff. That would be Weston.

A flicker of movement alerted Granville, and he spun out of reach of the taller second man. Turning slightly, he delivered another hard punch to his first opponent. "Who hired you?"

"None of your concern," the second man said, reaching for him.

"Wrong answer," Granville said, knocking the fellow out with a left-handed upper-cut that the thug hadn't expected. "Got a better one?" he asked the Cockney, watching him closely.

A shake of a head, the man peering muzzily back at him. "Not my place. I'm the messenger. Think 'bout it, or you'll be seeing us again."

"Your choice. Don't expect that conversation to go any better."

He blocked the anticipated blow. Then laid the Cockney out with a hard right.

Rubbing at his sore jaw, Granville left the sorry duo behind.

5

G ranville's mood hadn't improved much by the time he reached the Carlton. The main room was crowded and thick with the mingled odors of cigars, whisky and bay rum. Granville weaved his way through the revelers, who were beginning to focus on the stage where a spotlight was tracing idle circles.

Frances must be about to start her first show of the evening.

He eyed the inebriated crowd. Rowdy and increasingly noisy, they'd settle down when Scott's sister took the stage. He hoped.

Sure enough, the wail of a lone trumpet sounded and the spotlight vanished. It was Frances Scott's cue. Glancing at the far corner of the room, nearest the small stage, Granville recognized the blank faces and hulking bodies of two of Benton's toughs. Which meant he didn't need to worry about Frances' safety. Only his own and that of his informants.

Assuming he could find them, that is.

His eyes scanned the crowded, smoky room, looking for McAndrews' flame-red hair or Kerr's short, bony frame. Since he'd never met either man, it helped that they were easy to describe. Or it would have helped if either man had been present.

If Scott was right about there being high stakes gambling here, it was well hidden. There had to be a back room somewhere.

His gaze returned to Benton's bully boys. He'd assumed they were there to protect Frances, but Benton was subtle, too. Most things had a purpose beyond the obvious.

All eyes were glued to the stage, where a huge white-feathered fan had just appeared, topping a pair of shapely legs. No-one was paying any attention to him, and that included Benton's men. He moved at an oblique angle behind them, then along the far wall towards the back.

And there it was.

PUSHING open the section of paneling that didn't quite align, Granville slipped into a narrow corridor where the chill damp of a foggy night crept through the thin outside wall, overlaid the cigar smoke and whisky fumes from the main room. Under the beat of music and clapping from behind the inner wall, he could hear a murmur of voices and the clink of poker chips. It came from the far end of the corridor.

It was a familiar sight that met his eyes as he stood in the door-way, assessing the men gathered around a handful of round, felt-topped tables. Faces intent, hats pushed back, they concentrated on the turn of a card and the quickly placed bets.

Scanning the room, he noted two redheads, each seated at different tables, and a short, cadaverous looking fellow seated at the same table as the taller redhead.

"Mac" McAndrews and Toby Kerr, presumably. The only face he recognized was Scott's. His partner was seated at the same table as their quarry. With a grin, Granville sauntered over to stand behind him.

The way Scott played poker, he might need to step in before Scott lost their business on the turn of a card. It still amazed him how quickly his otherwise capable partner lost track of the run of the cards.

As if reading his thoughts, Scott half-turned and glared at him. "Bout time you got here."

"My apologies for the delay. Shall I sit in on the next hand?"

The question earned him a frown from McAndrews and a nod from Scott. He checked the four chips lying in front of his partner and the small stacks in front of McAndrews and two others.

Yes, it was definitely time to sit in.

By the time Scott stood up to let Granville take his place, the big man was down to two chips. "Don't say anything," he muttered into Granville's ear.

Granville's only response was a grin, which broadened as he picked up the cards he'd been dealt. His eyes sharpened and his shoulders firmed. "Shall we play, gentlemen?"

Three hours later, the stack of chips in front of Granville was larger than that of any other player. The last four inches of a cigar smoldered in the ashtray in front of him. His fellow-players looked resigned, defeated or angry. McAndrews was in the latter camp.

Realizing it, Granville had been subtly baiting him for the last hour and a half. His strategy was paying off. With every card played, the flush on McAndrews' sharp cheekbones grew redder.

The whiskey he swigged back with every lost hand wasn't helping him any. "Cards can't be running that well," McAndrews muttered.

"Excuse me?" Granville said.

Heads turned from Granville to McAndrews and back. Not a few hands moved to hidden guns. It wasn't legal to go armed in Vancouver, but then high-stakes poker wasn't exactly legal either.

"Nothing at all." McAndrews muttered and pushed some chips forward. "Call."

The other players folded.

"Full house. Jacks high." Granville said.

McAndrews threw down three aces. There was a murmur from the onlookers who now crowded around the small table. The tension between Granville and McAndrews, to say nothing of Granville's winning streak, had drawn them in.

Chips clattered across the table to where Granville sat.

Two of the other players were cleaned out. One pulled out a small notebook and raised an eyebrow at Granville, who had no choice but to nod. He just hoped the fellow had the resources to cover his IOUs. The second man stood, and reached across to shake Granville's hand. "Well played," he said, in an accent as crisply English as Granville's own.

Granville gave a quick nod of acknowledgement, noting the newcomer who slipped into the vacated chair as a new hand was dealt. Strain was beginning to show on the other men's faces. Despite the smoky air and the late hour, he felt invigorated, more alive than he'd felt in weeks. With a half-grin, he reached for his next hand of cards, checked them.

Across from him, McAndrews grew even more flushed. His eyes bored into every card that flew from the dealer's hand, then switched to Granville's face. "Well?"

In answer Granville placed a stack of chips in the center of the table. "Raise," he said.

Two men folded immediately, leaving McAndrews, his thin buddy, the newcomer, the poor fellow with the IOUs and one other. Granville could feel the tension in the room. It was what he'd been working towards, and it felt good.

Still, he was glad to know Scott stood behind him. His partner's eyes would miss nothing. They'd played this game before, though usually he didn't bait his opponents. This time, McAndrews' temper could be the shortcut they needed.

Granville discarded two cards, picked up, and the next round began. The others watched him warily. Good.

When his turn came around Granville placed a second stack of chips beside the first. "Raise," he said.

The newcomer matched, the others folded.

McAndrews paled, then flushed more deeply and his hands clenched on his cards. He pushed the last of his chips to the center of the table. "Call," he said, and laid down a full house, aces high on the green baize.

The newcomer laid down a flush. "Guess my luck's not in tonight," he said, scraping back his chair. "I'm done."

Granville exhaled a pungent cloud of smoke and drained his whiskey, setting the glass on the table with a thump. "Straight flush," he said casually as he laid the cards on the table.

"It's not possible." McAndrews stood and leaned across the table, glaring at Granville. "It just isn't possible."

Granville leaned back in his chair. "Are you implying something?" he asked in a very quiet voice.

Through the hush that followed his words, the wail of the trumpet and the thumping of the drums sounded clearly.

McAndrews met Granville's hard gaze, the thick veins in his neck standing out. "Implying? No. I'm accusing you!"

"Ah. Of what, might I ask?" Granville's tone might have been casual, but every muscle was tense, ready for action—and the men seated around the table knew it. Chairs scraped back as they moved to distance themselves from the inevitable explosion.

"You're ch..." the other man began, then took a good look at Granville's eyes.

"Yes? You' were saying?"

"Those cards can't have fallen so. Not twice in an evening."

"I think you need to finish your thought," Granville said, standing to tower over the other man. "And then I think we need to take this discussion outside."

McAndrews' jaw thrust forward. "Sounds like a threat to me, and I'm not one to sit still for threats. You're a cheater!"

Scott nudged Granville from behind. "Want me to check the cards?" he whispered, loud enough to be heard by half the room.

Granville shook his head, his gaze fixed on his prey. "I don't need to prove my innocence. But this fellow needs to answer for the insult."

"Check 'em," McAndrews spat out. "I'm not taking this man's word for anything."

"Man clearly can't see what's right in front of him," muttered Scott under his breath as he reached for the cards.

The sally was met by a wave of laughter, which was cut off abruptly when McAndrews knocked Scott's hand down. "You're his friend. I don't trust you, either."

Scott froze, his eyes pinning McAndrews. "Don't kill the fool," he said to Granville. "Leave that part to me."

"I think I have the prior claim. After all he named me a cheater."

"Well, I think he just did the same to me. And struck me, too."

"I have first claim," Granville said, his voice soft but deadly.

"You can break his legs, but leave it to me to end the miserable cur's existence."

A couple of the onlookers chuckled nervously.

McAndrews was pretending not to hear them, his eyes fixed on the men examining the cards.

Through the wall came the throbbing of the drums and the chanting of the spectators. "Fran-*ny*. Fran-*ny*. Fran-*ny*."

"I suppose I could let you have a piece of him," Granville said in a considering tone.

"Now you're talking," Scott said to Granville.

The two men examining the cards turned over the last card, running careful fingers over each side. "Nothing," said the one with a shrug. The other man nodded. McAndrews turned pale.

McAndrews turned back to the Granville and Scott. "I—I owe you an apology."

"And some money," Scott noted, pointing up the table.

McAndrews swallowed hard, scooped up the coins and dumped them in front of Granville. "I was wrong."

Granville glanced at the money, then back at McAndrews. "So you're satisfied I didn't cheat?"

"Yes."

"You're not going to let him off?" Scott said.

"He maligned my honor," said Granville at his most English. "And honor must be satisfied. Outside."

Scott grinned and reached for the coins. "I'll take care of these and meet you outside."

Granville nodded, his attention fixed on McAndrews.

Who stood and made his way to a small exit neatly concealed in the side wall, his back held stiff and straight.

Only once did he cast a glance back at Granville.

6

The door opened into a dimly lit alley stinking of rotting kitchen waste and stale urine. Granville was glad for the cold, or the smell would have been much worse. It was raining, a fine thin drizzle that beaded on his hair and eyelashes.

As he stepped from the lighted doorway into the dark alley, McAndrews spun and lashed out with a hard right hook. Granville had been expecting something of this nature and moved inside the blow, rendering it powerless. His own right hook caught the man off guard, flattening him on the filthy ground.

McAndrews lay still for a few seconds, then shook his head to clear it and launched himself at Granville again. This time he connected.

Granville danced back, shaking off the blow while watching his opponent closely. Judging his moment, he leapt in.

Another flurry of blows saw McAndrews back on the ground.

When it was clear the fellow was about to get up and attack again, Granville pulled his knife. As light from the doorway glinted off the blade, McAndrews froze.

"Got your attention, have I?" Granville said with a grin. "Good.

Now kindly stop attacking me, or I really might have to kill you. Or let my partner do so."

McAndrews coughed and spat blood. "So what d'you want?"

"Answers. Nothing more."

"I thought you wanted to kill me. Something about your honor?"

Granville laughed. He might even like this man. "I needed a chance to talk to you alone. So I confess I baited you."

"Didn't take much, did it?" the other man said ruefully. "Give me a hand up?"

Granville did so, keeping the knife in the other hand, in case McAndrews was more devious than he seemed. "I'd have thought a temper like that would be a problem for a gambler."

"You'd have thought right. It's why I end up taking so many risks."

"Hmmm. Well, if you can answer a few of my questions, we can lessen the risk of your current situation."

"What's it worth to me?"

Granville laughed aloud. He was starting to appreciate this fellow's style. "Your life. You get to keep it."

"Not sure that's such a good thing, given how much I just lost."

Under the light tone was a note that told Granville the fellow more than half meant it. He pictured Edmund's pale face and haunted eyes. If his old friend hadn't played one too many games, Edmund would still be alive.

"What's it worth to you?" he said.

"What is what worth?" McAndrews asked.

"Regaining what you lost tonight."

"Everything." McAndrews peered at Granville, seemed to be trying to read his expression. "But what do you want?"

"I told you, information."

"What kind of information is worth that much money?" McAndrews' wary tone confirmed what Granville had begun to suspect.

Despite whatever situations his temper might get him into, the man was honest. He deserved honesty in return.

"I understand you know a man named Weston. I need to know everything you know about him."

"Why?"

Even with far too much money on the line, McAndrews hadn't immediately agreed. Granville's respect for the man grew.

"I'm a private investigator, and..."

"Are you with Pinkerton's?"

It seemed everyone had heard of the Pinkerton's National Detective Agency, despite the fact that they were an American firm. He and Scott had their work cut out if they hoped to become the agency of choice in town.

"No, private. In any case, I need to find Weston to deliver some good news. From Home." McAndrews' accent said he was American, and from the east coast, if he didn't miss his guess. "From England," Granville clarified.

"Go on."

"Weston seems to have disappeared. I gather his health might benefit from a quick return to England, since I'm not the only one looking for him. I mean him no harm—I'm not so sure about the others. Will you help?"

"Perhaps. I'd need to hear more."

Granville nodded, glanced around him. "This alley is a decidedly unpleasant place for this discussion. Can I buy you a drink?"

"Appreciate it. But not here."

"No. The Taylor Arms?"

A QUARTER HOUR later Granville and McAndrews sat at a small table at the back of a pine-paneled lounge, whiskeys in front of them. Granville's eyes swept the place, looking for any signs of danger or of interest in them.

It must be a slow night—voices were low, the smoke was only a thin veil, not a blanket, and the leather-topped tables around them were empty. The few customers were either deep in their own conversations or too drink-sodden to notice anyone else. Which created exactly the privacy he needed for this conversation.

McAndrews tipped his glass towards him, took a long swallow, then sat back. Waiting.

Granville raised his own glass in acknowledgement. "Did you ever sense Weston's life was in danger?"

"In danger?" McAndrews sat straighter. "You really think he's in that kind of trouble?"

"What do you think?"

"At first I just thought him accident-prone, but I'd begun to think him one of those unlucky souls that bad luck seems to follow around."

"Accident-prone? Weston suffered a series of accidents?"

"Or bad luck." McAndrews downed another third of his whiskey, then considered Granville over the nearly empty glass. "But the fact you're asking the question suggests that it could be more than either, am I right?"

"That depends. What kind of accidents are we talking about?"

"Innocuous ones, at first. A tree branch falls in a high wind and narrowly misses him. He loses his footing on the wharf and nearly goes for an unexpected swim. In February." The other man gave him a wry half-grin. "And the man can't swim."

Granville watched McAndrews' face as he talked, looking for what? Honesty? "They sound like genuine accidents."

"They seemed that way, as I say. But then there was the runaway wagon that nearly ran him down, and the overloaded cart whose falling barrels nearly squashed him. Not to mention the time he found himself in front of a panicked horse that nearly stomped him."

"I gather Weston has good reflexes?" Granville said.

"He's very quick indeed. And good with horses, it seems, even panicked ones. He didn't fare so well in the bar brawl that broke out around him. Nor when his barber came to work drunk one day."

"Was he badly injured?"

"A sprained shoulder from the one, a cut that just missed his artery from the other. A few other bruises and strains from various other incidents, each seemingly happenstance."

"He was simply in the wrong place at the wrong time?" Granville suggested.

"Yes. Or so it seemed at the time," McAndrews said.

Granville downed a mouthful of whiskey while he considered that. "How close together were these accidents of Weston's?"

"Spread out a bit, but it went on for two weeks or more," McAndrews said.

"And how did Weston react to these accidents?"

"He laughed them off. Said maybe they'd use up his quota of bad luck and the cards would start running in his favor again."

"So he didn't take them seriously?" Granville asked.

"He doesn't take much seriously."

And if Granville hadn't been shot at and then warned off, he might not have taken McAndrews' recitation of Weston's "accidents" seriously. But he had been, and he was.

"I'll need a list of all the incidents you can remember," Granville said. "With the dates if possible."

McAndrews nodded. "I'll be as detailed as I can."

He didn't doubt it. "Do you know anything about a man named Norton? He was some kind of acquaintance of Weston's."

"The name doesn't mean anything to me," McAndrews said.

"Weston never mentioned him?"

"No. Why? Is this Norton important?"

"He was killed the other night, down on the docks. The police seem to feel Weston might be involved."

"It doesn't fit with what I know of Weston."

"What do you know?" Granville asked.

Another shrug. "I know a bit about his finances. He was often at low tide, considered selling investment shares for a mortgage company."

"You're an investor?"

"Me? Hardly." McAndrews gave a dry chuckle. "I'm an accountant. I work for Clarkson, Cross & Helliwell."

"So I take it accountants don't have a lot of money to invest."

McAndrews laughed then, and the tension went out of his shoulders. "Not usually—the honest ones, anyway."

"And you know about Weston's finances—how?"

"Weston and I gambled together," McAndrews said. "He did me a favor or two. When he got a job offer from the mortgage firm, he asked my advice. His financial background is a little lacking."

Not surprising. Weston's eldest brother would have been the one taught how to manage the estate. As a third son with no aptitude for the clergy, Weston would have received little attention and less training.

Which wasn't too dissimilar to his own situation. Which had made starting his own business more than a little challenging. Luckily he'd proved to be good at the business end of things.

Which didn't seem to be the case for Weston. "And what did you advise?"

"The numbers he showed me were too risky, and I warned him to stay clear." McAndrews grimaced.

"I gather he didn't much like the advice."

"He wasn't thrilled to hear it, no. He seemed rather—desperate for money. More so than I'd ever seen him."

Interesting. "But did he take your advice?" Granville asked.

"He said he was going to. But then he disappeared, so I don't know if he talked to them or not."

"So he disappeared right after you told him not to take that job?"

McAndrews stared at Granville for a moment. "Ye-es," he said slowly. "Yes, that's exactly right."

"Which firm was Weston talking with?"

A pause. "I suppose I can tell you, since Weston is missing. It was Vancouver Permanent Investment & Loan. Charles Putnam's the man in charge."

"I'll have a chat with them. Did Weston's circle include any new acquaintances around that time?"

"He was always meeting new people," McAndrews said. "No-one stands out."

"What about San Francisco? I gather he has some history there?"

"History? I wouldn't call it that. He got off the boat there, stayed a few weeks to gamble, then came north."

"Why?"

McAndrews shrugged. "He said it wasn't to his taste. That's all I know. And that his remittance got sent here, which I suspect was reason enough to leave Frisco."

"Would he have gone back to San Francisco?"

"I'd be surprised if he has—I never heard him mention it favorably," McAndrews said.

Which likely meant he'd found some trouble there. Granville wondered if it had finally caught up with him here. "What can you tell me about Weston? What kind of man is he?"

"Young. Restless. Too bold for his own good." McAndrews tapped long fingers against his glass. "He's arrogant, and makes too much of the class he was born into. And at the same time he's rebelling against everything it stands for."

Obviously McAndrews was a man who saw others clearly. "Go on."

"Weston is intelligent, quick to see an opportunity. Good company. A terrible poker player." A roughened laugh. "Not that he'd admit it. One of the things we have in common."

There was something the man wasn't saying. "You like him. Why?"

A shrug, a quick swallow and McAndrews' glass was empty. Granville caught the bartender's eye, signaled for another round.

"He's done me a few favors," McAndrews said.

"Favors."

"Sometimes the reckless ones are the best ones to have at your back," McAndrews said. The words came too fast, the tone hard. "He got me out of a rough spot or two."

"Would you call him a friend?" Granville asked.

"Aye, I would, God help me."

JUDGING THE MOMENT RIGHT, Granville retrieved their whiskeys from the bar, leaving a generous tip. He pushed one of the glasses towards McAndrews. The fellow grabbed it, downed a third of it. "Thanks."

Granville nodded. He debated telling McAndrews about the attack on him and Scott. Decided it wasn't necessary.

"I need to find Weston," he said. "Before anyone else does. Can you think of anything that might help?"

"I think so. But you're not going to like it,' McAndrews said.

"Go on."

"Weston vanished without paying any of his debts. And he didn't tell me or anyone else where he was going, didn't even hint that he might be leaving." McAndrews drained his glass. "He's probably dead. Or if he isn't, he likely wishes he was."

Granville hadn't expected that, or the depression in McAndrews' voice. "What makes you think so?"

"Weston vanished less than a week before his quarterly allowance from England was due to arrive. And he was dead broke."

Granville pictured that overflowing mailbox. "So where's the money?"

"Still at the Post Office," McAndrews said. "In a postal draft no-one else can cash."

"You're sure Weston didn't collect it? Or have someone else do it?"

"I'm sure. The clerk's a cousin of mine."

"Ah." So either Weston was dead, or he expected to be killed if he stayed in town. And he hadn't trusted anyone enough to have them collect his money for him. "Where would the fellow go without funds?"

"No idea."

Granville raised an eyebrow. "So what scared him off?"

"I wish I knew," McAndrews said. "He played poker most of that night, and lost, but that's nothing new."

"I hear he was in debt to Benton."

"Yes, but he was always in debt. He knew his allowance was due in six days. So did Benton, I'm sure."

No wonder Benton's men were looking for him now. "So Weston had no reason to run?"

A snort. "No more than usual," McAndrews said. "He wouldn't even leave a game that was running against him, much less leave town for what he regarded as a few losses."

Granville remembered the feeling, being sure that the next card would be the one to change everything. "And he didn't seem worried?"

"Not at all, he seemed in good spirits. Proud, if anything."

"Proud? Of what?"

"He didn't say," McAndrews said. "Dropped a few hints about making a fortune, but then he'd change the subject if you pressed him. He had that spark in his eye he got when he was about to make a big bet."

"When did you last see him? Was he still gambling?"

"He cashed in and left the gaming room a couple of hours after midnight. When I left an hour or so later, he was still in the main room, deep in conversation."

"With whom, do you know?" Granville asked.

"Sure," McAndrews said. "He was talking with that financier, Gipson."

Gipson again.

He and George Gipson had cordially detested each other since they had clashed in the Klondike. Gipson had tried to kill him over a gold mine then, and had done the same since over other business ventures.

Good thing he was hard to kill.

Unfortunately Gipson was proving equally resilient. The man seemed to have more luck than the weasel Granville had once named him. Even fraud charges slid off him.

Given the sad state of the local police force, that shouldn't be a surprise, but the provincial judiciary were relatively honest. It didn't seem to matter.

"Were Weston and Gipson doing business together?" Granville asked.

"Not so far as I know. I warned him against dealing with the man."

Good to know that Gipson hadn't fooled everyone in town. "Why are you being so straight with me?"

"Aside from the fact that I owe you more than I can afford to lose?" McAndrews downed the last of his whiskey. "Because at heart Weston's a good man, and I owe him. I think he's in trouble. And I haven't seen anyone else looking to help him."

7

MONDAY, APRIL 16, 1900

It was a cloudy grey morning, threatening rain. Granville switched on the gooseneck lamp on his desk and stared at the stack of mail Scott had put in front of him. "What's this?"

"Advertising mostly," Scott said.

"And why is it on my side of the desk?"

"It's your turn to deal with it. Since you say we can't afford help, and Trent isn't here."

Granville was about to deliver the response that statement deserved when the opening of the office door had them exchanging glances.

"Are we expecting anyone?" Granville said as he strode into the outer office, hand resting on the knife on his hip.

"Telegram, sir." The delivery boy beamed as he handed the familiar folded yellow flimsy to Granville. "Sign here, please."

Granville signed and tipped him. He opened the telegram with some caution, scanning the message as he walked back to his desk.

"Well?" Scott said.

"It's from my brother—the contract terms," Granville said. "They'll have a local lawyer draw up the official document once we agree."

"That was quick. They must have finalized it the minute they got your telegram."

"Hmm." Granville passed it to his partner.

Scott gave a soft whistle. "It's lucrative, anyway. Why are they willing to pay us so well?"

"Knowing my brother as I do, probably because there's a good chance of one or both of us losing our lives. Again, knowing my brother, it would probably be me, so you needn't worry."

That earned him a grin. "Seems easy enough, anyway." Scott flicked the letter.

"Seems, indeed."

"You've experience with your brother's schemes?"

"Oh, yes." It was all Granville could bring himself to say. Bitter experience.

"So do we accept? Or not?"

He nodded. "We accept. It's good money."

Scott gave him a searching look but didn't comment. "You're looking a little battered this morning. How did your discussion with McAndrews go?"

"That was the easy one," Granville said. "It was the two thugs that decided to deliver a message earlier that caused most of the damage."

"Why didn't you mention this before now?"

"Didn't seem important." He met Scott's scowl with a grin. "They weren't very good, and now we're certain that someone doesn't want us looking for Weston. Which is another reason to take the case, actually."

"Any idea who that someone is?"

"Not a one. And McAndrews wasn't much help. Though he did tell me Weston had dealings with Gipson," Granville said, and gave Scott the overview of his chat with McAndrews.

"Weston left before his money got here?" Scott said.

"According to McAndrews he did."

"So we just need to figure out what made him run so suddenly."

"Or at least where he ran to," Granville said.

"Hmmm. Shouldn't be too difficult." Scott glanced at his face again. "Not nearly as difficult as explaining those scrapes on your face to your fiancée. We are meeting her for lunch today, right?"

Granville gave a mock groan, not having considered that particular difficulty.

STROH'S TEASHOP NEVER CHANGED, Emily thought, noting Mrs. Smithers at her favorite table, her cowed-looking daughters in tow. She and her friend Clara Miles were seated near the rear, just behind a large potted palm. The thick fronds would give their conversation some semblance of privacy.

"Have they re-papered, Emily, do you think?" Clara asked as they settled their things and removed their gloves.

Emily glanced around. To her, it looked much the same as ever. "I doubt it. That wallpaper is a William Morris print, and you know how costly they are to import. They had one here before, so I doubt that is a new one."

"Something is different," Clara said, looking carefully around her.

Before Emily could respond, her eye was caught by the commotion at the door, as two very large men and one gangling lad crowded through the doorway. As usual, they looked out of place here—too large, too loud, too male to belong in this soft and rather frilly roomful of women. It never seemed to bother any of them, though, and in that moment Emily loved them for it.

Both Granville and Scott looked tired, though Trent seemed chipper enough. He caught sight of them, beamed, and only an opportune look from Granville stopped him from waving.

As they walked closer, she realized that part of what she'd taken for tiredness was bruises. This wasn't the right place to ask Granville about it, though. He'd tell her what had happened later.

Once they'd ordered, Granville filled them in on the details of their search for Weston, with a few additions from Scott and Trent.

"So after my chat with McAndrews, we have three leads to follow up—Gipson, this Putnam fellow and Benton again,"

Granville said. "I've appointments set with Gipson and Benton this afternoon."

"Are you a member of the Vancouver Club?" Emily said.

"No, I'm not. Your father has suggested several times that I join, though. Why do you ask?"

"Well from what I hear..." Emily began.

Clara rolled her eyes. "Which doorway have you been listening at this time?" she said.

"That's not fair," Emily said, feeling the heat rising in her cheeks. "You know that if I intend to succeed in my career, I have to understand how business is done in this city."

"And I still don't understand why you would want to," Clara said, picking up her teacup.

Emily wanted to say something sharp, but made herself take a sip of tea instead. What was bothering her friend?

"Tell me about this club," Granville said as the awkward silence stretched. "Do you think Weston would have been a member?"

"He might well have joined. A lot of business is transacted there, or so I've heard," Emily explained. "Though I gather that those involved with the financial community tend to become members at the Terminal City Club instead, so if he was thinking about selling financial investments, someone there might know something."

"That's an excellent idea," Granville said, giving her a private smile. "I would have to be introduced by a member, I expect. Does your father belong?"

Emily shook her head. "Yes. And I'm sure he'd be happy to introduce you."

"Mr. O'Hearn is a member. I'm sure he would introduce you, also, especially if you promised him a story."

Surprisingly, it was Clara who spoke. And there was a thread of bitterness in her last words. So her friend's problem lay with Mr. O'Hearn, Emily thought, putting her hand on Clara's arm in wordless support.

"Thank you, Clara," Granville said. "I'll talk to him. Though I'm not sure that there is a story, not until we find Weston."

EMILY TOOK A SIP OF TEA, and glanced around the teashop while she thought about the problem of Mr. Weston. They seemed to be attracting a fair bit of attention. Which wasn't really surprising, since Granville, Scott and Trent were the only men in the place.

Hiding a smile, she watched Trent reach for a pastry, while Scott held the handle of a delicate teacup in two large fingers. Clara and Granville had their heads together, apparently discussing Mr. O'Hearn's schedule. She sipped her tea, then put down the cup.

"Assuming Mr. Weston is still alive," she said. "Where might he have gone? Does he know anyone in Canada?"

Granville met her eyes. "You mean where would a young English gentleman with no money go in a mostly undeveloped province in February?" he said. "That's a very good question. And I don't know the answer. I've asked my brother for more details, but nothing has been forthcoming yet."

"If he has no money, he would have to borrow it, steal it or earn it," Clara said practically.

"I doubt he's much of a thief," Granville said. "And he's a poor gambler."

"Then what skills does he have?" Emily said.

"A fairly worthless classical education—as a third son, he'd have little or no training in anything useful. And probably not much of a head for numbers, or he'd be a better gambler. He'd be a good rider and a decent shot."

"He's probably dead, then," Trent said.

Scott glared at him. "We don't know that," he said, glancing pointedly at her and Clara.

Emily was pleased to see Granville stifle a grin at his friend's absurdity.

"It's still too early in the investigation to be sure of anything," Granville said.

Emily had more important things to focus on. "When did Mr. Weston vanish?" she asked.

"From what McAndrews told me, early February," Granville said. "Why?"

"Well, if he's a good rider and a decent shot, perhaps he joined up with Lord Strathcona's Horse to fight the Boers," Emily said. "I remember reading that they were recruiting in early February. And I think their commander was looking to the West for men who could ride and shoot."

"So Weston could be en route to South Africa by now?" Granville asked.

Scott nodded. "It's possible. There was quite a buzz when word went out that Steele was looking for good men to go fight the Boers."

"Steele? Not Sam Steele of the Mounties?" Granville asked. "The Klondike Gold Commissioner?"

"Yep. You didn't hear?" Scott asked.

"No. But Steele's a good man," Granville said. "When did this all happen?"

"It was pretty quick—they announced it in late January or early February, I think," Scott said. "They'd all left by mid-month."

"I was in Seattle around then, chasing down rumors on a previous case. I must have missed it," Granville said.

"Steele and his men arrived in Cape Town last Wednesday," Emily said. "The papers were full of it, and my father told us about it in great detail."

"Weston was last seen on February ninth, so the dates might fit," Granville said. "But who is Lord Strathcona? I don't recognize the title."

Granville glanced at Scott, who shrugged.

Emily smiled into her teacup, then looked up to see Granville watching her.

"Emily knows," he said. "Don't you?"

"I can't help but know," she said with a laugh. "He's Donald Smith, and he played a major role in building the Canadian Pacific Railway. My father considers him practically part of the family."

"So Smith's a Canadian?" Granville said. "How did he end up being knighted?"

"Services to the Crown," said Clara sweetly.

Emily ignored her. "He was knighted for his work in building a purely Canadian railway from coast to coast."

"And he made enough money to fund his own regiment?" Granville said. "Interesting."

"Isn't it?" Emily said. It was why business fascinated her. There was so much opportunity, especially in the West, because everything was still new and growing so fast. She wanted to be part of it, not just sit on the sidelines and be supportive.

Her mother insisted it was a woman's role to provide a calm environment for her family, away from the hustling world of commerce. Women were society's balance, Mama said. Emily rolled her eyes every time she heard it.

"So if this Mr. Weston might have enlisted, how will you find out?" asked Clara, apparently tired of all the details.

"I can ask around. I heard a couple of our fellow Klondike gold-seekers signed up," Scott said. "Remember Jarvis?"

"He was a crack shot, wasn't he?" Granville said. "And didn't he have a claim on Bonanza Creek?"

"Sure did," Scott said. "Pulled out a million or more in nuggets. Don't know why he'd want to get himself killed in some desert."

"For the Empire," Trent said. His eyes were gleaming. "If I'd been old enough..."

Emily felt a shiver trace down her spine. Any one of them could have signed up, gone off to fight a war and been killed in some land she'd never see. "I'm glad you weren't," she said.

Trent didn't look impressed, but she could see Granville understood. Emily wondered what he thought of this war that everyone was so fervent about. She'd ask him later if she got the chance.

"There will be full records of those who enlisted," Granville said.

"Sure," Scott said. "All we have to do is track 'em down, then convince some official to let us see them."

"There were some names in the papers," Emily said. "And I seem to remember something about the son of an English nobleman signing up. It might be Mr. Weston."

"That would simplify things," Granville said.

"Except they are already in South Africa," Clara said. "What if it was Mr. Weston and he did enlist? Then what? How do you get him out of a war?"

Emily threw her friend an exasperated glance.

Granville just smiled at Clara. "One problem at a time," he said.

"Sides, if he enlisted, it means he's still alive," Scott said. "That puts us ahead in this case. Right now, we don't even know that."

"And it gives us another direction to search," Granville said slowly. "Even if Weston didn't join the regiment, Emily is quite right that his riding and shooting abilities might qualify him for a similar job."

"Where?" said Scott.

"There's an estate called Cannington Manor in Saskatchewan that breeds thoroughbreds. It's become something of a haven for British remittance men," Granville said. "It's a long shot, but if Weston knew about the place, he might have headed there. I'll send Earnest Beckton a telegram and ask."

"Weston might've headed for Seattle or San Francisco, too," Scott said. "I have some contacts—I'll check if they've heard anything."

"I can visit the newspaper archives and look up the story that listed those who signed up for the regiment," Emily offered. "Clara, will you come with me?"

"What about your typewriting class?" her friend wanted to know.

"I'm ahead right now, and besides, I can catch up anything I missed on Monday," Emily said.

"Oh, I suppose so," Clara said indifferently.

She was definitely going to have a long chat with Clara, Emily decided and turned back to Granville. "You're going to talk to Mr. Gipson now?"

He nodded. "First Benton, then Gipson. Scott? Are you with me?"

The big man shook his head. "Nope. After I send that wire, I'll see if I can find Willis again. He was a little quick to get rid of us last time, and I have a few more questions for him. Odds are he can tell us what Norton got himself mixed up in, and whether Weston played any role in it. I'll take Trent with me."

Granville nodded and turned to Emily. "And would you care to join me at the racetrack next Saturday, Emily?"

"I'd adore it, Granville! Is this connected to Mr. Weston?"

"Yes. He was as fond of betting on the horses as he was of playing poker," Granville said.

"And he didn't win at either?" Emily asked.

"Apparently not." He glanced at Clara, sitting silent beside her. "Clara, would you care to join us?"

Clara looked pleased, and Emily gave him a quick smile. Then her friend frowned a little.

"Oh, I can't go," Clara said. "I have a previous engagement. Perhaps another time?"

"The next time we go," Emily said quickly. "We'll plan something soon, won't we, Granville?"

"Of course. I'm sorry you can't join us," he said to Clara. Then, to Emily, "If it suits you, I'll call on you at noon and we can dine first?"

"That would be perfect," Emily said with a wide smile. She loved spending time with Granville, and she loved even more being part of his cases.

And the horse track was a most amazing place; colorful, noisy, crowded and full of action. She hadn't been for nearly a year, and it would be good to feel part of that excitement again.

8

A fter the high-pitched buzz of women chatting at the teashop, Granville found Benton's fancy offices oddly quiet. A lone clerk tapped away on an adding machine in the outer office, while two burly men who looked like they'd feel at home loading lumber on the wharves played a silent game of cards. The more muscle-bound of the poker players stood, accompanied him to Benton's inner office, and announced him.

Benton looked surprised and none too pleased to see him, rising from behind that massive desk with a hand outstretched but a frown between thick brows. "Granville? I didn't expect to see you today."

"I had a few more questions," Granville said. "Were you aware that more than sufficient money to cover Weston's gambling debts is sitting in a box at the Post Office, waiting for him? And that it's been there since six days after he disappeared?"

"Yes, I knew," Benton said, reseating himself and waving Granville to a chair opposite the desk.

"So if Weston would soon have enough money to pay you back, then why did he run?"

"That's what I want to know," Benton said.

"Which is why your men are looking for him?"

"Well, I can't very well cash his postal order without him, now can I? But I've called my men off. I'm counting on you, now," Benton said with a sly smile.

It was an unsettling thought. "Weston seems to have suffered a series of potentially fatal accidents in the weeks before his disappearance. Know anything about that?"

"First I've heard of it. You think these accidents are why he vanished?"

"That would be my guess," Granville said. "Any names come to mind?"

"No. He didn't owe enough anywhere else to have a target on his back."

"And you knew his remittance was coming in, which made killing him first pointless."

Benton grinned and raised the half-full brandy snifter that sat beside him. "Exactly."

"So you've no other names for me?"

"None."

"You haven't heard any rumors?" Granville asked.

"Not about Weston," Benton said, then savored a mouthful of brandy.

Right. "How about rumors of someone looking to kill Scott or myself?" Granville said.

Benton didn't look surprised, which, while not unexpected, was not exactly reassuring. "The night Norton was killed?"

Granville nodded. "You know something?"

"Nothing that would help you. But I'm sure you'll figure it out," Benton said, drinking a little more brandy.

Which could mean anything. Still, Granville had what he'd come for. It probably wasn't smart to press Benton further. Not yet.

"Thank you. I shall," he said, and took his leave.

———

GRANVILLE'S JAW tightened as he climbed the carpeted stairs to

Gipson's second floor office. From what he knew so far, it didn't sound like Weston had learned much since being kicked out of Cambridge. Still, young fool or not, he didn't deserve to be a target in someone's game.

Least of all the dirty games Gipson liked to play.

Granville had made an appointment this time, which some would see as giving Gipson an advantage, so the man's sleek smile and general smugness were no surprise. It was hard to swallow, but Granville needed to know why Weston had been so deep in conversation with Gipson the night before he vanished. If letting Gipson gloat would get him closer to finding Weston alive, then it was worth it. Mostly.

"You are looking for a compatriot, I believe?" Gipson said, once the clerk had whisked himself out of Gipson's plushly appointed office. "One Weston."

"Yes. I understand you know him?" Seating himself in the low chair opposite the desk, Granville leaned back and nonchalantly crossed one booted ankle over his knee.

Gipson liked his visitors to feel inferior—hence the lowered chair—and defeating such petty attempts amused Granville. The resentment that flashed in Gipson's eyes almost made the entire visit worthwhile.

"I'd hardly say I knew him," Gipson said, letting his gaze rest for too long on the bruising on Granville's cheek. He smirked at Granville, then said, "I met with him once or twice, no more. He had hoped for information about a business opportunity he was considering."

"I see. And what was the opportunity?"

"It wasn't one I knew much about. Putnam would be the man you need to speak with. Charles Putnam. Which is what I told young Weston."

Granville didn't believe him, but it was interesting to see Gipson so intent on distancing himself from any involvement. "And where would I find Putnam?"

"He is with Vancouver Permanent Investment & Loan, with offices down on Hastings."

"Thank you," Granville said blandly, noting down information he already had. "I noticed you used the past tense in speaking of Weston. Is the fellow dead then?"

"I'm afraid I had assumed so." Gipson's face was serious but those narrow eyes mocked him. "I understand he disappeared some months ago. Since I gather he had little in the way of money or resources, I fear the worst."

What Granville wanted to do was reach across the desk and strangle the smug fool.

He took a deep breath and thought of Emily, who would not be pleased to see him in jail. His lips twitched slightly at the thought. She'd probably either try to dig him an escape tunnel at midnight or charm the jailor into letting him free. Still, he'd rather not put it to the test.

"You find something amusing?"

He did now.

That glint of humor had annoyed Gipson as no insult could have. He'd have to thank Emily later—she'd appreciate the joke. "Not at all. Merely the thought of the fellow I knew braving a Canadian winter," Granville said.

He didn't expect Gipson to believe him, and indeed was pleased to see the man did not. The twitch at the corner of that narrow mouth displayed the other man's growing irritation.

"However, I was told you were the last person to speak with young Weston before he vanished."

"And when was that?"

Was the fellow pretending ignorance? Granville couldn't tell. "He was last seen at the Carlton, on the ninth of February. You did speak with him there?"

Gipson's mouth tightened. "Yes, though I can't be sure of the date. But your information is faulty."

The mask slipped a little there, Granville thought. Time to press him harder. "Oh? Weston spoke with someone else after he talked to you?"

"He must have."

"And why would that be?" Granville asked.

"Because our conversation had nothing to do with his disappearance," Gipson said with a flash of irritation.

Right. "And what did it have to do with?"

"He simply asked me tell Putnam he was no longer interested in the business opportunity they'd discussed," Gipson said. "Then something about exploring other opportunities."

Had Weston not turned Putnam's offer down himself? And what had he meant by exploring other opportunities? "Nothing more than that?"

"Not that I can recall."

The fellow was as slippery as ever. "And how did he seem? Was he discouraged?" Granville asked.

"He seemed fine, especially given his financial situation. Excited, even."

Excited? Over what? "And nothing he said gave you any indication why?"

Gipson spread his hands wide. "I wish I could tell you more."

Of course he did. "I'll need to have a chat with Putnam, then."

Gipson didn't look at all concerned. "Yes, that would be best."

"Where did Weston go when your conversation finished?"

"He left the Carlton. Beyond that, I have no idea."

"I see." Granville made a note, looked back at Gipson. "One last thing. Do you know if Weston had an acquaintance with a man called Norton?"

"Norton? I don't believe I know the name. And I certainly didn't know Weston well enough to know who his acquaintances were," Gipson said.

"Then I thank you for your time." Giving the other man a brief nod, Granville turned to go.

As he descended the stairs, he reflected that although Benton was undoubtedly every bit as villainous as Gipson—and perhaps more ruthless—he much preferred dealing with the former. At least Benton was honest about his dishonesty.

Emerging into the grey drizzle that passed for late afternoon, Granville considered the difference between the two men. Benton didn't hide what he was, but Granville suspected Gipson would do anything to further his own ends. Rather like Brother William, in fact.

Which reminded him, he still had to send a telegram to his brother, accepting the terms of their new contract. Granville headed for the railway station before he could change his mind.

9

E mily turned over yet another page of newsprint with grimy fingers, trying to contain her frustration. The bare electric bulbs overhead dangled on long black cords, far too close to the worktable for her taste. They made the small, stuffy room hot, and they created too much glare on the pages, which were already yellowing.

At least the back-issue room for the *Daily World* was above ground, and it had been swept recently. She sighed, and reached for the next stack of papers.

She'd already gone through all of the January issues. Articles about the war were on the front page of every edition, but not a single one mentioned the recruitment for Lord Strathcona's Horse. Inside, there were brief mentions of any number of happenings across the country, but nothing of what she was looking for. When had she seen that article?

Dispatches from the front talked of the losses in South Africa, and there was talk of the need for a third regiment from Canada— Emily glanced over at Clara.

Her friend was sitting in front of several weeks' worth of the *World*, turning the pages far too quickly to be even skimming the

articles, much less the advertisements that usually caught her attention. "What's wrong, Clara?" Emily said.

Her voice echoed off the concrete wall behind her. For a
moment Emily thought Clara was going to ignore her, then her
friend looked up.

"Wrong? Why nothing, Emily."

"Something is bothering you."

"What makes you say that?" Clara asked.

"You're not even looking at the ads."

It didn't draw a smile. Clara just shook her head and turned back
to the stack of newspapers in front of her, flicking through several
more pages.

"Clara!"

"What? I told you, I'm fine."

"Have you found any mention of the war?" Emily asked.

"No, nothing so far."

Emily moved around to Clara's side of the table. Taking the
newspaper her friend was looking at, she flipped back to the front
page. Meeting Clara's defiant gaze, she pointed to the headline. It
screamed "Boers Winning Against Gordon's Troops" in large type.

"Oh," said Clara, and her eyes filled with tears.

"Tell me what is wrong."

"Oh, Emily. You wouldn't understand."

"I might not. But tell me anyway."

"It's easy for you. You're engaged, even if you don't want to be,
and you're training for a job too. Two jobs, if you count the work
you do for your fiancé. Not like me."

"But Clara," Emily said. "I thought you hated the fact that I was
training to be a typewriter. You disparage it every chance you get."

"I do hate it. I hate the fact that you're off doing something
interesting and I'm stuck home waiting to get married."

"But..." Emily wasn't sure what to say. This didn't sound like the
Clara she thought she knew so well—the one who was bored with
the business world and loved the social whirl. "But what brought
this on?"

"Father brought home yet another of his associates for dinner last night."

She was missing something here, Emily thought. "Oh?"

"It was awful. The man was a bore."

"And?"

"And they want me to marry him," Clara wailed. "Or if not him, the man from last week. Or the week before. And they're all bores."

Emily was beginning to understand, or at least she thought she was. "When did you last see Mr. O'Hearn?" she asked.

"I haven't seen him since February," Clara said. "But what does that have to do with anything?"

"I thought he was rather smitten with you,"

"Well, yes, he was. So?"

"And that you were inclined to like him as well," she said carefully.

"Me? Like a poor journalist? Where's the future in that? Besides, my father would never permit it."

And there we have it, Emily thought. "My father allowed my engagement to Granville."

"Only after you disgraced yourself," Clara retorted. "And besides, he's the son of a peer. It's not the same."

"Still. If you really wanted to marry Tim O'Hearn, they'd eventually have to give in."

"Not until I'm of age. That's years away. And what kind of life would I have, even if they did agree? He—doesn't earn much. And I'm used to living in the West End, and buying a new wardrobe every season."

"And you're miserable," Emily said, putting her hand on her friend's arm.

"Oh, and your life is so wonderful," Clara snapped, dabbing at her eyes with a lacy handkerchief.

Emily ignored that, patting Clara's hand. "Yes, you're right. It's really just too bad that Mr. O'Hearn will never amount to anything. He's not even a real reporter, after all."

"He is too," Clara said, sitting upright and glaring at her. "He's had several feature articles in the last two months, and even my father commented on the story he wrote about that photographer."

"Oh, so you do think Mr. O'Hearn's career might do well?"

"Yes. He's a good writer, and he's well-spoken and ambitious, and..." She broke off, and stared at Emily. "I see what you're doing. I knew you wouldn't understand."

"No, I'm afraid I don't. Explain it to me."

"I—I can't..." Clara clutched the now damp handkerchief in her fist, and made a sweeping motion. "It's just impossible. All of it."

Emily nodded. "I quite agree. Go on."

"Well—you see," Clara met Emily's steady gaze and one side of her mouth quirked. Unexpectedly, she began to giggle. "You're not supposed to agree with me."

Emily smiled back. "I thought that was my job as your friend. Especially when you defend him so well."

"You really think it might work?"

"Do you believe he'll build a good career for himself?"

Clara nodded. "Yes, I do. And you're right—eventually even my father will have to see that he's a good match for me. Especially if I keep refusing to consider any other option."

"Being stubborn is one of your best features."

Clara smiled and dabbed at her eyes again. "Thank you, Emily. Now, let us see if we can find these soldiers of yours."

"You mean of Granville's," Emily said as they turned back to their stacks of newspapers.

EMILY BLINKED HER EYES HARD, then turned another page. The combination of slightly blurred print, poor light and dust was making it hard to focus. They would have to take a break soon. A cup of tea would be welcome—her mouth felt so dry. She turned another page. And there it was.

Sam Steele's men had held a mass recruitment across the country for Lord Strathcona's Horse. They'd been in Vancouver on February fifth and six of this year.

She skimmed the details, then read them more slowly. It listed all of the men from the Vancouver area who had volunteered. Weston's name was not among them. But the article also stated that a number of men had enlisted in Victoria, in Nelson, Revelstoke and Kamloops.

If Weston didn't want to be found, it was possible he had gone elsewhere to enlist. It was also possible that he had used another name. But at least she'd found the article. She copied out the names.

"Emily, did you find something?" Clara asked.

She turned the page so Clara could read over her shoulder.

"No mention of Mr. Weston," Clara said.

"No. Did you find anything?"

"No, nothing. Emily..."

"What?" Emily said absently, as she finished copying the last name.

"I wonder if the *Province* would have more information. Now that we know what dates we're looking for."

Clara was volunteering to spend more time in a newspaper archives? She must be feeling better, Emily thought with relief. "I think you might be right. Shall we go?"

TUESDAY, APRIL 17, 1900

G ranville was at his desk the following morning, reviewing his
notes from the previous day and wishing he'd spent a little
more time learning about business. At the sound of the outer door
opening he froze, listening intently.

Scott and Trent were off trying to track down more information
on Norton's associates, and as far as he knew, they weren't
expecting anyone. He moved quietly towards the door, muscles
tensed.

A sudden waft of lilac scent overlaid the smell of ink and paper
and he relaxed. "Emily?"

She was wearing a navy ladies suit, which suggested she'd dressed
for her typewriting class, but the striking white trimmings and the
way the short jacket showed off her tiny waist were pure Emily. She
had a folded umbrella in a matching navy and white stripe tucked
over her arm, and was smiling at his surprise. "You'll never believe
what Clara and I found out."

"Don't you have a typing class this morning?" he asked as he
followed her back to his office.

"Of course," she said, putting the umbrella on the desk and
seating herself in Scott's chair. "This is our mid-morning break."

"You'll never make it back in time, and you'll end up failing your classes," he said as he took his seat across the desk from her.

She waved the comment off with a laugh. "In case you're interested, Clara and I spent most of yesterday afternoon going through back issues of the *World* and the *Province*."

"Your eyes must still be tired from reading all that small print. Did you find Weston?"

"You can thank me later," she said. "And no. He didn't join up in Vancouver, or at least not under his own name."

"Was there somewhere else he could have joined up?"

"Yes, they were recruiting in Victoria, Nelson, Revelstoke and Kamloops."

"Hmm. How likely was it that he could have joined up under another name, do you know?" Granville asked.

"I don't think it would have been too hard," Emily said. "But all the recruitment took place the week of February fifth. By the fourteenth, they were all in Ottawa. There must be records there."

"I'll find out."

"My father might know. He's been very interested in the whole matter, almost takes a proprietary interest. Because of the CPR connection, you see. Why don't I ask him?"

"He won't be upset that you're helping me?" Granville asked.

"I may not tell him why I want to know," Emily said with a sideways glance.

He laughed. "Probably a wise idea."

"So how was your afternoon? Was Mr. Gipson helpful?" Her smile said she knew he'd have been anything but. "And did you learn anything more about the investment position?"

"Gipson was singularly unhelpful," Granville said. "He's referred me back to Charles Putnam.

"Which firm is Mr. Putnam with? I don't believe you said at lunch."

"He's with Vancouver Permanent Investment & Loan," Granville said. "Why do you ask? You don't happen to know anything about them?"

She gave him a sideways glance. "Not officially."

Not for the first time, he wondered what was really behind Mr. Turner's enthusiasm for their pending marriage. Was it only his own connection to the English gentry, or was he afraid of what his youngest daughter might get up to next? "Oh?"

She grinned. "I overheard my father talking with a friend of his, who was considering buying property along the extension of the streetcar line. They had quite a discussion about the various mortgage companies that have sprung up with the possibility of rising property values."

Emily paused, eyed him speculatively. "Now that you have gold to invest, is buying property something you would consider?"

It was an interesting thought, and not something he'd considered before. "Perhaps," he said slowly. "I come from generations that valued property ownership over almost anything. But unless you are farming the land, it will bring in only what someone is willing to pay."

"The newspapers talk about land speculation. Is that what you mean?"

"Yes. It can drive prices too far beyond what most people can afford. The risk is that prices can fall even more quickly than they rose."

"Why?" Emily asked.

He shrugged. "Depends on why they rose. The lure of gold takes many forms."

"And you think that's what Vancouver Permanent is involved with?"

"I'm thinking it could be a possibility," he said. "McAndrews told me the numbers were off, which often happens in an economic boom. What did your father suggest?"

"To avoid investing with them. He didn't say why. Not loudly enough for me to hear, anyway. I can find out for you if you'd like," Emily offered, then made a face. "After my typewriting class, of course."

Granville wasn't even going to ask how she planned to do so—he had no doubt she'd accomplish it. "Yes, that would help," he said instead. "And I have a meeting with Putnam himself. I'll walk you to the streetcar."

"I'd like that," she said, standing and tucking her hand under his arm.

AFTER WATCHING Emily catch her trolley, Granville stopped in at the CPR station. He sent off his telegraph to Cannington Manor, then walked briskly up Seymour towards Hastings.

The four-story brick building at the corner of Richards and Hastings was one of the city's newest. Vancouver Permanent Investment & Loan was on the top floor. Elaborate gold script on the door identified the firm.

Putnam and company were either doing very well, or they felt they needed to present the appearance of prosperity. Granville wondered which it was.

A formal office, heavy with mahogany furniture and fringed draperies, spoke of respectability and success, as did the earnest young man at the desk in the outer office. As he was ushered in, Granville noted that Putnam's own office was even more elaborate. The expansive desk, glassed-in bookcases and silk draperies would have been impressive in London, let alone in this pioneer city.

Putnam stood up to greet him. A heavy man, with a florid complexion and a damp handshake, he was as prosperously dressed as his office.

"Mr. Granville, is it?" he said, holding out his hand. "A pleasure, a pleasure. How may I help you?"

"The pleasure is mine, Mr. Putnam," Granville said, shaking his hand. "George Gipson suggested I talk with you."

"Oh? Always happy to have a referral from George. Please, have a seat. I gather you are from England originally."

And Granville's Oxbridge accent would imply he had money. As would a referral from Gipson, at least in most circumstances. "I am indeed."

"And are you interested in purchasing property here?" Putnam asked. "A home for yourself and your fiancée, perhaps?"

Now how had the fellow known about Emily? He must read the social pages as well as the business ones. Which, in his business, probably made sense.

"Buying a home here is a possibility I'm considering," Granville said, though he hadn't thought of it until this moment. It was a good cover.

More than that, if he and Emily really were going to marry, he'd need a house to bring her to. It was an unsettling thought. "And I would want to be sure that I was buying a suitable house, in an area where my future wife would feel comfortable."

"I am sure we can provide you with a mortgage sufficiently flexible that you would be able to buy the house of your fiancée's dreams," Putnam said smoothly.

"That is indeed good to know," Granville told him. "However, while I am considering such a purchase, it will not be immediately, I'm afraid. Actually, I'm here today because I'm looking for a young countryman of mine, one Rupert Weston. Gipson told me Weston spoke with you about a business opportunity?"

"Ah. Yes, Weston had indeed talked to us," Putnam said. "The discussions did not get far, however."

"Oh?"

"He seemed to lose interest. And I'm not sure he was right for our firm, in any case."

"May I ask why?"

"We lend sums of money, often quite large sums, to people wishing to buy homes," Putnam said. "If the buyer over-commits and cannot meet his payments, then we lose money. The ability to judge our borrowers to a nicety is critical. It became clear in our discussions that—well, that the young man was a gambler."

Which was true enough, but given what McAndrews had said, it was probably far from the whole story. "I see," Granville said. "And did Weston have access to any of your financials during these discussions?"

"Some limited access. No more than a potential investor would see," Putnam said. "But I can't see how this is relevant to finding the young man."

Nor could Granville.

He couldn't see any logical connection between Putnam and the accidents Weston had suffered, either. "You say he lost interest in the opportunity. May I ask if he told you so directly?"

Putnam grimaced. "He sent a message through Gipson. It was all most odd."

So Gipson had been telling the truth, at least that far. "Do you have any idea what Weston intended to do next? He appears to have left Vancouver."

Putnam's eyebrows rose slightly. "He's left town? I hadn't heard. No, I'm afraid our acquaintance was very slight. I've no idea what his plans were."

It seemed this was yet another dead end. "Did Weston ever mention a man named Norton?" Granville asked, expecting to hear a no.

"Norton? Not that fellow who was murdered the other night? Down on the docks?"

"The same."

Putnam scowled. "I would hope a potential employee of ours was not associated with such a low-life, but in Weston's case, I can feel no assurance it wasn't the case."

It was an odd way to phrase it. "But you don't know it for a fact?" Granville asked.

"Not as a fact, no." Putnam seemed to be about to say more, but then clamped his lips together.

Interesting, Granville thought as he rose. Obviously there was more to learn about Norton. With a little luck, Scott and Trent were uncovering it now. "Then I thank you for your time."

As Putnam made to rise Granville said, "No, don't bother. I'll see myself out."

"Very well. It was a pleasure talking to you," Putnam said. "And please do keep us in mind when you are ready to buy that house for your bride-to-be."

IT WAS DRIZZLING AGAIN, and a chill wind was coming off the mountains on the North Shore. Quickening his step, Granville turned up his collar and turned down his hat brim, still thinking about his conversation with Putnam. Something was wrong there, but his gut said it had little to do with Weston's disappearance. The comments about Norton, on the other hand, suggested they had missed a connection.

Perhaps Scott and Trent had learned something useful while he'd been wasting his time with Putnam's half-truths. In a hurry now, Granville took the shortcut off Richards. The alley was dim and filled with discarded lumber and cardboard boxes, but there was a pathway of sorts.

A bullet zinged by his shoulder, knocking chips off the brick wall ahead of him. Granville dived low, landing on an uneven stack of old boards, and sliding with them as they fell with a clatter.

A second shot.

He rolled until he lay against the wall and froze. There was a moment of quiet.

The second shot must have gone wide. He'd hit his head on something, but it didn't feel like it was bleeding too badly. In the silence, he could sense the shooter, listening as hard as he was.

Granville moved only his eyes, assessing his situation in a quick glance. Luck had left him with a sturdy barrier of boards between him and the shooter. But he was pressed between the boards and the wall.

With only a knife as a weapon, he was trapped. Though perhaps his assailant didn't know where he'd ended up.

The third shot disabused him of that notion, and Granville ducked his head lower. Now what?

The men that had come after him on Saturday night had been clear enough, after all. "Stop looking for Weston, or else." Apparently this was the else, Granville thought with a wry grin.

He'd never thought they'd be bold enough to attack in daylight, though.

He began to elbow-crawl along behind the boards as silently as possible. If he could just get closer to the end of the alley...

The fourth shot stopped him cold.

But the shooter likely had at most two more shots before he'd have to reload. If he could get the man to waste those shots, he could rush him. Granville tossed a chunk of brick a few feet ahead.

It didn't work. There was no movement from the shooter. He felt a reluctant admiration. Whoever was after him, they were smart. Too bad.

He might have to take a bullet to have any hope of getting out of this one.

"Hey! Hey, you there!"

The strident voice came from the far end of the alley. "You can't shoot rats in the city limits. It's illegal! Get a dog," the same voice said.

Apparently four shots in the center of downtown did get noticed. Granville nearly called out, warning the man off, but he waited to see what the shooter would do.

"You hear that, rat?" came a hissed voice. "Want we should set the dogs on you? Give it up! You got lucky this time."

Then the sound of quick steps, and Granville was alone. There was no sign of the shooter, and the man at the other end of the alley had apparently gone about his business.

Granville brushed himself off, and headed for his office. He and Scott needed to talk about where this case was going.

And he'd be carrying his gun from now on.

———

GRANVILLE WAS AT HIS DESK—A cup of strong coffee in front of him—attempting to make sense of the notes he'd taken earlier when Scott and Trent finally returned. One glance confirmed that they'd also found trouble.

Both were covered with dirt. Scott had several small cuts on his forehead. And Trent was limping.

"What happened to you two?"

Scott cast a quick eye over him. "I might ask the same."

"I was shot at. He missed. A passer-by scared him off."

"Us too," Trent said. "Exactly that."

"In an alley?" Granville said, exchanging glances with Scott as Trent nodded.

"A little too convenient, you think?" Scott said.

Trent frowned as Granville nodded. "What d'you mean? Getting shot at isn't convenient," the boy said.

"Were you hit?" Scott asked.

"No, but..."

"It feels to me like they're still just warning us off," Granville said. "They had no trouble killing Norton in the fog, but the shooter missed us completely. And the two they sent to beat me up were either incompetent or not trying very hard."

"So why were they quiet on Monday?" Scott asked.

"Letting us think it over, perhaps?" Granville suggested. "And we may not have done anything they recognized as related to our search for Weston."

"Maybe they knew about Putnam's connection to Weston, so you got shot at after you saw him," Scott said. "Trent and I were asking questions about Weston along the dock, so we got shot at too."

"But why?" Trent said. "I still don't get it."

"Or perhaps that's the wrong question," Granville said.

Scott raised an eyebrow at him.

He grinned. "Not why, but who? Who would want to stop us from looking for Weston?"

"Same people that caused Weston's accidents, do you think?" Scott said.

"That's my guess."

"Seems there's a few of them involved," Scott said. "You didn't recognize the shooter?"

"No," Granville said. "So there are at least three men."

"Probably four. Trent and I must have been shot at around the same time you were—and he was good enough to miss by fractions of an inch. Several times," Scott said.

"And we weren't standing still for him, either," Trent added.

"In both cases, a passer-by just happened to come along and challenge them? And the shooters backed off?" Granville said. "I don't buy it."

"You think it was a set-up? All of it?" Trent asked.

"Well, it would have been easier to kill us," Granville said. "Likely easier to just shoot Weston, too. So why didn't they?"

"Maybe killing us would draw too much attention," Scott said. "And maybe they wanted Weston's death to look like an accident."

"Or they wanted to scare him away from something we don't yet know about," Granville said. "We must be getting too close to whatever Weston was involved in. Or maybe whoever told them about us led them to believe we'd back off easily."

"Someone like your brother?" Scott said.

"Exactly like my brother."

"So you think we can expect the attacks to get worse?" Trent asked.

"I think we should be prepared for that," Granville said.

And they'd leave Trent minding the office for a while. Or send him on unrelated errands.

WEDNESDAY, APRIL 18, 1900

E mily stood in the hall, holding the telephone tightly to her ear and angling her body away from the drawing room, hoping she couldn't be overheard. She could still hear the buzz of voices from the drawing room—her mother and her sisters, probably discussing some social event—but not what they were saying. It would have to do.

The line rang several times before he answered, and she found herself holding her breath. If he'd already left the office for the day, she'd have to wait until tomorrow to talk to him.

"Granville here."

"This is Emily. Mama has asked you for lunch on Saturday."

"Saturday?"

"We are still going to the racetrack on Saturday?"

"Oh, that Saturday," he said with a laugh. "Yes, indeed we are. They are predicting sunshine, too."

"That just means it will rain. It won't matter though, since the stands are covered against the weather. But about lunch?"

"Thank your mother for me, but I think it would be best if I took you out for lunch as we'd planned. I want to be certain that we don't miss the start of the races. Unless you would rather the change of plans?"

"No, of course not," Emily said before Granville could change his mind.

"Will you be joining us for church on Sunday, though? I know Mama will invite you for lunch after church. You could talk to Papa then about the signups for the Boer War. He may have useful contacts and I'm sure he'd be happy to share them with you."

"Thank you, I'll do that," Granville said. "And I'll ask your father to put my name forward for membership in the Vancouver Club at the same time. Perhaps we could stroll in Stanley Park afterwards?"

She smiled at the thought of it. "Yes, I'd like that."

"Which reminds me—since we're planning a real marriage now, it occurred to me we'll need somewhere to live. If I'm looking for a house, is there a specific area you'd prefer to live in?"

The very idea made Emily so breathless she couldn't speak for an entire minute.

"Emily? Hello? Are you there?"

"Yes, I'm here. You surprised me, that's all."

"It rather surprised me, too. But we should be thinking about it. When I talked to Putnam today, several of his comments started me thinking. Perhaps we can talk about it further on Saturday."

"Yes. We'll talk then," Emily said. "Goodbye, now."

She hung up abruptly, and sat down hard. If Granville was talking about buying a house for them, he really was serious. They were going to get married.

It shouldn't come as a shock, but it did.

Somehow she'd never envisioned herself as mistress of her own house. Much less with a man like Granville as the master of that house.

FRIDAY, APRIL 20, 1900

G ranville had just returned to the office after yet another morning spent fruitlessly tracking down leads on Weston. He was writing up his case notes, when the outer door creaked open.

He tensed, listening—and the ink blotted. Cursing under his breath, he jerked the inner door open. Enough of these games.

"I have two telegrams for you, sir." The delivery boy wore a green uniform and a tentative smile. He looked familiar. "Sign here, please."

Granville signed and tipped him well. It wasn't the boy's fault his nerves were on edge. He ripped open the first telegram. From Beckton at Cannington Manor. He hadn't seen Weston. Another dead end.

So where was the lad?

The second telegram was from his brother. A local law firm, Henderson and Pruitt, had drawn up their contract as per William's instructions and would expect to hear from him. They would have a first payment ready for him on signing. Granville stared at the yellow flimsy for a moment, then made several quick calls.

Time to learn something about Henderson and Pruitt. He

packed his papers away and was locking the desk drawers when the outer door creaked open again. Now what?

Heavy footsteps told him who it was.

"You look relatively undamaged today," Granville said as Scott came into the inner office. "No-one lying in wait today?"

"Nope, not a sign of them. In fact, the quiet is kinda unsettling," Scott said. "You?"

"Nothing since the attack on Tuesday. They're watching us, though. I can feel it."

Scott frowned. "Now that you mention it—I've had that itchy feeling too. Doesn't make sense."

"What doesn't?" Granville asked.

"We're still looking for Weston. Why aren't they shooting at us?"

"You feeling neglected?"

Scott ignored the sally. "Feels like they've got a new strategy. Wonder what they're up to now?"

"You don't think they've given up?"

"Not a chance," Scott said. "You?"

"No. We're missing something."

"Like what?"

Granville stood up, paced the room, thinking.

"Weston's been missing more than three months," he said. "The lad can't be dead, or there wouldn't be all this interest."

He reached the wall, paced the other way. "But if he's not dead, why are they still in Vancouver? Weston clearly isn't."

Scott watched him pace. "Maybe they can't find him," he said after a bit.

"Yes, but why would they think we can?"

Scott tilted back his chair and stared at the ceiling, humming a little under his breath. It always amused Granville when the big man did that. "Maybe they don't. Think that, I mean. Maybe it makes them look good if nobody can find him."

"You know that makes no sense, right?"

Scott grinned at him. "I know sitting here trying to figure out what some nameless bad guys that can't even shoot straight are up to is a waste of a rainy day. We don't know enough to ask good questions, much less guess what's really going on."

"So what do you propose?" Granville said with a quick spurt of temper.

"I propose," Scott said, emphasizing the word, "that we find young Weston. And while we're doing it..." He paused, sat back.

"What?" Granville said, grinning now.

"We lead our nameless admirers up a few stray paths."

Granville started to laugh. "Since they're so set on watching us, we'll offer a little misdirection?"

"Exactly."

"This could prove amusing," Granville said. "In the meantime, however, we have an appointment to sign a contract."

"Your brother came through?"

"Yes."

Scott nodded slowly, eyeing the telegram Granville held. "I'm guessing we want Randall to have a look at that contract before we sign it?"

Granville doubted there was a legal trick that Josiah Randall didn't know. "That's why we have an appointment with him in twenty minutes.

His partner gave him a shrewd look. "You haven't trusted your brother's request from the beginning. Now we're under attack. Or something. You still sure you want to sign?"

Give up now? Granville thought about the threats the shooter had made, the attacks on Weston. "More sure than ever. Let's go."

"Granville? And Scott. Is there more trouble?" Josiah Randall smiled as he stepped forward and wrung their hands, but his tone was concerned.

"Not directly, anyway," Granville said, returning the smile. "I don't need you to dig us out of a legal hole this time, nor to save a client—or at least not yet."

"I'm glad to hear it. But come in."

Randall waved him into an office that was decidedly less shabby than the one he'd been using when Granville had first hired him. And all of his law books were now respectably housed in glass-fronted bookcases, instead of on the floor.

"Nice offices."

It earned him a quick grin. "Working on your cases has increased my profile."

"You mean your notoriety."

"Whichever," Randall said. "In any case, my accountant thanks you."

Scott chuckled. "Yet you're still practicing on your own?"

"I've had offers from other firms, but I find I prefer my independence. Though it does keep me busy."

"I'm surprised you still have time for us," Granville said.

"You two are much more interesting than some of my clients."

Granville laughed. "Good to know," he said, then explained the situation with young Weston and the contract with his brother. "I wanted to know a bit about the lawyers my brother chose before I meet with them. Henderson and Pruitt. You know them?"

"Indeed I do."

"And are they interesting?" Scott wanted to know.

"Oh, they are interesting indeed. I'm simply glad I don't have to work with them." Randall said, then glanced at Granville. "Or at least, not often."

"Oh?"

"Hmmm. They set up shop when the Klondike money started to pour into town. Much of their business is in real estate, but they handle contracts and other work from time to time. Generally, they accept whatever will pay well. Their clients don't tend to have a reputation for scrupulousness."

That figured. "I'd like you to review the contract and suggest any needed amendments before I sign it," Granville said.

"And is there any question as to whether you will sign it?" Randall said.

"No. That contract will be signed today."

"We just need your help to be sure those expensive lawyers don't play fancy with the words," Scott said, his expression solemn.

Granville laughed. "That's it exactly."

"Certainly," Randall said. "You've an appointment set up with Henderson and Pruitt?"

Granville nodded. "I'm meeting with Henderson himself in an hour."

Randall glanced at the calendar on his desk, nodded. "Since I have the time available, I'll accompany you. I'm interested in observing their operation first hand."

"And keeping us out of legal trouble, too?"

A sideways look. "But of course."

SATURDAY, APRIL 21, 1900

With his first glimpse of the local racetrack, Granville could see what Scott had meant about the state of the infield. His gaze swept the charred stumps and outsize boulders that littered what should have been an expanse of grass.

The track itself looked good, though—a half-mile oval of hard-packed dirt, nicely leveled. The grandstands were clearly thrown together in a hurry, but they served. And he'd spent enough time around horses to approve the quality of horseflesh on display in the paddocks.

He drew in a deep breath. Crisp, fresh air that smelt as if it had come directly off the snow-capped mountains across the inlet, over-laid with the thick smell of mud and manure. The latter took him back to some of the happiest days of his childhood. His father had bred hunters, and he'd grown up surrounded by horses and men who knew them.

"I take it our race track is not quite what you're used to?" Emily said.

He tore his gaze from the ragged stumps that cut into their view of the mountains to the north. "I was attempting to picture the trees that left such enormous stumps behind."

"They were mostly cedar, hundreds of years old. When you're standing beside them, some of the stumps are wider than I am tall."

"What is this fascination you have with trees?" Scott drawled from the other side of Granville. "No trees left in London or something? We're here to find Weston, remember?"

"Oh, I hadn't forgotten. I'm simply amused by the newness of this town of yours. And by the size of these forests." He swept an arm towards the densely forested lands that marched downhill towards the inlet and the mountains beyond.

Emily rolled her eyes at Scott, who grinned.

Granville saw them, as he was meant to, and laughed. "You would be gaping even more in London."

"A lady never gapes," Emily said, copying her mother's most admonitory tone. "She observes, but never stares."

"Right. Then perhaps we should all be observing the other racegoers."

Emily half-lifted a shoulder and looked out over the crowd with mock-indifference. "And exactly whom are we looking for?"

"We're looking for anyone who knows something about the recent murders or about Weston. As it's fairly obvious Weston is no longer in town, I'm hoping to pick up information about why he vanished and where he might have gone. Since the fellow is fond of horse racing, someone here may know something."

"Then let us stroll," Emily said with assumed dignity, placing one hand on Granville's arm and holding her parasol at just the right angle with the other. "Mr. Scott, do you join us?"

"Nope. Think I'd best be talking to the ones who'd find your questions—unsettling. If you'll pardon my plain speaking."

Her eyes danced, but Emily only nodded. "We should be off then."

Granville and Emily strolled along the row of rough bleachers that served as the spectator stands. Their role today was to misdirect the attention of whoever was after them, while Scott tracked down Weston's bookie.

Granville's eyes swept the stands for any hint of their pursuers, but part of his attention stayed on Emily, who was clearly enjoying being here. Her eyes too searched the stands.

He wondered what she was looking for. And he hoped Scott and Trent were having some luck finding the elusive Todd Graham.

"Do you bet?" Emily said.

"I hadn't planned on it. Would you like to place a bet?"

"Me?" Her hand squeezed his arm. "Above anything."

It amazed him that Emily's spirit had not been quenched, given her very traditional family. Such spirit should be encouraged, and he was just the man to do so. "This way."

After a lively discussion on the merits of the various contenders for the next few races, they chose a horse for each race. As they finished, the horn sounded for the first race, and they made their way to the railing.

Emily had brought the box camera he'd given her for her birthday. She fiddled with the catch at the front for a moment, then the lens opened and she held it ready. Twitching her skirts out of the way, she leaned forward, putting one hand on the railing, the other clutching the camera.

"I can't see Morning Light, can you?" she said. Then the starting gun fired, and she leaned even further over the rail. "Oh, they're off!"

As the horses pounded around the first turn, Granville alternated between watching the other spectators and watching Emily's excited face and how carefully she was setting up the photographs she was taking of the horses as they swept past.

Morning Light was holding her own against the field, and it looked like they might actually have a winner. The filly seemed to run into trouble as they cleared the turn, with several of the front runners bunched together. As he tried to make out what was happening, he felt a tug on his sleeve.

"Granville, we have to go," came Emily's voice, her tone urgent. He looked down to see her gaze fixed just beyond the turn at the far side of the grandstand.

"Is there a problem?" he said as he watched her folding up her camera and tucking it away.

"I think so. I think I caught sight of something very odd," she said, and began to make her way through the crowd gathered at the railing.

"Tell me."

"No, I need to be sure first," she said, as she weaved her way through the crowds.

They finally reached the west exit, and she led the way out through the gate. His eyes scanned the area, but he had no idea what she might have seen.

"This way," she said, hurrying her steps. "I think she went this way."

She? Emily didn't seem to notice his surprise as she quickened her step still further.

"I hope I haven't lost her," she said, half to herself.

Granville's eyes scanned the few people entering and exiting the race ground. He couldn't see any women at all, yet Emily's attention was still focused on a small group right ahead of them, all men. He glanced at Emily's face, considered her intent expression. Was the woman she'd seen dressed as a man, then? It was hard to imagine.

As the group ahead of them slowed to greet another man just arriving, Emily slowed their pace. The men ahead of them stopped, and Emily slowed still further.

As they strolled by, she didn't even seem to be noticing them, but Granville could feel her intensity practically vibrating up his arm from where her hand clutched it. She was good at this, perhaps even better than he and Scott. It was an unsettling thought.

Very aware of her tension, he nodded to the men as they passed them, noting an expression here and a way of standing there. All males, or he'd eat his hat. So what had Emily seen?

"I thought I saw Frances," Emily said as soon as they were out of earshot. "Just for a moment, but I'm sure it was her. And she was wearing trousers."

As he'd suspected, but it wasn't the name he'd expected to hear. What would Scott's sister be doing here, and in such a disguise? Speaking of which, where was Scott?

"I'm not sure where I lost her," Emily said. "It must have been when there was such a crowd around the exit. Perhaps she is still inside. Shall we?"

"Indeed we shall. We can see how your horse did," he said as they turned back onto the race grounds. And he had a few questions for Scott.

"I hope Morning Light won, but I would rather find Mr. Scott," Emily said, unconsciously echoing his thoughts. "Perhaps he knows what Frances might be doing here in trousers. Do you think it might be connected to your missing lord?"

"What do you think?"

"It might depend whether Frances is here for herself, or for Mr. Benton," Emily said. "If she were here on his behalf, it could indeed be connected."

He nodded. "It will be interesting to hear what she has to say."

Assuming it was Frances that Emily had seen, or indeed a woman at all. She'd had only a glimpse in a crowd, and from some distance. Again she surprised him.

"I could have been wrong," Emily said. "But the 'man' moved like Frances would, were she to don trousers."

Impressed by her powers of observation, Granville wondered how she could know that. "Do you want to look for Frances now, see if she'll talk to us?"

"No, I believe she was heading towards the exit. I'm not sure how I missed her, but there were several groups of gentlemen leaving at once, and I must have followed the wrong one."

"Unless it was not Frances."

"Exactly. Oh, I see Mr. Scott."

His large friend was easy to spot. Granville made a path for her through the crowds clustered around the ticket windows. "We might as well place a bet while we're here. It looks as if Scott is doing the same."

"And we can find out if Morning Light won."

She hadn't, but the next three horses they bet on did.

Granville had to smile at his fiancée's enjoyment of the wins. It was to be the only satisfaction he got from the afternoon.

Scott knew nothing of his sister's possible presence at the track, was indeed inclined to be offended that they thought she might be present in male garb.

Several races later, Emily was taking photographs again, while Granville scanned the track and the crowded stands surrounding it. So far, this expedition had raised more questions than it answered. He hoped that Scott and Trent were having better luck.

"Oh," Emily said suddenly.

At the distress in her voice, Granville turned, his stance immediately alert and protective.

"What is it?" he said, one hand going instinctively to the gun he wasn't wearing.

She nearly dropped the camera in her distress. "Did you not see?"

His eyes searched the crowd. "What?"

"A man just fell—there—in the crowd."

Granville was pleased to note she hadn't singled herself out by pointing, but allowed him to follow her gaze.

"I think he was stabbed," Emily said. "And I'm almost sure I saw it happen."

"Did you see who did it?"

She shook her head, her face pale but composed. "Not clearly. It happened too quickly and his face was mostly half turned away from me. But Granville..."

He took her hand in his own.

"I am almost sure the knife-wielder was the same woman dressed as a man that we followed before."

"You think it was Frances?" He couldn't keep the shock out of his own voice. No wonder she looked so white.

"No," Emily said. "I don't think it was Frances we were following, before. Similar but not like, if you know what I mean?"

He did. "Yes. But why?"

"At the last moment, as he began to turn away, I saw his—no her —face. Not long enough to really recognize, just the impression of intense focus, and a bit of shock, too."

"Did he, or she, see you?" Granville asked.

"I don't think so," Emily said. "But there was another man that might have. Standing off to the side, but I think he was part of it, somehow. He—seemed to look right at me, but that might have been a trick of the distance."

"How far away was this?"

A cry arose from a small knot of people not more than fifteen feet from where they stood. Followed by a babble of concerned voices and a call for the police.

Emily let her gaze rest on them. "Just there," she said.

He watched for a moment, analyzing the movement of the crowd and the stillness of the victim.

He was almost sure the man was dead, and that Emily had witnessed a murder. And it had happened too close to where they stood. If Emily's attention—and her camera—had been noticed, she could be recognized.

He took a step back and considered her. The brown hair was unremarkable, but the willowy figure, the piquant face with the lively green eyes and above all the confidence and hint of daring in the way she stood—yes, she would be memorable. And particularly so to someone for whom she posed a threat.

"Best to put your camera out of sight, then."

She paled but nodded, closing the camera and putting it into her reticule without a word.

"And now I think we should leave," he said, putting a hand on her arm and beginning to guide her towards the gates.

The announcement for the fifth race blared from the speakers and the crowd turned back in the direction of the stands, as they neared the exits.

"Can we not stay, Granville?" said Emily, picking her way carefully through the rutted mud that the path had become. "Thunderstorm is running, and they say he is quite something to see."

He glanced at her face, still too pale, the bones standing out in sharp definition. Shock, he thought. And she probably didn't realize it. "Have you ever seen death before?"

"No. But I'm fine, really. You don't need to cut our day short. We haven't even talked to anyone about Mr. Weston."

"Scott and Trent will get answers if there are any here. They don't need us as well," Granville said. "Besides, I think it best that I not be here when the police arrive to investigate the stabbing."

"We can go to the station later to make a statement, if you like," he said, steering her through the crowds hurrying the other way so as not to miss the starting gate.

"You don't mean they would arrest you?" Emily sounded shocked.

"I'm not their favorite person at the moment," Granville said, smiling at her. "And I must admit, I do seem to stumble across murders rather frequently."

"It's your business," Emily said, stopping dead and nearly causing an older gentleman with an ornate cane to trip over her. "Of course you'd be there."

"True. I'm afraid, however, that the police would not agree with that clear sighted statement." Granville placed Emily's arm in the crook of his elbow and began to stroll towards the exit. "In their eyes, I am interfering at best and somehow involved at worst."

"That isn't fair! If you were a Pinkerton's detective, would you face the same prejudice?"

"Perhaps not. They are an internationally known and respected firm of private investigators. And they have a much longer history than my three months in the business."

"What would happen if you worked with them?" Emily asked. "Pinkerton's, I mean."

He noted she didn't suggest he work for them. Clearly she'd learned a fair bit about him in the last months. "It's an interesting idea. I don't know that they work with other agencies, though."

"An article I read the other day said they do," Emily said.

He noted her shocked pallor was fading. "Why are you reading about Pinkerton's?" he asked. And watched a blush spread across her face. Now what had she been up to?

"There was a rather good article on them in *Harper's*. I was curious to see how their business compared to yours."

"Oh?"

"You know a good typewriter has to understand business if she plans to get ahead."

"And do you? Plan to get ahead, I mean?" He'd thought she was growing rather tired of the typewriting business.

"Of course," Emily said. "I'd soon be bored, doing nothing but typewriting all day."

The more he learned of his fiancée, the more true Granville found that statement to be. "There are few women in business, I'm afraid."

"I quite like the idea of being a pioneer," Emily said. "It's why I've persisted with my typewriting lessons. Typewriting is a skill that can have many applications."

Which was true. Granville wasn't sure why it surprised him so much to hear her reasoning. He'd wondered why she'd persisted so long with her typewriting lessons—they seemed so foreign to her adventurous nature. "And are you drawn to any application in particular?"

"I was interested in the idea newspaper reporting for a time, and it's still a possibility," she said. "But what really interests me is the detective business."

It shouldn't have come as a surprise to Granville, but it did. Now what did he say?

He drew her closer as the crowds thickened near the exit gate, jostling them both. "It's a dangerous business, as you've seen."

As Granville spoke, he felt Emily jerk against him.

"Oh!" she cried out.

Turning quickly, instinctively sheltering her from the crowd, he examined her face, grown even paler. "What is it?"

"My arm..."

There was a rent in her sleeve, cutting through her coat and blouse, and a line of blood welling up on the fine skin of her arm.

His eyes darted beyond her, quartering the crowd, looking for anything threatening, anything out of place. The happy din of the racegoers was the same, the smell of mud and horses in the crisp air unchanged.

Yet someone had harmed Emily.

"You've been cut," he said, forcing his tone to gentleness when he felt like hunting down whoever had dared do this to her, and showing them real pain. If she hadn't been wearing such a thick coat, she could have been badly injured.

"It doesn't look serious," he told her in the calmest voice he could manage. "But it does need attention. Let's get you out of here."

She nodded, not pretending to misunderstand him, or playing down the incident, protesting it was nothing. It was yet another thing to value in this rather surprising fiancée of his.

"Who did it, did you see?" she asked. "Now would be the time to find him and question him."

"Later," Granville said. "That arm of yours needs attending to."

"It is a little sore," Emily said, and fainted.

———

TWO HOURS LATER, Granville found himself at the Beaver Tavern. The smoky air, the smell of spilled beer and the bite of whiskey were old friends. He'd had Emily's arm attended to at the local hospital, against her protests that it was nothing and he really didn't need to fuss.

Granville thought he had every need. It had shocked him deeply to see her injured. And it worried him even more that the attack was because of the murder she'd witnessed.

It was possible he was over-reacting. Probable, even. But how else to explain what was clearly a knife cut on Emily's arm, if a shallow one?

Granville had seen Emily home and extracted a promise that she would rest that evening and the next day. Unfortunately he'd learned the danger of believing Emily's promises when it came to her own safety. Which was why he'd made a point of telling her he'd call the following morning to see how she was.

She'd given him a look that said she'd seen right through him. Well, at least her mother would be pleased to welcome him.

Granville drained the whiskey and called for another. The glass slid down the scarred wood of the long bar. He shifted his stance, stopping it just before it reached the edge.

"Thanks," he told the bartender, who smirked, then slung a glass in the opposite direction. Its recipient was the worse for drink, and nearly lost his balance reaching for it.

Granville smiled a little, and raised his own drink in a salute. Then he tuned out the noise and the smoke, and went back to contemplating his current problem. What was he going to do about Emily?

Until he was sure he was imagining the threat to her, he wanted her safe. And even if he wasn't imagining it, he wanted her out of town.

One murder in the week since he'd begun investigating Weston. Three attacks on him. Two on Scott. And now Emily had seen someone murdered, then been attacked herself.

It was too much.

Over-reaction or no, he wasn't prepared to risk Emily being in danger. But how was he to make sure she was safe? Short of marrying her and taking her away himself.

He considered the idea for a moment, his lips quirking. There was no denying its appeal. But Emily was only eighteen, and while old enough to marry, he wanted to give her time to be sure she knew her own mind.

Granville had made up his own mind almost immediately, but he thought Emily had only recently begun to consider making their false engagement real. It had been only a little over three months since they'd met, after all. He wanted a lifetime with her.

And he didn't want to see her rushed into something she'd regret all her life. He couldn't live with that.

But if Emily was killed because he'd failed to act, he couldn't live with that, either. He'd never get over losing her, and in such a way.

He carried enough guilt over his lack of action in saving his friend Edward. Granville's mind flashed to the smoking revolver, the pool of blood. Edward had thought he had no options left.

He needed to make sure Emily always had options.

And he'd do whatever he had to do to make sure she was safe.

Decision made, Granville drained the last of his whiskey, and dropped a coin on the bar. He needed to know just how much danger Emily might be in.

15

Granville paced the increasingly small floor of his office, drumming his fingers against the .38 revolver at his hip. Where were Trent and Scott? He needed to discuss the incidents at the track with Scott. He wanted his partner at his back, and more importantly, at Emily's.

When the door creaked, he spun round, hand closing around his revolver, and strode into the outer office.

It was Emily, accompanied by a nervous maid. His fiancée looked very much better than she had a few hours before. She'd regained her color, though her face was still a little strained. And her eyes lacked their usual life.

"Emily? What are you doing here?"

"And good afternoon to you, too."

"You should be resting."

"I have rested. Now I feel much better, and I want to know what Mr. Scott and Trent have learned. May I sit?"

He pulled forward the most comfortable of the wing chairs and she sank gracefully into it. He knew the strength of mind it took to keep from showing pain. Emily's maid chose a small wooden chair on the far side of the room.

Emily shook her head at him. "Granville. I've had worse scrapes falling from my bicycle, for heaven's sake. Don't look so worried."

Before he could respond, the others finally arrived. Trent was looking very pleased with himself. Obviously they'd found something.

After a round of greetings, they all gathered around Emily's chair. Granville watched her closely, noting her posture—still very straight, but she was leaning her head against the high back of the chair, in a way that suggested weariness. He needed to take her home again, and soon.

His eyes met Scott's, conveyed a warning. "Well?"

His partner's stance went from relaxed to watchful. They'd been in enough tight situations—no words were needed between them.

Usually Granville found danger somewhat exhilarating.

This time he didn't. He didn't much want to contemplate why that might be so. "What have you found out?"

"Very little, I'm afraid," Scott said.

Emily looked from Scott to Granville. "I'm not fragile, and I don't need to be protected."

Despite her pallor, her face was determined. And he knew that set to her lips. His youngest sister used to look like that when she'd made up her mind. They'd never succeeded in changing it once she got that look on her face. "Very well. Go on."

"We found Weston's bookie," Trent said. He seemed to have missed the byplay between Granville and Scott. "Todd Graham."

"Go on."

"He was—persuaded—to talk to us," Scott said, shooting Trent a look that had the lad taking a step back. "Mostly because he liked Weston, and we were able to convince him that we had good news for him. He last saw Weston twelve weeks ago. Hasn't heard from him since. And he agreed with you that the man's left town, likely in something of a hurry."

"And does this Graham know for a fact that Weston left town, and that he was alive to do so?" Granville said.

"Not exactly," Scott said. "But he did tell us Weston had the money to go pretty much anywhere."

"I thought he was broke?"

"He was. But apparently an old bet got paid off, and Graham gave the money to Weston that afternoon."

"What afternoon? You mean the ninth? The last day he was seen?"

Scott nodded.

"And is that all Mr. Graham knows?" Emily said.

"No." Trent was grinning now. "He knew something about where Weston went."

Finally. "Where?"

Scott gave Trent another look and the boy looked away, shuffling his feet. "Apparently Weston intended to head north."

"North! What would attract him to the north?"

Scott grinned at him.

"Don't tell me?" Granville said with a groan.

"Yup. Something about gold."

"Not another would-be Klondiker?"

"Not this time," Scott said. "Seems our friend was headed into the northern interior."

He groaned. "We're working in a growing city in the midst of a business boom. Why do we keep running into gold-seekers?"

"Just lucky, I guess," Scott said.

"Well, at least you won't be headed for Cape Town," Emily said with a soft laugh. "And I won't have to spend any more time looking through dusty newspapers."

Maybe she'd rest, then. "True enough," Granville said.

But Emily wasn't done.

"So why would Weston tell his bookie all this?" Emily asked Scott. "I'd never heard that bookies were particularly discreet? And if Mr. Graham knew, why did no-one else know? And if he didn't tell anyone else, why tell you?"

"Whoa," said Scott, holding up a hand. "One question at a time. And Graham didn't exactly tell us all of this."

She tilted her head and laughed at him. "Of course he didn't. How silly of me."

Granville fought back his own laugh. She was definitely feeling better, and her eyes were brighter again. "And exactly what did he tell you?"

"He said Weston let slip something about heading north," Trent said. "But he seemed to think it was a joke."

"That's it? That could mean anything," Granville said.

Scott nodded. "Yes, but we also talked to your buddy McAndrews."

He hadn't seen him at the track, but McAndrews was a gambler too. It made sense he'd be there. "And?"

"And I asked him if Weston had ever talked about heading north. McAndrews said not, but that Weston had once said something about gold in the Interior," Scott said.

He grimaced. "You know anything about goldfields in the Interior?"

Scott shook his head. "Except that they're north of here."

"There was the Caribou Gold rush, mostly around Barkerville," Trent said with a smirk. "But that played out nearly fifty years ago."

Ancient history. Just what he needed. "So we have no clue where the fellow really was headed."

"I wouldn't say that," Trent said.

Granville eyed their apprentice. The kid was doing it deliberately.

He caught Trent's eye, and the boy flushed, then blurted out, "McAndrews was able to tell us that Weston was worried sick about something until he went to the Masonic Lodge one evening. He came home in high spirits. Two days later he was gone."

"Still doesn't tell us where he went, though," Scott said.

It didn't surprise Granville that Weston had been a Mason, but it irked him that he hadn't even thought to ask if there was a local lodge. Foolish of him. He should have checked long before now. And had he not been in full retreat from his oldest brother and everything the baron stood for, he likely would have done so.

Once he found the local Lodge, he'd need to find out who Weston had talked to. Which might not be easy.

"Do you know when your friend attended the Lodge?" Emily asked, a small frown between her brows.

Now what was she up to? And how had she known about the Masons? His fiancée's knowledge of anything related to the secretive organization surprised Granville.

"The day before he vanished, the Thursday. He was at the Carlton on Friday night, and we haven't yet found anyone who saw him on Saturday." Scott told her. "Why d'you ask?"

"My father is a member, you see," Emily explained. "A Mason, I mean."

Granville wondered with an inward grin if she'd been listening at keyholes again.

"And I know they sign in," she continued.

Which wasn't a usual part of the ritual. "I'll look into it," he said.

"I can ask Papa," Emily offered.

"No need. I'm a member myself," Granville said, smiling a little at her surprised look. He turned to Scott. "Did you hear anything about a death at the track?"

It was Trent who answered, straightening a little from where he leaned against the side of Emily's chair. "Hear about it? It was all people were talking about," he said. "And we were questioned by the cops."

"Everyone was," Scott added. "You must have left before they arrived."

Granville nodded. He wasn't ready to tell them about Emily quite yet. "Do you know who was killed?"

"You didn't hear?" Trent said.

"Hear what?"

"It was Graham," Scott said soberly.

"Graham? The man you'd just talked to? Weston's bookie?"

"Yeah. Probably why the police wanted to talk to us."

Granville could barely summon up a smile at Scott's wisecracks. "So that's two of Weston's acquaintances murdered since we began looking for the fellow," he said.

And now his investigation had touched Emily. And she'd been hurt.

It was enough. "Did you get any sense of who might be behind it?" he asked Scott.

"No. Rumors were flying', but I didn't get the sense anyone knew much more than we do," Scott said.

"And nothing Graham said gave you any clue?"

"Nope. And he seemed fine, too," Scott said. "Not nervous or wary or like that."

"The cops were busy asking everyone about the dead man's connections to some fellow named Heade. Runs gambling rackets or something," Trent added.

"Well, Graham was a bookie." Granville turned to Scott. "Do you know anything about this Heade?"

"Nope. Never even heard of him," Scott said. "He can't be a very big player."

"I wonder if Benton knows him," Granville said.

"Most likely Heade either works for Benton or has been marked by him," Scott said.

"Marked?" Emily said.

For a moment, Scott looked like he was regretting his words. Then he gave a little dip of his head towards her, and told her the unvarnished truth. "As a potential rival," he said. "Or a potential problem."

His partner had just given his fiancée his highest accolade; he'd treated her as an equal. Granville hadn't expected that to happen, ever. "You really think Benton's that ruthless?" he asked Scott.

"I know he is. His last serious rival..."

"Not counting Jackson?" Granville asked. Benton's former second-in-command had been the first body he'd discovered, or at least the first since his arrival in Vancouver. That particular episode had ended with Scott in jail and himself under suspicion from the police.

Scott waved that off. "Jackson didn't count. He wasn't any kind of threat to Benton. No, this was a gent from Boston, who'd been running a few rackets there and thought he'd set up something similar here. Brought a few of his boys with him, threw his weight around a bit, set up shop. Benton got word of it and made his displeasure clear."

"I've never heard anything about this."

"Before you got to town. Anyway, the fool ignored the warning. He was raking in the money for a few weeks, 'til the foggy morning they found him floating in the Fraser, beat so bad they almost couldn't identify him. No-one's been fool enough to challenge Benton since."

"I wonder if Norton had any connection to this Heade?" Granville said.

"Not that I ever heard. Doesn't mean he didn't, though," Scott said. "You think maybe these murders are because of Heade, not because of Weston?"

"I think it's worth looking into. And immediately."

"Why the urgency? Did I miss something?" Scott asked.

His expression grim, Granville glanced at Emily. His instinct was to protect her, even against his own fears for her. But how could he value her less than Scott just had?

He filled Scott and Trent in on what had happened at the track.

"You could have been killed!" Trent said to Emily.

"It was just a scratch," Emily said.

"But what if they try again?"

"I'm sure it was just an accident," she told him.

"It's my job to make sure she isn't injured again," Granville said.

"Our job," Scott said.

Granville nodded his thanks.

Emily looked flustered and about to argue with them. Apparently she thought better of it, because she sat back without saying a word. Her face had gone white.

He needed to see her home. Now.

"Scott, can you talk to Frances?" Granville said. "See if she was at the track today? And find out if she knows or has heard anything about Heade or the murder."

"I'll do that."

"I'll go too," Trent said.

"You're with me," Granville said. "We'll all of us see Emily home. Then it's time for me to have another chat with Benton. It will be less of a challenge if I don't confront him alone."

16

"You should come with me, talk to Frances," Scott said.

They had left Emily and her maid safely at her parents' home in English Bay and were walking from the streetcar stop towards the small bungalow Benton had rented for Frances. Granville pulled his cashmere muffler closer against the bitter wind as he considered the statement.

Scott never said anything without a reason, but he'd be damned if he could discern it this time. "Why?" Granville asked.

"It's Saturday."

Was Scott testing his temper? Given his state of mind over Emily's safety, that wasn't difficult.

It also wasn't smart, which Scott had good reason to know—he'd seen the results on the creeks of the Klondike when Hodgkins, Sanders and Mitchell had tried to bushwhack them and take their claim. Not that it would have done them any good, as the claim had proved to be barren, but that wasn't the point. "So?"

Scott grinned at him. "On a Saturday, around this time, Benton takes tea with my sister."

He had to smile back.

It was an incongruous picture—the gangster sitting down for a late afternoon tea with his inamorata. It didn't make the man any less dangerous, but it did make him human. "All the better. Benton won't kill me in front of Frances."

"Whoa!" The big man stopped, stared at him. "You're going to challenge Benton?"

"Whatever it takes," Granville said. "I need to know Emily is safe."

"You really think someone was trying to kill Miss Emily? And that they'd try again? That just ain't right." Trent's jaw had firmed and his eyes bore witness to the man he was becoming.

"I'm hoping that isn't true," Granville said. "But I need to be certain. And at the moment the only thing I'm certain of is that this particular case seems to have more dead ends and convoluted twists than one of my brother William's plots."

"You don't think he's involved? Your brother I mean?" Trent was back to being seventeen.

"I don't see how he can be from such a distance," Granville said. "However, I'm not ruling anything out until I have more facts. And Benton may have the answers I need. Certainly he didn't tell us everything the last time we talked to him."

"Then why would he now?" Trent asked.

Let the boy figure it out for himself. It would do him good. "We'll see."

———

BENTON WAS INDEED VISITING—LOUNGING in Frances' overheated and be-frilled parlor with a cheroot in one hand and a snifter of brandy in the other. Frances sat beside him in a day gown of plum silk that flattered her dark good looks, her rigid posture and the dainty china teacup she held an oddly proper contrast to her lover's casual sprawl. Neither rose when the houseboy announced them.

Frances gave them a strained smile and Benton waved the cigar at them and nodded.

Granville wondered what they had interrupted. The warm

crackle of the fire and the spicy incense that Frances loved did not disguise the tension in the air.

"Please have a seat," Frances said. "Would you care for tea? Brandy? Whiskey?"

"Brandy, if you have it," Granville said as he lowered himself into an overstuffed armchair across from the sofa where Benton and Frances sat. Scott and Trent both nodded as they seated themselves in chairs along the far wall. "But I think Trent would rather have a soda, am I right?"

Trent gave him an irritated glare but didn't contradict him. Frances motioned to the houseboy, who disappeared towards the back of the house.

"To what do we owe this honor?" Benton said through a cloud of pungent smoke, which was barely offset by the incense.

Benton was too astute, and probably too suspicious, to be misled by social niceties. He hadn't gained and kept his current position by trusting easily.

"The matter of young Weston continues to grow more complex," Granville said. "There have been two murders that I know of, and now I fear it may have touched my fiancée."

"The murders are not a surprise, but the matter of your fiancée is, I confess," Benton said. "What has happened?"

It was a sharp-edged demand, but Granville chose to overlook the matter of its delivery. He needed whatever information Benton might choose to offer.

"She witnessed the stabbing at the racetrack this afternoon," he said. "She didn't see precisely what happened, but afterwards someone jostled against her and her arm was cut. I fear someone may believe she saw more than she did."

"How dreadful," Frances said. "Is she all right?"

"The cut was not deep, and Emily is resting." Or at least he hoped she was resting by now.

"You're worried she may still be in danger?" Benton's tone was neutral, but he was frowning.

"I don't know. I can't ignore that she was hurt, and immediately

after seeing Graham's murder. I hoped you might have some
wisdom for me."

Before Benton could answer, the houseboy returned with the
tray of drinks. In the bustle of serving them, Granville lost sight of
Benton's expression. When he looked again, the shorter man's face
held its usual bland expression.

"I can tell you that Graham's death this afternoon was indeed
murder," Benton said.

"Why was he murdered?" Granville asked.

Benton's eyes didn't change, but he saw the tension in Frances'
hand where it lay on her lover's black-clad arm. "That isn't something I can answer," Benton said.

Which didn't mean he didn't know.

"My apologies—I asked the wrong question," Granville said
smoothly. "My concern for the moment is solely for my fiancée's
safety. Is Emily in any danger?"

"I can't tell you that," Benton said, puffing on his cheroot so that
his face nearly disappeared behind the resulting smoke.

He'd hoped for a denial. Benton's carefully worded phrase told
him exactly nothing, but the implications worried him. "What *can*
you tell me?"

Dark eyes met his, holding his gaze for a moment. "Nothing, I'm
afraid," Benton said. "But look after your lady."

It wasn't enough, but Granville knew better than to push Benton
for more. "I'll do that," he said, and turned towards Frances. "But
enough of such unpleasant things. Tell me, did you enjoy the races
today?"

"Today? I didn't attend today," she said. Her face showed only
polite interest, but her hand had clenched on Benton's arm.

"Ah, my mistake," Granville said. "Emily thought she caught a
glimpse of your face in the crowd."

Frances' face was still smooth and calm, but Benton was
frowning.

"I'm hearing rumors about someone named Heade," Scott said,
leaning forward and speaking directly to Benton. "You heard of
him?"

"He's from out of town, just visiting, I gather," Benton said smoothly. "Likely he won't be in town long." The smile that accompanied the statement was not a pleasant one.

Granville hoped it was never directed at him. "Is Heade someone Emily needs to worry about?"

"It's certainly possible," Benton said with a tight smile. "But not for long."

So Scott had been right. "Do I need to persuade her to leave town for a time?" Granville asked.

"That might be wise." Again the smile.

Frances's fingers were white with strain against the dark wool of her skirt, but she didn't say a word.

Granville gave a sharp nod, drained his brandy. "Thank you. I shall do so."

As they left the house, Scott put a hand on Granville's arm. He looked worried. "Wait. Frances wants to talk to you. After Benton leaves."

Would Frances tell them something Benton would not? "How did she manage to let you know without Benton hearing?"

Scott showed him the note. "The houseboy gave me this as we left. We might as well grab a drink. They'll be a while."

Granville could imagine.

There's a decent bar not far from here," Scott said as they turned the corner. "So, what are you going to do to keep Emily safe?"

"I think she has an aunt in Victoria. Perhaps she could visit there."

"And in the meantime?" Scott asked.

"I'll tell her to stay indoors until I can get her to somewhere she'll be safe."

"You think she will?"

"Not for long."

FRANCES STILL LOOKED PERFECTLY GROOMED when they returned,
if a little flushed.

"I'm glad you came back," she said, rising to greet them. "I
didn't want to say anything in front of Benton, but I have information I think you need to hear. But I need a drink first. Can I offer
you anything?"

"No, I'm fine. Thank you," Granville said as they all sat down.
Scott took his place on the sofa beside his sister. The others
resumed the seats they'd taken earlier.

"But what did you want to tell me?" Granville asked.

"Sam? Anything?" Frances asked, still playing the perfect
hostess.

"I'm good, thanks."

Frances nodded, took a sip of her brandy. Looked directly at
Granville. "You said Emily thought she'd seen me, at the track?"

He nodded.

"Was there anything—unusual—in what she saw?" Frances
seemed to trip a little over her words. Which was most unlike
Scott's usually poised sister.

"Yes," Granville said. "The person she thought was you was
wearing male attire."

Frances' face looked strained. She turned to Scott, put a hand on
his arm. "Sam, do you remember our cousin Ronald? Ronald
Trueman?"

"Ma's sister's son? Yeah, a little. Why?" Then Scott's face took
on a similar look of strain. "He's not...?"

"We lived near them when we moved to San Francisco. He was
lonely, I think. And for a jest, he'd sometimes dress in my clothes."

"Let me guess. He looked just like you?"

"Like enough, especially from any distance," she said. "Then he
got in with the wrong element. Since I left, I've lost touch, but I
hear things."

Granville, listening without interrupting, found it ironic to hear
Benton's mistress talk about the wrong element. He wondered how

she'd describe Benton, or whether she simply chose not to think about her lover's work.

"Is our cousin part of Heade's gang?" Scott asked.

Her answer, when it came, was terse. "He was," she said. "I doubt he'd have left him."

"Where is Heade from?" Granville asked Scott.

"I can tell you that," Frances said. "David Heade is from San Francisco. And he's dangerous. Very dangerous. He's been building a very specialized empire there since long before I left."

San Francisco again. Granville and Scott exchanged glances.

"What's Heade doing here?" Scott asked her.

She swallowed hard, drank a little of her brandy. "I don't know. But he was in town for a few weeks earlier this year. And back again this week. Benton isn't amused."

That much was obvious. "Then why has Benton allowed Heade's visits to go unchallenged?" Granville asked.

"I don't know that, either. But I do know he's watching him closely, and I can guess the reason." She finished off the brandy, handed the glass to Scott to refill for her.

"Heade has a lot of power—he's not one to take on if you have any choice. And he has some of his best men with him here. But you heard Benton earlier. I think if Heade doesn't leave town soon, Benton will take him on. And I'm afraid of the outcome." Her voice was hard, but her eyes were damp.

Scott handed her the refilled snifter, and a little silence fell between them.

"There is something you need to know for your own safety," Granville said after a moment's thought. "But I'll ask you to keep it to yourself, for Emily's sake—and for her safety."

Frances gave a jerky little nod.

"Emily thinks the man who looks like you is the one who stabbed Graham."

"Oh. Oh no." She'd gone pale, and the few light freckles on her cheeks were suddenly visible.

"When exactly was Heade last here?" Granville asked.

"Late January, I think. Perhaps early February."

Right around the time Weston vanished. What exactly had that young idiot got himself into?

"We'd just had an unexpected warm spell," Frances was saying. "And I can remember being annoyed that it was cold and rainy again, while Benton was ranting because he'd just got wind that Heade was in town. With a few members of his gang, and without the courtesy of checking in with him."

"That's a bad sign," Scott commented.

She nodded.

"How long did he stay?" Granville asked.

"A few weeks. It took a bit for Benton to track him down. Heade left after that."

Granville wondered if Heade had left because of Benton's threats, or because he'd killed Weston. Or lost him. "And now he's back?"

"Yes. With our cousin, this time."

"And Benton thinks Emily might be caught in the middle?"

"It's likely to get bloody," Frances said softly. "And our cousin— he has a reputation. He kills people. And he doesn't like to lose. I'd be worried for anyone caught anywhere near him. Or Heade."

"Any point my talking to Ronald?" Scott said.

"I doubt it. He's been with Heade a long time," she said.

Right. "Thank you for the warning and the information, Frances. Scott, we'd best be going," Granville said. "We have a few leads to run down tonight."

⁘

AN HOUR LATER, Granville approached the Masonic Lodge on Pender Street. Three stories tall and solidly built of rough-hewn granite, the Vancouver chapter's lodge had few of the carved flourishes he'd grown accustomed to in British lodges. Inside, though, the oiled mahogany panelling and the scent of cigars and port had a comforting familiarity, and the usual rituals gave Granville immediate entrance.

Nor did it take long to find the information he was looking for.

Emily was right about members signing in. Weston had been there in the late afternoon of February eighth along with a half a dozen others. Granville didn't recognize any of the names, and none of those listed were currently present. Weston could have talked with any of them.

Making a list of the names, he thanked the steward and made his way into the lounge, choosing a seat at the long mahogany bar that ran across the back of the room. Other than the bartender and one other man, drinking alone at a table near the large windows, the room was deserted. Which seemed odd. It wasn't that early.

"Whiskey, straight up," he said.

"Of course, sir."

It was delivered in a cut crystal glass placed on a silver coaster. The silver gleamed softly in the lamplight. Just like home.

London, rather. It wasn't really home any more. Odd as this upstart city on the edge of a continent had felt at first, he was beginning to feel like he belonged here.

He had a brief chat with the bartender, downed the drink, then went to find Emily and make sure she was safe.

17

SUNDAY, APRIL 22, 1900

The carved oak pews had been full today, and Emily had noticed they felt harder than usual as Reverend Dawson's sermon went on much too long. Despite the low hum of whispering from every corner, Granville had sat silently beside her for the entire time the minister droned on. She'd darted quick glances at him, but his expression gave nothing away.

Now they were strolling down a quiet side street with a chance to talk, just the two of them. The sun was even out, for the moment at least, and the warmth on her sore arm was welcome.

Her arm ached, though she'd never admit it to Granville. He'd only worry. And try to keep her far away from his investigations in future.

She glanced at the spacious homes with neatly laid out yards that lined the street. The kind she and Granville might live in one day. She felt her stomach jump nervously at the thought, and cast a sideways glance at him.

If it made her nervous, how did he feel about it? Now didn't seem the time to ask.

She smiled at him, squeezing a little where her fingers lay on his arm. There was a tenseness in him that she hadn't seen before, and he hadn't said a word since they left the church.

"Something is bothering you," she said softly, watching his hands tighten as she spoke. "More than an investigation usually does, I mean. Can you tell me what it is?"

"I'm worried about you," he said after a pause. "That knife came too close. And you should never have been touched."

His voice was carefully neutral, but Emily could see the strain in his face.

"Perhaps you could leave town for a time?" he suggested. "Just until I can resolve this situation and be sure you are in no danger. You have an aunt in Victoria, do you not? Perhaps you could visit her for a week or so."

Surely he didn't truly believe that her life was in danger? But he looked so worried. "Let me think about it," Emily said, trying to keep her voice neutral.

Judging by his expression, she hadn't succeeded. "But do tell me what you learned at the Lodge," she said.

It was an effective distraction. Apparently Mr. Weston had gone to the Lodge, but Granville hadn't recognized any of the names.

"Who was there that night?" As he paused, she smiled at him. "It's all right—I promise I won't tell anyone. Your Masonic secrets are safe with me."

He smiled back, and told her. "From what the bartender can recall, he chatted with several men, but spoke the longest with a fellow named Harrison," he added.

Emily felt pleased with herself, because for a moment the worry lines on his forehead had disappeared. They came back almost at once, though.

Then the name registered. She stopped walking, bringing him to a halt and turned to face him. "Mr. Weston spoke the longest with a Mr. Harrison? Judge Eli Harrison?"

He nodded.

"And didn't Trent say that young Mr. Weston had gone north to seek gold?" Emily said, aware that she was speaking too quickly. She was trying to sound business-like—she intended to convince him she'd be an asset to his business, after all—but she couldn't quite hide her excitement.

"Yes. Why? What have you thought of?"

"I met his wife, you know, several months ago. Judge Harrison's wife, I mean."

"Oh?"

"Mm-hmm. An interesting woman—she's from Victoria. Her family is extremely well-connected, as my sister Jane delights in telling me."

She took note of his expression and grinned. "Yes, I think so too. But Mrs. Harrison tells a wonderful tale of her husband and some of his travels with the Chinese court interpreter. And she also spoke of rumors of a rich goldfield in a region the Indians consider sacred."

"This region wouldn't be in the northern interior, by any chance?" Granville asked.

"I do believe it is. It seems Judge Harrison was one of the magistrates for the Caribou for a number of years, and so knows much of the area well."

"Which could explain why Weston headed north."

"I hope he didn't rely solely on such flimsy information," Emily said.

"Given what we've learned so far," Granville said. "I suspect he'd have thought it safer than staying here."

She felt rather sorry for the poor man. "I hope you can find a way to return him to England before whoever's after him catches up with him."

He nodded. "So do I."

"So what is next?" she asked, though she suspected she knew the answer.

"I need to talk to Harrison."

She nodded. "Is he still in town?"

"I gather he's currently in session in Nanaimo."

"That makes sense. I believe he's now one of the Provincial Judges with responsibilities there." She tucked her hand back into his arm, and they started walking again. "When will you set out?"

"As soon as I can make arrangements. Likely tomorrow. But I would prefer to see you safely off to Victoria first."

"Well, you do know the fastest way to Nanaimo, do you not?"

The mischief in Emily's eyes intrigued Granville. "Frankly, I have no idea where Nanaimo is. Why don't you enlighten me?"

"It's on Vancouver Island. You would take the ferry to Victoria, then the train up-Island," she said. "And since you are traveling that way in any case, perhaps you could escort me to visit my aunt."

He couldn't hold back a laugh at her evident delight, though his strongest feeling was relief that he would be able to see her safely away from here. "How convenient. Will you accept my escort to Victoria?"

"I'd be delighted to do so."

"And would you be ready to leave tomorrow?"

"Clara will be accompanying me, and I am sure we can both be packed in time."

"And does Clara know about this?" Granville said.

He must have noted her friend's uncharacteristic behavior at lunch the other day. She kept forgetting Granville didn't miss things.

"Not yet," Emily said. "But I'm sure I can convince her to join me. I will call on her directly after luncheon. And I'll see to my own packing early this afternoon."

"Then I will plan to collect you both at nine tomorrow morning."

"Perfect. And since Victoria is the provincial capital, you might want to pack a formal suit."

He groaned, but nodded. She was probably right. "You seem much more resigned to going than when I first suggested it?"

She grinned at him. "Well, I believe my aunt told me Mrs. Harrison is currently visiting friends in Victoria. If I asked her to tea, she might perhaps remember more of the story than she told me at the time. And I really do owe Aunt Alice a visit."

———

"BUT I DON'T UNDERSTAND, EMILY," Clara complained, batting at an over-familiar palm frond. "I'm pleased to see you, of course, but why do we need to go to Victoria?"

"Have you ever explored the city?" Emily asked, watching her friend's expression. Seated on a maroon velvet sofa in her mother's palm be-decked front parlor, Clara looked paler than usual, as if she hadn't been sleeping. "They have tea dances at the Crystal Garden. And splendid shopping. It is the capital, after all."

"Really? That sounds wonderful. Except you don't much care for any of those things," Clara said astutely. "Why would you want to go?"

"Well, I don't exactly want to go."

"But you're going? Is your father punishing you again? Oh, Emily, you haven't got yourself unengaged to Mr. Granville, have you?"

"No, why do you ask?" said Emily, knowing she was blushing and unable to control it.

Clara was the only one who knew that her engagement to Granville had started off as a temporary measure, designed to alleviate her father's wrath at her involvement in Granville's first case. He wouldn't be pleased to know how thoroughly she intended to involve herself in this one.

She was even a little reluctant to tell Granville himself what she intended, and that worried her.

Oh, Granville was supportive, and valued her comments, but she needed more than that. She needed him to truly recognize her abilities before she made a final decision to marry him. And she wasn't yet sure he could do that.

Their engagement had slowly become real, though she still couldn't quite believe that he really intended to marry her one day. She could think of nothing better than to be his wife. Except that she knew herself too well.

She couldn't be just the invisible wife that society expected her to be. The one whose role was solely caring for the home and eventual children. Though she could feel herself blushing again at the thought of creating those children.

She needed more in her life, needed to be involved and doing something meaningful. It wouldn't be enough to be his helpmate. She wanted—she wanted to be his partner.

"Whatever are you thinking, Emily?" Clara asked. "You have the oddest look on your face."

"Oh, well..." Emily's mind raced.

"You only get that look when you are thinking of Mr. Granville," Clara said. "Is he going to Victoria, too?"

"Yes, though he is going on to Nanaimo."

"Nanaimo." Clara sat back and pursed bow-shaped lips.

It was her most deceptively appealing look, but Emily's gaze was fixed on the sharp eyes above the pout. "Then you are investigating again. It is the only reason you would miss your typewriting classes. Are we still investigating Mr. Weston, Emily?"

Emily heard the "we" with relief. Clara loved to complain about their involvement in the detecting business, but she'd suspected for some time that her friend was secretly thrilled to be involved.

And it meant she could talk about the case and not Granville's odd concern for her safety. She'd never involve Clara if she felt there was any real danger.

"Yes, there is more information that may help us find him," she said, and Clara leaned forward, mannerisms forgotten.

"So you think Mrs. Harrison may know more than she told you initially?" she said when Emily finished telling her what they'd learned.

"She is a very entertaining speaker," Emily said. "I've noticed that when people are telling a story, they include only those details likely to intrigue their audience or move the story forward. Don't you do the same?"

Clara nodded. "I wonder if authors do that?"

"Most likely. Why?"

"Oh, no reason," Clara said, too vaguely for Emily's liking. She knew her friend well, and Clara at her most vague was also at her most devious. She wondered what Clara had been reading.

"What more do you hope to learn in Victoria, then?" Clara asked too quickly.

"I'm not sure, but I have the feeling that there was something that Mrs. Harrison was careful not to mention. Perhaps I can convince her to tell me what it was. Of course, it may be a waste of time." Emily shrugged. "Will you come, Clara?"

"Well yes, I think so. The tea dances, you know."

"Of course. You wouldn't want to miss those." Emily said, quelling the laugh she could feel somewhere under her rib cage.

Clara smiled at her, face innocently smooth. "Come upstairs and help me pack?"

Emily groaned. Clara's version of packing involved much trying on of possible outfits, complete with scarves, bonnets and boots, with long pauses for consultation. This could take hours.

Emily followed her friend up the polished staircase, all desire to laugh gone.

18

MONDAY, APRIL 23, 1900

They left Vancouver in drenching rain. The sea was rough and Granville braced himself for a difficult trip.

Emily didn't seem to care, settling herself at a table near one of the wide windows with a cup of tea and a plate of toast dripping with butter and honey. Even Clara seemed to be enjoying herself, which surprised him.

There had been no sign of anyone following them. Which was a relief.

He'd gone to the office as usual, then crept out the back while Scott and Trent departed very obviously by the front doors. The carriage he'd hired was waiting at Emily's home, and he insisted the driver take back streets, which hadn't pleased the man, but seemed to have got them to the docks without detection.

As the ferry wound its way through densely green islands covered in mist, the sea smoothed out and the sky began to clear. After a bit, the three of them went up on deck and took a turn around the ship.

He watched Emily facing into the wind, one hand to her bonnet and a wide smile on her face, and knew he'd made the right decision to get her out of town. Despite his continuing worry about her, he found himself enjoying the voyage.

It was beautiful in a way far wilder than England, yet less threatening than the bleak snows and driving winds of the Klondike. After weeks of grey skies, clouds and rain, the sun glittered off the water and the craggy islands thickly covered in cedar and fir had a feeling of invitation as well as mystery. At least to him.

Lately he'd begun to think that perhaps instead of chasing the will o' the wisp that was gold in the Klondike, he might have done better to travel.

What would his life be now if he'd gone East rather than West? He glanced at the two girls beside him. Perhaps it had worked out for the best.

They would reach Victoria soon.

He planned to hire a carriage to take them to the Emily's aunt's house before he went looking for the train station. Despite their uneventful trip, he still felt an almost primal need to see that Emily was safe. His hand fell to the pistol riding comfortably on his hip.

It was late afternoon by the time Granville was shown into Judge Harrison's chambers at the courthouse in Nanaimo. The imposing stone courthouse—which would be impressive anywhere—was especially so in a town this small. He continued to be intrigued by the contrast of modern settlements dropped amidst huge sections of wilderness.

The railroad journey up-island had been a perfect example—a seventy mile feat of engineering with several high trestles and a long tunnel, running through a vast rugged land much more heavily forested than anything he'd seen in Britain. A fellow passenger had informed him with great glee that Vancouver Island by itself was much the same size as the entire British Isles, which still made his head hurt.

As the clerk announced him, he focused on how much to tell Judge Harrison. The man himself was striding forward to meet him, an imposing figure with his upright carriage and full beard, now graying.

Granville changed his handshake into a Masonic grip. The judge's formality dissolved immediately, and he smiled.

"Mr. Granville, is it? Please, have a seat. How can I assist you?"

"I've been asked to locate a family acquaintance, who seems to have gone north without leaving a forwarding address. I understand he talked with you at the Masonic Hall in Vancouver some months ago. One Rupert Weston?"

"Weston? Oh yes, I remember. The fellow introduced himself to me one evening at the Lodge. Thought at the time he was too young to have that hunted look. He seemed better by the time we'd finished talking—didn't look so nervy."

Hunted.

That one word told Granville more about the man he was seeking than all the other conversations he'd had to date. Judge Harrison was clearly an astute observer of his fellow man—in his position, he probably had to be.

"Do you remember what you talked about, sir?"

"Indeed I do. He'd come to ask me a question. It seems he'd heard some version of a tale my court interpreter told me of undiscovered gold fields north of Hazelton, in an area forbidden to the local natives. I set him straight on the details. Boy looked much happier after that."

"Did he ask you where the find had been made?"

A nod. "And I gave him directions—to the best of my ability, anyway. From what I can gather, Ah Quan—my court interpreter at the time—was talking about a region slightly north of the Omineca, which had a gold rush of its own in 1869 and '70."

"Do you think your interpreter would be willing to talk to me?"

"Normally I'd say yes, especially as you're a fellow Mason, and I'd be happy to recommend you. But unfortunately I'm not sure if he is in town at the moment. I could write a letter of introduction for you, just in case, if you would like?"

Granville nodded. "Thank you. I'd appreciate it."

"I'll send it over before you leave. Where are you staying?"

Granville told him. "And did you suggest a route into the Omineca to Weston?"

"Yes, once I realized he didn't know the area at all. The lad was talking about renting horses in Vancouver." Judge Harrison shook his head. "Horses."

"I gather riding is not the best route north," Granville said.

"No, not the best," Harrison said with a sudden grin. "In fact, his best choice was by steamboat north from Vancouver to Port Essington, then by sternwheeler up the Skeena River to Hazelton. That's the place to rent horses."

The Judge leaned forward. "But I did advise him against heading north before the river broke up in late April. The Skeena is a dangerous river, and especially so at that time of year."

So Weston could have fled Vancouver only to drown in the Skeena. Wonderful, Granville thought as he noted down the names. Just like Weston's brothers had drowned off Swanage.

How accidental had those deaths actually been?

Granville realized again that he desperately needed to know more about the Earl of Thanet and his family. Without that information, he was thrashing around in the dark.

"When did you say Weston left Vancouver?" the Judge was asking.

"Mid-February."

Harrison clicked his tongue. "Fool-hardy. But perhaps he went only as far as Port Essington, and spent a few months there. Had he money, do you know?"

"More than enough for the journey."

"Even so, going north in February is a chancy proposition. Did his rush to leave have something to do with that hunted look he had?"

Granville feared neither of them would like the eventual answer to that question. "I suspect so."

Harrison gave him an assessing look. "And I suspect that you've been asked to do more than locate him, eh? I hope you can help him."

"So do I."

A nod. "Well, if he left in February, and didn't stay in Port Essington, he'd not have been able to take a steamboat up the river, because it would still be iced up. He'd have to go to the Haida or the Tsimshian and hire them to canoe him upstream."

"They can do that?"

"Absolutely, though it would be a most uncomfortable and somewhat dangerous trip at that time of year. The local tribes have been carrying freight up-river for the Hudson's Bay post in Hazelton for years, though. Their canoes are huge—made out of cedar or cottonwood—and sturdy, with impressive arrangements for steering. You can probably inquire in Port Essington, get some information from whomever he hired about where they took him."

"And are there places along the route that Weston could purchase mining equipment?" Granville said. "Or did you suggest that he take it with him?"

"There's always been mining in the area, and especially since the Omineca rush, so everything he needed would be available in Hazelton. I warned him it might be more expensive, but he didn't seem concerned."

"I suspect time was of the essence," Granville said, hoping Weston's haste hadn't proved fatal to him.

19

E mily let her eyes roam around her favorite teashop, and then had to hold back a smile. Mrs. Harrison was already there, seated at a prominent table towards the front of the teashop, as suited her position as wife of one of the Supreme Court Justices of the province. It was a little late for tea, and the establishment was nearly deserted, but that would not have mattered. She would have been given the right table under any circumstances.

Noting the woman's poise and her air of belonging, Emily felt suddenly young and gauche, and lucky that this woman had agreed to meet with her. An urgent hand on her arm reminded her that she had a reason to be here, and questions that needed answers.

"Emily?" Clara was saying. "Why are we waiting?"

"We aren't," Emily said, suiting action to words. "Good afternoon, Mrs. Harrison. I'm so pleased you could join us here."

"I confess I could not resist, my dear. Your invitation to share my stories with your friend was flattering. And I'm rather curious about the questions you hinted at, especially since you say you came to Victoria especially to ask them of me."

Before Emily could answer, the waiter returned and set the

gleaming tea service before them. "I took the liberty of ordering high tea," Mrs. Harrison said.

No-one did high tea like the Guilford.

A few Vancouver teashops served scones and dainty sandwiches and called them high tea. But as she'd promised Clara, those bore no comparison to the feast now spread before them. The scent of dark rich tea from Ceylon and buttery scones, thick with currants and sprinkled with sugar, the sight of crystal dishes of thick clotted cream and bright homemade jams, made from the tiny sweet straw-berries that grew wild and gooseberries carefully cultivated for the purpose, served to remind her of how much she too loved this very English ritual.

Mama served high tea from time to time, but somehow the meal as interpreted by their Chinese cook, delicious as it was, never tasted quite the same.

Looking at the bounty before her, Emily wondered if her Mama had ever thought to give Cook samples of the real thing to taste. Mama thought it was something to do with the flavorings, though she had watched every step of the preparation on several occasions, and found nothing amiss. Remembering that good lady's frustration, Emily hid a smile behind her white-gloved hand.

Mrs. Harrison gave her a questioning look.

"Oh, Emily, this looks wonderful," Clara broke in, her eyes on the tower of tiny, beautiful cakes and pastries. "No wonder you wanted to come here."

"You have not been before?" Mrs. Harrison asked politely.

"No, indeed. And it looks nothing like the kind of afternoon tea we can find in Vancouver."

"Then you should also try the tea at the Butterscone. They too do a superb job."

"Emily? Can we?"

"Of course, Clara. We are here for at least a week, after all."

Once the waiter had everything arranged to his satisfaction, he left them, and Mrs. Harrison poured the tea. Then she looked at Emily and with a little smile, quirked an eyebrow.

Emily smiled back. She liked this woman. She'd liked her when they'd met at Mrs. Smith's entertainment, and she liked her more now.

"I hoped to hear the parts of your story you left untold when you spoke with us at Mrs. Smith's last month," Emily said truthfully.

Mrs. Harrison sipped her tea and nibbled at a scone, as if considering her request. Then she smiled at Emily. "I am impressed that you noticed. And surprised. I thought I had better control of what I chose to conceal than that."

"She does not miss many things," Clara said. "It makes her an entertaining friend."

Emily shot Clara a look that promised retribution, but could feel herself flushing anyway.

Mrs. Harrison laughed. "I think we might become friends," she said. "I have too few friends who appreciate the humor in life. And perhaps I might join you for tea at the Butterscone when you go?"

"I'd like that very much," Emily said.

"I also," Clara said.

"Good. Meanwhile, though, I think I should answer what you came here to ask me."

"Thank you," Emily said.

"You are quite right, I was holding something back. In searching for gold, it seems this party of Chinese miners found something else, a cache that speaks to why the Indians consider that valley haunted and perhaps even sacred." She paused.

Emily glanced at Clara, whose rapt gaze was fastened on the storyteller. It was a skill, to hold your listeners' attention so thoroughly. Caught up though she was herself in the tale, a part of Emily stood apart and observed how the tale-spinner drew them in, building the tension with every pause and every detail added.

It was a skill she wanted for herself.

"Go on," Clara urged.

"The Indians tell stories of long, long ago, when a small party of foreigners came from a land across many seas. Can you guess whom I mean?"

"Captain Vancouver?" Clara suggested.

"No, from much farther away. They were small, and looked

something like the tribe who lived there, but with narrower eyes and a language spoken in tones that rose and fell."

"Chinese?" Emily said, surprised. "I had always heard that the Spanish discovered this coast, but that the English claimed it first."

"If the tales are true, this was long before the English or the Spanish," Mrs. Harrison said. "And the discovery made by these Chinese miners seems to prove that."

"What did they discover?" Clara demanded.

"Ancient Oriental disks. Round coin-like tokens with a square hole in the center, covered with very, very old Chinese characters. It's even possible that the tokens predate Columbus' discovery of this continent."

Emily drew a satisfied breath. She'd known there was something worth knowing in what Mrs. Harrison had left out of her original tale. And this was wonderful.

"But can it be true?" Emily asked.

"My husband was intrigued by the story and has made it a practice to enquire on his journeys. In many towns up and down this province, the same tale holds, that of a small group of Chinese explorers, led by a Buddhist monk, who found and explored this land long ago."

"Have you ever seen one of the coins?"

"My husband has one, given him by Ah Quan, the court interpreter. Would you like to see it?"

"Above all things."

"I will bring it with me when we meet again for tea," Mrs. Harrison said.

"Lovely. Would you care for a sandwich?" Clara said, passing the plate. Mrs. Harrison accepted a watercress sandwich and one of thinly sliced ham.

Emily, still caught in the unexpected outcome of the tale, waved the plate away.

"Has the coin any value?" Clara asked, looking up from her contemplation of the pastries.

"Why, I believe so. It is too old to be valued exactly here, but is certainly a rarity, which must give it value. And the Judge had wondered if a value would be placed on it were it returned to the Orient."

"In China?" Emily asked.

"Well, of course," Clara said. "It is their heritage, and if they have any kind of museum—do they?"

"I believe so," Mrs. Harrison said, with only a hint of a laugh in her voice. "It is a very old civilization." She glanced at Emily. "But now I think you are holding something back?"

Emily nodded. "Yes, I'm afraid I am. But it isn't my story to tell. When it is concluded, then perhaps I can share it, if you wish?"

"Yes, I definitely wish to hear any tale that intrigues you so much you'd come all this way to ask me about gold mines and Chinese coins," Mrs. Harrison said. "Can you give me any hints?"

Emily smiled. "Well, I think I can tell you that my tale involves missing heirs and lost gold."

"Even more intriguing. I look forward to hearing it some day."

"It's a promise," Emily said.

"Wonderful. Have a slice of teacake," Clara said.

GRANVILLE'S HOTEL room was adequate for his needs. It held a narrow bed, a wooden armoire for his clothes and a washstand with a white china pitcher and bowl. He had just shaved and changed and was about to go downstairs for dinner when there was a knock on the door and the bellboy informed him he had a tele-phone call.

Had something happened to Emily?

Tipping the man, he took the broad oak stairs two at a time down to the main floor, rather than wait for the elevator, and strode up to the main desk.

"I'm Granville in 302. There's a call for me?"

There was, and he was directed to a telephone table in an alcove just off the main lobby.

The wooden-box telephone attached to the wall beside the table was a little low and he had to bend forward to talk into the mouthpiece. Picking up the earpiece, he waited for the series of clicks to tell him the call had gone through.

"Granville here."

"Granville, it's Emily," came her excited voice. "I spoke with Mrs. Harrison, and as I had guessed, there's more to the story than she told me. Unless the Judge has told you already?"

He was relieved to hear the animation in her voice. No new incidents, then. She was fine. And obviously her visit was going well.

"I met with Judge Harrison this afternoon, and he confirmed he'd spoken to our friend about gold in the northern interior," he told her, careful with his choice of words. The switchboard operators could hear everything, and so could anyone else whose telephone shared the same line as Emily's aunt.

"So our friend was planning a trip?" Emily said, catching on quickly.

"It seems so," Granville said. "Presumably in search of this gold. Which ties in with the bookie's claim that our friend was talking of finding riches in the interior."

"The Judge mentioned nothing of ancient coins, though?" Emily asked.

"Coins? No, nothing. What have you learned?"

"Mrs. Harrison says that many years ago party of Chinese miners seeking gold in that area found a cache of ancient coins, or something like coins, buried under a tree. The court interpreter who told Judge Harrison the story gave him one of them, which is apparently a very, very old Chinese coin. And the story is that the coins were brought here by an explorer from China long ago."

Emily's excitement was bubbling through her voice. "Granville, if the coins are really old, would they not have monetary value? Beyond the face value on the coin, I mean."

"They might to a collector," Granville said slowly. "It would depend if there are any collectors interested in, and willing to pay for, such a curiosity.

"So could our friend be looking for more coins rather than for gold?"

"I'd say it is a possibility."

"Perhaps our friend doesn't care if it is coins or gold that he finds."

"Perhaps not." Granville stared at the thin gold stripe that ran through the maroon wallpaper surrounding the telephone, thinking. "I'll need to talk to the Judge again. And to find out more about the value of such coins."

"I visited the library here in town—it is even better than the one in Vancouver—but they seem to have nothing that is of any use."

"Interesting. I'm looking forward to talking to Judge Harrison again."

"The Chinese court interpreter was the one who told the Judge about the finding of the coins. He even gave him one. He might be willing to talk to you."

"Yes," he said slowly, his mind on what she had told him. "Mrs. Harrison has one of the coins?"

"And she has agreed to let me sketch it. I can send it to you when I'm done, if that would be helpful."

"Very helpful indeed. Thank you, Emily. And I should be back in Victoria tomorrow."

"Good," she said, leaving him grinning at the decided note in her voice as he hung up the earpiece, disconnecting the call.

TUESDAY, APRIL 24, 1900

The wind was cold and brisk off the water of the inlet, whipping their bonnets and the daffodils that made a brave show against a grey sky and grey water. Emily and Clara were walking along the footpath in Beacon Hill Park in downtown Victoria, no more than four blocks from the Parliament buildings locals called the Birdcages for their shape. Yet beyond the park was a wilderness of rough grey stone and red-barked arbutus trees leading down to the rocky beach. They walked into the wind, cheeks reddened and arms swinging.

"Isn't this marvelous, Clara?" Emily said with a delighted laugh. "It's so beautiful here, and you can smell the saltiness of the ocean on the wind."

"I don't know why you'd want to."

"You have to admit it's invigorating."

"You mean cold."

"It just gets us moving faster, which is good for us," Emily said. "Oh Clara, look at the way the daffodils are blooming around that cliff. I love the contrast against all that dark rock."

She stopped, and holding up her fingers to make a small square, seemed to be peering through them.

"Whatever are you doing, Emily?"

"Seeing if it will make a good picture. The man in the camera shop showed me—if I make a frame with my fingers, I can see if a scene will make a good photograph."

"Camera shop? Since when are you interested in cameras?" Clara asked. Then, after a pause, "Emily, what is that?"

Beaming, Emily pulled a small leather-covered box from her reticule and handed it to her friend. "My new camera. Granville gave it me for my birthday."

"I thought he gave you that lovely peridot silk scarf?"

"He did. He gave me this also."

"You never told me. And why have I not seen it before?"

"I wanted to ensure I could use it first, before I showed anyone. I've been practicing in secret, though I did take it when we went to the racetrack last Saturday. But look, isn't it beautiful?"

"It is beautifully finished," Clara said, turning it over in her hands. "But I don't see a lens. And where do the plates go?"

Taking the camera, Emily released a latch, and a bellows of red leather capped by a glass lens opened out. She handed it back to Clara. "Isn't that amazing?"

"Yes. And it's so light. But I don't see the negative plates. Is that why it is so light? Because the glass plates aren't in yet? My father always complains how heavy they are. And where do the plates go, anyway?"

Clara was peering at the back of the camera. "I don't see a slot."

"I didn't know you knew so much about cameras."

"My father loves them," Clara said absently. "I've learned a little."

"I'm impressed. And there are no plates," Emily said proudly. "This is a Hawkeye Tourist model and it's one of the new film cameras."

Emily pointed to another latch and a thin line. "If you opened this section here, you'd find a roll of twelve film negatives. They use those instead of glass plates."

"Twelve? In this little space?"

"It seems it should be impossible, doesn't it?"

Clara nodded, still examining the camera carefully. "The pictures must be tiny."

"No. They will be three inches by four," Emily said with gleefully.

Clara paused in her admiration of the lovely piece of workmanship she was holding and stared at her friend. "Why do you have a camera? And such a portable one? I've *never* heard you talk about photography."

Clara knew her too well. "I can take this one with me when we bicycle," Emily said.

Clara shot her a suspicious look and handed the camera back. "When did you develop such interest in photography?"

"I've been fascinated by what a camera can do since I read about Mary Vaux in the *World* last year," Emily said. "She climbs in the Rockies with her brothers, and she took photographs there that the CP Railway published in one of their brochures."

Clara groaned. "Please tell me you want the camera for your detective work, and not because you want to climb mountains."

"I see no reason why I shouldn't do both," Emily said with a laugh. Though in truth, she was still angry at herself for not making better use of her camera at the racetrack.

She'd been pretending to be a tourist, because she hadn't wanted to show Granville how much she'd learned. Not until she could prove to him that she could take photographs well enough to truly help him.

She knew he was reluctant to involve her too deeply in his investigations. So she'd wanted to prove she really could make a contribution to his work. If only she hadn't been so sensitive, she might even have captured a murderer on film!

Though really, the poor man's death had happened too fast to get a picture that showed anything at all. Which might be a problem in using cameras for detective work, now that she thought about it. Things often did not hold still long enough for her to get a good picture.

She'd have to practice more.

Emily couldn't share the thought with Clara though. Her friend was already uneasy enough with some of Emily's ideas for "detecting," as she called it. And Clara was still staring at her.

"But why did you bring it now?" Clara asked. "You want to take pictures of rocks?"

"Not just rocks. The flowers, too, the contrast between fragility and strength. And I'll need you to be in the picture."

"Me? But I'm untidy."

"You look lovely," said Emily sincerely. "The wind has brought out your color—it suits you. And you will be the focus of the photo, to give it meaning. Besides, I need to practice taking photographs of people outdoors. So I'll know how to take photos for Mr. Granville's cases when I need to."

"I still say that is a dangerous idea," Clara said, pulling her cloak tighter. "And does he know about it?"

"Well, he did give me the camera."

"Yes, he did. But did he know what use you mean to make of it?"

"Not exactly. At least not yet."

Clara shook her head. "Emily. You'll try the man's patience too far."

"I'll tell him when I've become more expert. Will you help me?"

"Oh, very well. Since you're going to do this anyway. Where did you want me to stand?"

"Just over there, half-facing the ocean," Emily said. "I'd like you to be looking past me and out to sea."

"I still say it will be an odd photograph," Clara said, but she did as Emily had asked.

After some minutes of deliberation, and much muttering to herself as she sought the perfect balance of Clara, rock, ocean and flowers, Emily depressed the shutter. "There. I am sure that will show all the elements clearly."

"Finally," Clara said, resettling her bonnet and wrapping her cloak more securely around her. "And will it be artistic as well?"

"Of course." Not that Emily cared about artistic, not really. She wanted to be able to take accurate pictures under all conditions, so that eventually she might even be able to record crime scenes.

"Good. Now perhaps we can go somewhere warm," Clara said.

"My toes feel icy, and I'm getting hungry. Surely it must be time for tea?"

Removing one cashmere lined glove and flinching at the icy bite of the wind on fingers already cold from maneuvering the camera fittings, Emily retrieved her watch on the end of its long chain and flipped it open. "You're right, it's nearly time. If we walk briskly, we should reach the teashop ahead of Mrs. Harrison."

THE BUTTERSCONE TEASHOP WAS BUSY. As they walked in, Emily's eyes flicked from the white-aproned servers wearing the frilled white mobcaps of an earlier century to the round table and fragile chairs that held a bevy of be-ribboned ladies in animated conversation.

A sideways glance at Clara confirmed her friend was already noting the various fashions and styles. Emily could look forward to an entertaining analysis of who had worn what well or ill later this evening. Though she couldn't bring herself to care about the latest fashions as Clara or even her sisters did, Clara's passion and unerring eye caught personality as well as style, making her commentary fascinating.

Mrs. Harrison was seated at a table near the window, with a view of Beacon Hill Park and a field of blooming daffodils. She wore a very fetching bonnet that Emily was sure Clara would approve of, and was raising a gloved hand in welcome as the hostess ushered them across the room.

Through the bustle of greeting the older woman and getting themselves settled, Emily had to restrain herself from blurting out a request to see the Chinese coin. Luckily Mrs. Harrison wasted no time in pulling out a small packet, carefully wrapped in a bit of white silk.

"Is that it?" Clara said, leaning forward.

"Indeed it is," Mrs. Harrison said, handing it to Emily.

Emily placed the material on the table, and carefully peeled back the cloth. The coin was smaller than she'd expected. It was an octagonal disc with a round hole in the center. Made of stone, it had a crack through the center, and was covered with thickly carved strokes of calligraphy, worn with time. It felt rougher than any coin Emily was used to, and very, very old.

There was a newer looking brass ring around edges of the coin, and Emily fingered it curiously.

"The Judge had the metal ring added for strength, as the disk is very old, and the crack made it fragile," Mrs. Harrison said.

"May I see?" Clara asked.

Mrs. Harrison nodded and Emily carefully passed the coin over. She couldn't find words for what she was feeling. Clara too was unusually silent as she examined it.

Mrs. Harrison seemed to understand what they were feeling. "It is extraordinary, isn't it? It strikes me every time I see it, that sense of age, and of a culture so different from our own."

"I have seen photos of Roman coins," Emily said slowly. "Most are very worn, but I imagine that they have the same feel of age that this does."

"Do you really think it could be so old?" Clara asked.

"Perhaps it might be half that old," Mrs. Harrison said. "So far, no-one seems to know for certain."

"Would it be possible to speak with the translator?" Emily asked. "With Mr. Ah Quan?

"Yourself?" Mrs. Harrison gave her a considering look, then a quick smile. "You remind me of myself as a girl. I was never one to be stopped by what others might think, either."

Her smile included Clara. "Unlike, I suspect, your friend."

"She will get herself in trouble, one day," Clara said.

Emily didn't respond, just waited for an answer to her question. It seemed perfectly logical to her that she talk to the man. She was here, after all, and Granville, who was not here, might need the information.

"I'm afraid that he will not talk to you."

"Because I am a woman? Or because I am English?"

"Neither, I am afraid." Mrs. Harrison said with a tiny laugh. "He only shared the information with my husband because they had worked together for so long, and because they are both Masons."

Emily was disappointed, but at least since Granville was a Mason, the information would not be wasted. "Then would you mind if I make a quick sketch of your coin?"

"Not at all."

After tea, they strolled back downtown along Broad Street. Clara kept pulling her closer to this shop window or that. Some of the displays were lovely, and they seemed to have a flair for hats that Vancouver shops could not quite match.

"I love the bonnet with the fur trim," Clara was saying. "Do you think that is mink?"

Emily glanced at the dark fur, shiny in the lights. "I think it is likely weasel, in summer dress," she said. "The color would look lovely on you."

Clara leaned a little closer. "Weasel? Oh, you mean ermine."

"Only when it has turned white. Have you never seen the brown before?"

"No. I have a bonnet trimmed in ermine, but nothing in this brown. I think I'll try it on."

"I'll wait here for you. I'd like to try to make a photograph of a street scene."

"On your own?"

Emily grinned at Clara's horrified tone. "I will be right here," she said. "It's still light out, and the street is hardly deserted. Besides, I'm not alone, you are with me."

"Inside the shop is not exactly with you," Clara pointed out.

"Don't be silly. You are just feet away. And the rain seems to be holding off," Emily said, glancing at the sky. "I want to get in at least one more photograph before that changes. Now, go and buy your bonnet. I'll be fine. No-one is going to accost me."

"You know what your mother would say. And I thought Mr. Granville was worried about you?"

"Oh, pooh," said Emily. "Don't be so staid, Clara."

Clara glanced up and down the street. They were in the heart of the shopping district, on a quiet afternoon. There were a few cloaked and bonneted matrons strolling from shop to shop, but no-one else in sight. "Well, all right," she said. "I'll be quick."

She would mean to be, Emily thought as she drew out her camera. She knew her friend well. Trying on one bonnet would lead to three.

Which meant she had plenty of time to practice making a street scene photograph.

Unfolding her camera, she considered the view in front of her, first with her naked eye and then through the viewfinder. If this were a case she was helping Granville with, what might she need to capture?

She considered the ornate fronts of several shops, with their carved stonework and curlicues. The shop windows were sonnets to the joy of shopping, but she couldn't see them being relevant to a case. The light was slanting towards late afternoon, casting long shadows through the small trees planted in boxes along the sidewalk.

She might be able to do an artistic composition of light and shadow, but nothing that would be meaningful in a court of law. Glancing into the milliners, she could see Clara deep in discussion with a shopgirl.

She had time.

It was lucky the rain was still holding off. She strolled a few feet further. A cluster of young women emerged from a cloth shop further down the street and stopped to compare parcels, seemingly deep in discussion. They hadn't noticed her. Emily raised her camera to waist level, looking down through the viewfinder. She had the group nicely framed, but they were too far away for clarity.

With another glance at her very involved friend, she strolled farther along the street, holding the camera half concealed by her purse, glancing through the viewfinder as she walked. She passed a narrow, fetid alleyway on her right before she found the perfect distance for her photos.

Pretending to glance in the window of a small bookstore, she rearranged the camera to the perfect angle. The girls had not moved. She held her breath—just—one—moment more.

And she had it.

The clicking of the shutter was satisfying. She had her photo, and her subjects had not even noticed her taking the photo. She couldn't wait to see the result.

As Emily looked up, smiling to herself, she had a sudden confused impression of someone too close behind her. Then she was off balance and being yanked backwards by one arm.

Shock and disbelief held her silent for a long moment.

Then she realized she was being dragged into the alleyway. She screamed, and kicked backwards. Hard.

She heard a grunt. A muffled curse. And then she was falling forwards.

Yelling for help, Emily half-fell against the rough brick wall beside her. She thrust her hands out to break the impact, but her head knocked hard against the wall.

Half dazed, she heard another curse and felt a sharp tug on her arm. Then she heard running feet behind her. And a chorus of horrified voices in front of her.

Taking a shaky breath, Emily put her hand to her aching head. Not finding blood, she slowly eased herself to an upright position.

Her head swam, and she leaned one hand against the wall for balance.

Before she could do more, she felt a hand on her arm, and Clara's concerned voice in her ear. "Emily, are you all right? Emily, what happened?"

"I'm fine," she said, hoping it was true, but not entirely convinced of it. "My head hurts a little is all."

"A little! Emily, you have a great bruise on your forehead."

"And will be very lucky if you don't end up with a black eye," came a brisk voice from somewhere in front of her. "Move back, please. Now miss, do you need to sit down?"

"I'm all right," she said automatically, still not sure if she was or not.

"Then can you tell us what happened?" the brisk voice asked.

Emily's gazed settled on the concerned-looking policeman, then moved beyond him to the small crowd that had gathered. She saw the girls she had photographed, and several of the shopkeepers.

"I'm not quite sure," she said slowly. "I was taking a photo-graph…" her voice trailed off as she realized she wasn't holding the camera. Her pursestrings were still looped over her arm, but the leather box was gone.

"My camera! Where is my camera?"

A small commotion ensued as the alley was scoured for the missing camera. No trace of it was found. As she listened, Emily relived the sensation of being pushed and falling forward, then the tug.

He'd taken her camera.

"You won't find it," she said, then swallowed hard. "I think my camera was stolen," she added in a slightly stronger voice.

"What's that? Stolen, you say?" The officer had heard her and came to stand in front of her again. "You have your purse, though?"

"Yes, it was over my arm. I was holding the camera, though."

"I see. And what kind of camera was it?"

As Emily told him, she watched him jot notes in a small note-book, his pencil jerking busily. I should have a notebook too, for my photographs, she thought.

Her mind felt a little disconnected from her body, as if nothing was quite real. Her head was starting to ache abominably, too. Granville wouldn't be pleased to hear about this incident, not after the racetrack. Maybe she wouldn't tell him, he'd only worry…

Suddenly, or so it seemed to her, Clara was at her elbow, tugging gently. "We need to get you back to your aunt's," she said. "Your color isn't good."

"I'm fine," Emily said, or thought she did, as the world suddenly went fuzzy.

'But I'm not one to faint' was her last coherent thought.

J udge Harrison was presiding over a full docket that day, so Granville had no chance to speak with him until late afternoon. He found him in a pub near the Nanaimo courthouse.

The Regal Beagle was clearly modeled after an English pub, and was obviously popular with the local businessmen. Built of local timber with a low roof, paneled walls and leaded glass windows, it boasted a cheery fire in a stone fireplace, and the choice of more than a dozen beers.

Granville felt himself relaxing. He spotted Harrison, looking less tired than yesterday, standing at a small table in the back, a hand-rolled cigarette in his hand and a half-full pint in front of him. Ordering a dark ale for himself and a refill of the Judge's beer, Granville strolled over to join him.

"I have a few more questions, if you have the time, Judge," he said, placing their drinks on the table.

"You do know it's illegal to bribe a judge in this part of the world?" Harrison said, sliding the lager across to his own side of the table.

Granville grinned at the sally. "I've heard as much," he said. "But

I wanted to thank you for the introduction to your interpreter. I received it earlier."

Harrison waved it off.

"And surely a curiosity about ancient Chinese coins can't be illegal, even here," Granville added.

The Judge gave a half laugh. "Now where did you hear about those?" he said. "I hadn't thought the story was well known."

"I have my sources," Granville replied, and repeated what Emily had told him. "So I'm wondering if you told Weston about these coins as well as the gold."

"I did indeed. Though they might more accurately be described as tokens, from what little I've been able to learn about them so far."

"And was Weston as interested in these coins—or tokens—as he was in the gold?"

"I wouldn't have said so, but then he began the conversation asking about the gold, and what I knew about it. I thought his interest in the coins mere curiosity."

"So he did ask about the coins as well?"

"Indeed he did. The fellow was surprisingly well-informed, too. He must have some knowledge of Chinese history, which is unusual. I thought he might have studied it at some point."

"He attended Oxford for a time, though I never heard that he was much of a scholar."

"Sent down, was he?" Harrison said with a chuckle.

"That's it," Granville said. "Perhaps he developed an interest in Oriental history somewhere along the way. Given the questions he asked, is it possible he was hoping to find more of these coins, do you think?"

"Certainly his questions could be interpreted that way. I can't imagine there'd be more than one such stash, though, can you?"

"I confess I know little of the history of the region, sir."

Judge Harrison laughed. "None of us do," he said. "The Spanish claimed it first, then the British. The Indians, of course, were here all along. But there are no records of the Chinese in that region before the gold rush in '57."

"Perhaps the coins date from that time?"

"They could do, I suppose. I tried to have mine dated and valued —but experts differ, suggesting an age anywhere from several hundred to several thousand years."

"Several thousand years," Granville said. "Is that even possible?"

"There are stories amongst the natives and the Chinese themselves of a long ago explorer from China, a Buddhist monk. But oral history like that is difficult to confirm," the Judge said. "If young Weston had an interest in Chinese history, though, perhaps he hoped to learn more of how the disks journeyed here, and when."

"It's a fascinating question," Granville said diplomatically.

"I've found it so," the Judge said. "Apparently this monk's visit is the reason the Tsimshian consider the area where the coins—and the gold—were found sacred, even haunted. Though I don't know if those views persist now, since there have been quite a few missionaries working to convert the natives in the area for the last twenty years or so."

"And it's this haunted area that Weston would be headed for?" Granville asked.

"Certainly it was the region he was most interested in."

"The one informant I've found who can confirm that Weston was leaving town thinks he was headed north to the Interior."

"When exactly did he leave town?

"He was last seen the night of February ninth, but logically he must have left early on the Saturday, the tenth," Granville said. If Weston had avoided Heade's boys long enough to head north.

"Two days after I spoke with him. And too early in the year to get there easily. Lad seemed pretty eager to leave." Harrison raised his mug, and drank off half of it. "He run into trouble?"

Granville nodded. "I'm not sure what he got mixed up in, but there are some pretty unsavory types from San Francisco after him."

"Sorry to hear that. I quite liked him."

Granville was surprised. First McAndrews, now Harrison, had been impressed by Weston. Both were good judges of character, both had taken to him. There was clearly more to the lad than his former life had allowed for.

"Do you know the area beyond Hazelton well?" he asked the Judge.

"No, my territory didn't extend that far north. Heard a fair bit about it from Peter O'Reilly, though. He was the Gold Commissioner assigned to the rush to the Omineca River, back in '71."

"Have you any advice for my journey there?"

Harrison paused, drained his mug. "Make sure you're equipped for the territory, especially at this time of year. You ever done any gold mining?"

"Eighteen months in the Klondike."

"Ah, then I don't have to tell you to go prepared. The snow will be gone on the coast, but may still be on the ground as you climb. That far north, and with the mountains, you'll need to be prepared for anything. They get storms up there that blow up out of nowhere."

Granville thought about the Yukon winters, and the thousands of pounds of gear he and Scott had packed in over the Chilkoot Pass on their way to the gold fields, and had to fight the urge to laugh. "Yes, sir."

Harrison caught his expression, and a broad grin split the solemnity he'd been showing. "I've seen the photographs from the Klondike," he said. "Guess I don't have to tell you much about the consequences of poor planning."

Granville sobered in a hurry. "I've seen too much of it."

"I suppose you must have at that. Well, I wish you great luck with your search. I hope you find young Weston."

He wasn't the only one.

L ying in the four-poster bed in her aunt's second best guest room, heavily embroidered white linens pulled up to her chin, Emily stared absently at the rain that had been drenching down almost since they'd brought her home. She was supposed to be sleeping, but she'd been reliving the attack, going over every moment of it—alternately shivering with the knowledge of how close she'd come to being really hurt, and a riff of excitement at the adventure of it all.

Which wasn't very grown up of her, she knew, but she couldn't seem to help it.

At first all Emily could think of was the loss of her camera, and the photos she'd taken. She'd never know, now, whether the photo of Clara had turned out as she'd hoped. Or how the street scene had looked on film.

Then slowly she began to remember the rest of it. And felt a nagging sense that in those chaotic moments of the attack there had been something that seemed familiar. What was it?

She ran through the scene in her mind, trying to relive every moment. The hands hard on her arms, the grunt he'd made when she'd kicked him, the curse she'd heard—those were frightening, not familiar.

She replayed the scene again.

She'd heard his footsteps as he left, she'd had the sense that he was taller than she, though not by much, she'd caught a glimpse of a rough tweed overcoat—and she'd smelled mint. That was what it was, the scent of mint, mixed with the smell of the sea.

Where had she smelled that particular combination before?

But no matter how hard Emily tried to remember, the connection wouldn't come. She knew she'd met someone who she connected with that scent. Somewhere. But thinking about it was only making her head ache worse.

Through the ache, she thought about what the attack might mean. And realized Granville might have been right to fear she'd be a target after witnessing the murder at the track. But he'd been wrong to think she'd be safer in Victoria than she'd been in Vancouver.

She could only be glad Clara hadn't been caught up in this.

But what if the attacker had been watching Emily, and waiting for the moment she was foolish enough to wander off on her own? She replayed the scene in her mind, pushing down the quiver that it caused.

Unfortunately, that made a great deal of sense. And it explained the uneasy feeling of being watched she'd had ever since the races. She'd thought that feeling was just nerves after the attack, and resolutely refused to acknowledge it.

A shiver traced down her spine as she thought about the way the cut in her arm had burned. Half healed, it throbbed anew at the reminder. Should she feel lucky she'd only lost her camera? Had she been closer to death than she'd known?

On the other hand, she'd seen no sign of a knife. It didn't take long to stab someone in a dark alley, and she'd been unscathed. Perhaps it was a failed kidnapping?

But then, there had only been one man and he hadn't been a very successful abductor. Unless he was after the camera, and not her?

She had been taking photos at the racetrack. Perhaps they thought she might have a picture that would incriminate someone? Emily tried to remember what pictures she had taken that day, but her thoughts kept blurring.

Well, if they had the film, at least they would leave her alone.

Except if they were after the photographs from the racetrack, they'd soon discover those pictures weren't on the camera they'd stolen. She'd finished the roll of film from the racetrack the following day, placed it in the little envelope that came with the film, and mailed it back to the company for developing.

Despite her aching arm, Emily had been thrilled to drop that film in the postbox. It was the first one she'd completed. And film cost sixty cents for a dozen photos—though that did include the developing as well as the postal charges—so she hadn't wanted to waste a single one.

It took more than a week for a film to come back, so the pictures wouldn't even be waiting for her when she got home. Just as well, or whoever had followed her might have broken into the house and stolen them.

Wait, though. The murderers wouldn't know the photos weren't developed yet. Once they found the picture wasn't on the camera, what would they do? Would they search her home?

And who might be hurt if they did?

But they wouldn't know the picture wasn't on the roll they had, would they? Not until they had that roll developed, the one on the camera now. And that would take ten days. Unless they could pay to get it developed faster? Then what?

Emily sat up too fast, and had to put a hand to her head, which swam. It would take her too long to get back to Vancouver, and she didn't think they would let her travel in any case. But she could telephone Granville.

He would know how to make sure her family and their household were safe.

She gingerly swung her feet to the floor and stood. All she had to do was to make the call.

As soon as she could stand.

GRANVILLE HAD JUST RETURNED to his hotel and was crossing the lobby towards the elevator when a male voice from the front desk stopped him.

"Mr. Granville?"

"Yes?" he said as he turned towards the hotel clerk.

"I have a Miss Turner on the line for you," he said. "Shall I put it through?"

Something was wrong. Emily knew he'd be in Victoria tomorrow —there was no reason for her to be calling now.

"Yes of course," he said, striding towards the telephone. He picked up the earpiece.

"Granville here. Hello?"

There was a silence in which all he could hear was a crackling on the line. Then Emily's voice, sounding faint with distance. Or at least he hoped that was the reason her voice sounded so small.

"Granville? Oh, I am glad you were in. I'm afraid someone might think I have a photo, from the racetrack, you know, and go looking for it. At my home. It isn't there, but they won't know that."

She was talking too quickly, and was obviously wary of the listening ears of the switchboard operators. Her soft voice and the crackling on the line didn't help either.

"Emily? Are you all right?"

More crackling. Then her voice again, louder, and with more life in it. "Of course. I'm fine."

Was she?

Now he was really worried. He wanted to demand if she'd heard something about—or worse yet, from—Graham's murderers. But his awareness of listening ears wouldn't allow it. "Has new information come to light?"

"Well—I have a sketch of a Chinese coin. Would you like to see it?"

"Yes, very much. But that wasn't why you called."

"Not entirely. I wanted you to know that the photo from the racetrack didn't turn out."

Which photo was she talking about? And why was she calling about it now?

Granville hadn't paid much attention to the photos Emily had been taking at the track, had forgotten them entirely after she'd been attacked. She'd been photographing the races, hadn't she? And the crowds.

Oh hell, she'd been taking pictures of the stands. Could she have caught the murderer on film?

If the damned camera had put her in danger, he'd never forgive himself for giving it to her. "I understand."

"Do you? Then you understand why I need you to make sure my home is safe?"

That was clear enough. She was worried about her parents and her sisters—presumably the murderer might think an incriminating photo existed, and that it could be at her parent's home.

But she'd never mentioned even the possibility of such a photograph before this sudden telephone call. Something was very wrong. "Emily, do you have your camera with you?"

A hesitation, but he couldn't tell if she was hiding something or if it was this thrice-cursed telephone line.

"Yes, I do," she said. "Or I did. I'm afraid I've lost it."

Lost her much valued camera? He didn't think so. If the camera was gone, it hadn't simply been lost. Someone had taken it.

Was she hurt?

"I'm sorry to hear that," he said carefully. "How are you holding up?"

"As I said, I'm fine now. A little shaken is all."

Shaken? So he'd been right. She was hurt.

In Victoria, where he'd insisted she go.

And he hadn't been there.

Scott would make sure her family was protected. And he intended to be on the next train back to Victoria.

Granville glanced at his watch. Dammit. The last train of the day had just left. "I'll take care of things in Vancouver."

"Thank-you. So much. Well, goodbye."

"Emily?" he said into the crackling as his hand gripped the earpiece even tighter.

"Yes?"

"Are you at your aunt's home?"

"Yes. And I'm fine." More crackling. "Really."

"Then I'll see you tomorrow morning. Early. Take care of yourself." It was all he dared say over an open line.

"I will," she promised, her voice fading a little.

Then the crackling increased and she was gone.

He thought hard for a moment, then dialed a familiar number.

"Scott, I have a job for you," Granville said when his partner answered. "And you'll need to get in touch with McAndrews. He has connections with the Post Office, and I think he'll be glad to help."

WEDNESDAY, APRIL 25, 1900

At nine-fifteen the following morning, Granville sat in a spacious bedroom on the upper floor of Emily's aunt's house in Victoria. Clara, looking nearly as pale as Emily did, sat quietly in an armchair by the window. Granville had barely remembered to nod a greeting to her, focusing on his fiancée's bruised face.

"What happened?" he demanded.

Emily smiled, but it looked strained to him. "I was walking by an alley. He wanted my camera."

"Only the camera?"

She was silent. Would she try to dismiss this incident too?

"For a moment I feared it was more," she said slowly. "But there were people close, and he grabbed the camera and ran."

"They didn't find him?"

"No. Nor my camera."

She looked defeated. He couldn't bear it. "I will buy you another."

And he'd make damn sure she only used it where she would be safe.

But the promise cheered her. Head tilted to one side, she smiled at him, a hint of mischief in her eyes. "I wagered Clara that you would forbid me ever to use a camera again."

He had to grin back. "She'd never accept a wager like that. No more than you would ever accept being forbidden to do anything." Much as he might like to, on occasion.

"Thank you. I do promise to be careful."

Until the first interesting subject came along. "Just promise you'll try," he said.

"That's a promise I know I can keep," Emily said.

With a smile that looked far too faint to his critical eye. "That was the general idea."

"You're good for me, Granville," she said softly. "I wish I were sure I was equally good for you."

This was a truth Granville hadn't been sure Emily would ever be willing to disclose. Just how badly had she been injured? "How can you doubt it?"

"Well, I'm determined. And impulsive. I will never make a conformable wife, and I fear I won't even really want to try. And you could choose anyone. Your father was a wealthy baron, after all. While mine is in trade."

Granville forgot Clara was even in the room. "All of them reasons I love you."

"You do?"

He hadn't expected it to be so easy to say. In fact, he hadn't meant to say it at all, most especially not in these circumstances. "Yes. It's why you are still wearing my ring."

"Oh."

It seemed to be all she could say for a moment. Then Emily drew in a quick breath and he all he could think was that she was about to tell him that the marriage was impossible. She'd never said she loved him.

"Emily," he began.

"Shush," she said, waving a hand at him. "It's my turn. I—I don't think I even know how to tell you. That I love you, I mean. Because I do. I do."

There were tears in her eyes, and the hand that wore his ring was clenched tight. He wanted to hold her, but he didn't know how badly bruised she was.

"Emily," he said again.

"No, let me finish. Or I won't get this out. Oh, I am making such a mess of it."

"No."

"Yes," she said, smiling through tears. "I'm not usually such a watering pot. It's this injury, that's all. And I am so happy to hear you say you love me. To be able to tell you..."

"What injury? I can see the bruises, but is there more? I thought you said you were fine, just shaken."

"I am."

"Fine, but injured?" He could hear the growl in his voice, and tried to restrain it.

"Yes."

"Exactly how are you injured?"

"I knew you'd react like this."

"Never mind how I'd react. Just tell me what is wrong with you."

"Nothing is wrong with me."

"Tell me about your injury." He wasn't letting go.

She sighed, glanced up at him through wet lashes. Being Emily, she couldn't do it with a straight face.

He grinned back, reluctantly. "I'll accept that you're fine, if you say you are. But I need to know the extent of your injury. If you please."

"Oh very well. I'm still a little dizzy, is all. But at least I don't have a black eye. The policeman thought I would develop one."

"A little dizzy?" Heaven save him. "You have concussion?"

"The doctor said only a slight one."

"Did the fellow hit you?"

"No, but I fell against a wall when he was trying to pry my camera away from me. It really is nothing."

He was never letting her out of his sight again. "You can't be taking these risks. I'd hoped you'd be safe out of Vancouver."

"Safe enough."

"You were attacked. What if he had used a knife, like the last time?"

Her face went even paler and he cursed himself for a fool.

Seeing his face, she hastened to say, "I have thought about it, and I'm sure all they wanted was the camera. But in any case, I'm very glad you have come now."

"Because of the pleasure of my company?"

Emily laughed, but blushed a little as she did so. "Well of course. In addition to that, I mean. Now that you're here, would you like to see the sketch of the Chinese coin?"

"Would I...?" Shaking his head, Granville held out a hand.

She smiled, and placed the sketchbook in his hand. "I thought of taking a photo, too, but didn't like to presume. Which is as well, given the theft of my camera."

"Indeed," he said as he flipped to the appropriate page. "This is very good."

"Thank you. I am no artist, I fear, but I can capture details of an object. It is useful, though not as quick or as accurate as a photograph."

"Which is why you are so intrigued by cameras?"

"I suppose it is," she said. "I hadn't considered that before."

"Don't undervalue your ability to do a sketch like this. This is still valuable," he said. "It captures a level of detail that a camera may miss."

"I wonder if you are right?" she said thoughtfully. "I haven't had enough experience with my camera to know which things are clear and which are not. It is something I will have to experiment with. Once I have a new camera, that is."

"We can order one tomorrow," he said, still examining the drawing. "Can you draw people this accurately?"

"I'm afraid not. You were thinking of the man I saw at the race-track? The one who reminded me of Frances?"

Her quickness still surprised him—at times she almost seemed to read his mind, which he found disconcerting.

Luckily for his peace of mind, her mental leaps mostly concerned his cases. "Yes. I'd be happier if we were certain it was

Frances's cousin you saw. The photo you took is still in Vancouver?"

She surprised him. "No. The photo is still being developed. I mailed it last week, and don't expect to receive the finished prints until the end of the week at the earliest."

"Which doesn't help us much."

"I'm sorry."

"Don't apologize. None of this is your fault."

"If I could draw people, we might know more."

"Never mind. You saw only the one man, and we know who he is." A beat, as he watched her expression. "Or was it just the one?"

She wouldn't meet his eyes.

"Emily?"

"Well, I don't know anything for sure."

"Emily."

"I've been thinking about it, you see," Emily said in a rush. "For the last day I've had nothing but time to think. And I keep remembering where we stood, and how I turned to look up at you when I felt that slash on my arm. And before that, before I turned to look up, I mean, I remember there being people all around. And I had the sense that one group was going to pass quite closely by us. It had become very busy there, all of a sudden."

"I remember," he said, feeling grim. "Go on. What did you see?"

"A group of men, all in black, gathered in a small cluster, as if conversing. I—I think the killer was there, but I'm not exactly sure. The cluster seemed to ebb and flow, as if—Have you ever seen crows gather?"

"A murder of crows?" he said sardonically.

"You know what I mean. They are everywhere in Vancouver. Have you ever watched them gather?"

He had, actually. It was a rather eerie sight, especially at twilight —when the sky darkened with flock after flock of the black-feathered birds. Crows landed everywhere, thick on the grass, while in the trees sentry birds sat, ready to shriek a warning at the least sign of danger. More and more crows constantly flew in while others winged away, yet there was an odd sense of order.

"Yes, I know what you mean."

"You know how they strut in small groups, seeming to talk, while the sentries watch for danger."

"Yes."

"It was like that."

"What you saw? Tell me how?"

"That group of men visiting first caught my attention when they were ten feet or more from me. I felt as if someone had just noticed me and fixed his attention on me."

"A sentry bird."

"Exactly. Not someone part of that little group, but someone apart, watching for trouble."

"And since you might have seen something, that sentry decided you were trouble and needed to be dealt with?"

"Yes. Except he missed."

"Thank God!"

"Yes." She paused for a moment, and he saw that this was harder on her than she'd been letting on. Yesterday's shock was still there, and thinking about the events at the racetrack wasn't helping any.

"Did you see this sentry?"

"No, I just had a confused impression of someone nearby. I hadn't even remembered it until I was lying here, trying to reconstruct that day. But the sentry was taller than I was, though not so tall as you. Dressed in black, wearing a rough greatcoat of some sort. And he bore the scent of the sea—salt, creosote and tobacco. And a hint of mint."

"Mint?"

She gave a half-smile. "I know. But you see why I think the man in the alley was the same man who tried to knife me at the track?"

She did? "Not many sailors smell of mint," he said slowly, watching her. She looked exhausted. "You're sure that both your attackers smelled of the sea and mint?"

She nodded. "Yes, I think so. And I think there may have been more than one of him. More than one sentry, I mean. Not more than one attacker."

"You're talking about a very organized group," Granville said.

"And something that had been planned ahead," she agreed.

It worried him, because he thought she was right. And it matched what Frances had told him about Heade's gang. Which meant they had been followed here—Emily had been followed.

A group like that had the resources, and the time, to track her down. "Do you recall anything else about the members of that group?"

"No. I wish I did. I'm sorry."

"Don't be. And don't try to think about it." He felt angry as well as protective, seeing her like this, and he stepped away and took a turn about the room. There had to be something he could do, some way to trap the villains. Why had she been attacked and not him?

She lay still, her eyes on him, and he suspected she guessed how he felt. "I'll remember more eventually, I'm sure of it."

"Indeed," he said, sitting down beside her again and taking her hand. "Now that you have reconstructed the scene to this extent, other details may come to you at any time."

She nodded. "I hope so."

HIS CONVERSATION with Emily churning in his mind, Granville checked into a traveller's hotel near the center of town and placed a call to Vancouver.

"Scott here."

"It's Granville. Have you heard anything about an arrest made in the case of the murder at the racetrack?"

"They've arrested a fellow named Jacobs. Apparently the man has a real temper. Rumor is that it was an argument over money owed that erupted into murder."

"Not anyone you know?"

"Nope."

So either Emily was mistaken, or they had the wrong man.

Which was interesting, given that the murder happened in front of a stadium full of people. "And there's no mention of the man your sister knew?"

"No, nothing."

"See what you can find out about this Jacobs they've arrested. Maybe there's a connection."

"Will do."

"And Scott? Keep an eye on Trent. You have to assume you're both being followed. And they're good. I saw no sign of anyone on the ferry coming over."

"They followed you? Is Emily OK?"

"She'll be fine."

"She'll *be* fine?"

"She has a concussion, but the doctor says it's not serious," he said, even more wary of saying too much over a party line. "And I think you and I will be heading out soon, but I can't leave town until she's fully recovered."

"We're leaving town?"

"We are indeed." He didn't mention that he wasn't yet sure if it would be he and Scott who went north, or Scott and Trent. He wasn't yet certain that Emily was safe, and he wasn't leaving her alone until he was.

"So you did find out where he went," Scott said.

"I have some idea," Granville said.

"Fair enough. What should I be packing?"

"Pack for Rabbit Creek. In changeable weather," he said, grinning to himself. It wouldn't be quite that cold, but once he mentioned the Klondike creek, Scott would know they were headed north and pack accordingly.

Hanging up the telephone mouthpiece, Granville stared thoughtfully at the notes he'd made. Graham's killer was a hothead, and the murder had come out of an argument with his bookie?

It made sense, but it didn't fit with what Emily thought she'd seen, or her description of the group at the track as being like a murder of crows. If this was a spontaneous incident, then why were there sentry birds posted?

And why pursue Emily to Victoria?

Granville was in a thoughtful mood as he locked up behind himself and headed for the courthouse.

AH QUAN OCCUPIED a small cubbyhole of an office on the third floor of an old brick building off Bastian Square. Compared the impressively new courthouse in Nanaimo, the Provincial Court-house was rather shabby, Granville thought with a grin as he climbed the worn stairs two at a time.

He'd offered to meet Ah Quan in Chinatown, but the inter-preter had preferred to meet in his own cramped space. There was room for a small desk, two straight wooden chairs and not much else. Granville didn't mind—it was information that mattered.

"Thank you for taking the time to talk with me," Granville said.

Ah Quan inclined his head. "The Judge says here that you are looking for a man who may have gone looking for the source of the coins I told him about so long ago?"

"Indeed. It is a task I undertook at the request of my elder brother, who does a service for a friend." Which was true. "Anything you can tell me that would help me locate the region, and young Weston, would be appreciated."

"And you too are a Mason?"

"Indeed I am. As is young Weston."

Ah Quan nodded slowly. "Yes, so he said."

So Ah Quan had spoken with Weston. "Can you tell me what you talked of?"

"As a fellow Mason..." A pause. "Yes. I will tell you what I remember," Ah Quan said.

Granville inclined his head. "Thank you."

"He came to see me in—February, I believe, and told me he had heard of the coins, and wished to know more of where they had been found. He explained he was something of a scholar, and inter-ested in the story told by the Indians of the long-ago voyage from my lands to this one."

"And what were you able to tell him?"

"I told him what my cousin told me—that he was prospecting for gold near Hazelton, and they decided to explore in new territory north of there. They wandered for some time until they came on a branch of either the Skeena River or the Peace River, they could not be sure which."

Ah Quan paused, looked at Granville.

The man was a natural storyteller. "Go on," Granville said.

"It was on the bank of that river that they found the coins. They had stopped to pan for gold, but found nothing, so took time to eat. A large tree had fallen, and they dug in the space left by the roots, to make their fire. The spade hit upon a stone jar, covered with markings and filled with these ancient disks."

"And was there anything else?"

"I also warned Mr. Weston that it was forbidden land for the Indians, and vast," Ah Quan said.

"I'm guessing Weston didn't heed your warning?"

"I am not convinced he even heard it. His attention was focused strictly upon the coins, and, I suspect, the lure of scholarly fame." A small smile crossed Ah Quan's face. "It is a condition well-known amongst our Chinese scholars."

It was an interesting thought. Granville had never met a Chinese scholar, but if they were as competitive as the dons at Oxford, and with a much longer history, he wouldn't want to cross one.

He still couldn't picture Weston as a scholar, though—not the lad he remembered, nor the one he'd been trying to find. "Did Weston ask anything more?"

"He had some good questions to ask about the coins, which I was able to answer. "And has anything more been learned about the coins?"

That earned him an interested look. "You also ask good questions. Yes, some were sent to China, to the excitement of our scholars. The coins are very old—with inscriptions in a language no longer spoken—they possibly even date from before the Han Dynasty."

He glanced over at Granville and his mouth twisted a little. "Before the time of Christ," he clarified.

Though the interest in all things Oriental was fading in Europe, still any item this old—and especially if the story of how it came to be found here could be established—could be very valuable, even if only as a unique curiosity.

Perhaps Weston really was looking for coins, and not gold. And not such a young fool after all.

"Can you tell me any more about where to find the site where the coins were found?" Granville asked.

Ah Quan shook his head. "You might talk to the Indians—the Tsimshian," he said. "They are the ones who know the story. And the land."

Thanking Ah Quan for his time and for the information, Granville walked towards the docks, where he knew he'd find the various shipping offices. He needed a little more information.

25

THURSDAY, APRIL 26, 1900

The following morning, Emily felt much better, and was determined to go downstairs for breakfast. She and Clara were in her aunt's sunny morning room, and Emily was peeling an orange when Granville was announced.

She looked up and beamed at him. "I'm so glad you're early. Have you eaten?"

"Yes, thank-you. Some hours ago."

"Then would you like some tea?"

He thanked her and seated himself across from her and Clara, accepting the cup Clara poured.

"You're looking a bit grim this morning," Emily told him.

Clara, seated in a wicker armchair beside her, choked a little on her tea, and gave Emily a shocked look.

Emily ignored her, keeping her attention on Granville.

"There has been an arrest in the case of the murder you saw at the races last Saturday. It was in yesterday's paper," he said.

Emily felt her eyes widen, and fought to keep the tears at bay. The attack had affected her more than she wanted to admit to anyone, least of all Granville. "They found the man who looks like Frances? I can go home?"

"Unfortunately, they seem to have arrested someone else. But you can go home as soon as you like. Since we were followed here in any case, there's no need for you to stay here," he said, his eyes resting on her. "Though you might not be ready to travel yet?"

"Of course I am." She smiled at him, hoping to reassure him, and hoping that the smile didn't look as pathetic as it felt. "Who have they arrested, then?"

"A man named Jacobs. The story is the killing was unplanned, the result of a quarrel over a bet."

At least it got Granville off the topic of her health. "And do you believe it?" Emily asked.

"Frankly? No," he said.

"Why would they have arrested the wrong man?" Clara asked.

"That's one thing I'm going to find out when we get back to Vancouver," Granville said to both of them.

"You're coming back with us?" Emily said.

He gave her a look. "Of course. I won't leave you unprotected. And I also want to know more about the man who stole your camera, and why he followed you all the way to Victoria."

Her camera. Emily set down her teacup and stared at the section of orange still lying on her plate. "I wonder..." she said slowly.

"Wonder what?" He was eyeing her with concern.

"I wonder what really happened at the track. You know I'm not completely certain the man I saw, the one who looked like Frances, was actually the murderer." She picked up the last bit of orange and ate it slowly, thinking.

Then Clara poked a finger in Emily's arm. Now what? Emily looked up and saw from Granville's expression that he hadn't understood what she meant.

"There was a lot of movement in the crowd," Emily explained. "It happened quickly, and I could have been wrong. But if I'm not sure, how likely is it that they think I saw what I'm not even sure I saw?"

She beamed at him. "I think we might have been wrong. I think perhaps I was never in danger, after all."

Granville put down his own teacup and watched her carefully.

He looked quite worried. From beside her came a slight choking sound. Clara was trying not to giggle.

Emily fought back a grin. Granville must be imagining that little bump on the head had caused more damage than just the ridiculously large bruise she'd tried—rather unsuccessfully—to powder over before coming downstairs. He didn't yet know that when she got excited by an idea, she seemed to lose her ability to explain it.

"The attempt at the racetrack failed, but it wasn't because he didn't kill me. It failed because he didn't get my camera," Emily said more slowly, making sure her words were clear.

Granville was still watching her with concern. "No, it was this latest attack that targeted your camera," he began.

Then he stopped and stared at her. He must have realized what she was thinking.

"Was your camera in your reticule then? At the racetrack?" he asked.

Emily nodded. "Yes, I'd put it away as you suggested. And I had the drawstrings over my arm."

"Over the arm that was cut?"

"Yes. And I think perhaps they were trying to cut the reticule strings and steal the camera that time. Only I turned to talk to you and so they missed and cut my upper arm instead of the reticule."

"I think you might be right," Granville said. "And it explains why the recent attack was focused on your camera."

No-one was trying to kill her. It was a huge relief. "So I'm not in danger," Emily said. "And Clara and I will come with you back to Vancouver."

She glanced sideways at Clara. Her friend just rolled her eyes.

"If you're sure you're up to it," Granville said. He glanced at his pocket watch. "And if you can be packed by ten o'clock."

Emily grinned at him, but didn't argue. She'd be packed. She wasn't so sure about Clara.

But more importantly, she'd figured out what was going on. She knew she was right.

EMILY COULD FEEL the thrumming of the engines right through her feet as they stood in the narrow passenger area on the steamship's deck. She glanced around to be sure they were out of hearing distance of the few sightseers on deck, then turned her back to the view of fog-draped islands, and studied Granville's expression.

He stood leaning against the deck rail, watching the fog roil and twist. For a moment he looked tired, despite all his energy. This case, and the worry over her, had been hard on him.

She felt a little guilty, even if it wasn't really her fault.

Drawing her coat more closely against the chill wind, she said, "So now we know where Mr. Weston went when he disappeared. And I was right about the coins being important. But there's still one thing about this case I still don't understand."

He looked over at her, and smiled. "Only one thing? Then you're ahead of me."

She laughed. "Hardly. But why did he disappear so suddenly? Mr. Weston, I mean. Especially when everyone seems to have assumed his so-called accidents were exactly that—accidents. Was there a more direct threat?"

"Not that we've been able to find. Which is the problem, because it doesn't mean there wasn't one. Just that we haven't found it." He held out his arm. "Shall we walk?"

She tucked her gloved hand in the crook of his elbow, and he matched his stride to her shorter steps.

"It seems this Heade and his gang may be behind Mr. Weston's accidents? And that perhaps the intent was to murder him, but to make it look accidental?" Emily asked.

"Yes, I'd say so, based on the facts we have so far. Especially given the threats against Scott and myself. But we still have no proof."

"But why? In everything you have told me, I haven't heard a reason for someone to try to kill Mr. Weston. Was there one?"

"We still haven't found one," Granville said. "But Weston spent a few weeks in San Francisco when he first arrived from England. He could have got himself tangled up in something dangerous then."

"Something serious enough that they'd pursue him all this way, after all this time?" she said skeptically. "And why the attempts to make it look like an accident?"

"That's exactly the problem I'm having with it. It doesn't make any sense." Granville stopped speaking for a moment as they rounded the corner and walked straight into the wind. A few steps further and it was possible to talk again.

"Heade apparently specializes in hired killings, among other things," he continued. "So the other possibility is that someone hired him to kill Weston and make it look like an accident. But I can't see why anyone would want Weston dead, and if they did, why hire someone all the way from San Francisco?"

"How are the two murders we know about connected to Mr. Weston's disappearance?" Emily asked.

"Norton and Graham? We're only speculating that they are," Granville said. "It's possible those murders aren't related at all, given that both deaths occurred after Weston vanished."

She thought about that for a moment. "Well, if you had to argue that the murders were a direct result of him leaving, what would you say?"

He gave her an amused look, but nodded. "As if I were arguing it in court? Very well. The first murder is easy. Norton was meeting us that night to talk about his dealings with Weston. And he was murdered before he could do so."

"By whom? And why?"

"And that is exactly the problem. If Norton had information about Weston being murdered, that could be the motive, but we don't know."

"And if that wasn't the motive?" she said. "Why else might this Norton have been killed?"

"Any number of reasons. The man lived on the edge and sold information for a living."

She nodded. "Then what was his connection with Mr. Weston?"

"Another very good question. We don't know."

"And the second murder?"

"The one you witnessed? Supposedly it was over a gambling debt, and on the surface seems to have little connection to Weston.

But neither of us believes that, since you likely saw a member of Heade's gang stab Graham. And since you were then attacked—twice—by another gang member." His hand tightened on her arm.

"So what do you think is the connection?" Emily asked.

"Graham was the only one who knew Weston might be headed north. Perhaps he wouldn't tell Heade's boys even that much."

"So they killed him? That hardly makes sense. And besides, he told Trent. Why wouldn't he tell them?"

"And that is exactly my problem with that line of reasoning. No, we're still missing something, something important. I just wish I knew what it was."

He looked frustrated, Emily thought, and a little angry. Some of that was still because of the attack on her, she knew. "So what will you do next?"

"Scott was going to try to find out more about Graham's death while we were gone. With luck, he'll have learned something. Failing that, our next move is to find Weston. And at least now we have some idea where to look."

He moved towards the nearest stairwell. "But the wind is growing harsher. Shall we go in for a cup of tea?"

"Yes, indeed," Emily said, putting one hand up to protect her bonnet from a sudden gust. "Do you think whatever is missing will become clear once you have found Mr. Weston? Or will we need to do more interviews when we get back to town?"

26

FRIDAY, APRIL 27, 1900

I t felt unexpectedly good to be back in Vancouver. Granville pushed open the door of their office, shook the rain from his coat and swiped at the moisture on his face. It still surprised him how similar this 'beastly climate' was to England's. He really should get an umbrella, though he hated carrying the things.

As Granville clicked the door shut behind him, Scott walked into the reception area, a broad grin on his face. "So you made it back," he said. "Just in time, too. There's mail for you, from England. It's on the desk."

Draping his dripping coat on the coat stand in the outer office, Granville reached out and clapped his partner on the back. "So, are you packed?"

"I think so. Where are we off to?"

"We're heading for a place called Hazelton initially, then into the Omineca gold fields. Ever heard of it?"

"Vaguely. It's not far south of Alaska, and it's cold. And the gold rush there played out decades ago. So why are we going?"

Granville explained what he'd learned about Weston and the Chinese coins and their possible value.

"Huh. So Weston's a treasure hunter, but he's not looking for gold? That's a new one."

"He might still be looking for gold. I'm simply guessing, from what I've learned about Weston, that he'll gamble on the other being worth more."

He paused, considered Scott's unhappy expression. "Of course, you could stay behind if it bothers you. I can always take Trent."

"That one!" Scott muttered something about uppity young'uns, then glared at Granville. "You trying to get out of taking me?"

Who shrugged. "I'd rather not head that far north without another gun beside me. You still interested?"

"Wouldn't miss it."

"You might regret that," Granville said as he led the way into their shared office.

"Yeah, probably. But I'm betting it won't be dull."

"Most likely not," Granville said absently, as he drew the three envelopes on his side of their partner's desk towards himself.

One was clearly a letter, addressed in his sister Louisa's familiar hand, the second, also from England, was larger. The third envelope was legal size, from Henderson and Pruitt. It must hold the final copy of the contract he had entered into with his brother and Weston's uncle.

Granville slit open the second envelope and the photograph he'd requested fell out—an image of a young George Weston. It was a formal sitting, likely done on the lad's nineteenth birthday. Weston looked much as he'd remembered him, with dark hair and eyes and a sullen set to his mouth.

Propping the photo up against the desk lamp, Granville slit open the largest envelope and glanced through it. Long-winded and abstruse as it was, the contract was everything Brother William had represented it to be. And Randall had made sure there were no tricky clauses, no hidden surprises.

The whole thing still made him uneasy. There was something he was missing, he could feel it. Why was William making all this effort?

And what was it William and his client really wanted from him?

GRANVILLE PULLED the smaller envelope towards him, noticing the thick texture and warm cream of the envelope. His eyebrows went up a little. Louisa's husband must be doing well. Louisa's hand was firm—black slanting letters with as much character as she had.

He felt a sudden burst of homesickness for his sisters and a way of life he'd enjoyed, even as he'd outgrown it.

He skimmed the letter, smiling at some of the family details she'd included before she got to the meat of his request.

"THE LOSS of both the two oldest Weston brothers was the *on dit* for months here," she wrote. "More than you might have expected, if you have never heard the old gossip.

ALICE, Thanet's Countess, was a beautiful woman, and the two of them were not suited. She presented her Earl with the requisite heir and a spare, and then contracted a liaison with Branford, the old Duke's heir.

ONE OF WESTON'S sisters may have been sired by Earl Thanet, but the other, to her misfortune, had the Branford nose, though of course no-one ever commented.

WESTON HIMSELF WAS ALSO THOUGHT to be Branford's son. When the Countess did not survive the boy's birth, the matter was quickly hushed up. And never settled of course."

GRANVILLE HAD THOUGHT there was some rumor, but all he'd heard was the occasional veiled jest. That Thanet had been cuck-olded was not so unusual—Granville remembered him as a choleric, frowning man—but the current circumstances, which left a bastard son in line for the title, were unusual indeed.

Thanet must be furious, though he would have little say in the matter. It was far too late to disown the boy, even if that were possible, given that he'd been born in wedlock.

So who inherited after Weston?

The question was an even more critical one than he'd first thought. He read on.

According to Louisa, Earl Thanet's much loved younger brother had been killed in a hunting accident at the age of twenty-two.

"Recently married, he left one child—a son—who was raised by Earl Thanet with his own sons. In fact, from what I could discover, the Earl far prefers his nephew to Weston," Louisa wrote.

"And of course, this nephew is next in line to inherit the title," Granville said aloud, earning as odd look from Scott.

"I'll fill you in later," he told him, unwilling to stop reading long enough to do so now.

Louisa confirmed his guess. Not only was the nephew next in line after Weston, he'd been trained in estate management by Earl Thanet himself and currently served as steward for the vast estates the Earl owned.

"I can't imagine why the Earl Thanet and William have asked you to return young Weston to England," she wrote. "Though I fear neither of them have the boy's interests at heart.

Granville cursed under his breath. Was he really supposed to find Weston alive? Or just to prove he was already dead?

Scott gave him another questioning look, but wisely didn't ask any questions.

I knew Weston a little," his sister had written. "He was wild, and cared for naught as a youth, though that was not surprising given the way Earl Thanet treated him. But he was a sweet boy."

She wasn't describing the lad he'd thought he was looking for. This was the boy McAndrews and Harrison had seen.

Granville folded the letter thoughtfully, and glanced back at the contract. Louisa's letter changed everything. If even his level-headed older sister thought Weston could be in danger, it was a serious problem. And an utterly impossible situation.

Weston had only his remittance to live on. If he chose not to return to England, he might live longer—unless it was his father who had hired Heade, which was looking like a distinct possibility— but he'd have no livelihood. No wonder he'd gone chasing after ancient coins and gold.

But as matters stood now, if Granville found Weston and convinced him to return to England, he'd be signing the lad's death warrant. And if he ended the contract—Heade and his boys would keep working to make sure Weston didn't survive to inherit.

He couldn't live with either possibility. So he'd have to find another solution.

"Granville?"

He looked up with a start. Scott was watching him over the pile of client accounts he'd been muttering over for the last twenty minutes or so. He knew that look. It was time to explain.

"We need to re-think this case," he said.

Scott grinned. "I didn't think that scowl you've been wearing was about everything working out for us. What's up?"

Granville explained. "So we still don't know who hired Heade. But I suspect we know why he was hired. And why Weston's death has to look like an accident."

"Huh. So Weston could inherit everything, even though he's not the old guy's son and everyone knows it?"

That summed up the situation rather well, if you left out the cruelty of it. "Yes, he could," Granville said.

"And there's nothing the old guy can do about it?"

"Nothing legal, anyway."

"So where would your brother stand in this supposed situation?" Scott asked.

"Either he's been duped, or he considers me appropriate gun fodder."

"Or maybe he thinks you can outwit Heade and protect the lad," his partner countered.

"I doubt that," Granville said. William had never thought that highly of him. "I'd be more likely to believe William's playing a double game, being paid by the brother-in-law to find his nephew, while helping Thanet make sure the boy never makes it home."

Scott nodded slowly. "Could be. But it's bad, either way."

"Yes. It is." If Granville let himself think about just how bad it was—first these ruthless schemers had harmed Emily, and now they would murder a man who'd been rejected all his life—he'd be too angry to think straight. So what was he going to do about it?

Granville stood, paced around their shared desk. Scott watched him. "The conclusion I'd drawn up to now is that Weston's an inveterate gambler with no regard for money and the attention span of a butterfly."

Scott gave a crack of laughter. "Sounds reasonable."

"I was selling him short," Granville said. "I should have known better, if only from my own experience."

He stopped dead, met Scott's eyes. "But with the information in Louisa's letter... What if the boy knew how much danger he was in, and was desperate to raise the money to escape it?"

"Then the facts point to a crazy kind of courage."

"Yes," Granville said. "They do."

"So what do we do from here?"

"We revisit those facts with new information. I need to talk to McAndrews. If Weston knew his life was in danger, McAndrews must have seen some sign of it."

"So what do you want me to do?" Scott asked.

"We still need to know more about Norton's death. The timing is too suspicious. And if Thanet—or my brother—sent Heade and his thugs after Weston, there are a few logistics and a lot of money involved. Someone must have known about it."

"And maybe that someone was Norton?" Scott said.

"I think it's worth asking a few more questions," Granville said.

The big man checked his gun and reached for his coat. "Yeah. I'll see what I can shake loose. What about Trent? You taking him with you?"

"Where is he?"

"Delivering bills. He'll be back soon."

"Have him take the photo of Weston and see if anyone knows where the lad went after he left the Carlton his last night in town. Tell him to be careful, though. And to make sure he gets loose from anyone who might be following him before he goes anywhere."

"Will do. We'll meet you at Mary's around two," Scott said. "I can already tell I'm going to need a steak after this."

"I'll see you there," Granville said, his focus already on the plan that was beginning to take shape in his head.

He was going to save Weston, if it was the last thing he did.

Bertie Wong, her parent's Chinese houseboy and Emily's sometime co-conspirator, had protested at the thought of taking Emily to visit his uncle again. He insisted that Chinatown was dangerous for a young woman.

Emily disagreed. It was mid-morning, after all. How dangerous could it be?

Besides, she hadn't been able to find more information on the Chinese coins anywhere, and she knew there must be more to the story than Mrs. Harrison had been able to tell her.

It was only this morning that she'd realized Bertie's uncle might well have answers for her—if he could be persuaded to give them.

And Emily needed to be busy. She couldn't stand to sit and do nothing while that poor young man was in so much danger. She'd tried to explain to her mother that she was feeling much better, that a small bump on her forehead was no reason to avoid her type-writing class, but Mama wouldn't hear of it.

So here they were. In the heart of Chinatown.

She and Bertie made their cautious way through inner stairs and along hidden passageways, where nothing looked, sounded or smelled familiar to her. The bright colors, the fabrics that shone or sparkled, the oddly shaped fruits and dishes that smelled of nothing she'd ever tasted, the language that rose and fell like a stream over sharp stones—it all fascinated Emily at the same time as it made her uneasy.

Wong Ah Sun's rooms, when they reached them at last, seemed even more mysterious and foreign to her. The scent of rich woods and the gilded gleam of golden dragons claimed her attention.

When Bertie's uncle's voice came from the shadows—where he'd sat unseen—she jumped. Bertie said something in their language, then both men looked at her.

Taking a quick breath for courage, Emily explained why she'd come, that she hoped to learn more about the Chinese coins and their origins. "Is there anything you are able to tell me?" she asked as she finished.

"I find your interest—unusual," Wong Ah Sun said slowly. "Before I answer you, can you tell me why you would know?"

Emily thought for a moment. "I would like to solve a mystery," she said. "I have heard a story of a man from your lands who sailed here many, many years ago. I wanted to know more, so I searched our histories. They tell of the discovery of these lands by my people. They say nothing of yours."

"And you would know what our history tells?"

She nodded.

"Why would you know this? What use would you make of the knowledge?"

Emily hadn't considered that, though she knew, of course that for a businessman information, knowledge if you will, was power. This man, from a very different tradition, one so alien to her own she could barely get her mind to encompass it, he too saw knowledge as power.

And for herself? Why did she seek to know? Why had she taken such a risk, for no-one other than Bertie knew she had come here.

"No use," Emily said. "I had hoped what I learned might help find someone who is lost."

She paused a moment, but his question deserved a real answer. "More than that, I need to know things. For their own sake. I—I think I want to understand how my knowledge about the past could be so different from yours. I had always understood that facts were facts, and that stories are just that. Now I don't know. And I don't like not knowing."

Finishing, she felt a little embarrassed.

She hadn't known she felt so strongly about it. And she was pretty sure she had just made a fool of herself in front of this very reserved old man. Steeling herself, she looked up to meet his steady regard.

Was that approval she saw in his expression? It was gone before she could be sure, but he was nodding slowly, his long fingers steepled together.

"You have the mind of a scholar," he said, his voice soft despite the rising and falling intonations. "Untrained, yes, but the love of knowledge for its own sake speaks loudly."

A silence fell and as the heavy scent of incense drifted between them, she was afraid to break it.

"I do not have the knowledge you seek," he said at last. "But there is one who might. I will inquire. If so, Bertie will bring you again."

And he nodded at his nephew, who came forward with a deep bow, so that his long pigtail fell forward and touched the deep piled carpets.

"Please come this way, Miss Emily," Bertie said, bowing to her also, though not so deeply.

MARY'S DINER was quiet by the time Granville arrived. The place smelled of grilled steaks and bacon fat, with an overtone of slightly burnt coffee. Moisture ran down the inside of the windows, and mud spotted the battered floors.

He joined Scott and Trent at a table on the far side, and ordered steak with all the trimmings. The other two were already eating. "You have any luck?" he asked.

"I think Norton was in on it," Scott said, his fork pausing

halfway to his mouth. "And when he arranged to meet with us, it made someone nervous. Which got him killed."

The morsel of steak completed its journey and an expression of contentment spread across Scott's broad face. Trent was too busy with his own steak to notice, but Granville choked back a laugh.

"What makes you say that?" he asked.

"Once I knew what I was looking for, I asked the right questions," Scott said. "Norton had money all of a sudden, after years of barely scraping by. And his interest in Weston was new, and obvious."

"What was the connection between them?"

"I doubt there was one. Norton was interested in Weston, not the other way around."

"And Norton's willingness to talk to us?" Granville said.

"Could be he saw a chance to find out what we knew, or he might have been ready to sell out whoever hired him—for the right sum, of course," Scott said.

Granville glanced around. There was no danger of being overheard. The lunch rush had passed and the only other occupied table was on the far side of the large room. "Heade?"

"Well, whoever it was, they weren't local. But that was the most I could get anyone to admit." Scott shook his head, swallowed some coffee. "I could chase a few more rumors, but yeah, I think it was Heade. He seems to have been the only big name in town at the time."

"But you told me Heade's boys are big-time," Trent said. "How'd they lose Weston?"

"If Benton's boys couldn't find Weston, someone from out of town probably didn't stand much of a chance." Scott used a hunk of sourdough to mop the gravy off his plate.

"Weston left town practically overnight. If Heade didn't have a tail on him, I can see the problem," Granville said.

"We found Weston, though," Trent said. Then he scowled. "But why are Heade and his boys back in town?"

"They showed up right after we got offered this case. Must've figured we'd leap at it," Scott said.

Granville frowned into his coffee cup. It made a bitter kind of sense. It still hurt to hear it, though, even when he'd already reached the same conclusion.

"They're hoping I can think like Weston, and find him where they can't," he told Trent. "It's why my brother and his clients hired us."

And he drained the bitter dregs of his coffee. Signaled for more.

"You mean you're supposed to find Weston so Heade can kill him?" Trent said. His scowl had grown as he listened.

"Something like that. Or at least arrange another accident—one that doesn't miss. I checked with McAndrews. Weston's first so-called accident happened a week or so after his brothers died."

"Right after Weston became the heir," Scott said. "It figures."

"Allowing just enough time for Heade and a few of his boys to get here from San Francisco, too," Granville noted. "Everything fits."

"But—then you have to stop looking for him," Trent said. "It's just wrong."

It was. But if Granville simply quit, they'd just find someone else, someone who didn't care what happened to Weston, and the lad would be in even more danger.

"If someone's put a price on Weston's head, they'll keep after him 'til they find him, whether we're part of it or not," Scott said to Trent.

"For the sake of a title?" Trent said.

"In England, a title like that one means land and money, but most of all it means power," Granville said. "Power over others, power enough to influence the course of the Empire. And such power is not easily given up."

"But—all that just because of who he's born as?" Trent shook his head. "What if someone doesn't want all that power?"

"The power, and the responsibility that goes with it, belongs to whoever inherits the title and the land, whether they want it or not," Granville said. "It's part of what made England a great empire."

Though he had to wonder if that would continue to be true. The

England he'd left was changing, and too many of the great aristo-cratic houses were not changing with it.

"Well, I'm glad I'm not English," was Trent's answer. "And it still doesn't seem fair that someone should be hunted just because of their birth."

It never had.

"Which is why we're going after Weston," Granville said. "He's in more danger if he doesn't know he's being hunted. If he does know, he could probably use some allies."

He turned to Trent. "How did you make out with Weston's photograph? Did you learn anything?"

Trent beamed. "I did." He put his fork and knife down and leaned forward, lowering his voice. "I lost the guy following me. And I was careful not to give anything away, too."

"Well thought of," Granville said. "How did you do it?"

"Yeah, I thought so," Trent said. "The guy following me doesn't know much about tracking. And I told people I was assisting O'Hearn on a story about remittance men."

Behind Trent, Scott rolled his eyes. Granville forced himself to keep his attention on Trent. It wouldn't do to laugh at the lad's earnestness. And he had been inventive. "Go on."

"Turns out a lot of people recognized Weston, but they didn't know him very well," Trent said. "He mostly hung out with the gamblers, but I doubt he talked to them, either. Most of them weren't up and about yet—too early—so I couldn't ask them."

"So how did you learn anything useful?" Scott said.

"Your sister. I went to see Miss Frances, and she recognized him, too. Only she could tell me that he was sweet on one of the other dancers, a Miss Minnie. So I went and talked to her."

It figured. "And what did Miss Minnie tell you?"

"Not much at first. She was pretending not to know him. But when I told her that Miss Frances had given me her name, and we were trying to help him, Weston I mean, then she started to open up. She got all weepy and everything, because she's so worried that she hasn't heard from him."

"Did she expect to hear?" Granville asked.

Trent nodded. "He promised her. That night he left the gambling early."

"The night before he left town?"

Another nod. "Yeah. That's why he was so happy when he was leaving that night. He was going to meet her. And he told her all about needing to leave town, and that when he had some money, he'd send for her."

"He said he needed to leave? Not that he planned to or wanted to?" Granville said.

Trent nodded. "That's what Miss Minnie says, anyhow. And she seems to have tried to remember every word, just as he said it."

Granville swallowed a laugh at the boy's expression at the very idea of hanging on someone's words like that.

Maybe Weston did want to build a new life with the girl. When Graham paid out that bet, Weston suddenly had enough money to head north, and chase the gold that might fulfill that dream. He'd been careful to keep that information from anyone except his sweetheart, though.

Had Weston been more aware of the danger he was in than they'd realized?

Though if Weston was in love with a dance-hall girl, his new title had complicated his life far more than Granville had realized. "Do you believe her?"

"Yeah. Miss Minnie was really upset."

"The question isn't whether she's telling the truth," Scott said. "It's whether Weston was telling her the truth."

"Aww, she's too sweet to lie to," Trent said.

Wonderful. Now the boy was smitten too.

"I had the feeling someone was following me today," Scott said, obviously feeling a change of topic was in order.

Granville had to agree with him. "You didn't see anyone?" he said.

"Nope. Just had that back-of-neck prickling thing going on. So I added in a few detours. Lost him on the second one," Scott said with a grin.

"I doubt they'll have learned much so far," Granville said.

"Nope. But we'll have to be careful we're not followed when we leave town."

"Hmmm. On the other hand, it might be useful to know who they are and where they are," Granville said, picking up his mug.

"You mean to make sure they follow you?" Trent said.

Granville added a dollop of cream to the black sludge in his cup. "Exactly. We stand to learn more than they do. And that they suffer a few uncomfortable detours."

Scott's guffaw was loud enough to make the three late diners on the far side of the restaurant jump. "Serve 'em right," he said. "Let's do it."

Trent leaned closer. "How?"

Granville pulled out a map, unfolding it and running a calloused finger over the route he planned to follow.

"Here's what I'm thinking," he said.

28

I t was very quiet in the parlor. Emily had been resting there half the day and was extremely tired of it. There had been no word from Bertie's uncle, and nothing from Granville. When the door opened, she looked up eagerly.

"Your mail has come, Miss Emily," the maid said, pulling a yellow kraft envelope from her apron pocket and offering it to her.

"Thank you, Jane." Emily opened the buff-colored envelope with shaking fingers.

Her photographs. It had to be her photographs. Had they turned out?

It was a good thing she'd bribed Jane with half a dozen new hair ribbons to bring her any mail addressed to her immediately. If Papa had seen this, he would have opened it, and who knows what he'd have made of the photos she'd taken at the racetrack. If she had caught the murder on film, she might even be forbidden to use her camera ever again.

Emily pulled out a little paper folder, opened it, and removed a stack of photos. Quickly sorting through them, she noted that several were either too dark or too blurry to see anything.

"Please, please, let the racetrack photos be good ones," she chanted under her breath.

And the first shot was. It showed the horses lining up at the start gate, and every detail was clear right down to the braiding on the jockey's whips.

Then there was one that was mostly blur, which was probably the photo she'd tried to take of the man she'd thought was a woman. She'd have to practice more. She flipped quickly to the next photo.

Taken seconds before the murder, this one was sharp and clear. It showed a circle of gentlemen in top hats, most standing with their backs to her, though one or two of the faces were clear, and several more were visible in profile. Emily peered at the photo, holding her breath.

She didn't recognize any of them.

She couldn't tell which man was the victim, Graham—or if he was even in the photo.

Holding her breath, she turned to the next photo. Would it show the murder?

It was blurred. As was the final shot that followed.

Emily flipped back to the shot taken just before the murder. Holding it a little away from her, she looked for the pattern she'd sensed when she'd seen that little group. Where were the sentry birds?

Now that she was looking for them, she quickly spotted one on the very far edge of the photo, his attention focused to one side of the group. It took her longer to find the other, because she'd caught only part of him.

He was in the foreground, also away from the group, with only his face, partly shadowed, and the right half of his torso showing. And he was looking straight at her.

Holding her breath, Emily brought the photo closer and stared at that face. He looked familiar. Was it—?

Her glance took in the frieze greatcoat he was wearing. Yes. It was the man who attacked her in Victoria, the one who stole her camera. She was sure of it.

Which proved she'd been right.

The two events were indeed linked, and it was her camera they were after. Not her.

Granville needed to see this photo.

LATER THAT AFTERNOON, Granville was making notes while Scott and Trent argued over the maps and schedules spread across his desk, when he heard the outer door open. He cursed under his breath.

They weren't expecting anyone, and they had no time for a new client. Not now that they'd finally got a line on Weston.

"Hello?"

Emily. Who was supposed to be resting at home. What was wrong?

Granville flung open the inner door, to see Emily and Clara calmly removing raincoats and scarves. Emily was folding up a preposterously large spotted umbrella that was dripping water everywhere.

They looked fine.

"Emily? Is something wrong?"

"Not at all," she said. "But I have new information, and I wanted to share it with you immediately."

"Good afternoon, Clara," Granville said courteously, then turned back to Emily. "New information?"

She smiled. "My photos came back. And they turned out. Well, some of them did."

"You mean the photos from the racetrack?" he said, standing back to let them precede him into the office.

"Yes," she said, nodding hello to Scott and Trent, then laying out four photos on the large partner's desk that Granville and Scott shared.

Granville gave Trent a look, and the lad was quick to move guest chairs into place for them.

"This is the one that matters," Emily said, picking up the last photo and handing it to him.

Granville looked at it with interest. It was in sharp focus, and some faces were clearly visible, but it just looked like a group of men talking. Unless you knew it was something else. "This was taken just before the murder?"

"I think so. Though I am not positive if it was taken just before the murder or even while it was happening. The scream came moments after I had pressed the shutter."

He studied the photo more closely. It was fascinating to see all that detail, knowing what it showed, and yet be unable to say with any certainty exactly what was happening. "This one man, here in the foreground. He seems to be looking directly into the camera?"

Emily nodded. "Yes, he does."

"Do you think he saw you?"

"I am very much afraid he did. Granville…"

What was she so reluctant to tell him? "Go on."

"I think this is the man who was in Victoria." It came out in a rush.

"The one who stole your camera?"

She nodded. "So you see, I was right. It was because of the photo I took at the racetrack, and now that the murderer has been caught, they should have no further interest in me. I wasn't impor-tant to them, only what my photographs could prove. And it doesn't prove anything at all, does it? And I mean, they've already arrested the murderer, besides."

"Calm down, Emily," Clara said, putting a hand on her friend's arm. "I am sure you're right, and besides, we can all see that the photo really doesn't show anything."

Granville wasn't listening.

He was staring at the photo, remembering Emily's description of the scene, the group all focused on their center, the alertness of the sentry birds. And in this photograph, she'd captured exactly what she'd described. You could see it clearly, if you knew what you were looking for.

"This fellow staring at you is one of the sentry birds?" he said finally.

"I think so."

He nodded slowly, caught up in the realization that this same sentry bird had likely been the one responsible for wounding Emily at the track, since he appeared to be the only one aware of her and her camera.

Then, aware of Scott's confusion, he explained Emily's theory of the behavior of crows and how she'd seen it reflected at the track that day.

"Huh. And this guy's the one attacked you in Victoria?" Scott said. "Pass that photo along, will you?"

"Just a moment." Granville looked at the photo again, looking beyond what had to be Heade's men.

What he didn't see was the heated argument, that moment of rage that supposedly had driven Jacobs to kill Graham. This photograph said that the police had arrested the wrong man, that whatever the killing had been about, it had nothing to do with Jacob's debts.

Which meant Emily's life was still in danger.

Scott would have to be the one to save Weston. Granville was staying here.

"Scott, you'll be the one heading north," he said, passing the photo to him. "Take Trent with you."

Trent beamed.

Emily looked worried, and started to speak, then stopped herself. Clara gave him an approving look. But Scott didn't look up from the photo. He was staring at it as hard as Granville himself had done. What was he seeing?

"Scott?"

"This sentry crow," Scott tapped the edge of the photo. "I've been asking around. He's definitely one of Heade's men."

So it was Heade. No surprise there. "Do you recognize any of the others?"

"There's one in half-profile here that I'm not sure of, but there are two others that are definitely also part of Heade's gang," Scott said. "And I think this fellow that's turning away might be my cousin. Could be right after the murder."

"What happened to the weapon?" Granville said.

"Left in the victim," Scott said. "It was Jacob's knife."

"Then I was right," Emily said. "And this was planned?"

"Probably," Scott said. "Way I hear it, Heade's boys have worked together for years, and they have a system that's worked for them for quite a while now. It's why Benton's keeping such a close eye on them."

"But why?" Granville said, turning to pace the room. "If they were hired to kill Weston, why kill Graham?"

"Wait a minute, what?" Emily said. "Heade was hired to kill Weston? When did you learn that?"

"We still don't know it for sure," Granville said, and filled her in on what he and Scott had learned that day.

Emily was every bit as horrified as Trent had been. "So Heade is here to eliminate an inconvenient heir? And your brother hired you to betray the very man you're supposed to protect? That's—that's beyond horrible."

"I know," Trent said. "He's worse than Gipson."

Emily's lips tightened and she cast a glance at Granville that he couldn't read. What was she thinking now?

Emily didn't leave him wondering. "So how are you going to save Weston?" she asked him.

"I won't be the one doing the saving. Scott is," Granville said. "I plan to stay in town and lay a false trail for Heade and his boys."

Emily narrowed her eyes at him. "You mean you'll stay in town and protect me. It isn't necessary."

"I admire your courage, but it is…"

"No, I mean it really isn't necessary. If the sentry crow followed me so easily in Victoria, then he or someone else probably followed you also."

"So they likely know I met with Judge Harrison."

"And that I met with his wife. It shouldn't be hard for them to put the pieces together."

Scott was nodding. "They may have had some of them already. Graham is the one who told us Weston was heading north. He could have told Heade the same thing. Could be why they killed him."

"Or because he wouldn't talk at all?" Granville said. "Either makes more sense than the story the police are telling."

"Then who is the man they've arrested?" Emily said.

"That's a very good question. And something else I'll be looking into while Scott saves Weston." The words sat bitterly on his tongue.

"Your brother is trying to use you to kill Weston. You need to be the one to save him," Emily said.

"And leave you here to be killed? I think not."

"Nothing of the kind," Emily retorted. "All they want from me is the photo. So we give it to them. They can burn it, for all I care. And since the photo doesn't show anything incriminating to them, they should have no further interest in me."

Except that the photo didn't show the kind of furious argument that might result in a death, either. And if Heade was sharp enough to create the kind of criminal empire Frances had told them about, Granville was sure he was also sharp enough to see the danger that photo could pose.

But only if it fell into the right hands.

Then he thought about Vancouver's current inept police force, who would never even think to notice what was missing. Heade and his gang were in no danger from them.

"She makes a good point," Scott said to Granville. "And I think we should ask Benton to deliver to the message. The photo, I mean."

Granville had to grin at the thought of Benton's likely method of delivery. It looked as if he might be heading north after all. "Heade isn't going to trust anyone's word. We'll need to give them the negative as well as the print," Granville said. "Emily, are you willing to give up both?"

"Of course," she said, and handed him the photo and a little envelope of negatives. "I should have thought of that. It's the last strip of three negatives you need. The photos before and after that one didn't turn out. Give him all three. That way they'll know that I'm not holding anything back."

"And they're numbered ten through twelve, so they'll know there are no more photos from that day," Granville said, glancing at the negative strip. "Good. Scott and I will talk to Benton."

And ask him to ensure Heade got the message along with the photo. Emily was off limits. He turned to Trent. "And Trent, I'm sorry, but you will need to stay here and keep the office open for us."

Trent's disappointment was etched on his face, but he simply nodded.

Emily was the one who protested, looking from one to the other, then fixing her gaze on Granville. "You'll need him," she said. "There are only three of you, and Heade has—five men?"

"Six," Scott said.

"Our firm is beginning to gain a reputation," Granville said. "The office needs to remain open, if only to make appointments for when we return."

"When do you plan to leave?"

"Tomorrow. So there is no time to train someone."

Trent had been looking hopeful, but at these words his face went blank. To his credit, he didn't argue.

29

As Emily, Clara and Granville strolled back to the West End, the soft light of late afternoon gilded the newly-leaved young trees along the boulevard. Luckily, it had stopped raining, so they didn't need the umbrella. Granville had courteously offered an arm to each of them, and Emily noted a few envious glances coming their way.

She almost smiled to see the younger Miss Smythe's glare, and even her escort, one of the Robertson twins, looked rather jealous of Granville. She tried to focus on how amusing it all was, but couldn't quite convince the hollow in her middle that was already missing Granville.

He'd insisted on seeing Clara and herself home before he and Scott went to talk to Benton, and she was glad of the extra time with him.

"What time do you leave tomorrow?" she asked him, keeping her tone light with an effort.

"Our ship departs for Port Simpson at nine."

"And from there, where do you go?" Emily said.

"Scott and I disembark in Port Essington, then make our way some two hundred miles up the Skeena River to Hazelton, and inland to the goldfields from there. We could be gone a month or more."

"A month!" Clara said. "So long? But why?"

"It will take at least three days to get to Port Essington. Then we board a sternwheeler to take us up the Skeena River. That's assuming the river is free of ice by then, of course."

"So there might be a delay in Port Essington?" Emily asked.

He nodded. "And possibly a further delay on the Skeena itself. It's apparently a treacherous river."

"So how long do you hope to be?" Clara asked.

"No more than a week going up river," Granville said. "If there's still too much ice on the river, we could hire some of the natives to canoe us up-river. Which would take nine days or so."

"Canoes? On a river you describe as treacherous? That doesn't sound safe," Emily said.

"These canoes can carry ten to twelve people, plus goods," Granville said, "And the local Indians are expert, and know the river exceedingly well. In any case, I doubt we'll need the canoes."

"Either way, you'd end up in Hazelton within two weeks." Clara said. "And then?"

"It depends what we find out in Hazelton. If we're lucky and find Weston there, then we could be home in another week."

Emily laughed. "You don't expect that kind of luck, do you?"

"No, I've learned never to depend on luck." He smiled at them. "I expect we'll be asking questions in Hazelton, then hiring Indian guides to take us another couple hundred miles inland."

"So another week?" Clara said.

"Depending on the terrain and how far north we have to go, at least a week," Granville said. "Possibly two."

"Then it really will be a month that you'll be gone. At best." Emily glanced over, met his eyes. "I do wish I could go with you."

"Someday I will take you," Granville said.

Emily was beginning to believe him. Yet even as she felt something in her melt at his tone, she bristled a little. She didn't want to be "taken" anywhere.

"We can go together," she said. "Mrs. Harrison accompanied her husband to the Barkerville goldfields in the Cariboo, and it was much wilder then."

Granville gave her a considering look, then grinned. "Very well. Together it is."

"You do know I will hold you to that?" Emily said.

"I'm rather counting on it."

On Granville's other side, Clara giggled. "You're really lucky, Emily."

"I know it," she said. "But why are you telling me now, in particular?"

"Because I suspect there are few men who would put up with you, let alone appreciate you."

"Hmpff," was all Emily said, but she squeezed Granville's arm a little tighter. Because Clara was right. And perhaps it really was time to decide to marry him, for real.

Not that she was going to give Clara further ammunition by telling her so, of course.

They delivered Clara to her home, then continued on towards Emily's. She thought Granville looked worried. "Is something wrong?"

"No, but I don't like leaving you for so long. If you need me, you can send word to Manson Creek, care of the mining recorder. I'll make sure the man knows how to get word to us."

"The mining recorder," she repeated. "I'll do that. Would it be safe to send any information I uncover about Weston or his quest that way also?"

"I think so." They had reached her house. Granville paused for a moment on the walkway, his eyes on her face. "I do still have a concern about Heade and his gang, though I believe they'll be more interested in where Scott and I are going than in you."

"They won't be interested in me at all, not once Mr. Benton has talked to Mr. Heade and given him the photo," Emily said.

"That's the plan."

"And you're sure this Heade is only interested in you as a way to find Mr. Weston?" Emily said a little anxiously.

"Yes. I'm in no danger. In fact, I think I've quite a bit more value to them as a credible witness to Weston's death than as a corpse."

"That's so—cold."

"It is indeed. But I have enemies in Vancouver, and our engagement is well-known. Please do try to keep a low profile."

"Of course I will," Emily said, trying not to sound like she was indulging him. It wasn't as if she rushed headlong into danger, after all.

———

When Emily entered the house, Bertie was in the hall to take her coat and scarf. "Word has come from my uncle," he said softly as hung them in the mahogany wardrobe.

"About the coins?"

"Yes. There is someone willing to talk with you. He is scholar," Bertie said in an awed whisper. "He visits from Frisco."

"San Francisco?"

A nod. "Their Chinatown much bigger. They have even scrolls." Seeing her confusion, he added "Histories. But it must be now."

"Now?" She thought rapidly. There might just be time before dinner.

"He leave tomorrow," Bertie was saying. "Has little time."

"He didn't stay just to speak with me?" She didn't know whether to feel honored or horrified.

The feeling didn't last however, because without a change of expression, Bertie somehow conveyed how humorous he found that idea. She felt silly, and ignorant. Suddenly she wished she'd told Granville what she was doing, and could somehow invite him to join them.

Chinatown, even with Bertie as escort, made her nervous at the same time as it fascinated her. She felt she'd walked into a different country, whose customs and history she didn't understand. Granville at least had travelled, and his education put hers to shame.

She hadn't even seen copies of many of the books he'd read. And she couldn't have read them in any case, because she knew neither Latin nor Greek.

But Granville was packing to leave tomorrow, and he would be at Benton's offices by now. There was no time.

She would have to manage.

———

BERTIE CONDUCTED her through Chinatown to his uncle's elaborate rooms, just as he had that morning. This time there was no sign of Wong Ah Sun.

Across the room a very old Chinese man wearing dark grey robes, his face a net of wrinkles and his eyes filmy with age, was looking towards her. At Bertie's signal, she moved towards him, bowing her head as a mark of respect.

She'd learned that much, at least, though it still felt odd to her.

The scholar—for it was he—asked a question, directing his gaze to Bertie, who apparently was to serve as interpreter.

"He asks what you would know?"

"Tell him that I wish to know the very earliest stories of your people in this country," she said.

"In Gold Mountain?"

"What is Gold Mountain?" It wasn't a term she had ever heard.

"Gold Mountain is Chinese name for this land."

"You mean British Columbia?"

He waved a hand. "All land north and south."

So it meant into America as well. Yet if the term had meaning to the Chinese, it might tell her more than if she tried to insist on country boundaries that had not even existed at the time she was interested in.

It was a novel thought. To whom did unclaimed land belong?

"I see. Why did they call it Gold Mountain?" she asked instead.

"Is seen as place of riches for my people, where gold lay about on ground. My town, my region poor, many starve. Gold Mountain means plenty."

"Then please ask him when your people first came to Gold Mountain?"

Bertie bobbed his head and turned to the old scholar. A spate of questions and answers ensued, all in their rising and falling language. Emily wished she could understand them, could ask the questions herself.

Finally Bertie turned to her. "He say a monk came by boat from China to Gold Mountain long before your people are here. At request of emperor of China. And that they explored, and spread word of the Buddha. They lived with the tribes for a time."

"Where?"

Another exchange of information, and Bertie ended up shaking his head and shrugging.

"Bertie? What did he say?"

A voice spoke from the shadows. Bertie's uncle. She hadn't realized he was there.

"It is difficult to translate. He said the Buddhist monk and his party lived with one of the tribes for long enough to father children before they moved on. He says they traveled south from land to land. To California, and also to Mexico"

"Why?"

"They came to spread word of their Buddha, but also for knowledge. The quest for knowledge can be a dangerous thing, as you will learn."

"*I* will?" Emily said.

No answer, just another exchange, this time between Bertie's uncle and the old scholar.

"Where this monk came from and where he went to are known, but the information cannot be shared."

"But surely, after all of these years?"

The answer and the accompanying head-shake were definite. "I am afraid not."

She had at least learned to accept defeat with grace. Her mother would be so proud, Emily thought with an inward grin. If she ever learned of it. And once she had recovered from being horrified that her youngest daughter had visited Chinatown at all, of course.

With a bow to both men, she left the room, and was relieved to find herself at length in the alley that bordered Chinatown, Bertie at her side. Whenever she braved the twisting passageways and hidden courtyards of that inner city, she had to fight the fear that she would never emerge from them.

It would be growing dark before long, and she needed to be home before either of them was missed. But she was glad she'd come. Despite how little she'd learned, the scholar's words had given her an idea.

"Bertie, I need to speak with you and Trent before dinner. Can you find him and arrange it? Without my mother finding out? I will be resting quietly by myself in the parlor."

"Yes, perhaps. I see," he said.

"Thank you. It's important," she said.

She just hoped he could find Trent in time.

BENTON SAT BACK in tall leather chair and looked from Granville to Scott and back again, his face perfectly blank. "Let me get this straight. You want me to play errand boy for you?"

Granville laughed. He couldn't help it, though Scott's expression told him it was a foolhardy thing to do.

"Not at all," he said. "I simply want to send a message to Heade, one that ensures Emily's safety. I also thought to use the message to lure the man and his cohort north, into the kind of trouble they're neither used to nor prepared for."

"A laudable aim. And why can you or Scott not deliver this message yourselves?"

"Because if we deliver it before we sail, there's a chance Heade could figure out what we're up to and buy tickets on the same steamer. If he gets the message tomorrow, he'll be delayed enough to miss his connection with the only sternwheeler currently plying the Skeena, and facing at least a three week delay.

If he's as smart as I think he is, though, he'll book passage on the new HBC sternwheeler, which leaves from Victoria early next month. He'll still be delayed, but only by ten days or so. Our strategy depends on that delay."

"And my role?"

"Well, given that our strategy might serve your ends as well as our own, it strikes me that the message would have a little extra—" Granville paused, eyeing Benton, "resonance, shall we say, if it was delivered by one of your men. And not someone in a low position, either."

Benton grinned. "I think this is the part of the conversation where I try to hire you again," he said. "What does this messenger of mine need to do?"

"I think it would be useful if they suggested, rather strongly, that Heade and company not attempt to follow Scott or me. Something about it being better for their health."

"I sometimes think you might be even more devious than I am," Benton said. "Luckily that doesn't happen often. Very well, I'll see your message delivered tomorrow."

He held out his hand.

Granville passed over the small package, then waited patiently while Benton read it. He'd been fairly sure Benton would agree, but the risk in offending the man was huge.

He didn't relax until Benton, reaching the last line, began to laugh.

"I think Heade might end up wishing he'd stayed to deal with me," he said. "But this is a far more fitting solution. I gather you'll have a few surprises waiting for him when he reaches this Port Essington?"

He grinned. "There, and elsewhere."

"He has at least five men with him, and I'm not sure about the sixth. Are you sure you can handle all of them?"

"No. But I'm fairly sure he won't have that many men left by the time he finds us."

"You're setting an ambush for him?"

"Not necessary. From everything I've learned, the country itself is more than enough for those not prepared for it. Particularly where we're going."

"I did some asking around," Scott added. "Heade and his boys are from Boston originally, and the lot of 'em are city boys through and through."

Benton shook his head. "I'll have Stanton deliver this, and make sure the underlying message is clear. And that Heade knows your lady is off limits."

Granville had been counting on it. He stepped forward and held out his hand. "Thank you."

Benton shook it and then Scott's. "Good travels, you two."

As the door closed behind them, Scott let out a groan. "I can't believe you pulled that off," he said.

"Why not?" Granville said. "And who is Stanton, anyway?"

"He's Benton's new second in command. That's quite a message you're sending."

"Good," Granville said, and clapped his friend on the shoulder. "And we have packing to do."

MONDAY, APRIL 30, 1900

"This place looks like the same kind of dump as Dyea in Alaska," Scott said.

Granville had to grin at his friend's mournful expression.

It felt good to be off the steamship after three days of steady chugging northward along the steep, heavily forested coast, threading between islands for part of the way. They'd seen few signs of civilization, and fewer that any human had ever set foot there. He knew it for an illusion; the Haida and the Tsimshian had hunted and fished this area for a very long time, but they'd left little trace to his Oxford-educated eye.

Port Essington, however, was—the word dismal came to mind. It was scenic enough—incredibly steep mountains on one side, a river on the other—but from what he could see, the town itself was built on a bog, with docks connecting to boardwalks that ran between the low wooden buildings. Low-hanging clouds cast a grey sameness over everything, while wisps of fog drifted here and there, and the air was chilly and damp.

"I think Dyea might have been more welcoming," Granville said.

Scott gave a crack of laughter. "You're still out of sorts because we hit a little uneasy water. It's no shame to be seasick coming through the Narrows."

"Uneasy water? Is that what you call it? I'll have you know I didn't get sick once all the way from England to this benighted country of yours. And that counts the storms that hit us on the open ocean."

"Uh huh. Let's find this hotel you were talking about. I could use a drink, a steak and a bed. Where did you say it was?"

"The Queen, on Dufferin, which is apparently the main street." Granville pointed. "And this looks a likely candidate. Come on."

The street he pointed out was broad but muddy. It paralleled the boardwalk that ran from the dock straight through the town, and was lined with noisy restaurants and busy shops. Picking up their bags, they strode out.

"Why's the place so busy, anyway?" Scott said.

"Tomorrow's sailing will be the first boat up the Skeena since the river froze last winter. Some of these folks have been in town for a couple of weeks already, so as not to miss the *Caledonia*."

"Then we were lucky to get a berth?" Scott said. "Wonder if Heade will be out of luck when he arrives."

"If he isn't smart enough to book on the *Strathcona* out of Victoria, he'll be stuck with ten days of canoes and black flies when he gets this far."

Scott grinned. "I really hope he's not that smart."

"Never mind. Our plan works either way, as long as he's at least a week behind us."

Scott glanced into an open doorway as they passed and Granville followed his gaze. He caught a glimpse of crowded tables, could hear the buzz of voices talking in many languages and smell the spilled beer and grilling steaks.

"Are you sure Weston isn't here?" Scott said. "February wouldn't have been a great month to head inland, and this place is hopping. How do we know he didn't just wait here, that he isn't sailing on the *Caledonia* tomorrow?"

"It's a possibility, but I suspect even this place is too close to

Vancouver if he has even a suspicion that someone like Heade is on his trail. We'll check with the ticket agent tomorrow, though."

"Let's dump our bags and come back here for dinner."

Granville gave him a look. "And information?"

A broad grin split Scott's face. "Nah. All I care about's a good steak."

"Right. Then let's see what we can do about that."

———

DINNER LONG OVER, Granville cast a quick look at his cards, then considered his surroundings. The rough board walls, the familiar smell of cigar smoke and whiskey, the rattle of the poker chips and the bearded, weather-beaten faces that surrounded him—he could have been back in Dawson City.

Instead he was in the back room of the best hotel in Port Essington. Not that that was saying much.

Some of these men were heading inland with them tomorrow, some were fishermen or worked at the sawmill or one of the canneries. Apparently none of them had encountered Weston, either in February or recently.

"I call," one of the players said.

There was a clatter of chips as some players made their bets and others folded.

With a quick glance at the faces of the players, Granville tossed in a few chips and laid down his cards. "Full house, Queens high," he said.

A collective groan rose, and the original bidder threw down his cards. "You're too good," he muttered.

"You implying something there, Parks?" the weathered man beside Granville asked, gathering up his own cards in knurled hands and passing them back to the dealer.

"No! Can't a man make a comment?" the unfortunate Parks snapped back, casting a wary look at Granville. "Man's in luck tonight, that's all. Makes it hard for the rest of us."

He'd learned all he was going to here, anyway.

Putting down his cards, Granville reached to gather the chips. "I'm cashing in, in any case," he said with an easy smile. "Maybe the luck will turn your way."

Parks muttered something else, but kept his eyes down. Granville stood, ignoring him. "Thank you for a good game, gents. I hope we cross paths again."

Looking around, he saw Scott deep in a game of blackjack. Bystanders lined the wall behind the game, watching closely and catcalling when a poor call was made. He wandered over and joined the group watching the game, leaning back against the rough boards.

The grizzled man standing beside him, a quarter-full glass of whiskey in hand, gave him a shrewd glance, and shifted over to make room. "You new in town?"

"Just here for the *Caledonia*."

A nod. "I figured. You don't have the look of those who stay in places like this."

"What look is that?" Granville asked.

"You still have hope. You a miner?"

"I've done some mining."

"But you're not on your way to the Klondike?"

"I've been, and don't see any point in going back."

"So you're going inland?" His new friend squinted up at him. "You know the Omineca's played out, right? She was big news in '86, '87, and she still attracts the losers and the fools, but there's nothing there."

"So I'd heard. Actually, I'm in search of a friend who may have taken it in mind to do a little mining."

"He a Klondiker too?"

Granville laughed. "He's what we'd call a tenderfoot in the Klondike. English, educated, never done any mining in his life."

That earned him a shrewd glance. "I 'spect that applied to you, too, and not that long ago."

He had to grin. The man was right. "You have a point, at that. Still, at least I got in early on the Klondike rush. This lad's nearly fifteen years late for the Omineca."

That earned him a chortle. "You said your friend may be mining. You're not sure?"

"All I know is he was headed to Port Essington. I've been trying to track him from here, and had no luck so far.

"Mebbe I know him. Boy got a name?"

"Weston. Rupert Weston."

"Doesn't ring any bells. You got a picture?"

Granville brought out the copy he'd had made of Weston's photo, and showed it to the old man, getting a slow nod in return.

"Yeah, I know him. He was here in February, or thereabouts. Haven't seen him since. He could still be here and me not know it, though, if he's found work somewheres out of town, like on a fish-boat, or favors a different local bar."

He paused to down the remainder of his whiskey. "But if he is still here, you can probably find him tomorrow when the boat leaves. The entire town goes down to the wharf to see her off. You'll find everyone there—Tlingits from Alaska, Haida from the Queen Charlottes, Tsimshians from Skeena, Kwakiutls from Vancouver, Chinamen, Japanese, Greeks, Scandinavians, Englishmen and Yankees. Some of 'em will be going up-river with you, but most are just there for the excitement."

Granville tried to picture Weston working on one of the shabby fish-boats he'd seen tied up at the docks, and couldn't do it. "Thanks for the suggestion. I'll make sure I look for him tomorrow."

"You do that. And if I happen to see him, I'll pass on that you're looking for him. What name?"

"Granville, John Granville." He held out a hand. "And you are?"

"Prescott Sutton. Pleasure." He laughed a little, and gripped Granville's hand firmly. "Folks round here just call me Press."

Granville wondered a little at the distinguished name, which didn't match the man's worn appearance, but the blackjack table cleared just then. Scott stood up, spotted Granville and came over to join them. Granville introduced them, then bade the odd little man farewell.

"We should be on our way. Thanks for the information."

As they reached the door, a big, burly man was coming in, and jostled against Scott, who was just reaching for the door. "Hey, watch yourself," the man said.

"Sorry," said Scott, stepping to one side.

"Sorry's not good enough. We can't have folks like you coming through, thinking they own the place."

Granville was amused to see that the newcomer, though as tall and broad as Scott, was decidedly unsteady on his feet. Scott had obviously noted the same, because he held the door wide. "Care to discuss this outside?"

"Yeah. You first," the bully said, then attempted to push Scott through the door.

Scott had anticipated the move, however, and moved more quickly than his opponent was prepared for.

Finding himself shoving empty air, the man overbalanced and tumbled down the stairs. "You thundering piece of rotted camel dung! You'll pay for that! Just you wait," he shouted once he got his breath back.

But by then Granville and Scott were well clear of him and sauntering down the street. "Well, at least the man has a way with an insult, even if he's none too steady on his feet," Scott said with a grin.

"Good thing you're not likely to see him again. I doubt you're one of his favorite people," Granville said, clapping Scott on the shoulder.

TUESDAY, MAY 1, 1900

T he following morning, the long, shrill blast of a steam whistle signaled the arrival of the *Caledonia*. The fog was thicker this morning, and the air felt damp and chilly. The temperature had dropped near the freezing point last night, and the fog kept it from warming quickly.

Granville pulled the lapels of his heavy mackinaw more snugly together. Glancing at the throng around them, he motioned to Scott. "If you stay with the bags, I'll see if I can get a line on Weston."

Scott nodded, his gaze fixed on something in the crowd. Granville nearly asked him what was holding his interest, then glanced downriver. He could just make out the black shape of the smokestack. There wasn't much time.

He strolled along the dock, letting his gaze move from face to face. He wasn't sure what he was looking for, but he'd learned on the unforgiving goldfields of the Klondike to trust his instincts about people. They seldom sent him wrong.

Half-way along the pier, an odd movement caught his eye, and he looked more closely to see someone apparently trying to duck out of his sight. He angled his path to intersect with that furtive movement. Whoever it was seemed to be moving backwards from him.

He circled around, trying to come up on them from behind, and caught a glimpse of a full skirt. A woman? But who would know him here?

A quick turn, and he was facing her.

"Emily?" He stared down at his fiancée's defiant expression, still not quite believing it was her. "And just what are you doing here?"

"Clara and I decided to do a little traveling," she said. "And a journey on the first boat up the Skeena after the breakup is apparently an experience not to be missed."

"Clara is here too?" Surely that wasn't possible. He looked quickly about him, but didn't see her.

"Oh yes, she's at the hotel with our bags. The porter will help her with them once the boat is docked." Emily tucked her hand into his arm. "She decided to stay for a second cup of tea. She doesn't like crowds, you see."

"Unlike you." He considered her in silence for a moment while she fidgeted with her reticule. "But how did you pull it off?"

"We simply stayed in our cabins."

"For three days?"

"The stewards were most accommodating. And it was a big ship."

Right. "And where do your parents think you are?"

"Ummm. In Victoria. Visiting my aunt again."

That wouldn't stand up for long. They were in for a difficult scene when they returned. And there was something Emily wasn't telling him, but he'd learned enough since they'd become engaged to know that further questions were unlikely to get answers.

She'd tell him when she was ready.

As if she'd read his thoughts, Emily grinned up at him. "Have you been able to find anyone who remembers Weston?"

"Yes, but he didn't know where Weston went," Granville said. "But why were you hiding from me?"

"I wasn't hiding! Well, not exactly. I'd hoped to surprise you, you see. Later, on the boat."

Granville considered the twinkle in her eye, and grinned back. "Of course you did. And it had nothing to do with any fear that I might send you home. The Skeena at this time of year is no place for a lady, you know. Much less a pair of them."

Emily widened her eyes at him, but the laughter in them told its own story. "But surely you wouldn't leave us here alone in this—frontier—town, would you? I hesitate to call it unsavory, but it is certainly no place for a lady or two."

He admired her spirit, and the way she so cheerfully turned his own words against him. And she was right, dammit. There was no way he could leave the two of them on their own in Port Essington, not after what he'd seen of the place the day before. Not even long enough to wait for the next steamship back to Vancouver.

He'd have to wait and personally see them onto the boat, which would mean he'd miss the *Caledonia*. And be stuck going up-river along with Heade and his men. Which would entirely defeat his own purposes.

"You're right, and you know it," he said. "But you and Clara will be staying in Hazelton. Going any further would be too dangerous for you."

At least he hoped that they could stay in Hazelton, that the place was safe enough for two young ladies.

"We'll see," said Emily. "But I'll need to collect Clara and our bags. Do you need to see if Mr. Weston is here? The boat will be docking soon."

———————

GRANVILLE WAS STILL SHAKING his head when Emily had vanished from sight. She was right, he did need to be looking for Weston—something her unexpected presence had almost made him lose sight of. He glanced at the crowd around him, recognizing a few faces, but no-one who could possibly be Weston, even if the lad were wearing some form of disguise.

He let his gaze wander from face to face. Weston's eyes would be the hardest to disguise, and, thinking back, his sister was right. The poor boy did have a modified version of the Branford nose—which must infuriate the current Earl. But there was no sign of a Branford nose in the crowd, either.

"So, you found him yet?" came a voice at his shoulder.

Granville turned and looked down to see Prescott, his acquaintance from the night before, eyes a little bloodshot but a wide grin on his face. "No sign of him. Why, did you see him?"

"Nope, not hide nor hair of him. But I do have a little proposition for you."

He'd learned to be wary of drinking companions who had propositions the morning after. "Oh?"

"Hmmm. I know a fair bit about lads like your missing boy. I c'n keep an eye out for him, if you like. Get word to you if'n he shows up, or jest let him know you're looking for him. For a fee, o'course."

Granville listened to this remarkable speech with a grin on his face. He was now convinced that the old man was far more than he pretended to be. But what was he up to? "Of course. And I'm sure the fee would be a reasonable one."

Prescott's eyes twinkled. "'Course it would. Commensurate with the effort expended, you might say."

"Though the lad in question may already have gone up-river."

"We might have to discuss contingencies."

Of course they would. And this man was no fool. In fact, he might be exactly what Granville had been looking for. "It's possible I might have a different proposition for you."

"Oh? Well, as long as it doesn't include gutting fish, I might just be interested. I've had my fill of that line of work. I wasn't raised to it, y'know?"

And despite the thick accent he seemed to assume at will, Granville didn't doubt it. "I'm expecting another party to come through here in a few days. They'll either be asking after Weston, or they'll be looking for me."

Shrewd eyes considered him for a moment. "And perhaps a little misdirection is in order?"

"That's it, exactly."

"Hmmm. And would you be wanting them stopped, or just delayed? It'll affect the fee, you understand."

Granville had to bite back a grin. "Of course. I think delay, and perhaps inconvenience, would be sufficient."

"I could add a soupçon of frustration, to top it off?"

"That would be ideal. And if a man or two happened to get left behind when they head up-river after us, well, that would be a bonus. Can you do it?"

"If the fee stretched far enough, I'd be bringing in a partner. He's particularly good at inconveniencing people. In fact, I believe your partner encountered him as you were leaving last night."

"The fellow with the inventive line in curses?"

"That's him."

"Oh, I think we have to include him in the fee. I doubt our friends have ever encountered anyone quite like him. Quite like either of you, come to that."

"Then please, step into my office," said Prescott, with a wave towards a nearby tavern. "We can discuss the details. And the payment, of course."

With a reluctant grin, Granville followed.

SEVERAL HOURS LATER, Emily watched the almost feverish movements of the *Caledonia's* crew as they finished loading the steamer and readied her for sailing. It was fascinating.

She couldn't quite believe that she was really here, and that Granville hadn't immediately found a way to send her home.

"You look pleased to be here."

Emily turned and smiled at Granville. "I am indeed."

If he was upset with her, he didn't show it, just put a hand under her elbow and walked with her along the deck towards the stern. "You'll want a view of the paddle-wheel as we get underway," he said. "I understand it's quite a sight. Here should do."

He stopped at a point a good ten feet back from the back of the boat. Emily was about to ask him why they weren't going closer, when steam began to screech from the funnel and the whistle blew. They were underway!

As Emily watched, the huge red painted stern-wheel began to turn, slapping at the river and throwing water up and over the wheelhouse as it spun. If they'd been closer to the stern, they would have been drenched.

"Oh Granville, look! You see, this is why I came. I'd never have seen anything like this if I'd stayed in Vancouver."

"You mean if you'd stayed safely in Vancouver?"

She grinned at him. "Now you sound like Papa."

He made a face. "Surely not. But venturing all this way alone..."

"But I had Clara traveling with me."

He glanced around the deck. "I haven't seen her yet. Did she make it on board?"

"Of course she did. She found the journey tiring, and is resting in the ladies' retiring room."

"As she was resting in the hotel? Are you sure she is actually here?" he asked, then continued before she could answer. "And I still do not understand how you managed to get yourselves and all of your luggage here on your own. Not to mention how you managed to get a booking so late."

"I don't know why you'd question it. I'm very capable."

"Yes, I know you are, of a great many things. But of something you've never done before? And with no time for error—if you'd missed this boat, you'd be waiting a week or more for the next. Not to mention traveling with Heade and his sentry crow."

Granville looked down at her, and Emily tried to keep the guilt off her face. "I'm here, aren't I?"

He watched her for a moment before he spoke. "Alone?"

"I don't know what you mean."

"I'd asked Trent to check in on you. Just exactly how did you manage to evade him?"

"Did I forget to mention that Trent came with us?" Emily said. "You did ask him to watch out for us, after all."

He groaned, and she hid a smile. They couldn't have left Trent behind. Besides, Trent was keen, and deserved an adventure.

"And she didn't exactly evade me," came a voice from behind them.

Granville closed his eyes. "It only needed that."

He opened them, and met Emily's eyes. "I suppose you had to corrupt my assistant."

"Hey..." Trent began.

"I hardly corrupted him," Emily said tartly. "It's not as if he didn't want to come in the first place. You're the one who was sure we'd be better off staying home. We just—corrected that misapprehension."

"Corrected it. I see."

His tone was dry, but was that a smile she saw, fighting to get loose? Emily lifted her chin a little, and grinned at him. "Absolutely. You can't always be right, you know."

"And just who is keeping our office open?"

"One of my fellow students. Laura Kent," she said, and proceeded to explain that her business course required each student to spend a month working in an actual office to gain experience. They would need to be paid only a small sum for the work they did.

"So Laura is officially your intern for the next month. And don't worry, she is very professional and extremely efficient."

It had taken Trent less than ten minutes to explain Granville and Scott's appointment books, and Emily had been hard pressed to keep her comments to herself. The system was adequate at best. No matter, Laura would soon have it set to rights.

"I'm sure she is," Granville said dryly.

He wasn't taking this as well as she'd hoped.

"You need me," Trent said, then glanced at her. "Us, I mean. Finding Weston in this wilderness isn't going to be easy."

"And since I have so little experience with wilderness, you thought you'd come along, and bring two women who are town-bred, with no experience at all."

Trent flushed a little. "I never said you had—I mean, I'm not forgetting your time in the Klondike."

Emily glanced from one to the other. "We'll be helpful, you'll see."

And to Trent, "How did you leave Clara? Is she feeling better?"

"Her maid is with her. I brought her some chamomile tea from the galley, which they seemed to feel would help."

Granville's eyebrows rose. "You brought Clara's maid with you?"

Emily grinned at him. "Of course. There are proprieties to be observed, after all."

"I see," he said, keeping a straight face with an effort.

"Can we go forward, though?" she asked. "I'd hoped to see something of the scenery as we go by."

Granville shook his head at her, but gave her his arm, and the three of them strolled towards the bow, which was crowded with other passengers with the same idea.

From where they stood, Emily could no longer see the paddle-wheel, but she could still hear the suck and splash as it churned its way up the Skeena River. As she watched the bank, cannery after cannery slid away behind them. The river was dark and cold-looking, but clear of ice, and not too high.

"They say the river is low for this time of year," she said. "Apparently the rapids upstream will be more treacherous if it rises."

Trent snorted. "Too bad it's a warm day, then. We'd best hope for rain."

"Rain? Wouldn't that just raise the river?"

"Nope. Sunshine will melt the snow off the glaciers higher up, and the runoff makes the river rise."

"Oh." She glanced at the water flowing by. "I've never seen rapids. It would be a shame if they proved too tame. And I'd rather be able to see where we're going."

G ranville stared at the river that boiled past the bow of the *Caledonia*. The banks were steep here, with fir and cedar clad slopes rising nearly straight up from the water. Here and there a small stream trickled down, before losing itself in the river.

Granville found it exhilarating, especially in contrast to the tamed fields and lanes of England, but some of the passengers had gone inside when they'd left the flatter land of the estuary behind an hour or so ago.

Emily had decided to go and see how Clara was doing, and he missed watching her fascination with everything she saw and heard. He couldn't help worrying about her, though. She had no idea what she might face on this journey, and as for bringing Clara, whose natural habitat was the department store…

"You're not mad at me, are you?" came Trent's voice at his elbow. "I really can be useful."

"What were you thinking, bringing Emily and Clara along?"

"Well, I couldn't very well leave them," Trent said. "Miss Emily was determined to come, and even her Papa doesn't manage to stop her doing things when she decides to do them. Not most of the time, anyway."

That was true enough. And Emily's unquenchable spirit was one of the things he loved about her.

"And I had Bertie book the tickets for us," Trent added. "So that Heade's men wouldn't know about us."

"And just when did you book the tickets?"

Trent flushed again, but this time Emily wasn't there to rescue him. "Well?"

"Ummm, well—I booked them that same day," he finished rapidly.

"Which same day?"

Trent scuffed at the deck with one worn-looking boot. "The day you and Scott found out about Thanet," he mumbled.

Granville had to strain to hear him over the chuffing of the steam engine. "You mean the day I told you to stay and look after Emily?"

"Yes, that day." He looked up. "Because if I was going to look after Miss Emily, I couldn't stay, could I? Because she was coming on this trip, no matter what."

"Even if you hadn't booked the tickets for her?"

"She'd have found a way, and you know it."

Yes, he did. Emily didn't let minor inconveniences stop her. Even when her father had locked her in her room, she'd helped him save Scott's life. Missing out on an adventure like this one just wasn't in her blood.

But he'd really like to know how she'd persuaded her friend to join her. Adventure was hardly Clara's style.

His silence was apparently making Trent nervous. "You wouldn't have wanted me to let her come on her own, would you?"

"No. But did it ever occur to you to tell me what was being planned, before you bought the tickets?"

"You couldn't have changed her mind."

"Maybe not. But Emily isn't the only one who didn't want to be left behind, is she?"

The boy grinned. "Can you blame me? And she was determined to come, so I was doing what you said and looking out for her."

"You made a decision based on what I'd asked of you. But I was still in town, and you didn't discuss that decision with me. Aren't you supposed to be my assistant?"

Trent returned to digging at the deck with his boot, and mumbled something.

"What's that?"

"Am I fired?"

"No. I admire your loyalty to my fiancée." And Trent's devious reasoning rather amused him. "But if you make a habit of similar poor judgment, I will fire you. You'll be too dangerous to work with."

"Poor judgment? When I got Miss Emily and Miss Clara here safely and on time?"

He almost grinned at the wounded pride in the boy's voice. "The poor judgement lies in not asking yourself what the consequences might be for Emily and Clara in joining me on this trip."

Trent scowled, and wouldn't meet Granville's eyes.

"Granville, there you are," Scott said, walking towards them from the other side of the bow. "Have you met Mr. Booth? He knows something about mining prospects where we're headed."

With a thoughtful look at Trent's stubborn expression, Granville turned to greet Scott's new acquaintance.

"THIS IS MR. SAMUEL BOOTH," Scott said, waving forward a prosperous looking black man, whose upright posture belied his white hair and seamed face. "He came up from Victoria last week. He and his party are headed for Lorne Creek, where he has placer claims."

"And where is Lorne Creek?" said Granville, as he shook the extended hands.

"It's part of the Omineca area," Mr. Booth said. "The gold rush thereabouts petered out in the mid-seventies, but some of the claims still pay out enough, if you're willing to work them. And I am. I come up every spring to oversee things."

"Mr. Booth staked a man named McDame to explore the area

some ten years ago, and he found several creeks bearing gold," Scott added.

"Lorne Creek was the best of them," Booth said.

"McDame was one of the four men who found the original Discovery Site for the Cassiar rush. They're now calling it McDame Creek," Scott added. "Booth here tells me there's men come up every year looking for another big strike, but no-one has found it yet."

"Which ties in with what Harrison told me," Granville said, then turned back to the old man. "I'm looking for an Englishman named Weston, who came north several months ago looking for gold."

"He must be most enthusiastic to come north so early in the year," Booth said.

Or most desperate. "Indeed," Granville said. "Did you hear any mention of him while you were in Port Essington?"

"Weston, you say? No, no I don't think so. You might find word in Hazelton. Unless you plan to go straight to the creeks?"

Hardly. And certainly not with Emily and Clara along. Not to mention their maid. "Thank you, I will inquire in Hazelton. But tell me, if you were an enthusiastic young man coming north to look for gold in this region, where would you go?"

Booth gave him a thoughtful look. "That depends. Do you have any personal interest in the matter?"

"My only interest is to find young Weston. I had enough of searching for gold in the Klondike."

That earned him a grin. "I see. Well, if your Weston is a young man, and one in a hurry, I would expect him to head towards Manson Creek."

"Which is where?"

"From Hazelton, it is hundred or so miles to the Omineca diggings. A series of trails will take you there by way of Fort Babine and Takla Lake. The creeks fan out across the region, as I imagine they did in the Klondike. Manson Creek is one of them.

"And why there?"

"It is currently one of the more popular of the gold streams, and is rumored to be where the next big strike will occur."

"Obviously you don't believe that."

A shrug, accompanied by a half-smile. "I am no longer young or particularly enthusiastic. I consider myself a businessman, and as a businessman, I value the investment that pays consistently and for a long time."

"But that's—that's not the point of looking for gold," Trent broke in.

"Exactly," Booth said, his smile widening. To Granville he said, "There are others on the *Caledonia* who are returning to claims on or near Manson Creek. It might be that they have answers for you."

Granville nodded. "Thank you. I do have one last question. Have you ever heard the story of very old Chinese coins being found somewhere near the gold diggings?"

The whistle blew shrilly as the boat rounded the bend.

Booth smiled and nodded. "Everyone has some version of that tale, it seems," he said, once his voice could be heard. "Some have it that such coins were found near Telegraph Creek, over on the Stikine, some that they were found near Barkerville, or even north of Victoria. Others call it a myth. The Indians will not discuss it. Myself, I do not believe the story. I have never personally seen such a thing in all my trips to the region."

Granville noted that the old man's gaze had moved beyond him. Before he had time to wonder who Booth saw, a hand on his sleeve gave him the answer.

"Mr. Granville, please forgive the interruption, but I have need of your assistance," a soft voice said.

Emily. And sounding not at all like herself.

"Excuse me," he said, receiving a slight bow in return, and turned to face his fiancée. "What is wrong?"

"Can you come with me?"

"Of course," he said, following as she turned to make her way hastily across the deck towards the inner door.

"I'm sorry to have interrupted," she said again.

They emerged into a corridor that seemed very quiet after the din on deck. "Emily. Tell me what's wrong."

"It's Clara."

"Is she ill?"

Emily shook her head. "No. It may be worse than that."

"Worse than that?"

"She wants to go home," Emily said. "She says she hates boats, and she hates travel and she thinks she might hate me too, for convincing her to go. And she wants to go back to Vancouver—immediately. Only not by boat, because she says she'll never take another boat so long as she lives. And she doesn't care if I come or not, but she says she'll take her maid, because she must have one, and I don't need one and this is all my fault anyway."

She paused to take a breath. "Oh, Granville. What am I to do?"

He bit back a smile at the melodrama, because her unhappiness was real. "Is Clara seasick?"

His calm response seemed to have an effect, because she drew in a deep breath and the tears that had glinted in her eyes disappeared. "No. No, just deeply unhappy, I think. Why, what are you thinking?"

"That a stroll on the deck will do her all the good in the world. Fresh air and new faces can shake the misery out of anyone. And I need to question several young men heading north to the goldfields. I thought perhaps the two of you could help me?"

Emily smiled at that. "And Clara just happened to pack one of her newer dresses," she said. "We will need to dress for dinner in any case, and it would be wonderful to stroll on the deck beforehand. Oh Granville, you are a genius. Having a reason to wear that dress and an appreciative audience will cheer her immediately. Thank you. We will see you on deck shortly."

Emily stretched up to kiss his cheek, then she was gone in a whirl of skirts. Granville was smiling as he headed back on deck, glad of the moment of levity.

The grin faded as he surveyed his fellow passengers. Who to talk to next?

A well-dressed man who looked like he had some native blood caught his eye. Scott had pointed him out earlier—he was one of the mining recorders for the Omineca goldfields. Jimmy—something. Anchoring his hat more firmly against the wind, he strode towards him.

"I'm John Granville, and I understand you know something about the Omineca diggings," he said on reaching him, and put out his hand.

"Jimmy Wells, and I'm glad to know you," said the other, pumping his hand. "And yes, I guess you could say I know something about the diggings. What did you want to ask?"

"I gather that the rush was over a quarter-century or so ago, and yet many of the passengers I've talked to are heading up there either to work existing claims or to stake new ones. Is there gold?"

"There is indeed," Wells said with a laugh. "And it is spread out over a number of creeks, right through the region. Not as much of it as in earlier days, not enough to drag starry-eyed youngsters from half-a-continent away, but enough to be worth your while if you're willing to work for it. And of course, everyone hopes for that one-in-a-million strike. It could still be there, y'know. The region's big enough, and even now it hasn't all been explored."

"What kind of mining?"

"Mostly placer, though Colonel Bech over there," and he indicated a tall man with a stiff posture, who stood with a large party against the railing, "Is with Kildar Mining out of Ottawa, and has hopes of developing a bigger operation in the area. For now, though, he's placer mining like the rest of them."

Granville was impressed. Placer mining was hard, dirty work that never ended. "I imagine it's pretty country up there."

"Sure is. It's God's country. Except for the blackflies."

Granville laughed.

"Pardon my asking, but I'm confused," Wells said. 'If you're not mining yourself, what brings you up this way so early in the season?"

"I'm searching for an old friend who came north looking for gold earlier, one Rupert Weston. I'm told he was headed this way. I have urgent news for him, and am hoping to get a lead on where to start to look for him. You ever heard of him?"

Wells' quick glance noted the quality of Granville's attire, and acknowledged the Oxbridge accent. "This news must be pretty urgent to come all this way with so little to go on. An old friend, you say?"

The mining recorder was no fool. "The son of a family friend. There is news for him, from England, that he'll want to hear. My brother asked me to find him, and deliver that news. I'm an investigator, you see."

"An investigator—you're with the Pinkerton's agency?"

Pinkerton's again. "I have my own firm, but am considering affiliating with them."

Emily was right about it being an interesting option for their firm, especially given how often the Pinkerton's name came up when he said he was a detective. As far as he knew, the Pinkerton's Agency had no affiliations in British Columbia, but since William Pinkerton—son of the founder and now co-head of the agency— was a friend of his sister Louisa's, it might be interesting to open a discussion with him. Some kind of connection might prove beneficial to both firms.

Wells nodded, seemingly reassured, though he now looked puzzled. "This—Weston, was it?—when did he come north?"

"He left Vancouver in February and made it as far as Port Essington. I'm not sure when he left there."

"And he's not on board?"

"No. First thing I checked."

"Then he's either still in Port Essington, or he hired someone to paddle him up-river. Have you talked to any of the Tsimshian?"

"Not yet."

Wells nodded. "Come with me."

3 3

Clara glanced down at the rapids, then out at the thick forests and snowy mountain peaks stretching beyond the river. Swishing her long skirts out of the way, she beamed up at the young miner who was guiding her along the railing.

"It is indeed beautiful here, but so wild and lonely. And mining—I simply can't believe you're going to spend the next six months doing such hard work, Mr. Barnes," Clara said. "It's—inspiring, I think is the word."

Emily watched the two of them, hiding her smile as the young man reddened.

"It's just what I do, Miss Miles," he said. "And when I hit the mother lode, why then it will all pay off. I could—I could even live in Victoria, and come calling one day."

"Thank you," Clara said. "Though I live in Vancouver."

"Oh, oh I'm sorry. I thought you'd be in the big city."

She smiled at him. "Vancouver will be the bigger city one day, you'll see."

"I'm sure it will. If you think so."

"But tell me more about your work," Clara said. "Where do you look for gold, and how do you know to look there?"

He laughed. "You do me too much credit, miss. No one really knows where to look for gold, but there are signs, you see."

"Signs?"

"Sure. The kind of gravel on a stream-bed, where glaciers might have been. Like that. That's why me and my partner filed a couple claims on Manson Creek. We'd heard it was proving a rich one, and then we found signs of long-gone glaciers. So we staked 'er."

"And are there still claims available on that creek, Mr. Barnes?" Emily asked.

He glanced over at her, and nodded, then his gaze returned to Clara, who was making little patting motions to adjust her bonnet against the wind coming off the river. "Yes, miss, though those of us working there like to think all the good claims are taken."

"I wonder," Clara began, then left off to fuss with the cherry ribbons on her bonnet, which kept coming loose.

"Yes, miss?" Mr. Barnes prompted.

Emily had to admire the way Clara kept his focus fully on her, but she wondered what her friend was leading up to.

"I promised my brother I'd try to find a friend of his, and pass on a message. A Mr. Weston. I don't suppose you've heard news of him?" And Clara peeped up at her admirer from under the bonnet's brim.

"Can't say as I have. Was he coming up this way?"

Clara nodded. "He told my brother he was heading north of Hazelton, and that he was going to find gold or die trying. That's the area you work in, is it not?"

"Well, 'north of Hazelton' isn't very specific, and it covers a big area, but yes, it is," Mr. Barnes said.

"I do hope to find him, and I'm not sure where to look," Clara said. "But tell me, if you were coming here for the first time this year, and determined to find gold, where would you go?"

Emily felt like cheering her on. Clara was inspired.

"Well, I guess I'd choose Manson Creek—it's still got the best payouts. But if I were feeling contrary-like, I might head to Lost Creek. Some say it's the least explored and hides the real riches."

"Thank you," Clara said, patting his arm. "And isn't that the dinner bell I hear?"

"Indeed it is," Emily said, coming forward to link arms with her friend. "We'd best not be late, since we're seated with the Captain tonight. It was very nice to meet you, Mr. Barnes."

"Miss," he said, doffing his hat to them both. "The pleasure was surely mine." And the glance he cast at Clara left no doubt that he meant it.

IN THE MAHOGANY-LINED DINING ROOM, passengers quickly made their way to the white linen-topped tables they'd been assigned. Above the lingering smell of wood smoke that clung to everything, something smelled wonderful. Emily thought she could smell roast beef, and something buttery. Mashed potatoes?

She watched the assembly of her fellow-diners with great interest. She and Granville, were seated at a round table for ten. Clara and Scott were at the same table, along with Mr. Valleau, the Gold Commissioner for the Omineca region, several investors heading for the mining fields, and a missionary and his wife returning to Kispiox, the Indian village north of Hazelton.

Conversation was general, and she was happy to talk with Mr. Valleau about his work—though she had to force herself not to stare at his enormous mustache, which he habitually stroked as he talked. He was very helpful in advising her on what accommodations she might find in Hazelton—useful in case she couldn't convince Granville to let her come north with him.

Their waiter, who was apparently on his first journey with the *Caledonia*, amused everyone by taking affront at one passenger's conviction that the tinned peaches served for dessert must have come from Ontario, as only Ontario peaches could taste so good. He took great delight in producing a can from the galley, clearly labeled "Cuttings Packing Company, California."

Fascinating as this odd social mix was, Emily couldn't wait for dinner to end, and for an opportunity to exchange information with Granville and Scott. And Trent, of course.

Finally the meal was over. As the other diners left the room in small clusters, chatting, the five of them gathered at the far end of the dining room, where there were chairs set out for those who wanted to sit for a time after dinner.

"Well?" said Emily. "Were you able to find any news of Weston?"

"Nothing so far," Granville said. "Which isn't surprising, since he went north some months ago, and most of our fellow travelers are heading north for the first time this year. I noted a large group of Chinese on the boat, so I hope to speak with them tomorrow. I'd be more comfortable with a better description of where Weston might have gone than I have so far."

"Mr. Barnes advised me that Manson Creek and Lorne Creek were the places he'd most likely go, were he only now heading north looking for his first strike," Clara said.

It surprised and pleased Emily to hear her friend speak up so quickly. Usually Clara had little to say at first, and made most of her comments in quick, seemingly frivolous asides.

Clara could deny it all she wanted, but she really was getting caught up in this investigation business.

"Excellent," Granville said. "Mr. Booth, who also has placer holdings, confirmed that Manson Creek is rumored to be the best bet for a strike. He made no mention of Lost Creek, though. Did Mr. Barnes tell you why he chose it?"

"Yes, he said people think it might hold real possibilities," Clara said.

"Thank you. Tomorrow Scott and I will see what we can learn of the country from the Chinese and the Indians on board. Trent..."

"I'll talk to the crew," Trent said. "Our waiter tonight—he seemed the sort to pay attention to what's going on. It shouldn't be hard to get him to talk."

"Just get him riled up," Scott said with a guffaw as Clara giggled. "Good planning, though."

"Since tomorrow is likely to be a busy day, I think perhaps Clara and I will adjourn to the ladies lounge for a quiet cup of tea before we retire. It has been rather a tiring day," Emily said, with a glance at her friend, who nodded. Clara was looking much happier than she had earlier in the day, but she was still too pale.

"In which case, we three will adjourn to the smoking lounge, and see what else we can learn," Granville said. "We will see you in the morning, ladies."

WEDNESDAY, MAY 2, 1900

Granville gripped the railing with both hands as the *Caledonia* drifted backwards down the rapids, bracing himself as the boat crashed into the rocks, lurching heavily.

"You think we'll make it?" Scott said.

Granville laughed, the wind driving the sound back into his face. Since this was the boat's third try at the rapids, Scott's concern was warranted.

After an uneventful first day of steady progress up-river, he'd begun to hope the trip would be an easy one for Emily and her friend. So far, their second day was proving to be a bit more challenging. And Clara was obviously no traveler.

"This boat's been making this same journey every summer for years. I'm sure we'll get there. Eventually," he added, bracing himself again as an attempt to run the fourth and final shallow channel resulted in another crash.

There was a loud grating sound and a clattering. He looked up to see the wheel throwing water and gravel over the pilothouse.

"What do you think they're doing now?" Scott asked, watching as the boat seemed to move sideways, and several of the crew raced to untie a skiff from the back deck. Then the engines slowed, the boat stopped moving, and the huge wheel stilled.

"I have no idea, but they seem to," Granville said, watching in fascination.

It was much quieter now, and he could hear the whistle of the wind and somewhere, the cry of an eagle. "Emily should be seeing this," he added without thinking.

"I quite agree," came her voice from behind him, and a hand tucked under his elbow.

"How is Miss Clara?" Scott said.

"She's drinking tea and pretending she isn't here," Emily said with a smile. "I can't believe she's missing this," and she waved a hand at the activity around them, the white-chopped water racing by, and the rugged, thickly green land around them. "But what are they doing?"

Granville looked to see the skiff being lowered into the water, then seven crew members clambered in and one end of a long heavy cable was handed down to them. They rowed ashore, then made fast to a huge fir tree that looked as if it had stood for hundreds of years.

Once the cable was securely attached to the tree and to the capstan, they signaled the captain, who nodded, and bellowed to the Indian pilot "Go 'head capstan."

The engine sped up, the wheel turned faster and faster, and the boat seemed to shiver from stem to stern. With a tremendous grating, the *Caledonia* began to move across the sandbar, and slowly but steadily upstream.

Emily clapped her hands. "This is amazing. I'm so glad I'm here to see this."

Despite his concern for her safety, Granville was glad for it too. The look of delight on her face would stay with him, no matter what else this journey brought them.

Scott was shaking his head. "We're going to have to keep doing this, you know," he said, waving a hand at the straining cable and the boiling rapids beyond it. "It could take forever to get to Hazelton."

"This is called lining. We do it whenever the river's too low," said a voice from behind them. "But the *Caledonia*'s flat-bottomed, built shallow so she can run this river; she only needs six inches or so of clearance. And the river's pretty good this spring—there should be deeper water ahead. We'll make better time then."

Granville turned to see the purser, smiling at Emily.

"Not to worry, my dear," the man told her. "Our captain knows this route well, and we'll be safely docked in Hazelton before you know it."

But in the next four hours, they had advanced only a hundred yards or so.

A hundred very noisy yards, what with the boiling of the river, the screeching of the steam, the grinding of the cable over the capstan, the grating of the boat on the rocks, and over it all, the Captain's shouted commands: "Stop steamboat." "Go 'head capstan." "Stop capstan." "Go 'head steamboat."

And Emily loved it. Every tedious minute of it.

Granville watched her—one moment fascinated with the process of getting the *Caledonia* through the sandbars, the next chatting cheerfully with the Gold Commissioner about the challenges of maintaining law in this wild country.

He'd known she had a questing imagination and an adventurous spirit but this—she'd have thrived in the Klondike itself.

"THE PURSER TELLS me that this canyon is easier now because the river's lower." Emily said some hours later. "And that we're climbing about five feet higher with every mile we go. You can feel the steam engine straining, can't you?"

She was right. The thrumming reverberated through the boat, and Granville felt it through his feet all the way to his eyebrows.

"I'm still amazed nothing was damaged, the way we kept falling back on the rocks. Apparently only a little of the wood trim was knocked off. And did you know that we've yet to face the Hornet's Nest Rapids and Devil's Elbow Canyon?" she went on, eyes fixed on the rapids ahead.

"Sorry you came?"

"Never!" Emily looked at him, eyes alight. "Don't tease. But, Granville? I've some information about the Judge's Chinese coin. Actually, it's part of the reason I wanted to come on this journey."

She hesitated. "I'm not sure if it's important, but I find it fascinating, and I think it might be."

Was she nervous? "Then tell me about it."

"I could find out nothing more about the coin in the libraries, so when we got back to Vancouver I asked Bertie. He looked worried and tried to change the subject, but eventually I persuaded him to let me talk with his uncle."

No wonder she was nervous. She must have gone to Chinatown with only Bertie as protection. Again!

But she was safe now, and he wasn't her father. "And what did you learn?"

Emily's face lit up and she leaned towards him. "Bertie's uncle and an ancient scholar of their people were able to tell me that they have legends of a monk from China who travelled to this country more than a thousand years ago. And that the Judge's coin came from this journey. Which confirms everything that Ah Quan told you.

And Bertie's uncle seems sure that this monk, traveling on behalf of the Chinese emperor, came to this area first, and then traveled farther down the coast to first California and then Mexico. If that were true, would it increase the coin's value? To a collector, I mean?"

No wonder she was excited. "If the coins were that old, and proved that an Oriental explorer discovered North America before Columbus, it could definitely increase the value of the coins."

"So it means we're right to think Weston might be looking for coins rather than gold?"

"It's a strong possibility. I just wonder how important those coins might be to the Chinese?"

"And to the local tribes. Mrs. Harrison says it is because of that Chinese monk that they consider those lands sacred. Presumably the coins would be considered sacred too."

"I'll have to see if I can find out anything more from our fellow passengers," Granville said.

"And I learned something more over tea in the ladies' lounge," Emily said with a smile.

"Is that where Clara is now?" Granville cast his eye over what he could see of the deck from where they stood near the bow. There were few women on this voyage, and the only bonnets he could see on deck, other than Emily's, belonged to native women.

"Yes, she finds it too rough. Not even Mr. Barnes is enough to persuade her to come up on deck," Emily said with a grin. "Then too, she has met a Mrs. Rowlatt and they seem to get along."

Emily glanced up at him, then her eyes were fixed on the churning water again. "But I've learned that there is a hotel in Hazelton, and it is quite safe. And also, a number of the old prospectors make their home there, and they have quite a knowledge of the area. They might know more of the coins or exactly where Weston might have gone."

As she said this, the *Caledonia* gave a mighty shudder, and her bow dipped, then rose high, then dipped again.

Emily gasped, and clutched his arm tightly, but didn't look away from the churning waters. "Look how close we are coming to that cliff. And all that snow. And then we turn, and barely avoid the islands. The purser said the captain knows what he's doing, though."

"He has done this before."

"No, apparently he is new to the *Caledonia*. This is his first run up the Skeena with her. The previous captain, a Mr. Bonsor, who made the run for the last fourteen years, is bringing up the new ship. So our friends will be in good hands," she said with a smile.

"Unfortunately," she added for his ears only.

Granville hid his smile and squeezed her arm in acknowledgement. It amazed him how good Emily was at gaining information from people.

It was too bad that women weren't detectives. She would have made a good one.

35

THURSDAY, MAY 3, 1900

I t was the afternoon of the third day when they reached Hazelton. With a long blast of her whistle, the *Caledonia* landed, scraping against the rocky bottom as she dropped anchor.

Emily winced at the sound, steadying herself as she looked ashore. What looked like the whole town had gathered along the waterfront to welcome them, all waving and cheering. She could see whites, Indians, a few Chinese—even the dogs were there, howling.

"Oh Emily, a town," said Clara clutching her arm. Then, after she'd looked a little closer, "But is this all? Was this what we've really come all this way to reach?"

"Well, most people who come here are going on to the goldfields or somewhere inland," Trent said. "It isn't exactly somewhere people plan to visit."

"And how are we to get ashore?" Clara demanded, having apparently realized that there was no wharf. "Don't tell me we have to get in *that*."

Glancing at the small boat that was rowing out to them, Emily stifled a grin. It looked exciting to her. "It won't be that bad. And at least it isn't raining."

"And see, the boat has a flat-bottom, so it will be stable," Trent said.

Noting Clara's brows twitching together, Emily said quickly, "If you were to write a letter today, I believe the *Caledonia* would take it back with her when she sails tomorrow. They're hoping to be back in Port Essington by late tomorrow evening, so your letter would reach town by mid-week. And Mr. O'Hearn should be back by then. I'm sure he'd be most interested in your impressions of a true frontier town."

Clara looked around her again, this time more slowly. "Yes," she said. "Yes, I could do that. And I could write about the voyage, too, and how the boat shook as we went through the rapids. And how I feared the ship would come to pieces when we slid into the rocks."

"That was nothing," put in Trent before Emily could shush him. "But I'll bet he'll wish he was here with you," he added, redeeming himself—even if he didn't know it.

Clara gave a decided nod. "Indeed he will. And so he should."

She watched the activity on the shore for a long moment. "This is quite fascinating, in a—primitive kind of way."

Emily hid a smile as her friend drew in a deep breath of the crisp, fir-scented air.

"It even smells different," Clara said.

"Are you three packed and ready to disembark?" came Granville's voice from behind them.

"We've been ready for hours," Trent said. "I can carry all our bags up when it's our turn."

"I HEARD an odd tale on the boat," Granville said, glancing down the battered wooden table at the seamed and weathered faces on either side. Each man had a filled glass and several empties in front of him, and most had an ashtray or a spittoon within easy reach.

"Something about a Buddhist monk being in America long before the British. Apparently there were Chinese coins and other objects discovered. And they were talking about the area somewhere near the Skeena. You fellows ever hear any of this?"

His question garnered a smile, a couple of winks, and raised glasses, which were promptly emptied. Apparently the town had run out of whiskey several weeks before, and the barrels of whiskey the *Caledonia* carried north had turned the hotel bar into the most popular place in town.

As soon as the sternwheeler docked, Granville had checked their party into the hotel. He'd seen Emily, Clara and Clara's maid to their chamber, and promised to be back in time to escort them to dinner. Then he, Scott and Trent had headed straight for the bar and this table of old miners.

He'd shown them Weston's photo with no result. It was heartening to see a stronger response to the Chinese coin story.

"Sure, I've heard that one," the fellow beside him said. "Not about the Skeena, though. Apparently a couple miners found a cache of coins near Cassiar."

"I heard the find was near Telegraph Creek," the man across the table said. "Friend of mine heard it from the Chinese interpreter for Judge Harrison."

He looked around the table, grinned at the grizzled fellow beside him. "Remember Harrison? He used to be the circuit judge up Barkerville way. Anyway, this interpreter found those coins at Telegraph Creek, up the Stikine River. The Judge had one of the coins valued in San Francisco, and it was said to be a really old Buddhist token."

Several others murmured their agreement with the second man's version.

It seemed that the story of an early Chinese discovery of the area was widespread, if not necessarily accurate. Granville wondered if the story variants gave it more credibility, or less? It was something he might enjoy discussing with Weston.

If he ever caught up with him.

"And is Cassiar anywhere near Telegraph Creek?" he asked.

That got a laugh. "Well, that depends how you count distance," the first man said. "They're in the same general area, but on different rivers, so maybe a hundred miles apart."

"It's tough country, though, so you're probably talking a six or seven day journey," someone else said.

"And whereabouts is Telegraph Creek from here?" Granville said.

"North and west a ways. Cassiar is even further north."

"And how would I get there?"

"You could go overland, but it's mountainous country between here and there. You'd be best to go back down to Port Essington, then go by canoe up the Stikine. It'd take you four or five days, at least," the first man said.

"Of course, you could wait for the end of the season, say around October," the second man added. "That's when the *Caledonia* takes the Indian cannery workers back up the Stikine to their homes in and around Telegraph Creek."

Granville hoped this particular story didn't prove accurate, or at least that Weston hadn't learned of it. It made the journey they'd already taken sound simple. And if Weston had decided to go to Telegraph Creek, it compounded the problem of how to keep Emily and her friend safe.

He debated telling his audience what the Judge and Ah Quan had told him, but decided to keep it quiet for now. If there was value in the coins, telling too many people where he thought Weston had gone could just make it worse for the lad.

To say nothing of making it easier for Heade to find him.

He'd have to make sure Emily knew about keeping her enquiries quiet, too.

***

"WHAT DO you make of their stories?" Scott asked as the three of them strode back along the plank sidewalk towards their hotel.

Granville shook his head. "Gold-seekers," he said. "Great story-tellers, but the truth gets embroidered out of all recognition."

Trent grinned at the two of them. "I know a few trout-fishers like that," he said. "They can tell you all the best fishing-holes, but they all pale in comparison to the monster fish that got away, the one that lurks in this deep, secret pool that only they know about."

Granville laughed. "Exactly."

"But are we any closer to finding Weston?" Scott said.

"Manson Creek would be a reasonable place to start," Granville said. "There seem to be plenty of conflicting rumors about Chinese coins, but we had the story direct from Ah Quan. And he told us to talk to the local tribes. They know the land.

We'll need to hire a Gitksan guide in Kispiox in any case, so I'd say we'd best hold off and ask any further questions there."

"Wonder what Ah Quan told Heade's boys?" Scott said.

"Even if they managed to trail me there and then find him, I doubt he told them much," Granville said. "I suspect it's our trail they'll be following. We need to stay well ahead of Heade."

"So when do we leave?" Trent said.

"Tomorrow, if the pack trains come in and we can rent horses," Granville said.

"Pack trains?" Trent said.

"The regions' fur traders, both Indian and white, have been out on their trap lines all winter," Scott said. "Everything they've caught will be heading here."

"Is that why the *Caledonia* hasn't left yet?" Trent said, his eyes bright.

"Yes," Granville said. "They're expecting quite a number of very heavily laden pack trains in the next few days."

"You mean all the available horses are used in the pack trains?" Trent said. "So we're stuck here waiting for the next one to come in?"

"That's it. But we'll pack up tonight, and hope to be able to leave first thing in the morning," Granville told him.

"The sooner we get underway the better," Scott said. "I bought most of our provisions earlier, while you were getting the ladies settled."

Granville nodded his thanks, his thoughts returning to his fiancée and her friend. He still couldn't decide what to do about them. He didn't feel right leaving them, and he had a nagging feeling that he should be taking them back to Vancouver on the *Caledonia's* return trip the following day.

The problem wasn't the town itself. Hazelton was proving even smaller than he'd expected, but for a frontier town, it seemed remarkably civilized. Emily and Clara might be safe here, but not in the town's only hotel. Not after the load of liquor the *Caledonia* had brought for the hotel's bar.

There had to be another solution, but he'd be damned if he could think of one. He looked up to find they'd reached the hotel.

"You want to check over the provisions?" Scott was asking him.

"Good idea. I've had a few thoughts about..." he began. Then stopped as a soft voice came from behind him.

"Mr. Granville? Is that you?"

"You go ahead. I'll catch up," he told Scott, and turned around.

"Mrs. Rowlatt?" he said, recognizing her from the boat and doffing his hat. "A pleasure to see you again."

"Thank you. It is mutual. And especially because I have a favor to ask of you."

STRIDING through the heavy glass doors of their hotel, Granville asked for Emily at the desk, then found his way to the private parlor, stomping mud off his heavy boots as he did so. Emily looked up at his entrance, putting down a tattered pamphlet she was reading. He was amused to note that it purported to be a guide to the gold fields of Omineca.

"Have you learned anything?" she said.

He grinned. "We have indeed," he said, looking around the small, cramped room. "But where is Clara?"

"She is upstairs, resting from the journey."

"Leaving you alone? Here?"

Emily frowned at him. "Don't be silly, it is perfectly safe. The owner's wife looks in on me from time to time. But tell me everything."

"We found nothing new on the Chinese coins. While the story seems to be fairly well known, the details vary, and many of them point to Telegraph Creek for the find the Judge told Weston about."

"How very confusing," Emily said. "You look tired. Would you care for tea?"

"Please."

He watched her while she poured, stirred in the sugar he preferred, and passed him the cup. "Thank you."

"So several people talk about Telegraph Creek as the site for that find?"

He nodded, sipping his tea. It tasted wonderful after the rain-thick wind he'd been fighting through all afternoon.

"How far is that from here?"

"It is north and west of here, almost as far west as Port Essington, and across two mountain ranges. Think of the mountains you saw from the boat, and imagine climbing over them."

"Most of those mountains were snow-clad. And when Weston came through here last month, it would have been worse." Emily took a sip of her own tea. "I'm sure there must be a more direct route to this place, if it is that far west."

"There is," he said with a grin. Her thought processes never ceased to amaze him—and she seldom missed anything. "Traveling up the Stikine River from Port Essington."

"But did Ah Quan not say his cousin travelled from Hazelton?"

"Indeed he did. And from there to a river that they believed to be a tributary of either the Skeena or the Peace River. The Peace runs quite a way east of here."

"So the Telegraph Creek part of the rumor is wrong. Unless there was a second find?" She looked excited. "Do you think that is possible?"

"I'm afraid not. Too many of the other details are the same."

"Too bad. Though it's probably easier if you and Mr. Weston are both looking for the same site," she said with a mischievous look. "And were the other stories any better?"

"No. But I've learned that both Fort Babine and Manson Creek are more-or-less in the center, if a little to the south, of the region that Ah Quan's cousin likely travelled to. Depending, of course, on if they were closer to the Stikine or the Peace. And since Manson Creek is also held to have the most potential of any of the current placer mining sites..."

"You will go to first to Fort Babine and then to Manson Creek, looking for news of Weston, as well as any more accurate rumors about the finding of the Chinese coins," she finished for him.

"Exactly," he said, delighted with her.

"So when do you plan to leave?" Emily asked him.

"Tomorrow, if the pack trains come in and we can rent horses."

"Pack trains?"

"The local fur-traders have been out trapping for fur all winter," Granville said. "Most of it will now be brought in by pack train and sold to the Hudson's Bay Company or to Cunningham's, the local store here, then shipped out on the *Caledonia*. The town will be filled with great long strings of horses and mules, laden with furs."

Emily glanced at her fur-lined gloves. "What kind of furs?"

"Mostly ermine and marten for the clothing trade, and beaver for top hats."

"I'll have to tell Clara. She'll be thrilled," Emily said. "Is that why the *Caledonia* is still here?"

"That's it."

"And—all the available horses are used in the pack trains? There are none for rent?"

He smiled at her. "Exactly. So we're stuck waiting for the next pack train to come in. But we hope to leave first thing in the morning."

She didn't look happy, but she nodded. "Very well. Clara and I will be here when you return."

"Not in this hotel. It's not the right place for the two of you. Not alone."

"But it's the only hotel in town."

"As to that, I think I have a solution about where the two of you can stay," Granville told her. "Mrs. Rowlatt has asked whether you and Clara would be willing to stay with her while I'm away. She has an extra room, and her husband will be heading to the goldfields with us. Clara's maid can share with her own maid. The Rowlatts are a very respectable couple, and she says she'll be glad of the company."

"But Granville..."

"I couldn't leave you and Clara here—it's too rough. And I can't take the two of you with us, as that's even rougher."

"But I'd be fine. In fact, I'd love it," Emily said.

He grinned. "Yes, you probably would. But would Clara?"

Emily's face fell, then a small smile peeped out. Probably picturing her fashionable friend in the wilderness, he thought.

"Clara and Mrs. Rowlatt get along very well," Emily said. "She could stay with her, and I could come with you."

He should have expected that. Granville thought quickly. "Yes, that would work. We'll have to find the minister that journeyed up with us, then. Pierce, wasn't it?"

"What? What do you mean?"

"Clara would be fine with Mrs. Rowlatt, but the only way you can accompany me, alone, into that back country is if we're married. I'm sure a brief ceremony can be arranged quickly."

Emily just looked at him, speechless.

"We are engaged," he added helpfully, imagining Mrs. Turner's reaction if her youngest daughter came back from this little adventure already married.

"But..." Emily began, then her quick mind must have laid out for her all of the implications of what she'd been suggesting. "Oh," she said, then laughed a little. "Mama's face," she explained.

He grinned. "Yes, I was picturing that myself."

"Fine, so I will stay here. And how can I best help your investigation, while Clara and Mrs. Rowlatt are discussing fabrics and comparing patterns?"

He didn't want to know how Clara and her new friend would manage to do that in this remote wilderness.

"Scott and I haven't been able to learn much so far. The lead we have on Weston is still a thin one. But there must be a wealth of local knowledge in this town," Granville said. "Anything you can learn about which gold areas Weston might have been directed to would be useful. And I've noted that you're very good at persuading people to give you information."

Emily smiled. "Thank you. It is a useful trait in a detective, don't you think?"

"Hmmm," he said. "I'd also like Trent to stay in town with you, but I'm worried he'll find an excuse to come after Scott and me."

"Take him along, Granville. He'd hate to miss this, and we won't need him. And it's enough that I have to miss it, without making him do so," Emily said. "We're safe enough here. And I'll be careful. I promise."

Experience had taught him that Emily's version of being careful didn't quite match his. But unfortunately Trent was no better. "Your word on it? I couldn't live with myself if I go after Weston and some harm comes to you."

She started to say something, then stopped and looked at him for a moment. "You really mean that, don't you?"

Granville nodded.

"Then I will be careful to bring no harm to myself. Or Clara," she added with a tiny grin.

"Thank you. Then yes, I will take Trent with us. If you need me, send word to Manson Creek, care of Jimmy Wells, who is the mining recorder there. I'll make sure he knows how to get word to us."

"Yes, I remember Mr. Wells from the boat," she repeated. "I'll do that. Would it be safe to send any information I uncover about Weston or his quest that way also?"

"I think so." He watched her face for a moment. "I do still have a concern about Heade and his gang. They should be reaching Port Essington themselves in a few days, though I hope it will take them some time to arrive here."

"I'm just glad I don't have that photo any longer," Emily said. "They won't care about me at all now.

She sounded more confident that he felt. "I doubt my associate in Port Essington will succeed in misdirecting Heade for too long, so I'm expecting that he and his gang will show up in Hazelton in the next week or so," Granville said. "Please try to keep a low profile, especially if you're asking questions about Weston. That could draw Heade's attention."

"Of course I will," said Emily.

36

FRIDAY, MAY 4, 1900

In the cramped bedroom the three of them shared, Scott looked up from the list he'd been checking off and scanned the jumble of packs and bags around them. "It looks pretty good to me. You think we're missing anything?"

A gleam of sun through the curtains reflected off the buckles of their canvas rucksacks. It would be a good day for traveling. "The mules to carry it all, perhaps?" Granville said.

His partner gave a quick laugh, then glanced at the pencil-covered pages he'd spread on one of the narrow beds, a frown pulling at his thick brows. "You think we're taking too much?"

"Relax. I'm just hoping the pack trains do arrive today."

The door swung open, and Trent burst in, bringing with him a hint of the cold freshness of early morning air.

"They're coming! The first of the fur trains, I mean. But there's a lot of men heading for the Omineca, so we need to get there fast, before all the horses are rented."

Without a word, Granville and Scott sprung to their feet and followed him out the door.

THE VILLAGE OF KISPIOX—HOME to the two men they had rented their horses and four pack mules from—proved to be an easy ten mile ride north and west from Hazelton, the trail wide and bordered with stands of alder and thick clusters of hazelnut shrubs.

Granville's tall black gelding shook his head and nickered as if in recognition when they reached the village. Long, narrow wooden buildings with sharply peaked roofs lay along the grassy riverbank, with tall mountain ranges on rising behind them on the west and jagged, snowy peaks to the east.

Granville sat forward in the saddle and tightened his grip on the reins, his attention caught and held by the towering poles of carved and painted wood that guarded the place.

Ah Quan had spoken of what he called the sinister totem poles of Kispiox, but Granville had expected something more ordinary. These were not ordinary. There must be more than thirty of them standing between the buildings and the river, and some of them had to be fifty or sixty feet tall. The wood was weathered, but the features of the fantastical creatures carved on it were clear, some of the paint still bright.

He wished Emily could be there to see them.

"What are those carvings supposed to be?" Trent's voice demanded from behind him.

Granville half-turned in the saddle to look at their assistant's puzzled face. "Never seen totem poles before?"

"Just from the boat, when we went past those islands on our way to Port Essington. Never up close like this. They're amazing. Kinda ugly, but—I keep looking at 'em, y'know?"

"The islands were the Queen Charlottes, and those were Haida totem poles you saw from the boat. I talked to a guy on the boat, knew all about them," Scott said, as he rode up alongside Trent. "These are Gitksan. Different thing entirely. I've no idea what the symbols mean, though. They look a little like the ones we saw in the Yukon—you remember them, Granville?"

"Yes, but they weren't nearly as impressive as these."

"You mean they were shorter. That's because they were Tlingit, and their traditions are different again. Colors are different too, and the totem animals."

"Totem animals?" Trent repeated.

Scott gestured at the carvings. "I think that one might be a frog. It looks kinda the same as the Tlingit carvings. It's probably the symbol of a family here."

"Like a crest?" Granville said, pulling his horse to a halt.

He hadn't paid much attention in Alaska—his focus had been on striking it rich, not on the local cultures, but there was something about these rows of carved poles standing silent guard on the village had him picturing the broad estates and sturdy manor houses he'd known in England.

"Yup. And apparently they tell something about a family's history, too, if you know how to read 'em," Scott said, reining in also. "Maybe Thomas can tell us more. Hey, Thomas!"

One of their Gitksan guides had stopped a little ahead of them, and seemed to be watching their reactions to his village. At Scott's hail, he cantered back. "Yeah?"

"What are the carvings?"

He must be used to the question, Granville thought, because Thomas just nodded.

"Here is Eagle, Raven and Frog. This is Killer Whale, Bear and Wolf," he said. "And here is Man."

"These are totem figures?" Scott said. "For your families? Clans?"

Thomas nodded again. "This tells who owns what. And remembers those who are gone."

"All that?" Trent muttered, staring from one pole to another.

Granville stifled a smile. Trent thought this was complex symbolism? He'd love to hear what their assistant thought of heraldry. Maybe he'd explain it to him one day.

After they found Weston.

"The village looks deserted," Granville said, then caught sight of a wisp of smoke from someone's fire. Cooking, most likely. "Where is everyone?" he asked Thomas.

"These are winter homes. It is Spring, and we go up-river to fish. Mostly salmon."

Which didn't get them any closer to finding Weston. When none of the Indians who'd been part of the pack train had recognized Weston's name or photo, he'd been counting on someone here remembering the man, or even knowing the story of the Chinese miners who had found the coins in the Gitksan's "forbidden land." Now what?

Scott apparently had the same thought, because he asked Thomas, "Is anyone still here who might remember the man we're looking for?"

"Maybe. I will ask, if you have photograph?"

Scott glanced at Granville, who nodded and handed over the picture.

"Come, there is food. You can eat, I go see if they know him," Thomas said, and he led the way into the village. "Or maybe Reverend Pierce can help you."

"Reverend Pierce?" Granville said to Scott as Thomas disappeared into the largest of the longhouses. Now they were closer, he could see there were also a few much smaller houses scattered in behind the larger buildings. "We met him and his wife on the boat, but didn't get much chance to talk. I don't know much about him. Do you?"

Scott shook his head. "No. I wonder how well he knows the natives."

"Pretty well," Trent said from behind them.

Granville jumped a little. Last he'd looked, their assistant had seemed completely engrossed in studying the totem poles, staring from one to the next as though determined to understand them. "Oh?"

Trent flushed. "Sorry," he said as he caught up with them. "Someone told me about the Reverend—on the boat, I mean. I'd forgotten. It didn't seem important."

"We're running blind," Scott told him. "Everything's important when you don't know which detail will matter most."

"I know," Trent said too quickly. "And it won't happen again, I swear."

Granville wondered just how worried the lad was that he might be sent back. Not that he'd go, anyway. Trent would find some way to be part of this journey, and all three of them knew it. But that flash of fear shouldn't surprise him—for most of the lad's life, things hadn't exactly gone his way.

"So anyway," Trent was saying. "This Pierce is a missionary, a Methodist I think, and he lives right here in Kispiox. Been here since 1895. And he's half-Indian himself, so I guess he understands 'em pretty well. Probably a good man to talk you, you think?"

"Probably," Granville said dryly. There was more he felt like saying, but from the look Trent was giving him, the boy knew he should have told them all this before the *Caledonia* docked in Hazelton.

On the other hand, he and the Reverend had been seated at the same table, and he'd not managed to learn any of this.

Scott was grinning at the both of them. He knew Granville rather well, probably knew exactly what he'd like to say. Still, as long as this Pierce was in town, they hadn't lost much time. The horses hadn't even been available earlier, and walking to Kispiox would not have got them here any faster.

THOMAS'S RETURN with the Reverend himself in tow ended their conversation. Pierce was a tall man with intense dark eyes and a friendly manner. Once greetings were exchanged, Pierce held out the photo of Weston that they had given Thomas. "I hadn't realized on the boat that you were seeking this man."

"Yes, we were trying to be discreet about our search," Granville said. "Do you know him?"

"We haven't met, though I do know of him."

"Oh?"

"Yes. He was asking questions of my brethren, both here and in Hazelton. I understand he seeks the region where a number of ancient coins were discovered many years ago."

"Yes, exactly. Do you know if anyone gave him directions to the place?" Granville asked.

"No-one admits to doing so—the taboo on discussing the place and anything related to it still lingers, I fear, even after this many years."

"What taboo?" Trent said.

Pierce smiled gently. "Our shamans—medicine men to you—had forbidden any talk of the ancient ancestors who came to this land many generations ago. According to our history, these ancestors ventured forth in a very large canoe—which was probably a boat of some sort, by the way—from a land far over the western sea, described as unimaginably distant, and eventually came to the hidden valley where the coins were found.

They taught us much, things which became part of our rituals. Discussion with outsiders of anything related to these old ones became taboo. Too many of our people are still reluctant to talk of it."

Clearly the minister didn't share that reluctance, which was lucky for them.

"And you? Can you tell us anything of this place and what was discovered there?" Granville asked him.

"Yes, indeed I can. I remember the story well."

"The story?"

"When the Chinese miners found the buried coins. Word passed from village to village, and we all talked about it. It was some years ago, before I became a Christian, and the shamans had much more power than they do now, not least because they held the stories of these ancestors."

Granville thought again of the family crests and accoutrements he'd known so well in his old life. "Go on."

"Our medicine men had particularly forbidden talk of the valley, where these ancient ancestors lived for a time. They kept their own knowledge close, along with the sacred symbols of the religion left behind by these old ones."

"And this is what the Chinese miners discovered?" Granville asked.

Pierce nodded. "They found the valley, and their discovery of the tokens simply confirmed it. Then one of us chose to tell them even more, and show them some of the other sacred things—Buddhist symbols, you would call them—even name them cousin. Which was further violation of all that had been held close."

"Do you, yourself, know where this valley is?"

A nod.

"Could you take us there?" Trent burst out.

Pierce smiled at him. "No, I have my duties here."

"Do others know of this place?" Granville asked. "Those who could guide us?"

Pierce nodded again.

"So someone could have agreed to take Weston to this valley?"

"Yes. And did," Pierce said, surprising Granville. "He hired two guides here."

Finally a direction. "Where were they going?"

A smile. "Manson Creek, officially."

"And unofficially?"

"He didn't say," Pierce said. "But he carried many provisions."

"And did they return?"

"The guides did, a number of months ago."

"But not Weston?"

"No."

So what had happened to him? "I'd like to talk to one or both of those guides."

Pierce smiled. "I wish I could help you, but now that the *oolichan*, the candlefish, have been brought in, both men have gone north of the Nass River for their summer hunting. I can tell you that they had little to say of the journey, only that Mr. Weston had hired someone else in Manson Creek and discharged them after they and this new guide had talked a little.

I suspect they were glad to return," he added softly, turning over gnarled, work-enlarged hands as though reading answers in them. "The old superstitions die harder than we like to believe."

"Weston was a true tenderfoot—I mean he knew nothing of surviving in this country," Granville said. "How could he have discharged the guides?"

"I gather this new man was very knowledgeable."

"Do you have a name?"

"McDame."

That was the man Booth from the ferry had hired, the one who'd found gold for him at Lorne Creek. What could have convinced such a man to join Weston on what was likely to be a fool's quest?

Granville considered Pierce for a moment. The missionary must know more about McDame than he'd told them, but if so, he wasn't telling them. Granville couldn't read the man, but he liked him.

There was a genuine warmth there, and even when Pierce spoke of the shamans whose way of life his own was displacing, there was compassion and understanding in him, and no hint of triumph or revenge. Granville had seen both reactions as industrialization swept across England, changing the old rules of who held power and who did not. It was one of the things that had driven him to the western wilderness to escape.

"But the family of the guides he hired might know something more. And our guide might know them?"

A slight smile. "Perhaps. But there you are beyond the scope of my responsibility here."

"Can you tell me whom Weston hired as guides?"

Pierce was happy to. And when Granville passed that information to Thomas, he soon had confirmation that Weston had, indeed, gone to Manson Creek and hired McDame there. It seemed neither man had told his family more than that.

"So we're off for Manson Creek, I gather?" Scott said.

Granville nodded. It would take them at least three days to get there, weather and conditions permitting.

And Thomas from Kispiox had agreed to guide them wherever their journey might lead. Which was a relief. His hire hadn't come cheap, but they needed him.

By early afternoon, the sun was out and the breeze had changed to a wind coming directly off the snow-capped mountains. Emily and Clara were comfortably seated with their afternoon tea in Mrs. Rowlatt's small front parlor, which had a view unique in Hazelton—an entire street lined with similarly cozy homes, each with a tilled garden with seedlings beginning to peep through.

Clara had been sorting through a stack of fashion magazines, while Emily stared out the window, wishing she were outside exploring this odd little town. Finally she'd lost patience, and convinced Clara to come for a stroll with her.

"But Emily, I don't understand," Clara said as they walked back towards the harbor. "I thought staying with Mrs. Rowlatt meant we'd spend time with her. And she has all the current magazines, and a lovely eye for patterns."

Emily rolled her eyes.

She couldn't even pretend an interest in fashion magazines, not today. It had been hard enough to bid Granville safe journey that morning. She couldn't face the idea of sitting quietly all afternoon.

"We'll have plenty of time to spend with Mrs. Rowlatt," she

promised her friend. "As soon as I find out these few things for Granville."

Clara sighed noisily.

Emily stopped and listened for a moment. "What was that?"

"Don't be sarcastic with me. You know I hate that."

"No, I mean it. Did you hear anything unusual?"

Clara listened for a moment, then drew her scarf closer around her neck. "Just the wind. Brrrr. I'm going to freeze before we get home."

"It's been warming up nicely. They say it's almost spring."

"That wind comes right off the glaciers up the valley. And it's only warm when the sun is shining and there's no wind, which only happens for about fifteen minutes a day," Clara said. "Can we go?"

"I think I heard a steam whistle."

"But the *Caledonia* just left at noon. And the new boat isn't expected until the week after next."

"I know. But listen."

They could hear what sounded like all the dogs in the village baying. It came from the direction of the harbor.

"They barked like that when the *Caledonia* came in, too. And when she left," Emily said. "Let's walk down to the dock. I want to see what's happening."

As they came out onto the main street, they could see the townspeople gathered along the waterfront, all cheering and pointing. And in the distance was a white sternwheeler with a black funnel, bearing down on the town.

"Something must have gone wrong," Clara said.

Emily raised a hand to shade her eyes, and squinted a little. "I don't think this is the *Caledonia*," she said. "Could Heade's boat have made it all the way from Victoria this quickly? Let's see if we can find someone who knows."

A few minutes of brisk walking along the main street brought them to a slight rise, just above the river, with a clear view of a sternwheeler coming into the harbor. Judging by the throng around her, it was a popular place to watch the boats unload.

She turned to an older, weathered man standing beside her, his eyes fixed on the approaching steamer. "I hadn't thought the *Strathcona* was due in yet?"

"You're right. This isn't the *Strathcona*," he said. "Far's I know, she's still in Victoria. There's a third one, now. Cunningham down at the Port, he's put one over on the Hudson's Bay Company. Got tired of paying their freight rates, he did. He's not only bought his own sternwheeler to beat their tariffs, he hired their captain to run it."

"Captain Bonsor?" Emily said, suddenly putting together what the purser had told her.

"That's him. Knows this river better than anyone. And made good time too, by the looks of it."

"But when I bought tickets, they didn't say anything about a third boat on the Skeena."

Another chuckle. "You probably bought your tickets from a Canadian Pacific Railway ticket agent, right? And CP deal exclusively with the Hudson's Bay Company boats, at least for now."

It could be disastrous for Granville's plans, if Head and his thugs were on board this sternwheeler. But would they be?

"Come along, Clara," Emily said. "Let's go see if we can get a little closer," she said.

EMILY AND CLARA managed to get a little closer to the river, close enough to have a clear view of the *Monte Cristo* and her disembarking passengers. Emily could just make out individual faces as the passengers were rowed ashore.

She stood watching carefully, one hand holding her bonnet low over her eyes, ostensibly against the wind that was gusting down the river. She was glad she'd packed her warmer clothing for this trip. Not only could she wait here without freezing, her narrow navy traveling skirt and plain grey wool jacket were quite different from what she'd worn that day at the racetrack—was it only two weeks ago?

The new sternwheeler was tied up now, and the passengers were being rowed ashore. Built along similar lines to the *Caledonia*, this boat was obviously new and had had an easy run up-river—every surface gleamed with polish or fresh paint.

She craned forward a little to see better, and smiled to see Clara doing the same. Her friend was every bit as curious as she was herself, if much more reluctant to admit it.

If Clara did marry Mr. O'Hearn, as Emily was now convinced she really should, what would that marriage make of her? Would she follow her curiosity, or would she be content to read the fashion magazines and gossip about her family? It wasn't a question Emily had asked herself before, and she found it unsettling to think about now—if only because she feared her friend's answer would be too different from her own.

A shout from the crowd focused her attention on the figures that had stepped onto the beach. A small party of men in business attire were unloaded, followed by a party dressed in the rough clothing of miners. Emily watched both sets of faces carefully.

She'd never seen Heade, and had no idea how he and his gang would present themselves here. They could look like businessmen, as they had at the track, or they could be dressed as miners because they planned to pursue Weston into the mining regions.

Scanning from face to face, she didn't spot anyone she recognized.

"What are you looking for, Emily?" Clara asked. "Do you know someone on this boat?"

"No, of course not," Emily said with a laugh. "I'm just interested in the kind of person that chooses to come north like this, and wondering what their stories are."

Clara gave her a skeptical look. "I see," she said, taking a quick look around them. "Is this another of those things that we should discuss when we are out of this crowd?" she said in a low voice.

Perhaps Clara would decide to become a detective, too? Or help Tim with his journalistic investigations? She had a flair for seeing beneath the surface.

Or maybe her friend just knew her too well, Emily thought, with a tiny grin and a nod at her friend. "Yes, I think that would be prudent."

"You can't tell me that Mr. Granville didn't make you promise to stay safe, because I know he would have. Is this safe?"

Clara definitely knew her too well. "Of course it is."

"Hmmpfff," Clara said. "Are we looking for anyone in particular?"

"Just tell me if you recognize anyone."

They watched in silence for a time. The stretch of beach where the passengers were landing was now thronged with passengers, and it was getting harder to see any of them individually. Emily was just about to suggest going home for tea, when a hiss from Clara had her looking to see what she saw.

"I've seen him before," Clara said. "That thin man, the brown-haired one wearing rough garb."

Emily followed her gaze. "The one beside the taller, black-haired man?" They both looked like miners, and Emily didn't recognize either of them.

"That's the one."

"You've seen him in Vancouver?"

"No, in Victoria."

In Victoria? That meant he wasn't likely connected to Heade.

"I saw him in the park, the day you were attacked," Clara continued. "When you were taking pictures."

No wonder she hadn't noticed him herself. Was it a coincidence?

Granville had said he thought he'd been followed, and her assailant had some way to find her. Had this man been following her that day?

Emily looked more closely at his companion, but still didn't recognize him. Just then the man turned to speak with someone behind him, and she realized the two were part of a larger group.

As she watched, she spotted one whom she was certain was the sentry-crow from the track. Behind him stood the man who looked like Frances. So Heade was here.

"I think that's them," Emily said in an undertone. "Good work, Clara. But don't let them see you looking."

"Of course not," was the quick response. "I'm not a fool. Who are they?"

There seemed to be four of them, with a fifth man a little distance back from the group, and turned the other way. Could that be Heade himself? Emily couldn't see his face, and she didn't dare watch him for too long.

"Later," she said to Clara. She'd need to get a letter to Granville, and quickly. He'd need to know Heade was here nearly a week earlier than they'd expected.

"Then what now?" Clara was asking.

"Hmmm? Oh. Now we try to keep an eye on them, see how many there are, and where they are going. The clothing suggests they plan to head for the Omineca fairly quickly, but Granville might find it useful to know what they do first."

"I thought so," said Clara with a little nod, looking pleased about something.

"What?"

"Are you supposed to be investigating?"

It was a whisper, but it still made Emily nervous. "Of course I am," she said, casting a quick look about them.

All eyes were fixed on the new arrivals, thank goodness, and no-one seemed to be paying them any attention. "Now shhhh."

"Oh very well," said Clara with a little flounce. "Why don't we stroll in that general direction, staying well back, of course."

She didn't have to look so pleased with herself, Emily thought. "Excellent idea."

And they set off to shadow a group of killers that made even Granville nervous. Emily worked very hard at not thinking about what his reaction would have been.

She needn't have worried. The only thing on the group's mind seemed to be food and drink, judging by the speed with which they made for the bar at the hotel. There seemed to be five of them walking as a loose group, chatting easily with each other. None of them seemed to pay any attention to their surroundings on the way, not even the sentry-bird, which struck her as odd.

Perhaps they thought Granville and Scott too far ahead of them to be still in town. Which they were. And the town itself was too small to pose much of a threat to this deadly team.

Just then Clara pulled at her elbow. "Emily," she said very softly, "That's not Heade and his men, is it? The ones who were after you?"

Oh no. Emily hadn't realized Clara had even been listening when Granville told her what he'd learned. "Um," she said, then stopped, not sure what to say.

"Never mind. It clearly is. And we're going home. Right now," Clara said, striding in the direction and towing Emily along with her.

Clearly there was no point in arguing. And she'd learned what she had wanted to know, anyway. Her quarry was unlikely to venture far tonight.

And tomorrow she'd find some way to learn their plans.

38

SATURDAY, MAY 5, 1900

The following morning, Hazelton was wrapped in gray again, the wind flinging huge drops against the windows of Mrs. Rowlatt's cozy house. Emily peered through the rain streaks on the window, watching the street. No-one was about, which either meant it was too early or too wet.

She hoped for the former, because she intended to find out everything she could about Heade and his crew today. If it was raining too hard, she might have to stay indoors.

On the other hand, an umbrella could provide a very good screen for someone who didn't want to be noticed. That bore thinking about. She went looking for Clara.

Who proved to be holed up in the parlor with Mrs. Rowlatt, a cup of hot chocolate, and a stash of fashion magazines. Neither of them had any interest in stirring that morning, even when Emily suggested checking the new stock at Cunningham's, which should be unpacked by now.

"You can go," Mrs. Rowlatt offered. "It's safe enough, just take Molly along."

Molly was the housemaid. Emily considered for a moment. This could serve even better, since Molly would be familiar with the town, but unlikely to argue with her, which Clara was sure to do.

"Thank you, I appreciate it," she said with a smile. "And I'll have her back before lunch."

Mrs. Rowlatt nodded, her attention mostly on an illustration Clara was pointing out to her. Perfect. Emily headed for the kitchen, where she was likely to find Molly.

Despite the weather, Molly seemed happy to be freed from her duties for the morning in order to accompany this odd guest. She couldn't be more than fourteen, Emily thought, glancing sideways at the slim Gitksan girl, but she was a hard worker. Mrs. Rowlatt's little house gleamed.

Emily had spent some time the night before thinking about what Heade might need to do if he planned to follow Granville. He was already several days behind him, and he had to know that. "Do you know where one can rent horses and pack animals to get to the goldfields?" she asked Molly.

The girl didn't look surprised at the question, which Emily found interesting. "No, but I have a cousin," she said, darting a shy glance at Emily. "He might know."

"Is he here in town?"

A nod. "He works at the hotel. In the kitchen."

Perfect. "Then let us go and talk to your cousin."

With a little persuasion, Molly agreed to fetch her cousin onto the back porch, out of view of the street and any curious guests. When he appeared, Molly's cousin was only a few years older than she was, and even shyer.

"You asked about renting mounts?" he said without once looking at her.

"Yes. Are there many places in town that do so?"

One shoulder lifted slightly. "Most of my cousins and their pack trains have left town. There are a few places in town who may still be able to help you."

"There are five men in this group." She had counted, and thought that Thanet must indeed be very rich, or very desperate, to pay for so many men for so long, and that Granville, Scott and Trent were badly outnumbered.

"Then there are only two who could help. One is good. The other," he shook his head. "Greedy."

"Does Molly know where they are?"

He turned to his cousin and they had a quick exchange in a language that sounded harsh—full of quick stops and starts—to Emily's unaccustomed ears. Turning back to her, he said "She can take you there. But only in day. Not safe at night."

"We'll go this morning," Emily told him. "If they are close enough?"

"Yes. Not far," he agreed.

"Thank you. Molly?"

The girl nodded, and led the way down the steps and along the wooden planks leading away from the hotel. Several blocks along, they stopped in front of a general store with a prosperous air. "Cunningham's Dry Goods" was freshly painted above the door, and the air smelt of fresh hay.

"This—good," Molly said.

Emily nodded acknowledgement and led the way inside.

"Help you?" came a holler from the rear. A large man in a two-piece suit came forward, and ran a quick eye over Emily's stylish bonnet. "I'm sorry, I hadn't expected to see ladies here today. What can I do for you?"

"I understand that you will arrange rentals of horses and pack animals?"

"That's correct."

"Have you booked a party of five recently?" Emily said. "My uncle had planned to leave for the Omineca, but forgot to tell me which stables I was to meet him at. He is planning on leaving today or tomorrow."

It sounded weak to her ears, but it was the best she'd been able to come up with on short notice. It seemed to pass muster, though.

"No, I'm sorry, I've had no bookings since the *Caledonia* came in."

"Nothing from the *Monte Cristo*?"

"Not so far, anyway."

"Well, thank you. Can you suggest whom I might be best to talk to next?"

He gave her a cautious look. "Well, normally I'd suggest a place called Crawford's, as they can handle that many people, but that's no place for a lady like yourself."

She smiled at him. "Thank you. Perhaps I will wait for my uncle at the hotel, in that case."

"That might be best."

He looked relieved, and Emily wondered just how bad Crawford's was.

As they reached the street again, she turned to Molly. "Was Crawford's the second name your cousin gave you?"

"Yes. We go there?"

The rain had stopped and a little sunshine was struggling through the cloud cover. Emily decided it was a good sign. "Yes. Which way?"

"This way."

As Molly led her down a block, across another block and down a narrow back alley, Emily began to wonder if the man at Cunningham's had been right. Still, she'd faced down Mr. Gipson without any ill results. How much worse could this be?

She had her answer when Molly slowed and nodded towards a run-down looking store—its rough wooden walls festooned with old snowshoes and battered mining equipment—several doors down and on the other side of the alley. The place looked badly lit and dirty, even from here.

"Crawford's," said Molly.

"Oh." Emily said. "Well, let's get this over with."

As they got closer, she could smell horses, rotting manure and filth. She'd never rent horses from a place like this one—they'd founder before they ever made it ten miles. In fact, if she ever had money, she'd hunt down places like this, buy all of the horses and force them out of business.

Taking a deep breath, and nearly choking on the stench of it, she pushed open the doors and walked into the gloom with Molly trailing behind her.

All was quiet. The inside—even more crowded with old implements than the outside—looked deserted, which was a relief. The last thing she needed was to run into Heade or one of his men.

"Hello?" she called out, her voice coming out more tentative than she'd intended.

"What c'n I do for you?" said a grubby man who'd been standing unseen in the shadows behind the counter.

"Oh, good morning," she said, and told him her story about her uncle.

"Hah," was the response. "If your "uncle" did business here, and I'm not saying he did, I'd not be sharing that information with any pretty bit that walked in. Now, get on with you."

Emily felt her face flush. She wanted to ask more questions, but a glance at the leering look on the man's face changed her mind. He'd practically admitted that he had a new booking, after all. And at a guess, they weren't leaving today.

That would have to do.

Emily nodded to Molly, and they left the shop. Molly led them quickly back to the main street. Emily let out a sigh that she hated to admit was relief once they reached it.

It was probably a good thing Clara hadn't joined her today, she thought, and put up her umbrella when the first raindrops fell. She checked the time on her watch-pin. Half an hour before she had to go back to Mrs. Rowlatt's for luncheon. What now?

She'd learned nothing for certain, and her guesses would only be helpful if Granville knew about them. She needed to ask more questions at Crawford's, but her skin crawled at the thought of going back there. It wasn't safe, and she wasn't a fool.

Was there some other way to find out when Heade planned to leave?

"Molly," she said, turning to the girl, "would your cousin or someone else at the hotel know how long a guest planned to stay?"

Molly's head bobbed. "They'll know at the desk."

"And is there any way of learning that information while making sure that the guest will never hear about it?"

The girl gave her a cautious look. "Mrs. Rowlatt says you are engaged to a man gone to the goldfields," she said. There was no question in her phrasing, but something in the way she watched Emily that told her what was needed.

Emily nodded. "Yes. I'm worried about him. That's why I need the information."

A smile was her reply. "I know who to ask, and he will never tell."

Emily smiled back. "Thank you."

"It is not easy, when they are gone."

"No, it isn't. You are engaged also?"

Another bob of the head, a shy look. "He is very brave, and he too has gone to the goldfields. When he earns enough, we will marry. Now, come."

When they reached the hotel, Emily again waited on the back porch. She'd told the girl who she was looking for, and she thought she could trust her, but it was hard to be the one who waited.

After Molly had been gone nearly fifteen minutes, Emily started to pace, then stopped herself. She couldn't afford to draw any attention, even if she was mostly out of sight. But she was feeling guilty for sending Molly alone. And it was hard to wait.

Finally she heard footsteps coming quickly down the hall and Molly appeared.

Emily let out a sigh of relief. "Did you find out anything?" she asked.

Molly bobbed her head. "Heade and four men—all leave tomorrow. There is poker tonight, a big game, and they stay for that. That is what you need?"

"Yes, and thank you so much. Now, I will need to get a letter to my fiancé. How would I best do that?"

"You know where he has gone? The goldfields are big."

"He was going to Manson Creek." Or in any case, that was where he'd planned to go first. She thought there would be no harm in revealing this much. And she did need to get word to him about Heade.

Granville would be thinking he had more time before Heade showed up. But he was already here! Emily drew in a swift breath to calm herself and focused on what Molly was saying.

"The post will get it there, but not swiftly. Is your letter urgent?" the girl asked.

Emily thought about the cruel lines in Heade's face. "Yes, it is. Very urgent."

"Then you want to send it with someone going that way. Sometimes Cunningham's will help. Or Crawford's, for a cost."

Emily glanced back towards Crawford's, then checked her watch. "We'll need to go to Cunningham's," she told Molly. "But I think we'll go back for luncheon first, and I'll write my letter. Could you show me the way again, this afternoon, please?"

Molly nodded, and led the way, looking pleased.

39

TUESDAY, MAY 8, 1900

The town that had sprung up around the gold workings at Germanson Landing and Manson Creek was bigger than Granville had anticipated finding twenty years after the main rush. He should probably have expected something of the sort from the number of miners he'd talked to on the *Caledonia* who were planning to come here, but he hadn't made the connection.

Where the hills sloped down towards the creek, one room log cabins with steeply sloped roofs marched along both sides of a wide dirt road. He could see the Hudson's Bay Company sign on a cabin that had been painted white with red trim. The Gold Commissioner's office would likely be in another. A few hastily built shanties and canvas tents stood on the far edge of the settlement.

It was still early—they'd made good time from Takla Lake—but the streets were already crowded with people moving quickly about their business.

"This is amazing," Trent said as they slowed the horses to a walk.

"You've seen gold towns before, haven't you?"

"Not really. Not like this."

Scott pointed towards two large cabins with carved wooden

signs over their doors. "I see the saloons, where we'll undoubtedly find gambling, but where are the ladies?"

"They'll be here."

"Just look for the red lanterns, right?" Trent broke in.

Granville glanced over at him. "I thought you had a girl."

Trent's ears went red. "I do. I mean—I sort of do." He bent forward to adjust his gelding's bridle, easing the bit in the sensitive mouth, and effectively hiding his face. "What do we do next?"

It came out muffled, and Granville bit back a grin. What do you know, the boy was fun to tease.

Scott elbowed Trent, making both of their horses sidestep a little.

"I'm going to look for Jimmy Well's office," Granville said. "I'd like to make sure he knows how to find me in case Emily tries to get in touch. Why don't you two get rooms for us? We'll need to stay for a day or so, until we establish whether Weston's been here or not. And find out more about McDame."

"I'll meet you over there for lunch." And Scott waved towards the closer of the saloons.

Granville glanced over, nodded. "The Nugget. Seems appropriate, somehow."

―――――――――

JIMMY WELLS' cramped office was in the front part of a small log building on what passed for the main street. Just big enough for a desk, two chairs, a small wood stove and a kerosene lantern, it faced the entrance and had no door.

Granville noted a wooden door off to one side, currently closed, that likely led to a larger office in the back, since this small building served as headquarters for the Gold Commissioner as well as his clerk. Despite the cold air sneaking in through chinks in the logs, the room was close, heavy with the smell of kerosene and wood smoke.

Wells was seated behind a desk covered with papers stacked every which way. He seemed glad of the interruption, coming forward with his hand outstretched. "Nice to see you again, Granville. And I have a letter for you."

It was the last thing Granville had expected to hear. "A letter? From Hazelton?"

Wells nodded. "Rider came in early this morning. Man was exhausted, but in a hurry to get to his diggings. He left it at the HBC store, and they passed it to me just a few minutes ago." He handed over a sealed white envelope.

Granville glanced at the handwriting—Emily's. What could have gone wrong so soon? He turned slightly so Wells couldn't see his face, and tore it open. Scanning the lines, he let out a breath of relief.

Emily was fine and nothing had gone wrong. Except that Heade and four of his men had already arrived in Hazelton and were preparing to leave town for the Omineca. They were a week early.

How had they managed that?

Rubbing his forehead, he read the brief note again. Wait a minute. Heade only had four men with him? He'd started with six. What had happened to the other two?

He started to grin. Despite Scott's skepticism, Prescott had apparently been as good as his word. He looked forward to finding out how his temporary associate had managed it.

Four ruthless killers on their tail—well, five if you counted Heade—was certainly better than seven of them. He turned back to Wells. "Did the fellow who brought this letter happen to mention the arrival of the *Strathcona*?"

"Yeah, he did. He was chuffed to have seen the day when three of 'em are making the Skeena run. It really puts us on the map." He paused. "Only, this wasn't the *Strathcona*—don't believe that one's left Victoria yet. This was the *Monte Cristo*—Cunningham's new sternwheeler.

So that was how Heade and his boys had arrived so quickly. Granville read through Emily's short letter again, more slowly this time. It had obviously been written in a hurry, but she didn't seem worried or upset. Good.

Still, it was critical to their plans that he and Scott find

Weston before Heade did. This news meant they'd have to re-think things, but at least—thanks to Emily's warning—they had a little time. Scott wouldn't be impressed by a change in their plans, though.

Granville folded the letter carefully and looked up to see Wells watching him.

"Not bad news, I hope?" the mining recorder said.

His tone was a little too careful. Granville realized Wells had noted the feminine handwriting, and assumed the worst. "No, not at all. From my fiancée, with some information I needed."

Wells beamed. "She's a lovely lady, Miss Turner. You're a lucky man."

"I am indeed," he said.

"You let me know if I can do anything for you whilst you're here."

Granville glanced at the date on Emily's letter. Three days ago. "There is one thing. You said the man who brought this was exhausted. I gather he rode faster than usual to get here. How long would it take a party who left Hazelton on Sunday to arrive in Manson Creek?"

"Depends on how late they drank and how hung over they were," Wells said with a grin. "But you could probably expect them to arrive sometime late tomorrow or the next day."

Granville nodded his thanks. "Oh, and while I think of it—have you any record of a man named Rupert Weston? He might have recorded a claim, or merely come in for information. He would be a tall man, with light brown hair."

"Weston—that's the man you were talking about on the steamer."

Wells thumbed through a stack of papers on the counter in front of him, not waiting for Granville's nod. "He a youngish gentle-man? British, like yourself?"

"That's him."

"I didn't meet him myself, but I gather he was here round about early March—we didn't officially open until this month. You might want to ask for Alfred, the bartender at the Nugget. He always hears all the gossip, and fills me in on anything mining-related that occurs earlier in the year."

"He's the one who told you about Weston?"

"That's it."

"Then I'll look him up. Anyone else I should talk to?"

"There's a few old miners that hang around the store in the afternoon. They might be able to help. They'll talk your ear off, though."

"Thanks, I'll risk it," Granville said with a grin. "Oh, one last thing. If I needed to leave a forwarding location for mail with you, would there be any problems?"

Wells glanced at the neatly folded letter Granville still held. "None at all. Happy to help," he said with a grin.

GRANVILLE CAUGHT up with Scott and Trent at the Nugget, a sprawling, rectangular building of skinned logs, with a shake roof and the kitchen in a lean-to off to the side. Lit by oil lamps which had darkened the low ceiling, the place smelled of lamp oil, spilled beer and old cigarettes, all overlaid by the richness of cooking bacon. His stomach rumbled and he could almost taste a hot, crunchy slice of fresh bacon.

Scott and Trent had taken a table towards the back, where the rotund bartender—who was ostentatiously polishing a very clean tankard and trying not to look like he was listening—couldn't hear them. He pulled up a rough wooden chair and downed half the ale that they'd ordered for him, then filled them in on Emily's note.

"Heade and his gang of thugs are where?"

Granville hid a grin at Scott's roar. Hands fisted on the table, scowling—his reaction had been even stronger than Granville's own. "At most a couple of days away. You find any news of Weston?"

Now Trent was scowling too. "We've been busy getting a hotel room. Which is not easy in a place like this, you know. When were we supposed to be finding out stuff about your missing lordling?"

Granville chuckled. Trent's expression got darker, but Scott glared at him for a moment and then broke out laughing.

"He's got us, lad. We didn't ask about him at the hotel and we should have."

"No matter. I've got it on best authority that our friendly publican," and he nodded towards the saloon-keeper when Trent looked confused, "not only talked to Weston, but is also the best source of local information."

Trent still looked resentful, but Scott exchanged glances with Granville. "You want to take this one, since our missing heir is your countryman?"

"That was my thought." He drained his mug and stood. "You hungry?"

"I am," Trent said. "Breakfast was a long time ago."

And hardtack with gritty camp coffee on the trail had been less than satisfying. They'd been traveling light and fast. "I'll see if they can find some bacon and eggs for us," Granville said. "Maybe even some coffee."

"I've got your back," Scott said, moving his chair slightly to the left to improve his line of sight.

Granville nodded. He didn't think it would be needed—it was still early, so the heavy drinkers weren't here yet and the bartender looked friendly—but this was a hard land, and the Mounties who'd been so present in the Klondike were nowhere to be seen. He was glad of the familiar weight of the gun on his hip, and his partner's watchful presence.

The bartender—Alfred—was watching him, eyes alert. But the man's hands were above the counter, his arms relaxed. No gun, then.

"More ale then?" Alfred said.

"Please," Granville said. "And coffee if you have it. I think we could all do with double orders of eggs and bacon as well, if you've any available."

"I think we can manage that, and bacon-fried toast with it, if you've a mind?" At Granville's nod he hollered the order, presumably to someone in the kitchen, and turned his attention back to Granville. "Food'll be right out. You just ride in?"

"This morning."

"Miners?" Alfred said as he placed three mugs of beer in front of Granville.

"Not anymore."

"Oh?"

His interested look invited details. Wells was right, this man loved gossip. And Granville intended to encourage him. "Klondike."

"Ah." A pause. "I heard there was real money to be made up there."

He grinned at the man. "True enough, but not for everyone. We came away frostbit and broke."

"We?"

He waved towards the table. "My partner. And our apprentice."

Alfred's eyes were trained on their table. He looked like he was trying to memorize every detail of their appearance. "You're a long way from anywhere, if you're not here for the gold."

"Yeah." Granville knew this type. The harder he had to work for information, the more he'd value it.

"Let me get you some coffee." And he turned to the stove behind him. "So what line of work are you in?" he said over his shoulder.

"We do investigations. Private," he said as Alfred put a full cup of coffee in front of him.

"Really?" Alfred's expression grew even friendlier. "You with Pinkerton's?"

What was this fascination with the Pinkerton's Agency, anyway? Did the whole world read too many Penny Dreadfuls?

"We're affiliated," he said, thinking again that it was worth looking into, since it seemed to be so effective. He had gold now, after all. Perhaps he could buy into the company?

"And you're here to investigate someone?"

"More like to find someone." Granville drank a mouthful of coffee, then leaned forward a little, lowered his voice. "Can I trust you?"

It amused him to see the fellow echo his actions. "Of course. I can keep a secret, ask anyone."

Right. He already knew exactly how well Alfred could keep secrets. "I'm on the trail of a man named Weston."

"Weston? But..." The face grew avid. "What'd he do?"

Granville shook his head. "I can't disclose that, I'm afraid. But it's urgent we find him, before..."

"Before?"

When he didn't speak, the bartender's eyes narrowed a little. "Someone else is after him too?"

Perhaps the Penny Dreadfuls were useful after all. "You didn't hear it from me."

"Is there a bounty on him, then? Or..." the hiss of indrawn breath. "Is he in danger?"

A slight inclination of Granville's head had Alfred arranging his features into a mask. "No-one will hear anything from me," the bartender vowed. "Even torture won't make me talk."

Right. "Actually..." Granville said, lowering his voice still further.

Alfred leaned forward again. "Go on."

"You might be able to help us—if you were willing to?"

"Yeah, I would."

"Thank you. But you'd have to tell everyone about our conversation."

"I'd have to talk? Tell people about it?"

A curt nod. "Yes. Every detail—up to a point."

"Ohhh. Leading them on, like."

"Exactly."

"So what can't I say?"

"You can't tell anyone that this man..."

"Weston?"

So he hadn't missed that. Good. "Yes. That Weston is in danger, or that there are men after him even now."

"There are?"

"I had word this morning that they are heading here even as we speak." It pained him to speak in such ridiculous phrases, but his target's eyes got brighter and brighter.

Granville proceeded to describe Heade and his minions in detail, leaving out their names. "Remember, these are dangerous men, and they will stop at nothing."

Which was true enough, if over-dramatic.

"I'll remember," Alfred promised. "And don't worry, I'll be careful what I say. But what will you do next?"

"I have to get to Weston before these men find him. Problem is, I know he came north, but I don't know where exactly he's gone."

"But—I can help you with that."

"You can?"

"I know where he's gone. Or at least, I know where he was going."

"Go on."

It was all the encouragement Alfred needed. "He was here, oh, six weeks or so ago. The Indians had brought him north in their canoes, though they'd had to portage more than usual, then he hired a couple of them to bring him here. He stayed a few days, but he was determined to go north, into the goldfields, despite the weather. It was too early to pan for gold, some of the rivers were still iced over, but nothing would stop him."

"North?"

"Well, not really. There's an old Indian trail that runs up the north branch of the Skeena. He found someone stupid enough—I mean he found someone who knows it well to guide him. Paid him pretty well, too, from what I hear. Well, he'd have to, wouldn't he? To go that far north in early March?"

"How far is it?"

"Journey would take five, six days. Probably longer in that weather."

"And he hasn't been back?"

"Not here, anyway. What d'you think it means?"

But they both knew what it could mean. The weather this far north was both unpredictable and unforgiving, especially for a young Englishman with little experience. "Who did he hire?"

"An old gold-hunter, a black man. Name of Harry McDame. He knows his stuff." It was a grudging acknowledgement.

McDame. So Pierce had been right. At least Weston'd had the

sense to hire someone with the experience he lacked. And it seemed Alfred didn't much like Harry McDame. "And is McDame back in town?"

The bartender looked startled. "No. No, he isn't. But he mightn't have come back here. He could have headed for Lorne Creek again, or even Lost Creek. McDame knows people working those creeks."

"At that time of year?"

"Maybe not."

The probable fates of McDame and young Weston lay between them.

Granville wasn't giving up on the lad yet, though. "Still, you said McDame is an old hand in this country?"

A nod. "The man's found gold a few times, too."

Which is what Booth had said. The fellow must really know how to spot gold in this part of the world. "So maybe he got them through. Where do you think McDame would be more likely to go?"

Alfred looked pleased to be asked. "Well, Lost Mine is closer," he said after some thought. "I think he'd most likely have gone there."

"Then that's where I'll look for him. Although..."

"What?" Alfred looked a little nervous. He struck Granville as one of those men who like to be 'in the know', but lived in fear that they'd be found wrong.

"Well, it seems to me I heard a few stories about McDame on the sternwheeler coming up. Isn't he the fellow that made that big strike up Cassiar way? And then found gold again on Lorne Creek?"

"Yeah, that's the man," the bartender said.

"Well, what if they didn't find gold wherever it was Weston wanted to look? Would this McDame be likely to guide him into the regions he already knows have gold, rather than come back here?"

Alfred was nodding now. "You mean up Cassiar way or to Lorne Creek? Yeah. Yeah, he would. He likes to talk about how well he knows the country, how there's still gold out there that no-one's found. He'd not miss a chance to dig if someone else was paying for it."

"Which one would he head to?"

"Well, if they haven't found gold, they're probably in the Cassiar by now."

"Then that's where I'll look for them. And I thank you for your insight."

Alfred beamed at him. "You're most welcome. But—what do I do if these men that are after Weston come here asking questions?"

"Tell them we went south. Beyond that, I'll leave it to your discretion."

"South? You mean to Howellstown?"

"They pan for gold there?"

"Yeah, or at least they did."

"Then that will do. Just don't tell him we think they've gone to the Cassiar area."

Alfred nodded, and Granville wished he could hear what Alfred ended up telling Heade. If he'd read the bartender right, Heade would have the story about Weston heading for Cassiar out of him in no time. With any luck it would slow Heade and his boys down by quite a bit.

From everything Granville had been able to uncover, Heade was a city boy. He'd not be prepared for this country, even in May. "And I think that's our eggs coming now. I'd best sit down. But thank you again."

It was waved off. "I'm happy to help. And I'll keep mum."

Granville nodded soberly and returned to his table.

"Learn anything?" Scott said.

He nodded. "Later," he said. "Breakfast is here."

"So where are we going now?" Scott said as they headed back up the main street towards the hills.

"And why couldn't we talk while we ate?" Trent said. "Those were some good eggs."

"I couldn't risk being overheard," Granville said. "And we're going to look for someone who knows their way along an old Indian trail, and who also knows McDame."

Scott grinned at him. "And where does our too-friendly bartender think we're going?"

"Somewhere else."

Trent glared from one to the other. "I don't get it. How could he not know you'd follow wherever he told you Weston was going?"

"Because I explained why I thought Weston and his guide would end up somewhere in the Cassiar region, so that's where we're heading. Officially," Granville told him.

"But where's Cassiar? I've never heard of it."

"Neither have I," Granville said as Scott started to laugh. "But we need to find Weston before Heade finds him. Or us. So we'd best get our plans in order."

THE HUDSON'S Bay store stood a little separate from the other buildings, surrounded by tall evergreens that provided shade and some protection from the wind that swept along the valley. And out front, smoking and shooting the breeze, were the old-timers he'd come to find. Right where Wells had said they would be.

Wiry, tanned, and grizzled, hair faded by age, there was little to tell the three apart. But they all liked to talk. Especially about Harry McDame.

It seemed McDame was well known in Manson Creek.

"Man moved north with a bunch of other blacks being persecuted in San Francisco, back in the late '50's," one of the grizzled old men said. "I guess most of 'em settled in Victoria or thereabouts, but McDame always had a feel for gold. He worked pretty much every gold rush we had up here. Found gold more than a few times, too."

"Did a lot of exploring, all round the Peace River country when that rush was on, too. He seems to like the north, which is odd, because he was born in Jamaica. You can still hear it in his speech."

"He worked Germanson Creek, few miles south of here, back in '70, '71," added another. "Found some color, but not enough to hold him here when the Cassiar rush was on."

"He's the one McDame Creek in Cassiar is named after," a third man put in. "He and his partners took $6,000 out of that creek in the first month. Then he came back to these parts and found gold on Lorne Creek."

If Weston was really looking for gold and not Chinese coins, it sounded as if McDame was the man who might be able to help him find it, Granville thought. It wasn't clear how much help he'd be finding more coins.

The real problem though, was that no-one knew where McDame might have gone. Nor could they suggest any way to find him.

"Plays his cards close, that one," added the third man.

Three heads nodded in unison. The first man lit up a hand-rolled cigarette, offered Granville one, which he declined.

The old men sat in their patch of sun, smoking in silence. He handed them the photo of Weston, and they passed it around.

"Looks kinda familiar," the second man said, holding it at arms' length and looking at it carefully. "Haircut and clothes don't match, but—might just be the young feller crawled in here a few months ago. Whadda ya think, Jim? This him?"

The first man—Jim—looked at the photo again. "Cleans up nice, if it is. But yeah, I think you're right. He had the same accent you do," he told Granville.

Who nodded. "I'm told this man hired McDame to guide him. What I don't know is where they went."

"Wherever it is, there'd be gold in it somewhere, for Harry McDame to take it on. Especially that time of year," the third man said.

"O'course, McDame is crazy anyhow."

"Anywhere in particular McDame had been prospecting lately?" Granville said.

"I think he spent some time in the Cassiar, up Telegraph Creek way, a few years ago," said one. "Don't know much about where he's been since."

That generated a round of shrugs, much wagging of heads, and murmurs of "tight-lipped, that one" and "he don't talk much."

"Y'know, I think McDame might'a been working up along the western branches of the Peace," the second one said slowly, after a bit. "He knew that river really well, and from things he let drop, he was doing some looking near where the Peace and the Skeena run close to each other, the last year or so."

Which tied in with what both Ah Quan and Pierce had said, and was probably the best Granville was going to get. He just hoped he could trust Thomas to guide them there.

"But you couldn't trust much that man said," Jim put in.

"Too afraid someone'll stake a claim ahead of him," the third one said with a crack of laughter. "Just like the rest of us fools. You mine?"

Granville nodded. "Klondike."

"Ah. Then you understand." A pause. "Find much?"

"Nary a thing."

That was received with more laughter.

Well, at least Heade wouldn't get much out of them, either.

Still, the fact that McDame had been in Telegraph Creek was interesting, given the stories about the Chinese coins being found there. Maybe McDame might be interested in more than gold, if someone convinced him there was money in it.

"Someone like Weston, perhaps?" said Scott when he reported back. The big man was stacking the additional provisions he'd been purchasing with Trent's assistance.

It was a good thing they had the packhorses, Granville thought, looking at the sizable load the two of them had now assembled. If he hadn't had spent time in the Klondike, he'd think they had bought too much. Now he could tell with one look that prices must have been high, and the choices few. He just hoped the food would last until they could find game or buy more.

It left him wondering how well Weston had been able to provision. It was good he'd hired McDame—on his own, the lad would likely have starved before he could find his way back here.

Maybe he had, anyway.

That time of year, the cold would have been fierce, the game scarce and hard to find.

40

WEDNESDAY, MAY 9, 1900

S everal days later, Clara found Emily in Mrs. Rowlatt's parlor, lit only by thin grey daylight, staring out at the rain. It had been raining heavily for two days straight, and an east wind blowing off the glacier had kept the two friends inside.

"Emily, when are we..." Clara began.

Then she stopped, and Emily could feel her moving closer. Watching her.

"Emily, what is wrong?" Clara asked.

"I hate this," Emily burst out, unable to contain it. "Since Heade left here, I've got nowhere with the case. Granville's gone off into danger—again—and there's nothing I can do here. I haven't been able to uncover anything at all about Weston, or even about the Chinese coins. And even if I learn something now, Granville will have left Manson Creek, and the information will wait there until he returns. By which time it will be too late."

Clara patted her hand. "What do you find the hardest to bear?"

It was a good question, but it took Emily no thinking at all to come up with the answer. Indeed, it practically burst out of her.

"That I can't do anything useful! Here they are trying to save this poor man whose own father is plotting against him, and facing a gang of thugs from San Francisco and who knows what kind of hardships, and all I can do is sit here and watch it rain."

"You were able to send word to Mr. Granville about Heade and his crew arriving here before anyone expected them to," Clara said. "That is no small thing."

"Yes, if he got it," Emily said. "I don't know if he did, or even where he might have gone after he left here. I don't even know if they are alive."

Clara patted Emily's hand again. "You didn't sleep well last night, did you?"

"How did you know?"

"Because you sound tired and out of sorts. You haven't been outside yet today, have you?"

"No," Emily said, beginning to smile at her friend's solicitous tone.

"I'll ring for a cup of tea, then we can talk about where we should go this afternoon."

As Clara patted her hand once more, then rang for tea, Emily considered her friend. What was she up to?

Clara was far more than she allowed most people to see, and one of these days she was going to end up ruling a very successful household. If she ever did marry Jimmy O'Hearn, he would probably end up even richer than Clara's own father, because Clara would make sure of it.

The tea was ready in short order. Clara passed a cup of tea with just the right amount of milk and sugar to Emily, who sipped it slowly. There was something soothing in the ritual. And she was increasingly curious what her friend was going to say next.

"Did you know that the boat is leaving for Port Essington tomorrow? And they expect the return trip to take only a single day," Clara said, putting her own teacup down and watching Emily intently.

"Oh?"

"Emily, we could be back in Vancouver by Tuesday. Mrs. Rowlatt has a friend who is going south with her husband, and we could travel with them, so it would be safe enough. And you have to face the facts. Although I am enjoying my visits with our hostess, you are bored to tears," Clara added with a small smile. "There is not enough for unmarried women to do here, and I've given up hope that you will develop an interest in fashion."

She paused, as if waiting for a response. When she didn't get one, she continued, "And besides, we have been gone more than a week already. You said yourself that Mr. Granville could easily be away another week or even two. By the time we return to Vancouver, we will have been away an entire month."

Still Emily made no response.

"And you know as well as I do that if we stay here too much longer, our mothers will learn what we have been up to. And we will never hear the end of it."

Which was true, if not helpful. Emily had been avoiding thinking about it. "But I can't leave," she said. "I have yet to find an answer to the problem of the different stories on the Chinese coins."

"Then after tea we can go and interview people who might know the answers," was Clara's surprising answer.

"But how?"

"Mrs. Rowlatt has some contacts that she is sure would be willing to help."

Which Clara had definitely not mentioned before. For a moment Emily felt annoyed, then she started to smile. It was so Clara. And she had another lead. "Thank you, Clara," she said, smiling and taking a sip of her tea.

"And we while we're out, we can check into the availability of tickets back to Vancouver," her friend finished.

Which didn't mean they would be leaving just yet. Not at all. "Yes, of course."

IT TURNED out that one of Mrs. Rowlatt's close friends had been born in the region, and knew all of the miners who still lived in

Hazelton. She'd been happy to help, and could tell them which of the older miners were still in town.

Their first call was a small trim house with white-painted shutters just a few doors down from where Emily and Clara were staying. Mr. Turcotte lived there with his daughter and her husband, and he was delighted to have a chance to reminisce.

"I knew some of the men worked Telegraph Creek, back in the '80's," the grizzled old man said, reaching for his tea. "And they did find some old coins and the like, buried in the bank of the creek there."

"And were the coins found in a stone jar?" Emily asked him.

"No'm. They was on a rope, kinda—or it might have been a wire of some kind—that disintegrated the minute they dug it out."

"And can you describe these coins any more clearly?"

"Well, they were old bronze coins. Very old. I had heard later that they might have been as much as three thousand years old."

She thanked him, and she and Clara set off under their umbrellas to talk to the next name on her list. The wind had eased off enough that they could talk as they walked.

"You know, Clara," Emily said. "It would have helped if you had told me about Mrs. Rowlatt's friend on Monday. Then I wouldn't have wasted all this time."

"I was sorting patterns and fabrics with Mrs. Rowlatt on Monday," Clara said. "And you would have wanted to come and talk to these men immediately. You know you would have."

"I could have taken Molly," Emily said, but a side glance at Clara's stubborn look confirmed what she'd suspected. Clara enjoyed investigating almost as much as Emily did, and she hadn't wanted to be left out.

Of course, she hadn't wanted to miss out on her time with Mrs. Rowlatt, either.

Three-quarters of an hour and two visits later, the pair found themselves in a shack-like building on the far edge of town. Old Bill, for so he'd introduced himself, had the stove burning for warmth, and several oil lamps defeated the gloom.

Clara didn't look too happy about being there, and declined the proffered tea with haste. Emily was fascinated, and quick to ask him what he might know about the Chinese coins.

"Well, I was up in Cassiar, nearly a hundred miles north of Dease Lake," he told her. "We wasn't finding much at first, not until McDame and that crew found the seam on what they're now calling McDame Creek. So it was big news when they found those old coins. Everyone was talking about it."

"Was that find anywhere near Telegraph Creek?"

Old Bill gave a crack of laughter that wheezed off into nothing. "Depends what you consider far. It's a hundred miles or so, give or take."

"And did you ever see the find?" Emily said. She knew the value of first-hand information. And in dealing with miners, she was learning that the further they were from having actually seen a find themselves, the wilder the tales grew.

"Oh sure. A few of us rode over special. And it was odd to see these things, looking so foreign, y'know, and dug out of that kinda country."

"Can you tell me exactly what you saw, and where they were found?"

"Sure can. It was a bunch of coins, bronze ones, y'know, threaded onto some kind of iron rod. The rod had pretty much disintegrated, and the coins were worn, but in good condition. You could see the writing clear as anything, and it was characters like the Chinamen write on your laundry tickets."

"And a few years later," Old Bill added, "the Chinese interpreter from Victoria, from the court there, y'know?"

Ah Quan, thought Emily. She nodded.

"Well, he was up here, near Telegraph Creek, in fact, and met some Indians who showed him some silver ceremonial dishes and some brass coins that had been found in the dishes. And they'd all been found buried in the roots of a large tree. Way I heard it the Indians gave him one of those coins, and he later gave it to Judge Harrison, who he worked with."

Well, it was something like the story they'd heard from the Harrisons and Ah Quan, especially if you'd heard about two different finds and jumbled the facts together. "How far is Telegraph Creek from any branch of the Skeena River?" Emily asked him.

"About a hundred fifty miles," was the answer. "But there's a few mountain ranges and some really rough country in the way."

Interesting. There were just enough differences in the stories, which at first had sounded so similar, to make her question her first assumption, that it was word of mouth confusing things.

Was it possible there had been more than one cache of Oriental coins found?

"So what do you make of the stories you've heard?" Clara asked, once they were back at Mrs. Rowlatt's and enjoying what Clara called a "proper tea."

Emily tapped a finger against her lips, then took a sip of Earl Grey tea. "Well, if you combine what we heard today with what Granville learned, what Bertie's uncle told me, and what Ah Quan said, they all have similar elements, but in different combinations. It's really very confusing.

Even Ah Quan's story, if we assume it to be accurate, is both second hand and remarkably thin on specific details as to where anything was found. It seems to me that finding further artifacts in this enormous region would be very difficult, and I wonder how Mr. Weston hopes to find anything. Unless he stumbles over something, of course."

"So that's taken care of," Clara said. "Can we plan our return to Vancouver now?"

Emily took another sip of tea, and smiled at Clara. "But don't you find it fascinating that there may have been two or more discoveries here of Chinese relics that date well before the known discovery of the region? Just imagine how they might have arrived here, and how difficult the voyage would have been."

"I don't think there's anyone left to ask questions of," her friend said.

"Well, no-one has spoken with the Gitksan yet."

"Oh, Emily," Clara said. Before she had a chance to say more, the parlor door opened, and Mrs. Rowlatt came into the room, followed by a woman with light-brown hair and a sweet face.

"You remember Mrs. Pierce, who was on the *Caledonia* with us, do you not?" Mrs. Rowlatt said. "I don't know if you were aware, but she works with the children in the village at Kispiox, where her husband does missionary work. She has some stories for you about the Chinese coins."

Clara sighed quietly. Emily ignored her, rising with outstretched hand to meet the visitor.

THAT EVENING EMILY sat down by lantern-light to write to Granville. It was a hard letter to write. She found herself repairing the pen, and polishing smudges off the ink-bottle as she tried to find the right words.

She wanted to be part of his adventures, part of his life, not left on the periphery while he went off with his partner and their apprentice. Was that so wrong?

Maybe it was time to set the date, to marry him. But he was already talking about building them a house, and would that become a reason to leave her behind, as the "lady of the house?"

She thought about Granville, the glint in his eyes, the way he had of including her, and thought that probably marrying him was a risk worth taking. For a moment she considered including it in her letter, but it felt too risky.

She needed more time.

Better just to send the small bits of information she had learned today, let him know she'd be staying in Kispiox with the Reverend Pierce and his wife until his return. That was probably shock enough for one letter, she thought with a private smile.

He'd get her letter when he returned to Manson Creek, whenever that might be. Then when she saw him again, she could tell him her decision.

Unless she'd changed her mind.

41

THURSDAY, MAY 17, 1900

Granville eyed the trail that wound steeply downwards, through spindly trees and thick grasses. Steep granite cliffs jutted out on both sides, and the wind was sharp and cold.

He drew the thick muffler more closely around his neck and glanced behind him. Scott was his usual stoic self but Trent's lips were blue.

He could see a glimpse of river glinting along the bottom of the valley in front of them, and hoped it was a branch of the Skeena. They'd been riding hard for most of the morning, but none of them was sure exactly where they were. Not since their guide from Kispiox, Thomas, had vanished during the night, without a word to anyone. Still, if Heade was on their trail, they couldn't afford to lose time.

Granville was happier than ever that he'd talked Emily out of joining them.

He glanced at the trail ahead and the hairs on his arms rose. They'd been warned. This was the valley that the Gitksan considered haunted.

Their legends spoke of Others who had claimed this land and made it theirs, many hundreds of years ago. Granville had been curious to see the place since he'd talked to Ah Quan, but he hadn't expected to feel anything himself. He dragged the heavy muffler closer around his throat.

"We're losing time. And we don't know how far behind us Heade and company are," he said, looking back to where Scott and Trent rode some distance behind him.

"If they're there at all," Trent said.

"We need to assume Heade and his boys are right behind us," Granville said. "Never underestimate an opponent. It can get you killed in a hurry."

"Do we have any hope of finding Weston or whatever it is he's searching for without our tracker?" Scott asked as he rode up beside him.

"We were warned the man might disappear. Nothing has changed."

"Not what I asked."

Granville laughed. "My answer would be the same as yours. This was a foolhardy venture from the start. And when has that ever stopped us?"

"Just checkin'."

"Of course."

"This place feel creepy to you fellows?" Trent said from behind them.

Scott grimaced at Granville. "Why d'you ask?"

"Cause it does to me. And our guide has vanished."

"We were just discussing that. You've never heard any of the legends of this area?"

Trent shook his head. "Nope."

"The local tribes won't go near it. Hasn't kept a few gold hungry fools from trying their luck."

"Like Weston?"

"Maybe not so desperate," Scott said.

"Exactly like Weston," Granville said with a quelling look at Scott. "People hoping for a windfall of gold to solve all of their problems."

"Like us. Only we found it," Trent said.

"And did it solve all your problems?" Granville asked.

"No. Having this job did most of that. Anyway, you won't let us have most of the gold."

"You don't look like you're suffering any. If you had the gold from the lost mine, you'd have to leave town," Granville said. "Too many questions would get asked if you started spending that money. And there'd be those who would line up to take that mine away from us."

"Which is why you never staked a claim to that mine."

"Exactly." Aside from the fact that it wasn't their mine.

"Huh," Trent was silent for nearly a minute. "But I still don't understand what we're doing here."

"Looking for Weston," Scott said.

"We didn't need to take the job," Trent muttered.

"Then how do we explain our income?" Granville asked him.

Trent thought about that one for a bit. "Investments?"

"Investments. That's Gipson's specialty," Scott said, in a voice heavy with sarcasm.

"Oh." The boy thought about it for a mile or so as their horses picked their way along the narrow, uneven track. "Well, we don't want to do anything his way."

———

"ARE we sure this is the place?" Trent said several hours later. With hard riding, they had left the steep cliffs and were now moving amongst the thick brush growing along the river. It proved even slower going than the rocky slopes had been.

"We're not sure of anything," Scott said. "But if Thomas was right, this is the place."

"You mean the Thomas from Kispiox who seems to have deserted us?" Trent said. "That Thomas?"

The lad had been spending too much time around him and Scott. He never used to be able to achieve that sarcastic edge. "Thomas' vanishing act might actually prove that this is the right place," Granville said. "If this isn't their Forbidden Valley, why would he run?"

"Dunno," Trent said, scowling around him. "He didn't like the company?"

The wind howled down the valley, and Granville caught something in its sound. He held up a hand to the others. "Listen."

"Is that voices?" Scott said.

"I think I hear it too," Trent said. "But which way is it coming from?"

The wind gusted, then died, then gusted again. The voices, if they were indeed voices, seemed to vanish, then Granville thought he heard them again, but from a different direction. "I can't tell."

Trent had his head cocked to one side. "I think it's coming from up there behind us," he said, his voice low. "And I can—maybe—just make out several voices. And hooves on rock, too, I think."

Which put whoever it was on the path just below the crest of the last mountain. Far too close behind them.

"You think it's Heade?" Scott said quietly.

If it was, he'd made good time. Too good. "Who else is likely to be up here?"

"Indians following the fishing?" Trent suggested. "Pierce did say the tribes follow traditional fishing routes in May."

"In what they consider to be a haunted valley?"

"Oh. Maybe not."

The lad looked embarrassed, which had not been his intention. "It was a reasonable possibility, and good use of local information," Granville said.

"Well, half of it, anyway," Trent said with a reluctant grin. "So now what do we do?"

"We find out who it is, and we make sure they don't see us."

"If it is Heade, how did he get here so fast?" Scott said. "We've been riding hard, and I thought your local barkeep was feeding them false information."

"So did I." Which just meant the bartender was an even bigger idiot than Granville had given the man credit for being. Or that

Heade was wilier than he'd thought. Which was an unsettling thought.

"They must have a tracker with them," Trent said. "We wandered pretty far before we found this branch of the river. If they've been tracking us, and have some idea of where they want to end up, they could have saved a lot of that time."

His partner grunted, which was pretty much how Granville felt about this turn of events.

* * *

IT WAS HEADE, all right.

From behind a stand of alder at the crest of a low hill, they had a clear view of the party of five, no six, men making their way down the trail from the peak.

Granville held his binoculars to his eyes, careful to hold them so the sun wouldn't flash off the lens and warn the gangsters they were being watched.

The horses were lathered, the men were travel-worn and a couple looked ill. Four were Heade's men. One of them was their Indian guide. It seemed Emily was right, and Prescott in Port Essington had managed to reduce the number of Heade's party, at least by two men.

Granville wondered what he'd done with them.

Heade himself was in better shape, but his lips were a firm line and his jaw was hard. He looked angry.

And very determined.

It would take Heade the better part of the day to reach this vantage point, and until he did so, none of his party would be able to see the three of them.

The wind was gusting steadily towards them now, bringing cold air off the snow-topped peaks. They could hear snatches of conversation, but couldn't make out what was said. Which meant Heade and company couldn't hear them.

He passed the glasses to Scott. "Seems they've had a hard journey."

"Good. Means they'll be more tired than we are."

Trent was examining the position of the other group through the scope of his rifle. "We've got a good angle on them. Can't we just shoot them? Solves our problem right there."

"No we can't just shoot them. So far, no-one's proven they've killed anyone. And we still have no proof they're even after Weston. For all we know, they're looking for gold," Granville said.

Trent scowled at him. "That doesn't make any sense. And we know they're after Weston, or else why would they be all the way up here?"

"So your answer is to kill them all?"

"Yes!" But Trent wouldn't meet Granville's eyes.

"We'd be no better than they are," Scott said.

"And where's the glory in that? This way, we get to watch them bumble around up here. Do they look like they're having any fun to you?"

Scott passed the glasses to Trent, who took a long look. "Maybe not, but you know they're dangerous. They wouldn't hesitate to shoot us."

"Not until we lead them to Weston, they wouldn't." Granville just had to figure out how to avoid doing that.

"Who've they got guiding them?" Trent was saying. "He doesn't look Gitksan, so the valley probably won't scare him off. He might be our real problem."

"If they listen to him."

"He looks Indian, not black, so it isn't McDame," Scott said. "Think McDame is still with Weston?"

"If they found gold, or something else valuable, he will be. I hope so, anyway. If McDame's spent as much time in the goldfields as our informants say, he'll know how to cover their tracks."

"Won't that make him harder for us to find?" Trent said. "I mean, we still have to find him before Heade gets to him, and we don't have much time. Faster is better, isn't it?"

"I agree," Scott said. "We're still outnumbered, in case you hadn't noticed. Maybe not as badly, but we know they're all good shots."

"And they won't hesitate to shoot to kill," Trent put in.

Scott ignored him. "So keeping Weston away from them until we work out a strategy makes sense."

"That is our strategy," Granville said.

Scott cuffed him on the shoulder. "Not helpful. You're supposed to be the man with all the ideas."

"Since when?"

"Since your brother hired us for this little farce. Same man who hired these idiots," and Scott gestured towards the men currently straggling down from the peak, their boots sliding in the loose earth and gravel that passed for a trail.

"You have me there. "Though technically, it was probably Thanet who hired them. We shall simply have to out-think this other guide. And McDame. It shouldn't be difficult," he said in his most upper-crust tones.

Scott shook his head at him. "Good plan. We'll just out-think the locals, the ones who know the terrain."

"We have time to lay a false trail."

"It's a little late, don't you think?"

Trent had been scanning the valley below him with the glasses, seemingly ignoring the byplay. "Didn't you say the Chinese coins were found where the stream widened?"

Granville turned to see what Trent had noticed. "Yes."

"But these guys won't know that?" and he gestured dismissively towards their pursuers.

"No. It's unlikely that either Ah Quan or Judge Harrison would have talked to them, and certainly not in that kind of detail."

Trent nodded, still staring at something below them. "Good."

"Why? What have you seen?" Scott demanded.

Trent handed him the glass, gave Granville a cocky smile. "Stream narrows as soon as it enters the valley, don't it? And the trees are too small. None big enough for what that interpreter described."

Granville surveyed the vista spread before him. He was right. It was all alder and young spruce trees. There must have been a fire at some point, but the growth wasn't new enough for the fire to have happened after the discovery of the Chinese coins.

So this wasn't the right part of the valley.

"We'll need to carry on up the valley until we find either the widening of the stream or Weston," Scott said, having apparently come to the same conclusion. "With Heade's gang behind us all the way, just waiting for a clear shot at Weston. That's helpful."

Trent flushed. "No, I meant..."

"The lad's right," Granville said. "Have a look, Scott."

Trent handed over the glasses, and Scott surveyed what he could see of the river. "At what?"

"Remember what Rabbit Creek looked like before they began digging?"

His partner grunted. "Not much. Shallow little trickle heading off into nowhere, just before clumps of grass widened into graveled shallows. How Carmack ever figured there was gold up that little excuse for a creek I'll never know. Man was a genius..." He trailed off, turned to meet Granville's steady gaze.

"Just like this place," Granville said.

"You think?"

"Don't you?"

"But I thought you said the interpreter's cousin and his party did some panning in the area, didn't find anything."

"Gold can be fickle. Don't forget that according to our informants, McDame has found gold on previously unknown creeks in this country more than once," Granville said. "I don't know how Weston talked him into coming on this wild goose chase of his, but I have to give him credit for it. Might even pay off for both of them."

"If Heade doesn't get to them first," Scott said with a grimace.

"Heade seems to be following us. Making pretty good time, too. And if he's got a tracker with him, they're watching for any faint traces they can find."

"And we swept our back trail when we came back to check on who this was," Trent put in. "So they'll think we've gone on up-river, walking in the water to hide our tracks."

"And since they don't have a gold-seeker amongst the lot of them, they'll probably miss a small creek," Scott said. "So we let them go on up-stream, then follow well behind them until we find that creek."

"And the creek will lead us to Weston. It's genius," Trent said.

"Unless we're wrong about that second creek," Scott said. "Or Heade does find it."

"In which case, we're the fools who got our client killed. Again," Granville said.

4 2

"There it is," Scott said in an undertone, pointing to a small trickle of a creek that ran into the Skeena twenty feet or so ahead of them. "Right before the river widens out. Looks like you were right, Granville."

They'd let Heade and his thugs get ahead of them, then gave them a two hour lead before making their own way back down the valley to follow the river north. It had been the hardest waiting Granville had ever done, watching Heade and his men pick their slow way down the rocky path and along the muddy shallows of the river.

Now they were the ones picking their way. There was no path along the banks, and the mud made slippery footing for the horses, though the mules didn't seem to mind.

Eventually they left the river and made their way along the forest edge. Overhanging pine and thick stands of fir made it tough going in places. A thick screen of branches covered with budding leaves made it seem as if they were the only humans within a hundred miles.

They all knew Heade could be miles away, or only feet, so they kept their ears open and their voices low. When they reached a point where the river narrowed and a small stream flowed into it, all three of them stopped, their eyes measuring. Granville noted the change in the gravel along the river bottom, and the way the stream had spread out into streamlets before it reached the river.

His heartbeat grew faster. This could be it.

"I don't think Heade turned off here," Trent said at last, eyeing the mud along the riverbank. "There's one set of footprints goes up a little way, but the stream narrows to almost nothing and the footprints don't go any further."

"Good tracking," Scott said with a thump on his back.

Granville smiled at their interplay as he slashed his way through thickets of blackberry canes with wicked thorns that seemed determined to bar their passage. Was the boy right? Had Weston and McDame made it this far, then turned inland here?

If they had, somebody had good instincts.

Two months ago, this would have been covered in several feet of snow, the creeklet hidden and likely frozen solid. Perhaps Weston had got as far as Manson Creek, then he and McDame had waited for the first thaw? It was one question he hadn't thought to ask.

"Second guessing yourself, Granville?" Scott said, coming up behind him.

His partner knew him too well. "What do you think of affiliating with Pinkerton's?" he said.

"Whoa. Where did that come from?"

"I keep getting asked if I'm with Pinkerton's when I start asking questions. I gather they have a good reputation?" As he spoke, Granville continued to make his slow way through the thick undergrowth and upwards along the creek.

"Yeah, they're pretty well thought of," Scott said thoughtfully. "I knew one or two of 'em, back in Chicago. Decent guys, and deadly when they had to be. They wouldn't be a bad lot to be associated with. Would they be interested?"

"Why not? They don't have a presence on here. Newspapers report they've been called in on a few cases in Toronto and Ottawa. It might be to their advantage to have connections out west."

Granville kept his voice low, though he suspected the burbling of the stream would drown out their voices. Which was just as well—he wasn't ready for their young hot-head of an apprentice to hear these plans.

"Huh. It might be worth exploring at that. How would the money work? Granville?"

For Granville had stopped dead and put up a hand. Both Scott and Trent froze, and all three listened in silence.

Over the sound of the brook, Granville heard the call of some bird he didn't recognize, answered moments later from the other side. His mate? Then a ringing sound that he knew well.

"Axe," said Scott. "We found them."

"Well, we seem to have found someone," Granville said, grinning. "Let's go see who it is."

THE STREAM WIDENED TO A CLEARING.

It wasn't obvious at first glance that it was inhabited. A small canvas tent was tucked up against the base of a huge fir tree, the doused campfire tucked into the shadow of another. Granville heard the axe again, but couldn't see the man wielding it.

Further upstream he saw a figure crouched over the gravel, the flash of a gold pan. Two horses and a mule were tethered to a young cottonwood just beyond the gold panner.

"You think that's Weston?" Trent said softly.

"Time to find out." Granville strode towards the man. There was no point trying to be subtle—they'd hear the three of them, even over the sound of the stream. As he got close enough, the man working the gold pan began to look familiar, despite his heavy beard. He was pretty sure it was Weston.

The snick of a rifle being loaded from within the screen of trees to his left froze him in place.

"No trouble," he called out just loud enough to be heard, raising his hands. Hoping Trent and Scott had the sense to do the same.

Weston—if it was he—dropped the pan, drew his revolver and

half-turned to cover them in one quick motion. Then he stood and came forward, eyes fixed on Granville's face.

"I know you," he said. "But from where?"

"Weston, right?" Granville said with a grin. The other man didn't deny it. "Try Oxford."

The gun didn't waver.

"That isn't necessarily a recommendation," came the precisely rendered vowels they'd all spoken, which seemed so out of place here. "Who are you? And why are you here?"

Where to start? The minute Weston heard they'd been hired by his uncle, or possibly by his father, he'd distrust them. Looking at the man's tight face, Granville thought he'd be more likely to shoot them. On the spot.

"We were hired to find you," came Scott's voice from behind him, the tone calm. "But we came to warn you instead."

"What?" The revolver wavered a little in Weston's hand, and all eyes fixed on it.

Weston's hand steadied, the gun still aimed at them. "What do you mean, warn me?"

"Not that you need the warning. You already know that you're now your father's heir apparent, don't you?" Granville said, very aware of Weston's revolver and the rifle that was still trained on them from within the woods.

"But would it help to hear confirmation that your father is behind the attempts on your life before you left Vancouver?" Or that the men he hired are still looking for you, in fact have taken a wrong turning earlier and have gone farther up-river looking for you?"

"Who are you?" Weston demanded.

"John Lansdowne Granville. Fourth son of the sixth Baron Granville. A remittance man, just like you. And, to my misfortune, brother to the current Baron Granville, who is a low and sneaky coward with no morals."

Despite his tension, Weston smiled a little, though the gun never wavered. "Let me guess, your coward of a brother somehow knows my coward of a father."

"I gather they do business together," Granville said.

"Naturally, they would do," Weston said.

The gun slowly lowered, though Granville knew the rifle was still trained on them from the woods. "And I think I remember you—you were a few years ahead of me, until you got sent down."

He grinned. "There's a reason I was shipped out here." It wasn't quite true—he'd chosen to try his luck in the Klondike—but he suspected Weston hadn't even had a choice.

Weston's gaze didn't soften, and his knuckles still showed white on his gun. It appeared fellow-feeling only went so far.

"Why'd you run?" came Scott's voice from behind him again.

Weston relaxed a bit, grinned. "Well, since you're good enough investigators to have found me, I suspect you already have a pretty good idea. Am I right, Granville?"

"You might be."

"So?" It was a challenge.

"You owed Benton enough money to take care of most of the remittance money you had coming to you," Granville said.

"And?"

He smiled. "After one too many accidents, you heard about the deaths of your two brothers. Or should I say your two half-brothers? How did you hear, by the way?"

"Former schoolmate had just received a letter from England. He told me."

"In the circumstances, no-one who knows your father well would put it past him to hire men to kill you. Which is when you ran."

Weston grimaced. "I'm impressed you uncovered all of that. So why are you here?"

"My coward brother—whom I don't trust for a minute, in case that isn't already clear—hired us to bring you the news and send you back to England."

Weston just looked at him. "Why take the job?"

"To find out what my brother was up to."

"And your conclusion?"

"That the purpose of the exercise is to see you dead and your father's nephew confirmed as his new heir," Granville said.

"Your brother expected to hire you to kill me? That's not the reputation you held when I knew you."

"Thank you. Nor is it the reputation I hold now. And my brother knows that. No, I think he's playing a deeper game. I expect my role will be to confirm your death for the authorities."

"But..."

"And possibly to lead his hired killers to you."

Weston's hand whitened around the revolver's grip. "You don't look like a fool, so why tell me this?"

"I make it a point never to play my brother's games."

"And yet your partner tells me my would-be killers are already here. How *did* they find me?" His words were an assault.

"They followed us."

Weston leveled his gun on Granville. "Why are you really here?"

McDame was probably covering the other two. "Because I don't think either your father or my brother deserve to get what they want, do you?"

"You're talking about revenge?"

Granville smiled. "I like to think of it as justice."

Weston gave a crack of laughter, but the gun didn't move. "And you thought leading my would-be killers up here would help?"

"Well, what did you have in mind? You intended to just disappear forever?"

"Yes."

Granville hadn't expected that. It didn't change anything, though. "These men won't give up. And your father has deep pockets."

Weston gestured to the rocker box that sat beside the stream. "So do I, now."

Granville could feel his eyes light up. He couldn't help it "You found gold?"

"Yes. So what'll it take to buy you off?"

"We're not the ones you need to be worrying about." Trent sounded—angry?

No, the boy sounded offended, Granville decided, with a private smile. And Weston looked confused. He couldn't blame him. It was an odd situation.

"Look, I know you don't trust us," he said. "But Heade and his boys went up-river this morning, following what they thought was our track. They could decide to turn back at any point, and it would be good if we weren't still standing here arguing when they did so."

A movement in the trees had them all looking that way as a man walked out, rifle held in a deceptively casual hand. The gun was a Winchester repeater—they were lucky the fellow hadn't just decided to shoot first. He was old for a prospector, likely in his late sixties, weathered like old teak, but still broad-shouldered and strong.

"Name's McDame," he told them. And to Weston, "If what you told me before's right, these men are telling the truth. We need to get ourselves gone from here."

43

FRIDAY, MAY 18, 1900

After some arguing, McDame had the last word. He'd looked at Weston, waved his rifle at the camp. "We need to erase all trace we've been here and get this claim registered. Unless you're fond of being broke and dead?"

Once Trent told him about the native tracker Heade had with him, McDame helped them clear their tracks all the way back to the river, then led them downstream for a while.

After a time he turned due east, away from the river, leading them through thick stands of lodgepole pine and Douglas fir.

"You need to get that mine registered as soon as possible," Scott said. "Why are you heading east?"

"Fastest way back to Manson Creek is down the Omineca River," McDame said.

"But I thought that was southeast of here? And we're going northeast," Trent said.

Granville was impressed the boy had such a good sense of where they were in this vast country.

McDame must have been impressed as well, because he grinned, saying "You're right. But there's a tributary of the Peace not too far north of here. If we do it right, we should be able to confuse your city boys into following it a long way east, even with that tracker of theirs. With a little luck, we'll be long gone by the time they make it back to Manson Creek."

"They're traveling light," Granville said.

"Not prepared for a long journey, then? And I'll bet they'd have trouble with the cold in the mountains," McDame said. He glanced over at Weston. "Even better. Though our pack animals could slow us down some."

"I still think we should have shot them," Trent muttered. "They couldn't follow us then."

They rode single file. A thick floor of needles kept the underbrush down, but picking their way through fallen trees and gnarled roots made for slow going.

More than an hour later they were following McDame along a path even narrower than the deer trails Granville had occasionally hunted back home. McDame said it was a shortcut, and none of the rest of them could argue, though Trent had a few rather loud thoughts as to where the sun needed to be if they planned to get back to Manson Creek in his lifetime.

"You mean your short lifetime, if Heade hears you," Scott said.

They rode in silence after that.

Eventually the trees thinned a little and their pace picked up. It seemed to Granville they were making good time. But with trees thick around them and not a mountain peak in sight, they could have been riding in circles for all he knew.

By nightfall, McDame decreed they'd ridden far enough that they could risk a campfire. Ably assisted by Trent, he built a campfire that was invisible from a distance and gave off almost no smoke. They were boiling coffee and roasting fresh-caught trout, and the mingled scents had Granville's stomach rumbling. Scott was making flat bannocks of flour and water, adding the pinch of salt that somehow made them delicious.

Granville looked across the campfire at Weston. "One thing I'll say about this land. It may be tough going, but you eat well."

"I love it here," Weston said over Scott's chuckle. "This is a land that's big enough for me, with work that's meaningful. Unlike the life I left in England."

His words left a moment of silence. Granville and Scott looked at each other, then back at Weston. "You were serious, then? About not returning to England?" Granville said.

"Yes," Weston said. "There's nothing for me there."

"You're the heir apparent. You stand to gain lands, title and wealth."

Weston grinned. "I have a death sentence on my head, remember?"

"Can you look to your uncle for help?" Granville asked.

Weston laughed harshly. "Against my father? Surely you jest."

"Your father can't live forever."

"Even if he died tomorrow, and I inherited everything, I wouldn't want to go back," Weston said. "This place fits me in a way England never did."

Granville felt the same way. But Weston had to be sure. "You've thought it through? And this is truly what you want?" he said. "Because if you're serious about choosing this life, there will be no going back to England. The life you were born to will be gone. Forever."

"Yes, I'm sure. Sure enough to have new identity papers." Weston gave a sharp bark of laughter. "Losing that life forever is the best thing that could happen to me."

"How'd you manage the papers?" Scott said.

"You can buy anything in Port Essington, if you know who to ask."

"So who are you now?" Trent wanted to know.

Weston stood, gave a little bow. "James Groves. Pleased to meet you."

McDame, silently watching this performance from the opposite side of the campfire, smiled a little.

"But what of your son, should you have one?" Granville said. "He would by rights be the next heir to your title and the land."

Weston stared at Granville, a peculiar look on his face. Clearly he'd never thought about having a son, and the rights of that son.

Best he do so now, before making the decision to throw that birthright away.

"If I'm lucky enough to have a son, he can make his own way in life," Weston said at last. "Better for him than to live the life I had in England. And I plan to build something here. He will inherit that."

Granville nodded. "Then the new Lord Weston needs to die," he said.

Weston looked stunned, then began to grin. "But how?" he said.

"I have a plan."

"Food's ready," McDame said. "And it sounds like we'll be needing full bellies for this discussion."

IT WASN'T until after they all had full plates and were sitting around the fire that Granville began to explain his plan. And Weston panicked.

"You're going to tell the authorities I'm dead? But you can't prove it. And why would you lie like that for me?"

"Because it's likely the only way to keep you alive," Granville said. "And you don't deserve to die, any more than your father deserves to have his plan succeed. In this case, the lies hurt no-one —except perhaps Heade and gang, who will likely be deported over this."

"And since Heade and his boys should hang for Norton's and Graham's murders—and likely won't—you could say they're getting off easy," Scott said.

"But I've left debts," Weston said. "And I promised—someone— I'd send for her."

"That's easy," Granville said. "Write a letter appointing our lawyer to cash your remittance and disperse the funds for you. There should be enough money to pay your debts and her fare north. We'll witness the document and take it back to town with us."

Weston looked like he was considering it. "So how will this plan of yours work?"

"We need to split up," Granville said. The campfire flames licked at the encroaching darkens, flickering over each face. "We'll make that false trail a real one, confront Heade and his boys, convince them you're dead. You and McDame get that claim registered."

McDame didn't react, calmly eating his trout, but Weston put his plate down and stared at Granville.

"So you'll risk death for me? A man you've just met?" Weston said. "What do you gain in this? How do I know this isn't an elaborate plan to steal our gold? Maybe you're all in it together."

"To be quite blunt, you have a party of killers on your trail. I hardly think your gold—no matter how valuable—is worth more than your life," Granville told him.

"Besides, we already know where your claim is," Trent blurted.

Scott elbowed him into silence.

"Without that gold, I have no life," Weston said bitterly.

"But what about Miss Minnie? Your girl. I know she's worried about you. You have her," Trent said.

Weston glared at him. "And just how do you know about her?"

"Frances—Franny—is my sister," Scott said. "Minnie trusts her. And therefore us. You could do the same."

"Franny from Frisco? Benton's lady?" Weston asked.

"That's the one," Scott said.

"She's your sister?"

"Uh huh."

"She was kind to Minnie." Weston looked from face to face in the uneven light. "How can I believe you'd do this for someone you don't even know?"

When his own father—or at least the man who'd raised him—was trying to have him killed, Granville thought. The words lay unspoken between them.

"What do you get out of it?" Weston asked again.

"My brother hired me," Granville said with a grin. "Remember? Thwarting him is payment enough. Besides, he's paying us a hefty fee, which counts as a bonus in my eyes."

"Mine too," Scott put in.

Weston gave a cracked laugh. "I believe you mean it. Are you really that crazy?"

"Yup," Scott said. "And life was getting kinda boring, anyway."

"A little excitement adds spice," Granville put in.

Weston shook his head, and looked at McDame. "What do you think?"

"You spend long enough looking for gold, you learn to read people," McDame said. "Or you die."

He reached down for a stick, poked at the fire until it flared orange-red. "I say we get some sleep. Tomorrow we split up, just like the man said."

44

SATURDAY, MAY 19, 1900

"I don't see how there's any revenge in your plan," Trent said, holding the reins tighter as his grey objected to the narrowness of the trail. "The Earl gets exactly what he wants—his nephew will be his heir. I liked your old plan better."

Granville raised the collar of his mackinaw under the thick scarf. The day was beginning to warm, but it had been close to freezing overnight, and the sun wasn't yet high enough to provide any warmth under the trees. "But the old plan sent Weston back to England. He doesn't want to go."

"He could still go once the old Earl is dead," Trent said. "We help him disappear until then."

"He's chosen to build his life here."

"He might change his mind."

"I don't think so," Granville said. "Weston never expected to inherit the estates, has no training to do so. He'd hate the life. And do you think Heade and company will give up?"

"Still. How is this fair?" Trent said.

Had Trent been thinking about this all night? Glancing at his troubled face, Granville suspected that was exactly what he'd done. "Fairness often doesn't look the way we expect it to. Weston has freely chosen what kind of life he wants. You think we should disregard that?"

"No. But..."

"And he found gold—which few men do—enabling him to build the life he wants. As for Weston's cousin, the new heir—he will own the land he's spent his life learning to manage. Isn't that fair enough for you?"

"But Weston's father hired men to kill him," Trent burst out. "That's just wrong."

Trent's own father hadn't exactly looked out for his welfare, either, but Trent didn't seem to see it that way. Unless that's what was behind his outburst. "Yes, it is," Granville said.

"And he should pay!" Trent said.

"How?"

"He should be arrested."

"The Earl has too much influence," Granville said. "And Weston would have to die first, remember?"

"What about attempted murder?"

"Nothing would ever be proved."

"So he just gets away with it?" Trent's jaw was squared and he was wearing his stubborn look, the one that alternately amused and irritated Granville.

He'd slept well despite the cold, so today Granville found it amusing. "No. It will have cost Thanet a lot of money—and our fee will be no small part of that."

"It's just money."

Granville smiled at that. The boy was right. "Yes, it is. And now Thanet's third son—the boy he hated—gets to build his own life, one entirely free of him. If Thanet hadn't tried to have Weston killed, maybe Weston would still be a remittance man, gambling too much and wasting his life waiting for that next remittance check."

"Oh."

"Stop it, you two. All this talk about what's fair this early in the morning makes my head hurt," Scott said. "But Granville, I do have a question about this master plan of yours."

"Oh?"

"For this to work, we have to report Weston's death to the authorities, right? And make sure all the evidence points to Heade's men. But we don't have a body."

"We buried him where he died. Of blood loss. Tragic."

"The local Constable will grab the nearest coroner and head north to unbury him."

"All that way?"

"Yeah. From everything I've heard, the provincial police force is just as determined as the Mounties. And just as good."

"Annoying of them."

"He could be carried away by the river," Trent put in. "There's places a body can get caught up and not surface for years."

"One, we don't know the rivers 'round here well enough to know if our story would hold," Scott said. "Two, how do we know he's actually dead if the body washed away before we found it?"

"Oh." Trent thought for a moment. "We saw him shot in the head and fall in the river, but he was gone before we could get there?"

"Right. In the middle of a gunfight, you see someone shot clearly enough to know where the bullet hit. They'll believe that one for sure."

"You don't have to get all sarcastic about it."

Granville had been only half-listening to them bicker, pondering the problem of how to pull off Weston's fake death without getting shot themselves. But Scott had a good point about not knowing the terrain.

He considered the path they were following, the gaps in the dense underbrush. "It's pretty steep around here," Granville said.

Scott grunted. "Yeah. So?"

"I figure we're at least three or four hours ahead of Heade. D'you think we can find a deep, narrow ravine that isn't too far from a plausible gold stream?"

"Now you're going to drop the body in a ravine? It's still the same problem. How do we know he's there?"

"Because we saw him teetering on the edge," Granville said.

"But for that to work, Heade or one of his men would have to see the same thing. How do you plan to stage that?"

He grinned. "Remember John Bray? In Dawson City?"

"That the one walked around for a few days with a bullet in his brain before he died?"

"That's him."

"You're crazy, you know that?"

"Yeah, but I'll never forget the details of that one. Will you?"

"Huh. It could work."

"What? What could work?" Trent demanded. "Why do I get left out of everything? I hate it when you two do that."

IT WAS NEARING dusk and growing colder by the minute when Trent's sharp ears picked up the sound of hoof beats. They'd ridden hard until early afternoon, mostly due east. For their plan to work, they needed a likely looking stream not too far from a steep cliff or two. And they needed to find it before Heade and his men found them.

They were all beginning to doubt they could actually pull it off when finally they'd found the place.

"Y'know, if I were prospecting for real, I might take a hard look at this place," Scott had said, casting an approving look at the shallow stream bed and the finely ground gravel, white with quartz, lying just under the water.

"Good. It only has to look real."

"You think I don't know a gold stream when I see one?" Scott said as he dumped a pile of Weston's belongings under a tree.

"Based on your efforts in the Klondike? No," Granville said. "Put up this tent, will you?"

It was Weston's tent, suitably battered by mud, frost and rain in the months he and McDame had spent prospecting. By Granville's reckoning, they had less than two hours to make this site look as much like McDame's real find as possible, before Heade and his

team showed up. And every minute counted—the oncoming dark-
ness would help hide the freshness of the site.

He was only off by about half an hour. The clop of hooves and
the slight jangling sound alerted Granville. They were here.

He glanced over at Scott, saw his partner was in place. "Trent.
Go," he said.

Picking up his rifle, the boy vanished into the stand of trees on
the far side of the campsite from where they'd ridden in.

Scott was very visibly washing gravel at the lower end of the
stream.

He himself was upstream, wearing several days worth of beard,
dirt-stained dungarees and one of Weston's oldest flannel shirts
under his mackinaw, as well as the lad's battered hat. He had to be
careful not to split the shirt at the shoulders, but otherwise it was a
decent fit. Weston was taller than he looked.

As soon as Heade's scout was close enough to glimpse them
through the trees, Scott called out the alarm—just loudly enough to
be heard over the breeze—and the two of them ghosted into the
brush that had swallowed Trent.

Granville waited behind a thick screen of alder, silent and still
enough that the birds would begin calling again soon. He'd be too
easy to spot otherwise. He knew Scott was doing the same.
Listening hard, he tried to discern what Heade and company were
doing.

When the exultant cry went up, he couldn't hold back his grin.
They'd found at least one of the nuggets McDame had given him.

"Might as well make it look real," McDame had said, handing
over a half dozen small gold nuggets, probably worth fifty dollars or
more at the assayer's office. "Wherever you set up, salt the creek."

When Granville had protested, McDame had waved him off.
"That's a good morning's work, no more," he'd said.

Their claim was that rich? "But you're taking in flour gold to
register the claim."

McDame had grinned at him. "Because I've staked claims
before. Even flour gold will spark a small rush. Nuggets are likely to
cause a stampede."

Nuggets worked well to distract a gang of city toughs, too. Town boys or no, someone on Heade's crew couldn't resist checking the creek banks for gold.

"Forget the gold," a rough voice shouted. "The boy's worth more."

Heade.

A second cry went up. Weston dead might be worth more to them than one nugget, but how about two? Or six?

Time to remind them why they were here.

In his guise as Weston, Granville backtracked until he could see the campsite. One man was searching the tent, while a second man stood watching, arms crossed. That had to be Heade.

Granville was pleased to see the remaining three up to their knees in the creek. One of them was actually using the gold-pan Scott had discarded.

There was no sign of their Indian guide. Had the fellow had deserted them because of the sacred valley, or maybe there had been a difference of opinion? Whatever the reason, the absence of their tracker was definitely in their favor.

Raising his .38 Smith and Wesson, Granville aimed carefully, let off a warning shot, then retreated back into the forest. From a few hundred yards to his right, another shot put a hole in the crown of the gold panner's hat. Scott.

The message was clear enough. We're here, and we're prepared to defend our find. The response was predictable.

All five men leaped for cover, reaching for weapons as they did so. A barrage of shots peppered the forest.

Then silence fell.

From behind a gigantic moss-covered fir, Granville waited for the silence to get on the attackers' nerves. It didn't take long.

First one shot, then several, then another barrage was fired, without any response from Scott or Trent. As the silence stretched out again, he listened hard.

Finally he heard the crackling of needles, the crack of a small branch underfoot. They were going to risk a search. Perfect. He leaned around the trunk, aimed for a near miss, and shot.

Dead silence, then a shot from Scott's location, followed by another from the area where Trent had headed.

That set off the barrage again.

This time, only Scott and Trent shot back. They fired and kept firing. Their fire was returned. When they paused as if to reload, the barrage increased.

It was time to implement the second part of the plan.

45

THURSDAY, MAY 24, 1900

Two trail-worn prospectors rode into Manson Creek early on a May morning, and registered a claim in an area that had never been staked before. By the time Granville, Scott and Trent rode into town two days later, the word had spread that Harry McDame had done it again.

Jimmy Wells at the Gold Commissioner's office was spilling over with the news as he handed over the letter that was waiting for Granville.

"McDame?" Granville asked him. "And a second man?"

"Yeah, a fellow named Groves. James Groves. He's not local. McDame seemed to know him from his time mining in the Peace River country."

"You think they found another major strike?"

Wells grinned. "Knowing McDame? Probably. No nuggets this time, but he found enough flour gold to register a claim, anyway. And there's more than a few miners putting their kits together to follow him, just based on that. You never caught up with him, then?"

"Who, McDame? No, but I might as well have a word with him while he's here."

"I'm afraid you're too late. He stocked up and headed back north. Man's got a claim to work." Wells paused. "No, I meant the fellow you were looking for. Wallace, wasn't it? You ever find him?"

About to open his letter—a glance had told him it was from Emily—Granville paused and looked up. "Weston. And yes, I found him. Too late to do him any good, I'm afraid."

At his tone, Wells gave him a quick glance, then looked away. "I'm sorry. He didn't make it?"

"No, he didn't. Didn't leave anything to bury, either."

Wells looked shocked. "What happened?"

"We finally tracked him to a camp on a creek north-east of here. Gave him the news."

"He was alone?"

"Yes. He and McDame seemed to have gone separate ways pretty early on. I didn't ask why." You didn't, in gold country.

Wells nodded. "He find anything?"

"Yes. He showed me a handful of nuggets he'd found."

"He hadn't staked it?"

"He was intending to, and he wrote up some papers that night. Asked us to accompany him back here, then take the documents to his lawyer in Vancouver."

Wells stared at Granville. "What happened?"

"Our camp was attacked late that afternoon. We fought back, but they'd got the jump on us and drove us off. We headed for higher ground, planned a surprise attack for early the following morning."

"So what happened then?"

"We didn't know Weston had been shot," Granville said

"He wasn't bleeding?"

"Only a little. He said it was a scalp wound, that the bullet just creased him, and bound it up."

"I gather it wasn't?"

"No. We found out later the bullet was still in his head. Anyway, he seemed fine that night, but in the morning as we prepared to attack, he was complaining of a crushing headache, and his behavior was erratic. My partner took a look—there was an entry wound above his ear but no exit wound. Hell of a thing."

Wells looked a little green. "But he was walking? And talking?"

"Yes, he was, which amazed all of us. I don't think Weston even realized he'd been hit. Well, we got the wound bandaged, then talked it over with him. Decided we'd forget about retaking the camp, just get him to a doctor."

Wells nodded, looking grave. "It was too late?"

"We never even got to make the attempt," Granville said. "Weston took off when we weren't looking, climbing up as fast as he could. Next thing we knew, he was teetering on the edge of what turned out to be a ravine."

"You...?"

Granville nodded. "We saw him fall. By the time we got up there, there was no sign of him. We called, but no answer. And that ravine was deep. Even if we'd had ropes, I don't think we could have got down to him."

Wells was shaking his head. "Terrible."

"It was," Granville said. "Our guide had vanished three days into the journey, so we had no-one who knew the country. We could do nothing but say a prayer over what was surely Weston's grave."

"It's hard country. Whereabouts did you find him?"

"The best we could tell, it was on a branch of the Peace, north and a bit west of here. Two, three days ago."

"You'd be in the Skeenas, most likely. Treacherous mountains, those, even at this time of year. You're lucky you three made it back, with no guide." Wells paused. You've reported this?"

"Not yet. Who do we talk to here? Would it be the Gold Commissioner?"

"Yes. Valleau serves as magistrate here as well as Gold Commissioner. You met him on the boat, I think?"

Granville pictured the genial man with the handlebar mustache, whom Emily had found so entertaining. "Yes, I did."

Wells nodded. "Thought so. Well, he'll report it to the Provincial Police—they're brought in on any suspicious death.

Constable Kirby should be in Hazelton this week—Valleau will send for him. Kirby's good people."

"I'll do that," Granville said.

"If anyone can get your man out, he and Valleau will do so," Wells said. "They'll likely need an opinion from the coroner, too, especially given how Weston died."

"Right. And is Valleau in?" Granville indicated the closed door.

"No, but I expect him back this afternoon. He'll be anxious to talk to you when he hears about this."

Granville nodded. "Thanks. I'll be back this afternoon, then. And you might take note of anyone new to the district staking a claim for that area. Especially if they have nuggets to prove it with."

Because Granville was sure at least one of Heade's men would try to register the claim, using the nuggets he'd salted into the creek.

Wells nodded, eyes fierce. "I'll do that. What can you tell me about the party that attacked you?"

"Not a lot. It was twilight, and they were screened by the trees. There were five of them, though. At least a couple of them are crack shots. And from the glimpses I had, they'd been traveling a while."

"Got it," Wells said, scribbling in the notebook on the counter. He glanced at the letter Granville had just opened. "Everything OK?"

Granville scanned the lines. Emily sounded happy, but she was in Kispiox with the minister and his wife. What was his name—Pierce? What was she doing there?

He hadn't expected that news, even if it had been three weeks since he'd left her in Hazelton. And where was Clara?

"Yes, it's fine," he said absently. "Looks like I'll be heading back to Hazelton early tomorrow, though." Not that Emily needed rescuing, but her letter left too many questions unanswered.

"Safe travels."

"Thanks."

THAT AFTERNOON, Wells gave a brief knock on the heavily knot-holed pine door beside his desk, then opened it and waved Granville into the Gold Commissioner's office.

"Granville," Valleau said, coming forward with his hand outstretched. "It's good to see you again. Please, have a seat. Wells tells me you have quite a story to share. What happened?"

Seating himself in a hand-built chair that was surprisingly comfortable, Granville explained how they'd finally caught up with Weston. "He'd found what he was convinced was a gold-rich stream some five days ride north-east of here."

"It's pretty slow going up that way."

He nodded. "Thick forest, and pretty steep."

"And did you see gold?"

"He showed it to me. He'd found a handful of small nuggets, but you know how it can be. They get carried downstream, mix with the gravel. It doesn't mean there's more in that site. But I didn't like to quash the young man's hopes."

Valleau smiled. "It might be a false kindness, but it was a good thought. I've seen any number of these sites—a little gold, and the newcomers think they've found the next Bonanza Creek. Only to wind up a year or two later with nothing but sore muscles and calluses."

He grinned. "You know the business well, I see."

"You don't happen to have any of these nuggets?" Valleau said.

"I'm afraid not. Weston kept them in a small bag that he wore around his neck."

"There were so few?"

"Yes. And they were that small."

"I see. And I'm assuming that the bag is where the young man is —at the bottom of a ravine, I understand?"

At Granville's nod, he continued, "But tell me more about this attack. How did Weston end up in the ravine?"

Granville told him the same story he'd told Wells. "There was a neat, dark hole going into his brain," he said with a shudder.

The horror he'd felt at the sight of Bray's injury several years before had stayed with him. "It was bleeding, but only a little, and he didn't seem to feel it. His comments were a little off, though, and Scott and I decided to override what he wanted and bring him straight back here to a doctor.

"Then how did he end up in the ravine?"

"We were breaking camp in a hurry, and didn't think to watch him. He seemed to have taken fright at something, because the next thing we knew, he was climbing straight up into the mountain behind the camp."

"You gave chase?"

"Indeed we did. It only made him climb faster. I don't know how he managed it, but the bullet seemed not to slow him down at all. But if he heard us yelling for him, either he couldn't understand us, or the injury was making him paranoid and he thought we were the ones after him."

"And were you?" Valleau said.

Granville was impressed. The man's genial attitude and portly bearing was deceptive. This was a lawman in disguise.

"Yes. We'd been hired to find him, give him the news of his inheritance, and see him back to England if that's what he decided. Losing him to a head wound and a ravine was no part of our plan."

"Inheritance?"

"Yes. There's no point keeping it a secret now. Weston's two elder brothers both died unexpectedly in January, and he became Lord Weston, the heir apparent to the Earl of Thanet."

"Ah. Poor man," Valleau said, and it wasn't clear if he was talking about Weston or the Earl. "Tragic all around, then."

"Yes." It was, more so than the Gold Commissioner had any idea.

"So tell me about these would be claim jumpers."

Granville did so.

Valleau listened intently. "I still find it odd that both McDame and Weston found gold, given that they set out together," he said when the tale was told. "And you know what the odds are."

"None better. There's nothing like being a failed gold-seeker to shove that point home."

"I'm sure."

"But it sounds like McDame's claim is the real thing. I don't believe Weston's was, even though he found a few nuggets. Nothing about the location was right, even given the little I know about gold streams. Did you ask McDame about it?"

"No, he was gone before you arrived."

"Yes, I learned that. I had wanted to talk to him, too. I just wondered if anyone had asked what he did with his former client."

"Ah. Yes, actually, Wells asked him that. McDame just said the client had found a stake he wanted to work, and McDame chose to go on." Valleau paused. "Which probably meant he didn't agree with his client about the stream's prospects."

"Probably," Granville said. "The funny thing, though, is that Weston was apparently chasing a potential mine site he'd been told about, which sounds a lot like the site McDame found. My guess is Weston gave up too soon."

"Wouldn't be the first time. And a seasoned hand like McDame could tell the difference, probably at a glance. He seems to have the eye, given the number of successes he's had," Valleau said. "Well, I wish him well. But what shall we do about this untimely death of young Lord Weston?"

"You'll look for the body?"

"Yes, I'll go myself. Along with the local Constable, and possibly the Coroner, though I don't think the good doctor will be up to the climb. You didn't have a guide with you?"

"No, he'd left us a few days out of Manson Creek," Granville said.

"Hmmm. Well, we'll need to sit down with you and your friends and a map, and figure out where you were when you saw him fall. It's a bad business, this."

"Yes. What happens when you find him?"

"We'll bring the body back for an autopsy, and hope that the fall hasn't done too much additional damage to the deceased's head," Valleau said. "Given the manner of his death, this will be a hard one to prove. If we don't have a body, though…"

He shook his head. "We can't make a case. What's your sense of the ravine? Is it too deep to climb into?"

It was. They'd made sure of it. But before Granville could answer, there was a sharp rap at the door and Wells burst in.

"They're here," he told Valleau, then glanced at Granville. "I'm glad you haven't left yet. You can identify them."

"Who is here?" demanded Valleau.

"The claim jumpers?" Granville said.

"Yes. Four of them are, anyway. Supposedly they left one behind with the claim," Wells said.

Valleau stood up and loosened the revolver strapped to his hip. "You armed?" he asked both of them.

At their nods, he turned to Wells. "Let's get them locked up until we can sort this mess out."

EXCEPT FOR TWO HAND-MADE CHAIRS, the log-walled room was empty. Poorly insulated and lined with rough wooden shelving, it was small and cold, clearly intended for another purpose. There were no windows, and the outer door was thick, with the heavy iron bar on the outside and a shotgun slot at eye level.

Granville stood with his back to that door, watching as the inner door opened and Heade came in, looking travel-worn and weary. Leg irons clanked with every step he took.

Whatever hardship he'd been through, it hadn't lessened the intelligence gleaming in the hard eyes considering Granville now. The door slammed behind Heade, and he leaned back against it, his eyes fixed on Granville.

Granville rested his hand on his holstered revolver. "We might as well sit. You look like you could use a rest."

Heade shrugged as if it didn't matter to him, but he winced as he sat down.

"You're the one who was following us," Granville said as he took his own seat.

"And you didn't make it easy," Heade replied. "Especially after our guide deserted us. And did you have to wade up all those creeks? It made your trail damnably difficult to follow."

Granville raised his brows. "That was the point. I wondered what had happened to your guide, though. Did he vanish just before you reached the valley, by any chance?"

Heade looked surprised. "How did you know?"

"Our guide disappeared in the same region. I knew the natives considered it haunted, but it seems I didn't take that knowledge seriously enough."

"Our information didn't stretch that far, but since your knowledge didn't do you any more good than our lack of it did us, I'm not going to concern myself." As he spoke, Heade's eyes were assessing Granville.

He seemed to be looking for any weakness, any crack in Granville's defenses. Which was interesting, given that it was Heade who was in chains.

This man was a predator, and neither chains nor imprisonment were going to change that fact.

"Why did you want to see me?" Heade said. "After you've gone to all the effort to make sure I'm locked up here."

"We both know you were after Weston," Granville said. "And we both know your mandate was to kill him, but to make it look like an accident. It's too bad your men were so trigger-happy. There's nothing accidental about a bullet through the skull."

"We only have your word that he was shot," Heade said. "Or that he's dead, since I understand the ravine you say he fell into is too steep, too narrow and far too deep for any retrieval. Too narrow to confirm that the body's there, do you think? Or even that there is one?"

"Which would be lucky for you. If they find the body, you'll hang for it."

"They'd have to prove we shot him, first. And that it wasn't self-defence."

"It was his claim," Granville said. "Which, I might point out, you just tried to stake."

Heade smiled a little. "Again, that's your story. Without a body, I don't even believe that we hit him. All those trees, after all."

He gave Granville a hard look. "That must have been a pretty lucky shot for us, you know, given that we were shooting blind."

"You set off enough bullets. It's perhaps more surprising that you only hit him once."

Heade watched Granville closely, his mouth set in a tight line, but neither his face nor his posture displayed any other sign of emotion.

This was a ruthless man. He'd probably have much in common with Weston's father, had they been raised in similar circumstances. Though perhaps Thanet would come off the weaker—he'd been driven to these extremes by anger and injured pride, if what his sister Louisa said was true.

"It's really too bad, after all this effort, that you won't be able to claim that bounty offered by the Earl of Thanet," Granville said. "It is Thanet, is it not? Your client, I mean."

"I don't know what you mean," Heade said. "But if I did have such a client, collecting the reward would be a simple matter. Given that you've sworn to poor Weston's death. You being a gentleman and all, no-one will question your word. Now will they?"

Heade was sleeker than Benton, but just as dangerous. In fact, he reminded Granville more of the weasel he named Gipson to be— sleek, quick and deadly—though beneath the trail dirt, this man had an arrogant confidence Gipson only pretended to.

Heade gave Granville an amused look. "I wonder if that's your game? Is the boy dead?"

"Few survive a ravine," Granville said.

"And a bullet in the skull. Don't forget that little detail." Heade was definitely amused now.

"Have you ever seen anyone walking around with a bullet in their head? I assure you, no one who has will ever forget it," Granville said.

"Hmmm. And the beauty of it is, no one who has heard your tale will ever forget your horror in the telling of it, either."

"Including the jury."

"True. It is a most compelling and intense story you tell," Heade said. "How sad that no jury will ever hear it."

"Now you're counting on them not finding the body? Ten minutes ago you seemed to be hoping they would find one, if only to prove you hadn't shot him," Granville said.

"Yes. But this conversation has brought me to realize the benefits if they don't."

"Oh?"

Heade leaned back and started to cross one leg over the other. It was clearly a habitual move, because he looked momentarily startled when the weight of the leg irons prevented the move. The clanging of the weights had the jailor opening the door to check all was well.

Granville waved him off, and the door closed again.

Heade grimaced. "Definitely. There's no question now that the boy is dead, but how did he die? With no body and no autopsy, the authorities can't prove anything. All they have is hearsay, and I'm assuming you didn't even see him shot? No? I thought not. So they'll have to let me go."

"They'll deport you," Granville said.

A shrug. "I get to leave this ridiculous frozen land and go back to San Francisco, which is far more civilized than anything you colonials can offer. And, as you've pointed out, I'll still collect my quite large fee."

"Based on my word," Granville said, his tone neutral.

"Which no-one will question. Lord Weston is dead. End of a short, sad story."

"Very sad," Granville said. "But over, poor lad."

"And everyone gets what they want." Heade eyed the heavy leg irons. "Once these are removed."

"There will still be a question mark against your name in these parts," Granville said.

"That's nothing new."

"But you won't be welcome north of the 49th any longer."

"After this little escapade, that will be a relief," Heade said.

That's what he said now. If Heade's only dealings had been with the Vancouver police, he might not realize just how efficient and determined the provincial police could be. But as long as this man was no longer interested in Weston, Granville would let it be.

46

SUNDAY, MAY 27, 1900

T he Tsimshian must have had word he was coming, somehow, because as soon as the totem poles that marked the village came into sight, Granville could make out a slight figure in a full skirt standing by them, watching the path. Emily.

As they got closer, she waved, her smile brilliant. He dismounted from the winded black mare and Emily ran forward, putting a hand on his arm. "I'm so pleased to see you. You are well?'

He nodded.

"As you see." He held her tight for a long moment, then released her to look into her face.

"And you? You've been fine here?"

"Yes, indeed I have, and I've enjoyed it immensely. But tell me, what of Mr. Weston?" Her eyes scanned the trail behind him, landing on Scott, Trent, then the three mules, but no-one else. "Did you not find him?"

He passed the reins to Trent with a request to see to his horse. Tucking Emily's hand into the crook of his arm, he led her along the path bordering the river.

Once they were out of earshot of the others, he paused and

turned to face her. "No, I found him. About a week north and east of here, working what might well be a profitable gold strike. Officially, he's dead."

She considered his face for a long moment, then her smile broke out. "Good," she said, squeezing his arm. "And unofficially?"

For of course she'd guess what his words meant. "Very much alive, but under a different name."

"But whatever does he plan to do?" Emily asked.

"He's partnering on a mine with the fellow who helped him find it. And he's planning to buy a farm near a settlement on the Skeena. We passed it on our way to Hazelton. Kitselas."

"Kitselas? Is that where we stopped to pick up goods the second afternoon? I remember seeing a few homes there, with farms behind them. And the people seemed nice. But it was very rough. And won't the land need to be cleared?"

"Yes, Weston—Groves now—will be a true pioneer. But he likes the people there, and apparently farming is a life he's always wanted, and couldn't achieve in England. He'll probably split his time between mining and farming, at least until the farm begins to pay."

Emily smiled at that.

"And he's sending for his girl to come north and join him," Granville added. "Scott and Trent will escort her north for him."

"But how wonderful. And the girl—she's from Vancouver?"

He nodded, wondering what was going on behind that expressive face. There were little lines between her brows. She was worrying about something.

"And she knows about the life he's planning?" Emily asked.

It was a very diplomatic way of asking if a city girl was going to find herself suddenly expected to be a pioneer. Granville wondered whether Emily had her own worries about what her life would be if she married him.

This didn't seem like the time to ask. "She does. Apparently having their own farm is her dream too."

"But how perfect. I'm glad you could help him find his dream."

"And stay alive."

"Well, yes, that too," she said with a gleam of fun in her eye. Then she turned to greet the minister and his wife, who were strolling over to greet him.

SEVERAL HOURS LATER, after a mouth-watering meal of salmon grilled on cedar planks, bannock and the greens the children had picked that morning, Emily strolled arm-in-arm with Granville along the river. They'd left Scott and Trent with the Reverend—finally she had him to herself. And after the hubbub of voices in the long house, all chattering at once, it was lovely to hear only the rush of the river and the wind soughing in the trees.

"Have you enjoyed your stay here?" he asked once they were out of hearing distance of the longhouse.

"Indeed I have," she said. "Granville, it is fascinating. This village, I mean, and the way the Reverend and Mrs. Pierce work with the people here. Reverend Pierce is half-Indian himself, you know. He cares so much about converting his people. He is Methodist, and he was explaining to me how the tribes are gradually finding God, even the shamans.

And when they do, they let go of all the symbols of their old religion—carved masks, and rattles, and beautifully embroidered and colored clothing. Some of them sell them, while others just burn them, because the old belief was that through fire the sacred objects return to the spirits. I thought that was beautiful, that even though the shamans no longer believe that these objects are sacred, they still honor the traditions that created them—even as they discard them. I am so glad I came north with you."

"I must say, I was a little surprised to get your letter saying you were visiting Kispiox," Granville said. "And even more surprised to learn you were still here."

Emily turned to stare at him. What was he saying? Did he think she should have stayed in Hazelton?

"But seeing you here, learning so much, and so at ease, I just have one question." His eyes were laughing at her.

She relaxed and smiled at him. "Only one? I was sure you'd have quite a few more than that, when you learned I was here. What question did you want to ask?"

"What did you do with Clara?"

At that she burst out laughing. Whatever she'd been expecting him to ask, it wasn't that. "I left her in Hazelton, with Mrs. Rowlatt. Granville, I couldn't stand it one more minute. They are kindred spirits, you know, and can happily discuss fashion for hours on end. Especially when it is raining."

He grinned. "Why do I get the sense you were bored beyond tolerance."

"I even cried one day, I got so blue." She could feel her face heating. "Mama will tell you I'm not good at distracting myself."

"It sounds as if you just prefer your distractions to be non-domestic ones."

"Yes. Is that awful?"

He smiled at her. "Unusual, perhaps. Not awful. You and Mrs. Pierce seem to be getting along just fine, though."

"She is so fascinating. She was born in the East, you know, and came here as a schoolteacher to help the Indians. She and her husband have lived in so many places in the North. How could I be bored talking with her, or helping her teach the women and children."

She paused to take a breath, then corrected herself. "Well, some of the women and children. Mostly they are all gone fishing, and the men will also hunt. They have a summer camp along the Nass River, you see. One day I hope to go there and see what it's like."

"I can't take you this time, I'm afraid." Granville said. "We have to get back to Vancouver to see Randall about Weston's legal matters."

He grinned at her. "And besides, I suspect Clara would have little interest in joining us. Since we're not married yet—I doubt your mother would understand."

Emily laughed. "She's not going to understand this journey at all, and I expect to pay for it when I return home. But I didn't mean now, and you know it. Besides, I've had a wonderful time here. I learned so much about the Tsimshian history. I'd never heard any of it before."

Granville wasn't surprised. He wondered what her father would think of her new knowledge. And if he'd ever learn of it.

47

FRIDAY, JUNE 1, 1900

Vancouver now seemed a bustling, noisy place compared to Hazelton. The buildings felt too tall, the streets too noisy with the yells of the delivery men and the creaking of their carts, and Granville found himself missing the fresh green smell of the forest. He'd probably find London completely overwhelming now, compared to what he'd grown used to, he thought with a grin.

They'd returned to Hazelton just in time to board the *Caledonia* on her second return trip. The trip home had been a fast one—the sternwheeler had made it back down the river in ten hours. They slid through the canyons, the wheel churning up water and flinging it over the pilothouse, rocking and swaying merrily.

On the steam-liner from Port Essington, they'd eaten the best salmon he'd ever tasted, freshly caught and poached in seawater and kelp. Even Clara had been unstinting in her praise. The five of them had sat on the rear deck after dinner and watched the boat's wake in the starlight. It had felt like a celebration, but it also felt premature.

They'd found Weston, and he was safe, at least for now. But Granville still had work to do to make sure he stayed safe.

It wasn't enough to have called off Heade. The Earl of Thanet would never give up—he had to believe his son and heir was dead. And Weston had a new life to build, free of the threat of discovery.

Which was why Granville's first priority, after he'd seen Emily and her friend safely home, would be a visit to Randall. He hoped the lawyer could provide the answers Weston would need.

———

FOUR HOURS AFTER THEY DOCKED, Granville sat in Josiah Randall's outer office, freshly bathed and appropriately dressed for conducting the somber business he had in hand.

"Mr. Granville?" the clerk said. "You can go in now."

Granville nodded his thanks.

"Granville. Good to see you," Randall said, rising from behind his desk, hand outstretched. "I hope you have good news of the young man you were searching for?"

"Not exactly," Granville said, handing him several sheets of battered-looking paper covered with fine copperplate. "But at least he'd put his affairs in order before they started shooting."

"He's dead then? I'm sorry," Randall said, seating himself behind his desk and rapidly scanning the pages he held. "And what have we here? His will?"

"Not quite. A request for you to act as his lawyer, and instructions for dispersal of the funds from his last remittance. You are authorized to pay his existing debts, to buy a certain young lady's passage north, and to pay out the balance to one McAndrews."

"And McAndrews is?"

"A friend of his. Local man."

Randall glanced up and raised an eyebrow. "He didn't have time to sign a will?"

Granville told him the same story he'd told Wells and Valleau.

"So there is no body?" Randall said sharply.

"No. They couldn't see far enough into the crevasse to see where Weston had landed," Granville said. "And it didn't sound as if they planned to even try to recover his body."

"That may prove tricky," Randall said, before returning to the documents. "I thought the fellow you were looking for was called Weston. This document is signed Lord Weston."

"With the death of his two brothers some months ago, Rupert Weston became his father's heir, hence Lord Weston."

"Ah." Randall finished reading, then put the document down. "Is there anything else I should be aware of?"

"Weston wrote and signed these documents before they attacked us. I believe Weston's remittance money—since it arrived here well before this letter was signed—would not then be part of his estate?"

"That would be correct. But tell me more about his inheritance."

"Weston had become the heir apparent to the Earl of Thanet, but had neither money nor property of his own. Most of the estate is entailed, I believe, and will pass to the next male heir."

"So the remittance payment, which I gather was sent before he inherited?"—Randall glanced at Granville, who nodded—"that remittance was the only money that was fully his. I see you and Scott have witnessed all three documents," Randall said thoughtfully, his eyes retracing the words Weston had written. "The fellow was coherent?"

"Very. And sound of mind and body. Then."

Randall was nodding. "Good enough. Yes, I'll take him on."

"Do you have any concerns if I share this information with young McAndrews?"

"Not in this case. Just leave his directions with my clerk, so we'll be able to contact him."

"I'll do that. First, however, I have a hypothetical question for you."

"Go on."

"Could our conversation about a hypothetical matter be used in court if I asked you to keep it confidential?"

"Since you're my client, and—I'm assuming this is a legal matter you're asking my opinion on?"

"Yes, it is."

"Then no. Whatever we discuss will remain between us."

He'd thought so. "Very well. If a man had obtained false papers under a new name, is there any way to make that name change legal?"

"Yes, one need merely advertise their intent in the local papers for a week, which makes the change legal."

"So no other documents are required? Or court appearances?"

"No."

"And if the name change is because the fellow wants to disappear?"

"And not be found?" Randall clarified.

"Yes."

"There are very obscure papers, with almost no distribution. If the fellow resided in a locale with an obscure paper for a period of time, say six months or so, he could make the change that way."

"And do you happen to know where I might find a list of such locales?"

"I happen to have one. It's all quite legal," Randall said with a small smile.

That was good to know indeed. "Mmmm. But, hypothetically, if the fellow wished his old name to die, and to actually write a will under that old name..."

"I'm afraid that wouldn't be legal," Randall said. "In order to probate a will, the testator must be deceased."

"I see."

"Hypothetically speaking, there might be other options," Randall was saying, "Depending on why your fellow needed to vanish, of course. If he'd committed a crime, for instance, and was on the run, there wouldn't be much to be done. But if he had an inconvenient inheritance, it might be simple enough to renounce it."

From what he now knew about Thanet, Granville doubted such a simple solution would satisfy the man. It was too open to later challenge, and the man was too determined to keep his supposed youngest son from inheriting.

"Thank you for dealing with my hypothetical problem with your usual thoroughness," Granville said. "I'll just be needing a copy of that list of obscure papers this time."

"My clerk has the general list and can supply you with that, as well. However, I think you might be more interested in the list of those papers that are particularly obscure. Just a moment."

Randall turned to the cabinet behind him and after some shuffling of papers handed Granville a single sheet covered with entries in a fine copperplate. "There you are."

"Thank-you. I will leave the matter of Weston's request in your capable hands. I'm sure he'd have been very pleased indeed with his representation."

"Mmmm," said Randall, and his eyes were twinkling as he saw Granville out.

E mily was seated in a very stiff chair in the front parlor when Granville called, a half-full cup of tea on the table before her. The Turners' diminutive maid showed him in and left them alone.

"Granville," she cried, rushing across the room towards him. "How did it go with Mr. Randall? Were you able to hire him?"

"Not exactly. Lord Weston hired Randall as his last legal decision. And I've just sent a telegram to my brother, advising that I found Lord Weston and told him the details of his inheritance. And also conveying the news of the new heir's unfortunate death."

"Details. I want details," she said as she led him to her father's comfortable armchair by the fire. "Here, sit."

He had to laugh. Then he told her what she wanted to know.

"So," she said at last, leaning back against the chaise where she'd perched and giving a satisfied sigh. "It is over. And you won."

"Well, I'm not sure you'd call it winning," he said. "Weston had to die, after all."

"No, Lord Weston had to die," she said. "Weston himself will live quite happily under a new name, thanks to you."

"He already had a new name," Granville said. "Without my help, Heade might never have found him."

"Really? And yet from everything you've told me, neither Mr. Heade nor the Earl of Thanet sound like the kind to give up. Ever."

She was right, of course. Not that he'd won, though.

"And what of you?" Granville asked. "How have your parents taken your news that you and Clara travelled to Hazelton with me, rather than to Victoria for another visit with your aunt?"

"Ummm," she said, suddenly very interested in the pale green embroidery on her sleeve.

"Emily? Was it that bad?"

"Well, it wasn't good," she said, in a voice that didn't quite sound steady.

"What happened?"

"Oh, Papa ranted for a time, but he will calm down. He always does, and he never means what he says."

She hadn't turned away, but she wasn't meeting his eyes, either, and she seemed to be trying not to let him see her expression. "And your mother?"

"Well." More staring at the embroidery. "Mama was horrified. And she thinks..."

"Yes?"

"Mama says we need to set a date for our wedding. Immediately. Or both our reputations will be shredded. Not just mine, but Clara's too. So I'd told her I'd always dreamed of being a June bride."

Today was the first. They were to be married this month? "You want to get married before month-end? I'd marry you tomorrow, of course, but I doubt I can find a house for us by then."

"You've never been part of a wedding party, have you?" she asked with a wicked grin.

"No. Why?"

"Because no self-respecting mother of the bride would allow a wedding that took less than a year to plan."

"Then—you mean June of next year?"

"Or the year following. Mama's plans sounded extremely complex, especially considering she's not yet had a chance to discuss them with her friends."

He stared at her, thinking about his sister's all-too elaborate wedding. The only thing he remembered clearly was drinking too much at the reception, and his relief when it was over. But for Emily...

She was laughing, reaching out to put a hand on his arm. "Don't worry. I won't let her turn us into a circus."

That wasn't why he felt suddenly uneasy. Did Emily even want to marry him? Or was this a way to put off telling him no? "Would you rather wait for a year or two before we marry?"

"No," she said decidedly. "That's much too long. We'll just let Mama announce a date now, then when we're ready, we'll choose the real date."

And she stepped into his embrace and wrapped her arms around his neck.

"Of course, if another case came along and we needed to travel, we could always elope," she added as she reached up to kiss him.

AUTHOR'S NOTES

I have been particularly fortunate in the number of original source documents that are now available online—including Sam Steele's original journals on the creation of the Lord Strathcona's Horse regiment, which I spent way more time reading than the plot called for. Not to mention everything I learned about traveling up the Skeena River by sternwheeler, or the Omineca Gold Rush. Did you know that they're still bringing gold out of the region? This for me is one of the joys of writing historical fiction—I get to travel down any number of fascinating byways, and I never know where some of that research will lead me.

I have made every effort to respect the timeframe and keep the historical details as accurate as possible. I have used historic figures for a number of minor characters, and kept them as close to the historic records as possible. In a number of cases, however, I've created incidents and conversations specific to the plot of this book, though in doing so I've tried to stay as close to what is known of the historical figures as possible. Judge Eli Harrison and his wife Eunice existed, as did Sam Steele—formerly Steele of the Mounties, black pioneer and prospector extraordinaire Harry McDame,

Victoria entrepreneur Samuel Booth, Omineca Gold Commissioner Frederick Valleau and Omineca Mining Recorder Jimmy Wells.

The story of discovery of ancient Chinese coins or tokens in Northern British Columbia in the mid-1800's continues to fascinate me. These coins or tokens are real, though the specific details of their discovery tend to conflict, and the age of the coins is still a matter of controversy. The tale of visits by Chinese or Asian explorers to the west coast of North America long before the arrival of the Spanish or the British—including stories of the voyages of Buddhist monk Hoei Shin in 499 AD— are numerous, and varied, with versions of them showing up in a number of communities in northern British Columbia, as well as down the California coast and as far south as Mexico. Again, I've listed sources I used specific to my story on my website, at www.sharonrowse.com

Thanks go first to my friends and family for their support. Particular thanks go to my first readers for insightful comments on early drafts of the manuscript, and to Linda Roggeveen for her exceptional copyedit. Any errors or omissions are mine.

I am also indebted to the resources and helpful staff of the Vancouver Public Library Special Collections and History divisions and the University of BC Special Collections division. A number of historical works and on-line sites have been invaluable to me in researching this book; many of them are listed on my website at www.sharonrowse.com

THE SERIES CONTINUES...

THE TERMINAL CITY MURDERS
A John Granville & Emily Turner Mystery

I

MONDAY, JUNE 11, 1900

John Lansdowne Granville glanced up from the sheet of flimsy yellow paper he'd been frowning over and cast an annoyed look at the ceiling fan overhead. It wobbled slightly as it revolved, making a thumping sound and casting odd shadows across the room in the early morning sunlight. His office was warming up, the erratic fan barely creating a breeze.

And the open window wasn't helping at all. It wasn't even eight o'clock yet, but already the air was hot and still. From the street below rose the rattling of delivery carts, the hoarse yells of their drivers and the rank smell of horse droppings mixed with hot tar. Cursing his landlord and whatever idiot had put in the fan, Granville shut the heat and noise out of his mind and turned back to the problem posed by the telegram.

Or maybe it was an opportunity?

He glanced at his desk calendar. They'd only been back in town for a week, and already they had several investigations underway. Most were new clients who had requested their services last month, while he, his partner Sam Scott, and their assistant Trent Davis had been up north, searching for a missing heir. That case had been an unusual one, taking them away longer and much further afield than they'd anticipated, but it had been lucrative. And oddly satisfying.

Being home again felt confining, somehow, after three weeks in the wilderness north of the Skeena River. And spending time in the office felt even more restrictive, like a too tight coat. It had affected the others, too. All of them were a little tense, though they weren't admitting it.

So far, their new cases were bread and butter—background checks on employees and the like—which didn't provide much distraction. Or challenge. None of the new cases would take long, none was likely to hold their interest.

What they all needed was another big case, a gripping one. Like the one they'd just finished. The kind that would take all their efforts to solve. The kind of case that built a big reputation.

He looked thoughtfully at the telegram, and re-read the blurred type for the sixth time. Could this be the answer?

The slamming of a door and raised voices in the outer office put an end to his attempt to concentrate. Granville frowned as he listened to the escalating argument. This was supposed to be a professional office, dammit.

"Trent!" he called out.

There was no answer from the outer office, just louder voices.

Tucking the unanswered telegram under the blotter on his side of the large oak partner's desk he shared with Scott, Granville strode to the door. Clearly he needed to sort things out here first.

He hadn't seen Scott that morning, but Trent was supposed to be in the front office, welcoming visitors. Their growing reputation as investigation agents meant that potential clients expected there to be someone in the office when they came to call. The sounds he was hearing didn't sound very welcoming.

"You can't just barge in..."

It was Trent's voice, far too loud, right on the other side of the door. Who was he talking to?

Granville wrenched the door open.

And had to stop himself from laughing out loud.

Trent was standing—freckled face set and arms akimbo—in front of Mac McAndrews, barring him from Granville's office. A sturdy five foot eight, the lad looked like a bantam cock facing off a stork. McAndrews had to be six foot two, an inch over Granville's own height, but he was thin almost to the point of gauntness. Add in McAndrews' flaming red hair and it was an image from a Gilbert and Sullivan opera. All that was missing was the singing.

But what was McAndrews doing here? He'd met the hot-headed accountant two months before, in pursuit of that missing heir. Their first encounter had been anything but friendly, though once sure that Granville meant his friend Rupert Weston no harm, McAndrews had been both helpful and knowledgeable. He'd also proven incredibly loyal to Weston, and Granville had ended up liking the fellow.

None of which explained McAndrews' current presence, or the stand-off he was engaged in with Trent.

"McAndrews?" he said. Both heads spun towards him. Apparently they hadn't heard the door open. Trent looked annoyed. Their visitor looked worried.

"Granville," McAndrews said. "I'm glad you're here. I need your help."

"Then you'd best come in," Granville said, opening the door wider. "Thank you, Trent."

Trent scowled, glaring at McAndrews, then stomped back to his desk.

Granville waved McAndrews to one of four straight-backed wooden chairs lining the wall beside the door. "What seems to be the problem?" he asked as he sank back into the over-sized leather chair behind his desk.

McAndrews collapsed onto one chair, dumping his hat and briefcase on the chair next to him. "I have a client who's about to be arrested for fraud. And I don't know how to keep him out of jail."

Granville put up a hand. "Whoa. Start at the beginning, please."

McAndrews shot him a wry grin. "That's why I'm here. I'm not cut out for the investigative stuff." He leaned forward. "You know I hoped to set up my own accounting practice?"

Granville nodded.

"Well, I've done so, though it's only part time. My most recent client..." McAndrews paused, shook his head. "Actually, he's more of a potential client at the moment. Because the thing is, I think he should be hiring you, not me."

"And why is that?"

"Because he's being framed."

THE TERMINAL CITY MURDERS
is available through retailers everywhere

Made in the USA
Coppell, TX
08 January 2020

14220702R10210